Acoustic Kitty

"Technical Specialist Arthur Monroe," Kricks said, "this is Special Agent Wyman Coleman. He's from Field Ops. Seems you've somehow managed to get yourself selected for some kind of special project. Even though nobody asked me if you were available. And nobody even told me that Agent Coleman was coming to visit you today." These last comments clearly were directed toward Coleman, even though Kricks continued to look at Monroe.

"I wasn't aware of any special project," Monroe said.

"Don't care," Coleman said, wobbling forward and wedging his shoulders through the doorway and around Kricks. "Special project is aware of you. Welcome aboard, soldier."

"I'm not a soldier," Monroe said.

"Don't need excuses, pipsqueak," Coleman said. "No room for 'em on this project. You know what you get when you make excuses?"

"Um...no."

"Bay of Pigs."

"I don't get it."

Coleman looked slightly perplexed. "Field Ops is not a joke, son."

"I'm sorry," Monroe said. "I really have no idea what you're talking about."

Coleman stared at Monroe for a moment. "Doubts," he said, to nobody in particular. "I have doubts."

Bob Rybarczyk
2007
brybarczyk@sbcglobal.net

For my melon.

Acoustic Kitty

Bob Rybarczyk

Note from the Author

In the 1960s, the Central Intelligence Agency, under its customarily copious amounts of secrecy, experimented on cats in the hope of turning them into surveillance devices.

The codename for this undertaking was Project Acoustic Kitty.

No, really.

Beyond what I've already told you, very little is known about the program. There's a little more public information than that, but sharing it with you at this point would pretty much ruin the surprise of this story, so Google the phrase "acoustic kitty" at your own risk.

What follows is an almost entirely fictionalized account of how Project Acoustic Kitty might have happened. A few facts are sprinkled in here and there, but they're so few and far between that they're likely to be as noticeable as a half-eaten dog biscuit in a satellite photo of Nebraska. Unless by some small miracle I guessed something right, it should be considered as historically accurate as an episode of *Mama's Family*.

My apologies, in advance, to the fine folks of the Central Intelligence Agency, anyone who loves cats, and all housekeepers named Carmelita, regardless of whether or not they have a tendency toward prostitution.

- Bob.

Chapter 1

Washington, D.C.
April, 1967

Yevgeny wasn't allowed to open the window to his office. Most days, this fact of his professional life didn't bother him. Today, it was driving him crazy.

It was mid-April in Washington, one of the few cities he'd experienced with weather as consistently dreadful as Moscow's. But on this particular day, the world outside his window looked downright delightful.

The sun shone on the park across the street from the embassy. A slight breeze danced its way through the few leaves that had begun to sprout on the trees. People in the park were walking around with their jackets draped over their arms.

It was a gorgeous day. And Yevgeny's windows were bolted shut. For that matter, he was fairly certain they also were bulletproof. That, he didn't mind. Americans were a bit too gun-crazy for his taste.

Still watching the park, he picked up his phone and dialed an extension.

"Sokolov," said the voice on the other end.

"Boris," Yevgeny said in Russian. "It's Yevgeny. Do you have a lunch meeting today?"

"I do not believe so. I was considering a haircut."

"Forget the haircut. We should go for a walk in the park."

"The park? The one across the street?"

"Yes, the one across the street. Have you looked out your window today, Boris? It is like Kiev in the spring. The air would do us both good."

"Will I be able to bring a sandwich? I brought a delightful sandwich today. I was very much looking forward to eating it."

Yevgeny rubbed his forehead and rolled his eyes. Boris was always worried, first and foremost, about food. "Yes, you may bring your sandwich."

1

"And you will have your own sandwich? Mine is not large."

"Yes, I will have a sandwich of my own. Meet me downstairs in ten minutes."

"Will it be safe? Perhaps we should bring security."

"Look at the park, Boris. It is populated at the moment by squirrels and cats. We will be fine. I just want to enjoy some fresh air. I don't want to have to fill out security request forms simply to take a walk. You worry too much, Boris."

"The Americans, they allow their citizens to carry guns. The Clint Eastwood, in his movies, he is always shooting."

"Boris, those movies are garbage. And the stories, they occur 100 years ago." Gun-crazy Americans be damned; Yevgeny wanted to feel that breeze on his old man's scalp.

"But in America, Yevgeny."

"Just meet me downstairs in ten minutes."

Boris hesitated. "Okay," he finally said. "It would be nice to walk in a park, yes?"

"Yes. Very good. I will see you then."

"Do not forget your own sandwich. Mine is not large."

"Goodbye, Boris," Yevgeny said as he hung up. God forgive you if you happen to ask Boris for a bite of his sandwich because his looks good and you have none. You will hear about it from him for decades.

~

"You were right, Yevgeny," Boris said. "It is delightful today. Hard to believe in this time of year. This is my third winter in this godless city, and never have I seen a day this perfect in April."

"This is why I suggested we take a walk today," Yevgeny replied, unbuttoning his shirt sleeves and rolling them up. "You see? Sometimes it would not kill you to listen to me."

"I would listen more often if you were not wrong so often."

"And to think I once suggested that you marry my sister," Yevgeny said. "She was fortunate you said no."

"Your sister, she was the size of a buffalo. I was the fortunate one."

"The doctors say she has a condition," Yevgeny said. "It is not her fault."

"Her doctors must be American. Americans never want things to be their fault."

"True."

"You brought your sandwich?" Boris asked.

Yevgeny turned his head slightly so Boris could not see him roll his eyes. "Yes, I brought a sandwich."

"What kind?"

"Chicken salad."

"They make salads from chickens here?" Boris asked.

"Yes. It is not really a salad. It is chicken, mayonnaise, and…I don't know, other things. It is good."

Boris gestured toward a nearby bench. "We should sit. I will try your chicken salad."

~

On another bench in the same park, a young man named Vic Tombrowski took a bite of his own sandwich – his was salami and turkey on rye – and froze in mid-chew.

His eyes had spotted something after he'd taken the bite. The two men on the bench, who appeared to be arguing over a sandwich, looked exactly like Yevgeny Repin and Boris Sokolov.

Vic stared in disbelief. During all the time that he had spent in the park, observing the Soviet Embassy across the street, he had never once seen Repin or Sokolov exiting the compound on foot. It was always by car, with a full security detail.

And yet, there they were, less than 100 feet from where he sat with his salami and turkey on rye. He wasn't even technically on duty. He had been assigned today to observe the Embassy from a nearby rooftop, but it had been such a nice day that he decided to enjoy his lunch in the park.

Vic was dying to get closer, to get a better look, to confirm with total certainty that the two men were Repin and Sokolov. The way they seemed to be arguing over Repin's sandwich – it appeared as though Repin was refusing to allow Sokolov to take a bite of it – was giving him doubts. But he'd seen their pictures enough times to know that it was them. Sokolov was raising his voice as he continued to reach for Repin's sandwich, and he was clearly arguing in Russian.

Vic debated with himself for a few moments, then decided that trying to get closer was too risky. He didn't want to blow his cover. Instead, he jumped up from the bench and sprinted at full speed toward the nearest pay phone.

~

"Look at that," Yevgeny said, gesturing toward the young man running headlong out of the park. "You are making such a scene that you are driving others entirely out of the park. Clearly that man had grown weary of your irritating voice."

"I do not understand why you are being so difficult," Boris said. "I simply am wanting a bit of the chicken salad. You are at fault for your selfishness."

"You have not shared a sandwich with me since the war, you old hyena!"

"This is why I did not marry your fat sister! Your family is overrun with stubborn dogs!"

"Here, you mule!" Yevgeny said, shoving the entire sandwich into Boris's hands, causing chicken salad to ooze out from between the slices of bread. "You have ruined my appetite! I do not wish to eat it. I hope you suffer food poisoning!" He shifted his weight on the bench so that his back was facing his companion.

Boris looked down at the half-smashed sandwich in his hand, then looked at Yevgeny's turned back. He had been about to say something else, but instead closed his mouth and carefully scooped a spilled hunk of chicken back onto the sandwich before taking a bite and chewing it slowly.

The men sat in silence for several moments as Boris chewed. The warm breeze fluttered the paper around Yevgeny's sandwich.

"This sandwich," Boris said, "it is shit. Here," he said, setting it down on the bench.

Shifting back around, Yevgeny glared at Boris as he picked up the sandwich.

"You were right about the park, though," Boris said. "It is lovely today. We should eat here often."

"Tomorrow I am bringing soup," Yevgeny said as he bit into his mangled sandwich.

"Soup?" Boris asked. "What kind?"

Chapter 2

Arthur Monroe closed the door to his apartment and tried, for the tenth time since waking up that morning, to forget about last night. He wasn't going to be able to concentrate on his work if he kept replaying what he heard in his head. Marie had been...well, she had been on fire. No other way to put it. He might have heard it all even if he hadn't planted microphones behind her headboard.

He hoped he could find a way to set it aside by the time he got to work. The problem with the Soviet compound wasn't going away. Not that the problem was his fault. He couldn't help it if the field agents couldn't figure out a way to plant the bugs in the compound. But he was expected to deliver a solution. Field agents always expected the Science and Technology guys to perform magic when they themselves couldn't get a job done. Of course, when the S&T guys routinely performed such magic, the field agents accepted all the praise for a job well done.

Comes with the territory, Monroe reminded himself. Being invisible is better than being shot at.

Monroe hoisted his briefcase, which felt heavier than usual. He expected to be working late that evening and had packed two sandwiches and three apples instead of the usual one-and-two. Another day, another sandwich. In today's case, two sandwiches.

He scuffled down the steps of his apartment building. Halfway down, he spotted Marie near the mailboxes. Marie was by far his favorite neighbor. She was a little too much of a free spirit for his tastes, but he loved the way she was put together. Skinny but not too thin, and with long toned legs that she showed off at every opportunity. He had often wondered how good her long blond hair would feel if it were brushing against his skin, even though he was entirely certain it never would.

Apparently Marie was just now digging yesterday's mail out of her box. Arthur stole a quick glance at the curves under her sweater and the tightness of her skirt, then nailed his gaze to the floor. It was hard to look her in the eye. A girl like her had to think there was very little that was appealing about a guy like him. He was too short. He wasn't fat, but not really in great shape either. His hair was dark and unruly and always looked like it had been recently exposed to a Category Four hurricane. About the only thing he had in his favor was that he didn't have to wear glasses. Just his luck that he could see precisely how delightful Marie's body was but not have a chance at actually making contact with it.

"Morning," Marie said as Arthur dashed past. He felt his cheeks flush as he sped by her, heaving open the heavy front door before escaping into the street. She watched him go, perplexed as always by her upstairs neighbor's decidedly anti-social ways.

Arthur wondered, not for the first time, if Marie knew about the microphones. No, he decided. Her greeting was too normal, too everyday. He wasn't surprised that she was in a good mood. He would have been if he were in her place.

Monroe ducked into the Dunkin Donuts on the corner and ordered his usual, a small coffee with lots of cream and lots of sugar. The woman behind the counter handed him a large black coffee. Arthur looked at it for a moment, hoping the cream would start floating to the top, to turn the coffee his preferred shade of beige. Instead, it just stayed black. It was like looking at a cup of piping hot anger.

The woman who had handed him the coffee, a heavy-set woman with a jaw like a suitcase, noted the hesitation. "Got a problem with your coffee, sir?" she asked. To Monroe it sounded like a threat.

"No," he said as he hefted his briefcase and dashed for the door. The woman with the jaw like a suitcase watched him go, convinced that he must have done something perverted that she was fortunate enough not to witness.

Traffic wasn't too bad. The highway wasn't nearly as backed up as it sometimes got. Monroe was only cut off three times and given the finger once. He didn't respond. He heard about some guy in California who gave someone the finger on the highway. The other guy turned out to be an ex-con who enjoyed administering beatings. The guy who gave the finger spent the next year in a coma. Something like that.

Monroe never gave the finger to anyone on the highway.

As usual, Monroe had a difficult time finding a parking spot and ended up parking near the back of the lot, practically a quarter-mile from the front door. He reminded himself that his inability to wake up early lately wasn't his fault. Marie and her boyfriend – what was this one's name? Dave? Dale? Dick. Yeah, that was it. Dick. That figured. Marie and Dick had gone at it until nearly midnight. He didn't understand how Marie could have sounded so cheery this morning; she probably got less sleep than he did.

Monroe liked to get in early. Most of his coworkers rolled in between 8:00 and 9:00. He preferred being at his desk by 6:30. But since Marie moved in five months ago, he'd barely been able to get to the office by 8:30. As a result, instead of getting a decent spot near the front of the lot, he was resigned to slumming it in the back of the lot with the lazier people. He usually stayed later to make up the time, but that didn't help when it came to getting a good parking spot.

Monroe promised himself that he wouldn't listen that night. He would get to bed early, like he used to do, before Marie and her carnival of lust set up camp in Mrs. McCloskey's old apartment. Mrs. McCloskey never told anyone that she thinks she gives her best head when she's tripping on acid. Mrs. McCloskey was easy to turn off.

Marie was not.

Monroe sighed. He knew better than to tell himself he wouldn't listen.

~

The guard at the building's entrance said good morning to Arthur, as did the guard stationed by the reception desk. As usual, both were courteous but not exactly friendly. At CIA Headquarters, security guards who are too friendly tend to not stay security guards at CIA Headquarters for very long. It was generally considered a wise career move for a guard to aim his sidearm a visitor at least once a month. Not that the lack of friendliness bothered Monroe. He appreciated it, especially since he had so far managed to avoid having any weaponry aimed at him.

Monroe flashed his ID to both guards and didn't say anything in response to their terse greetings. He didn't understand why so many people said good morning to him. Marie, the guards, the scary woman at the donut shop. More people should appreciate silence.

The woman sitting at the reception desk, the actual receptionist, now there was someone who appreciated silence. She'd given up on saying good morning to Monroe years ago. After a while, she had even stopped bothering to make eye contact. Monroe had a great deal of respect for her ability to properly interpret nonverbal signals. She was truly a rare bird. Whatever her name was.

~

Monroe flipped on the light to his lab and listened for a moment to the low hum it gave off. He was fortunate enough to have his own lab. It was small, but he didn't mind. It was easier to keep clean, and he liked a clean lab. On that morning, he noted with some disdain that the lab was not quite as tidy as usual. He'd rushed out the door the previous evening, knowing that Marie had a date, and her dates always ended up the same way. He hadn't wanted to miss it, so he didn't clean up quite as thoroughly as he preferred to.

The bug he'd been working on was still in the clamp, directly under the magnifying glass that was similarly clamped into place above it. He was getting close to finishing it and hopefully would be able to begin field testing in a couple more weeks. It was his best effort yet, almost as small as a quarter and only a quarter-inch thick. Monroe leaned in to peer at it and remind himself where he'd left off last night.

"Trying to see if it has tits?" boomed a voice, causing Monroe to jump.

Mitchell Kricks stood in the doorway and laughed, rubbing his crew cut with a beefy hand. As usual, Kricks was wearing a tie that was both too short and a total mismatch with his short-sleeved oxford shirt. No matter how old he got, he always managed to look like a neighborhood bully who had been forced to wear his father's shirt and tie. "Sorry, Monroe, that was just too good of an opportunity to pass up. You looked like you were about to lick that damn thing. You shoulda seen yourself jump. Priceless!"

Monroe said nothing.

"Damn, boy, sometimes you are simply no fun," Kricks said. "I've met livelier corpses. You sure you aren't simple?"

"Yes," Monroe said, waiting for Kricks to get bored and leave. It was a tiresome game that Monroe had to play every morning. He once made the mistake of engaging Kricks in a conversation, and for the next two weeks the man kept coming into his office and talking non-stop. Monroe had stopped saying anything back to him after the third day. It had taken seven more for Kricks to notice.

"You coulda fooled me," Kricks said. "How much longer till you finish that thing, anyway?"

"Two weeks," Monroe said. "Maybe three."

"Try for two," Kricks said. "Anderson's latest is turning out to be hunk o' shit. It's small enough, but it picks up every god damn thing in the room. Even picks up all the god damn noise from the street outside. All that ambivalent noise."

Ambient noise, Monroe thought. The word is *ambient*. Kricks considered vocabulary to be a detail not worthy of his robust attention. "Anderson's bug, it's shit. I make better bugs on the can after hitting El Guapo's on Nickel Burrito Night." Kricks burst out laughing. "Get it?"

Monroe said nothing.

"Damn, boy, ain't you ever heard of a joke? Anyway, we gotta show the boys upstairs that we're making some progress down here in the pits, and right now you're it."

Monroe shrugged.

"Aren't you just a regular Jerry Fuckin Lewis this morning," Kricks said. "You are one strange bastard, you know that? Well, whether I think you're weird or not, you're gonna have to be my sign of progress this quarter, so get going on it. Maybe I'll grab a couple of Anderson's guys to give you a hand."

"No," Monroe said with more urgency than he'd intended.

"They'll let you get the thing done quicker. I'm sending a couple guys down."

"They'd just slow me down. I'll have it done next Friday."

Kricks paused. He squinted at Monroe, as if he could divine further understanding of his employee if only he could focus on him more clearly. "Fine," he said. "But I'm gonna hold you to that promise. Next Friday."

"Next Friday."

"It's lucky for you that you're the best I've got," Kricks said. "Say hi to all your buddies for me," he added, gesturing toward the equipment strewn across the tables in the lab as he turned to leave.

Monroe looked back at his bug and sighed. Next Friday. He hoped Marie kept to her usual schedule and didn't start in with Dick until after 9:00. Maybe he could catch the second round. There was always at least a second round. Sometimes even a third if Marie had had enough to drink.

~

Monroe pushed open the door to his apartment and glanced at his watch. 9:45. He'd put in better than a 12-hour day and was exhausted. But he smelled the incense burning in Marie's apartment – her incense always stunk up the entire first floor, to the eternal aggravation of everyone living around her – and she only lit incense when she was having sex.

Monroe hurried up the steps. Maybe he wasn't too late after all.

He quickly undid his tie as he unlocked his front door. He hurried to the listening station and yanked off the tarp that covered it during the day. He never noticed anymore that all the furniture in that part of the living room was covered with similar tarps. The paint cans had similarly been stacked around the room for so long that he had gotten into the habit of setting his Coke on one stack of them.

He flipped the station on and waited as the lights dimmed, then came back to full brightness. He was continually surprised that nobody ever asked him about the frequent power surges in the building. The wiring wasn't designed to support a listening station that required large amounts of power upon startup. Three times he'd blown fuses, which was why he kept a full supply of them in his coat closet.

Monroe headed to the fridge while he waited for the station to finish warming up. This version, a custom model he'd built himself, only took about 30 seconds to warm up. Plenty of time to grab a Coke out of the fridge and pop the top.

The sound of knocking on his door froze him halfway to the kitchen. He dashed over to the listening station and reached for the power switch, then thought better of it and left the power on. He scrambled to get the tarp over the station.

"Mr. Monroe, I know you're in there," the gravelly voice from the hallway said.

Monroe sighed and slowed down, taking his time to finish putting the tarp over the station. Corkels could wait. Old bastard.

"Mr. Monroe, I need you to come look at my toilet," Corkels croaked from the hallway. "It's been running all night and won't stop. I've had to wait until nearly 10 o'clock for you to get hoooooome, so now I need you to please fix it."

Monroe slid the chain off the door and pulled it open. "Mr. Corkels, is it something that can wait until morning? I had a long day at work and I'm really tired."

Corkels looked like he hadn't shaved in three days. His thick gray-black beard appeared rough enough to chew through wood. The faded blue plaid robe had fallen open, exposing the man's pale chest and curly gray chest hairs. It took a force of effort for Monroe not to stare at the disturbing vision of the frail man's revolting flesh.

"No," Corkels croaked, causing the Marlboro attached to his lower lip to bounce like a stripper's cleavage. "It's driving me *crazy*. You need to fix it tonight. Don't make me suffer for the fact that you agreed to take on the super's job in your spare time."

"Hang on," Monroe said with a sigh. "Let me go into the back and grab my toolbox." He walked toward his bedroom.

Corkels stepped halfway through the door while he waited. "Some super you are," he grunted as he peered at the tarp-covered furniture. "You've been painting that same wall for months. I'm beginning to think you're never going to finish it."

Monroe emerged from his bedroom with his sizable toolbox in tow. "I never get time to finish the job," he said. "Too many toilets to fix."

"Lazy is a bad thing for a super to be, Mr. Monroe," Corkels said, pulling his robe closed.

"Lead the way, Mr. Corkels," he said.

~

By the time Monroe returned to his room, he was exhausted. Sighing heavily, he grabbed a Coke out of the fridge and pulled the tarp off of the listening station. He sat in front of it for a moment, then glanced at his watch. 10:25.

Taking a pull of the Coke, he hesitated. It occurred to him that he should get some sleep. Screw it, he thought, sliding the headphones on. He reached over to the unlabeled switch that represented Marie's apartment – he didn't label any of the switches, forced himself to memorize which switch represented which apartment – and flipped it up.

He immediately heard the sound of a bed creaking. Monroe sat up in his chair, considerably more awake now. His free hand went to the right earphone, pressing it against his ear as he took another drink from the Coke.

Creak. Creak. Creak.

Dick was going at a pretty good clip. Or maybe it was Marie who was doing the moving. Either way, it was far too rhythmic to be mistaken for anything else.

The sounds of Marie moaning and almost growling came over the headphones. Monroe had flipped in just in time; she usually didn't start getting noisy until right before her big finish. Dick began making some kind of noise as well, but Monroe tried hard to ignore it. He never liked it when Marie's partners made noise.

Dick moaned loudly and said something that sounded like "Creamed spinach casserole." Dick always spoke during his climaxes, Monroe had learned, but never anything intelligible. Two nights ago it had been something along the lines of "My monkey is the bushman."

Once Dick was done with his latest ecstasy-induced statement of gibberish, the creaking noise immediately slowed, then stopped. Other than the strange outbursts, Dick was generally quiet. Marie's last boyfriend – what had been his name? Mark? No, Alan. Mark was the guy before that. Monroe had a hard time keeping them in order. Anyway, Alan had been one of those guys who felt the need to describe in excruciating detail what he was doing to his partner. "I'm boning you so hard," he'd say, or "I'm grabbing your *tits*." Monroe could never figure out whether Alan said those things out of bewilderment that he actually found a girl willing to let him do those things to her, or simply because he felt the need to have points of emphasis made during his carnal performances.

Things had gone quiet in Marie's apartment. Monroe took the final drink of his Coke and set the empty bottle down on the nearby stack of paint cans. He pressed the headphones to his ears and turned up the volume just a tad. He was careful not to turn it up too far. He once made the mistake of jacking up the volume on a bug, only to have someone in the bugged room walk past the concealed microphone and sneeze loudly. It had sounded like a shotgun blast to Monroe, and his ears had rung for nearly five days. His doctor had told him he was lucky he didn't have a pair of ruptured eardrums.

Sometimes Monroe wondered if having intact eardrums were actually lucky in his case.

"That was a lot," Marie said. "See, baby, I told you those herbs would help."

"I think I hit your dog," Dick droned. He always sounded like he was seriously incapacitated by some kind of illegal substance. Tonight was no different.

"Serves him right for poking his nose around every time we're in here. Here, use this. You want something to drink, baby?"

"You have any Coke?" Dick said.

"You want a Coke at 10:30 at night? It'll keep you up half the night. Besides, I don't buy that stuff. Nothing but a bottle of chemicals."

Monroe looked at his empty Coke bottle and wondered if the chemicals in it could possibly be worse than whichever ones Marie and Dick ingested earlier that evening.

"Good point, man," Dick said. "Water's fine."

"Okay...you stallion," Marie cooed.

"You know what would be good right now, man? A cheeseburger. With mayonnaise. And onions. And...whoa, doggie, hey, stop licking that..."

Monroe flipped the switch for Marie's apartment back to the down position. The during part was fine. The after part, he could never really stomach. The only thing less appealing than hearing Dick moan was hearing him talk.

As tired as he was, Monroe wasn't quite ready for bed. The Hendricksons down in 1D were sometimes entertaining, if only because they were two of the most unpleasant people he'd ever encountered, and hearing them curse each other out for hours on end was fairly entertaining. He flipped their switch up.

Nothing. A little snoring, off in the distance. Monroe flipped the Hendricksons' switch back down.

He hesitated for a moment, then flipped up Mr. Corkels' switch. At first he heard nothing, so he dialed up the volume a touch. A faint noise was steadily repeating. Monroe pushed the volume up another touch. The noise became more distinct. It was...wet, somehow. Rhythmic, and wet.

Corkels was beating off.

"Oh God," Monroe said, jabbing off the switch to Corkels' apartment and simultaneously yanking the headphones off. Next time I'm down there I'm taking out that bug, he thought as he shut down the station's main power.

Chapter 3

Monroe happened to pass Marie in the hallway again the next morning. She was in a long tie-dye t-shirt, heading back to her apartment with the day's copy of the *Washington Post* tucked under one arm. Keeping his head down, Monroe noticed that the shirt, while long enough to keep her decent, did a poor job of covering her slender legs.

"Morning," she said in her slow, somewhat dreamy style as she passed. Mistaking Monroe's glance at her legs to be a glance at the newspaper under her arm, she tapped it with her free hand and said, "Gotta keep close watch on what authority is up to, you know?"

Monroe flashed a perfunctory half-grin at her – it actually was more like a quarter-grin – and kept walking toward the door and out into the street.

~

Monroe had been at work for several hours and was deep in focus on a schematic when he heard a loud knock on the frame of the door to his lab. He didn't bother to look up. Kricks always knocked on his door frame. The more Monroe would appear to be in deep concentration, the louder Kricks would knock, hoping to see him jump.

"What can I do for you, Mitch?" Monroe said, still hunched over his sketch.

"Nothing," Kricks said. "Somebody else wants to see you." The way he said it seemed odd. It told Monroe that something was up, and whatever it was, Kricks didn't like it.

Monroe looked up from his schematic and turned around. Behind Kricks, in the hallway, was a brick wall of a man, leaning on a cane. Despite his mostly bald head – what little was left was trimmed shorter than most toothbrushes – he didn't look old enough to need a cane. His bland dark suit told Monroe that he definitely wasn't somebody from the S&T wing of the building.

"Technical Specialist Arthur Monroe," Kricks said, "this is Special Agent Wyman Coleman. He's from Field Ops. Seems you've somehow managed to get yourself selected for some kind of special project. Even though nobody asked me if you were available. And nobody even told me that Agent Coleman was coming to visit you today." These last comments clearly were directed toward Coleman, even though Kricks continued to look at Monroe.

"I wasn't aware of any special project," Monroe said.

"Don't care," Coleman said, wobbling forward and wedging his shoulders through the doorway and around Kricks. "Special project is aware of you. Welcome aboard, soldier."

"I'm not a soldier," Monroe said.

"Don't need excuses, pipsqueak," Coleman said. "No room for 'em on this project. You know what you get when you make excuses?"

"Um...no."

"Bay of Pigs."

"I don't get it."

Coleman looked slightly perplexed. "Field Ops is not a joke, son."

"I'm sorry," Monroe said. "I really have no idea what you're talking about."

Coleman stared at Monroe for a moment. "Doubts," he said, to nobody in particular. "I have doubts." He turned on Kricks. "You can leave now."

"I can, huh?" Kricks said. "Gee, thanks. But I still haven't heard how I'm supposed to meet my group's deadlines when I'm down one of my better engineers."

"Ever been shot?" Coleman said.

"No," Kricks answered slowly.

"Want to be? I'm armed. Enjoy shooting people. Haven't gotten to in a while now."

"You can't shoot me," Kricks said, though something in Coleman's gaze caused him to take a step toward the door. "I'm a supervisor."

"Only makes me want to shoot you more."

"You're a maniac," Kricks said, taking another step toward the door. "Who's your supervisor? I'm not going to take this."

"Assistant Director Henderson. Phone's right there," he said, pointing to the dust-covered one on Monroe's seldom-used desk.

Kricks' expression changed to one that Monroe had never seen. He had the look of a man who thinks he's picking up a bag of trash and realizes that instead he has lifted a bag of disgruntled live snakes. "I want him back as soon as this project, whatever it is, is done," he said, trying but failing to retain his dignity.

"You'll get him back when we're done with him," Coleman said. "Might be a while. Go do something else now." He made a shooing motion with his free hand.

Kricks opened his mouth to say something more, then seemed to think better of it. Shooting a look at Monroe, as if the situation were somehow his fault, he left.

"Absolute disgrace," Coleman said, looking around the lab. "Man's not capable of running a kindergarten, much less a department in the finest intelligence agency this planet has ever seen. And you manage to be his subordinate?"

"Yeah."

"Doubts," Coleman said, addressing the walls again. He shook his head. "No matter. Team's selected. Moving forward. Right?"

Monroe shrugged. "I guess. I'm sorry."

"For what?"

"I don't know." It had been a knee-jerk-reaction thing to say.

"Low self-esteem. Unfortunate. No room for low self-esteem in Field Ops, pipsqueak. Knew a man once who was burdened with self-doubt. Got shot. Tragic."

"He got shot because he had self-doubt?"

"Of course. I shot him. Can't have self-doubt on my team. Owns a gas station now. Good man."

"I'm sorry, I'm really confused. What's this project you're talking about? I haven't heard anything about being transferred."

Coleman looked Monroe up and down, from head to foot and back up to eye level. "How many pushups can you do?"

"On a good day?" Monroe smiled, enjoying his little joke.

Coleman didn't answer. He just stared at Monroe, waiting for an answer.

Monroe's smile faded. "None," he said.

"None? Are you crippled?"

"No."

Coleman stared at Monroe again with an expression of mild disbelief. "Come on, I'll arm-wrestle you."

"I'm sorry?" Monroe asked.

Coleman ignored the question, yanking a nearby stool and pulling it up to the table next to where Monroe was sitting. Coleman heaved his way down onto the stool in a way that was so awkward Monroe was afraid the man might collapse to the floor.

He dropped a beefy arm onto the lab table with a loud thump and lifted the forearm up so that only the elbow was touching the steel surface. The fingers of his hairy hand wiggled in Monroe's face.

"I really don't want to arm-wrestle," Monroe said.

"Negative," Coleman said. "Can't work with somebody unless you've arm-wrestled them."

"I've never arm-wrestled anybody I've ever worked with."

"I beat Bulgaria's top arm wrestler once in a bar in Bucharest."

"Isn't Bucharest in Romania?"

"Your arms are sticks. I'm surprised you can even lift a glass of water. Come on, pipsqueak, time for *mano y mano*."

Monroe realized the man was not going to take no for an answer. He sighed and put his elbow on the table. Coleman wrapped his meaty hand around Monroe's.

"Haa, okay. Here we go. Ready?"

"Sure," Monroe said.

"One…two…*three!*"

Coleman sent Monroe's hand crashing onto the table almost instantly, with enough force that it made most of the equipment on the table bounce.

"Owwww!" Monroe said, yanking his stinging hand back. Coleman shot up off the stool, stood tall, and raised his arms above his head. "Sweet American victory!" he shouted. He then pointed at Monroe and yelled, "Ha! Son, you arm-wrestle like you're Swiss. Are you Swiss?"

"No."

"Might want to check to make sure. Usually the Swiss aren't very interested in admitting to it. They tell you they're German. Your folks tell you you're German?"

"My mom is half German."

"There you go." Coleman grabbed his cane. "Show up in Assistant Director Henderson's office at one o'clock."

"I still don't know what this is about," Monroe said, rubbing his throbbing hand and hoping nothing inside it was broken. "Who's Henderson? Why does he want to see me?"

"Sorry, pipsqueak," Coleman replied. "Henderson wants to tell you that himself. Don't worry. Lots of glory in this mission."

"Glory?"

"Of course. Assignment's no good if it doesn't have glory. This one has enormous amounts."

"Of glory."

"Affirmative. Glory. Marvelous American glory. Your nation will be proud."

Monroe had no idea how to respond. The two men looked at each other for a moment.

Coleman broke the silence. "You're good with bugs?"

Monroe shrugged. "I suppose so, yeah," he said. "Speaking of which, I'm supposed to finish this prototype by next Friday. How long…"

"Negative," Coleman said, picking up and inspecting a voltmeter.

"No offense, but I'm really having a hard time understanding you."

"You're not finishing that proto-whatever by next Friday. You're on special assignment. The other thing is irrelevant."

Monroe looked at the sketch in front of him. Suddenly this special project idea didn't seem so bad. "But I won't know what this project is until I meet with Henderson?" he asked.

"Affirmative," Coleman said, shifting his weight around on his cane as he headed back out of the lab. "Your consistent bewilderment needs to go. I don't tolerate the bewildered. Act like you're in charge and you will be. Advice from me to you. You're welcome."

Monroe watched him leave, then glanced at the clock. It took him a moment to realize that he had three hours to kill before his meeting. He looked back at his sketch, then grabbed a file folder, slid the sketch inside, and tossed the folder into his filing cabinet. For the first time in his tenure at the CIA, Arthur Monroe left his lab to enjoy a three-hour lunch.

~

Every day, on his way to and from work, Monroe passed a little diner. He had passed the diner every day for years but had never eaten there. Every morning and afternoon, he wondered how good the food was there. He imagined it being full of diners between the hours of 11 and 1, all of them rubbing their bloated bellies as they walked out afterwards to suffer through another afternoon at work, when all they really wanted to do was take a nap.

The diner had been empty when Monroe had arrived. He was served by an openly hostile fat woman whose yellowed name tag identified her as Patsy.

Monroe wanted a chicken salad sandwich, but without the tomatoes that the menu said would be thereupon. He ordered the sandwich and asked for the tomatoes to be held.

"You can just pick them off," Patsy said, writing on her pad.

But the tomato juice will be on the bread, Monroe thought. Slime and seeds.

"I'd really just prefer no tomatoes at all," he said. "Please."

Patsy had lowered her pad of paper and stared at him. For a brief moment, Monroe feared that she might strike him. Instead, she simply turned and sauntered back into the kitchen.

When the sandwich arrived, Patsy practically shoved the plate into his midsection. She glared at him again with the kind of contempt people usually reserved for the homeless. He waited until she left before lifting the top piece of bread to begin picking off the twelve tomato slices he found there.

After he had finished and paid his bill, making sure to leave a generous tip lest he anger the already discontented Patsy, he stood outside the diner and looked at his watch. His first-ever three-hour lunch was only thirty-seven minutes old.

Monroe looked around the parking lot. It was still mostly empty.

He looked around at the area around the diner. Traffic on the road, a few nondescript buildings, and several weed-infested fields, the mere sight of which made his allergy-riddled sinuses twitch.

Monroe got in his car and drove back to work.

Chapter 4

Assistant Director Henderson's office was nicer than Monroe was expecting. He'd never been inside an AD's office. It even had a waiting room with enough space for six comfortable chairs and an L-shaped desk, at which sat Henderson's secretary. She appeared to be in her mid-fifties and practically reeked of professional assistant-ness. Floral, shapeless dress, salt-and-pepper hair stacked into an invulnerable helmet, faux-pearl necklace, the whole bit.

The name plate on her desk read DOROTHY. No last name. That was how it was at the CIA. Men had last names on their plates; women, all secretaries and receptionists, had none.

"May I help you?" Dorothy asked.

"Arthur Monroe," he replied. "I have a one o'clock appointment with Mr. Henderson."

"Very good. Have a seat. You're the first to arrive."

It only took a few minutes of waiting for Monroe to become thunderously bored. His three-hour lunch had exposed him to a level of boredom he never knew existed. After leaving the diner, Monroe had bought a *Life* from a drugstore and sat in his lab. *Life*, as it turned out, was as boring as actual life. President Johnson had visited Britain. Jackie Kennedy had attended a party. Some woman with no legs had learned how to surf. An article about Roger Maris was the only one that held his attention. His life, apparently, had been fairly miserable since he broke Babe Ruth's home run record. The article improved Monroe's mood somewhat. He ended up reading it twice.

Sitting on one of the chairs in Henderson's waiting room, Monroe glanced at his watch. 12:56. He looked around. No magazines on the end tables. The only pictures on the walls were of President Johnson and Vice President Humphrey and a painting of Niagara Falls. Monroe looked at the painting of the Falls and tried to imagine going over it in a barrel. The thought of the drop made him a little queasy.

Another look at the watch. 12:57.

The door leading from the hallway opened and a short man with an ample belly and curly red hair burst in. Monroe recognized him but couldn't remember his name. He was another employee of the

Directorate of Science and Technology, but in a different group, Specialized Electronics. Monroe worked in Surveillance Electronics. Only in the Agency could the phrases "Specialized Electronics" and "Surveillance Electronics" be considered to mean vastly different things.

"Hi there, ma'am," he said to Dorothy in a booming voice. "Jimmy Kendall here. I have a one o'clock with the Assistant Director."

Dorothy glanced at Kendall's badge, then at the large appointment book laid on her desk. "Thank you, Mr. Kendall," she said in a tone that managed to strike a perfect balance between interested and uninterested. "We're still waiting for other members of the party to join us..."

"Hey, I didn't know I was coming to a party!" Kendall interrupted. "How about...um...that?" he said, his enthusiasm bursting against Dorothy's stone face. "Sorry," he said. "I'm a little nervous. Sometimes I make jokes when I'm nervous. It keeps me from getting too nervous, because when I get really nervous, I get all sweaty and gassy and I can't shut up."

Dorothy's expression refused to change. "You can take a seat while we wait for the rest...for everyone to arrive," she said.

"Am I in trouble?" Kendall asked. "You can tell me. I can take it."

"Sir, I just make the appointments. You can take a seat."

"Okay," Kendall squeaked. Monroe could see sweat beads glistening on his scalp.

Kendall turned toward the chairs and saw Monroe. His face brightened with such force that Monroe found it mildly alarming. "Hey there, fella," Kendall said, snapping his fingers. "I know you. Hang on, I'll come up with the name. I'm a name guy. Never forget a name." He made a popping noise with his lips and snapped his fingers a final time. "Morrison!" he said, jabbing a finger Monroe's way.

"Monroe," he replied.

"Yeah, right. What did I say?"

"Morrison."

"I was close! I told you I'm a name guy," he said with a dismissive wave. "Andy, right?"

"Arthur."

"Close again! See? Never forget a name." He ambled over and dropped himself in the chair next to Monroe's. "So how are things? You're in surveillance, right?"

"Yeah. They're good."

Kendall grinned at Monroe and nodded his head.

"Thanks," Monroe added.

"For what?" Kendall said.

"Um…for asking. You know. About how things are."

"Oh, yeah! Right. So things are good?"

"Yeah."

"Super. So are you in this meeting with the AD, too?"

"Yeah."

"Are we getting fired?"

"I don't know. I don't think so. I was told this was about some kind of new project."

Kendall snapped his fingers again. "Oh yeah, that's right! Maybe I'm not in trouble. Oh, that would be so good if I wasn't in trouble. Mom wouldn't be able to handle it again. Last time she hit me with an iron, right in the neck."

Monroe winced. "Really? That had to hurt."

"You're telling me. She could have at least let it cool first. But hey, that's a mom for you. Always caring enough to hit you with an iron. So what do you think it's about? The project, I mean? All that Coleman fella would say is that it was a special project, and that there was glory involved. Glory! How about that? I've never worked on anything glorious. I think it sounds fun."

"I suppose so," Monroe said. "To answer your question, I don't think I know any more than you do."

"I don't know why they aren't telling us anything," Kendall said. "You don't think they're sending us behind the Iron Curtain, do you? I couldn't handle it if I were behind the Iron Curtain. I hear they don't have toilet paper there. I need toilet paper."

Monroe took a long look at Kendall. "They're not sending you behind the Iron Curtain," he said.

"You think? I hope not. I'm allergic to vodka. It makes me turn all red and puffy, and then I throw up everywhere. That's all they drink over there, I hear."

"I think that's just Russia. Not the whole Iron Curtain."

"Yeah?" Kendall asked. "That helps, I suppose. So did you arm-wrestle him? That Coleman fella?"

"Yeah," Monroe said. His hand was still sore from the experience, and he absent-mindedly rubbed at it.

"You got whipped too, huh?" Kendall said, noticing the gesture and pointing at Monroe's sore hand. "I thought that guy was going to pop the tendons right out of my shoulder and use 'em for a necktie. I was certain that he broke my arm, but I went to the emergency room and they said that I need to stop bothering them."

Monroe really had no idea how to respond, so he said nothing.

"So you don't know what this is about?" Kendall asked.

"No, I'm afraid not."

Kendall fell silent for a moment. Monroe appreciated it; he was quickly finding Kendall's energy to be exhausting.

Then Kendall began making a soft whimpering noise. Monroe had to resist the urge to groan audibly in response.

The door from the hallway opened again, and through it came Coleman and a man wearing a suit so expensive that Monroe didn't have to see his visitor's badge to know that he didn't work for the Agency.

"Hello, Agent Coleman," Dorothy said. "Hello, Dr. Westcott."

Dr. Westcott, a well dressed, tall man with a long, angular face and sweeping white hair, did not bother to acknowledge Dorothy's greeting. He shot an impatient glare around the waiting room, spotted Kendall and Monroe, and very literally looked down his nose at them.

"Hello Dorothy," Coleman announced. "Such a fine, broad-shouldered woman. How are you on this wondrous afternoon?"

"I'm fine, thank you, sir," she said with professional blandness. She pressed a button on her intercom. "Mr. Henderson?"

"Yes, Dorothy," said the voice through the intercom.

Coleman wheeled around and saw Monroe and Kendall. He jabbed an almost violent thumbs-up at them. "Afternoon, soldiers," he said. "Glory awaits, does it not?"

Monroe shrugged.

"Exactly what kind of glory do you mean?" Kendall asked. "Because I really need toilet paper."

"Everyone for your one o'clock is here," Dorothy said into the intercom. "Shall I send them in?"

"Yes, thank you, Dorothy."

"Son," Coleman said to Kendall, "I don't know what on God's green earth you're talking about, but there's no room in my CIA for a whiner with a wiping problem. Shape up!"

"I see your agency spared no expense in finding the absolute best men for this project," Westcott said, apparently to Coleman, though his gaze never wavered from the door to Henderson's inner office.

"The Agency brooks no criticism," Coleman noted.

"I don't have a wiping problem," Kendall said. "I just..."

Dorothy cleared her throat loudly, effectively ending the conversation. She stood and almost ceremoniously walked toward the door to the inner office. The formality of it made Monroe suddenly feel nervous. He'd almost forgotten that this meeting represented uncharted professional waters for him.

Dorothy opened the door. "You gentlemen may go in for your meeting," she said.

"Thank you," Westcott said, striding in ahead of Coleman. As Coleman walked in behind him, he turned toward Kendall and Monroe and jabbed a solemn thumbs-up toward them. He mouthed the word "glory," then went inside.

"I guess we're up, huh?" Kendall said as the two of them stood.

"I guess so," Monroe said.

Henderson's office was even nicer than his waiting room. Mahogany was everywhere. The huge desk, the numerous bookshelves, even the six-chair conference table, all mahogany. Monroe wondered which was greater, his annual salary or the cost of the mahogany.

Henderson stood up behind his desk and walked around. He was a remarkably short man, maybe five-foot-three at most. What he lacked in height he made up for in sheer girth. The man had the physique of a partially melted bowling ball. His head was topped by a flowing mane of hair so perfectly white that Monroe wondered if Henderson dyed it.

"Sit, gentlemen," he said, gesturing toward the mahogany table.

Everyone sat. "Good to see you again, Morton," Henderson said to Westcott. "How's Ethel?"

"A total lunatic," Westcott replied without humor. "She seems bent on spending me into bankruptcy, and if I could legally kill her, I would." His tone left some doubt as to whether or not he were kidding.

"If you change your mind, let me know," Henderson said. "Maybe we could bury the two of them next to each other!" He burst out laughing, as if he had just told the funniest joke in the history of jokes.

"Nah, they'd probably enjoy that too much," Westcott said, clapping Henderson on the shoulder. "As loud as they are when they're together, we'd probably get complaints from the gravediggers about all the noise!"

Henderson and Westcott laughed uproariously. Monroe and Kendall looked at each other, wondering what they were missing. Coleman simply sat still and watched them, like a man waiting for a bathtub to fill.

Eventually the two older men's laughter faded. "So has everyone here met?" Henderson asked.

"We've met enough," Westcott said. "This one is obsessed with toilet paper," he said, jerking a thumb at Kendall.

"I am not," Kendall said.

"Really, Walter," Westcott continued, ignoring Kendall entirely, "I don't know how you expect me to work with some of your people. I can barely tolerate Agent Coleman. Now you add to my team a sniveling man obsessed with toilet paper..."

"Am not!"

"...and the other one hasn't said a peep yet, but I'm not expecting much."

"*My* team," Coleman said.

"I'm sorry?" Westcott said. "I hadn't yet mentioned gunplay, so I assumed you weren't paying attention."

"Not *your* team," Coleman said. "*My* team. Facts are important things to keep straight, doc."

Westcott sighed as if he'd just been informed by a director that a 34th take was needed on his last scene. "Forgive me, Agent. *Your* team. Which of course could not exist without me. I don't see anyone else raising their hand for your rather gruesome little experiment here."

"Morton," Henderson interrupted, "I thought I had made it clear to you that this project was in no way gruesome."

Another sigh. "Yes, of course. Not gruesome. I forgot where I was for a moment."

"Morton," Henderson said, his expression growing more serious, "that's quite enough. We are here for business."

"My apologies," Westcott said. "I simply wanted to weigh in with my...concerns."

Coleman's eyebrows shot up. "Concerns," he said, glancing at Monroe and Kendall and nodding.

"Hey," Kendall said. "Why are you looking at me when you say that?"

"Gentlemen," Henderson barked, "That's enough."

Westcott raised his hands in surrender and stopped talking. Coleman seemed not to notice the rebuke at all and continued to keep an eye on Kendall.

Henderson turned his attention to Monroe and Kendall. "I'm sorry, gentlemen. As you probably have surmised, you're at the disadvantage here, being the new members of an elite covert operations squad..."

Kendall whimpered and elbowed Monroe under the table. He kept doing it until Monroe smacked his hand away.

"...but I'm getting ahead of myself. Introductions are in order. As I'm sure you know, I am Assistant Director Walter Henderson. Yes, the same Walter Henderson who coordinated the Sub-Carpathian Assault of 1928. I'm sure you were wondering. I'm asked about it all the time."

Henderson fell silent for a moment and stared at Monroe and Kendall.

"Um, yes," Monroe said. "We, uh, had just been talking about the Sub...um...the Assault. In the lobby. Right, Jimmy?"

"It's one of my favorite assaults," Kendall said. He was sweating profusely.

"Is it now?" Henderson said. "That's very good. Good to see a young Agency man keeping in touch with his history."

"Thank you, sir."

"Now then, as for the others in the room, you've met Agent Wyman Coleman here. He's the lead Operations agent on this project. He will be ensuring that the project stays on course and will report all progress to me."

"In charge," Coleman said, jutting his thumb into his chest and eyeballing Kendall, Monroe, and in particular, Westcott.

"And this," Henderson continued, "is Dr. Morton Westcott. He is an old friend of mine – as well as a friend of the Agency - and happens to be the president and CEO of Westcott Research Corporation. I'm sure you've heard of it."

"It's my favorite corporation," Kendall blurted.

"He will be the surgeon on this project. Three decades of veterinary surgical experience, sitting right here at this table."

Kendall tentatively raised his hand.

"Mister...I'm sorry, I don't yet know which of you is Mr. Monroe and which is Mr. Kendall."

"I'm Jimmy Kendall, sir."

"Very good. Mr. Kendall, this isn't fifth grade. If you have a question, just ask."

"Sorry. I didn't want to interrupt."

"What is your question, Mr. Kendall?"

"Are we going to be maiming animals?"

Henderson stared at Kendall. He seemed to be weighing his answer. "Who told you that?"

"Nobody," Kendall said, his eyes widening with panic at apparently having stumbled across something he shouldn't have. "I'll stop asking questions. I promise. I'm sorry. I know better than to ask questions. I don't know what got into me. Please don't fire me or send me where there's no toilet paper."

"See?" Westcott said.

"I think we're getting ahead of ourselves," Henderson said, still staring heavily at Kendall. "I'll finish the introductions, then we can begin discussing the nature of the project. Morton, as I assume you have surmised by now, these are the gentlemen from the Directorate of Science and Technology who will be participating in the project."

Westcott grunted in disdain.

"Mr. James Kendall, I'm told, is quite competent in the field of remote control electronics. And Mr. Arthur Monroe – you are Arthur Monroe, I assume?"

"Yes," Monroe said.

"Very good," Henderson said, shooting a glance at Coleman. "Mr. Monroe is trained in the area of surveillance technologies."

"What exactly does that mean?" Westcott said.

"He builds bugs," Henderson replied. "Microphones in the houseplant, that sort of thing."

"Ah," Westcott said.

"Very good then," Henderson said. "Now that we've all been introduced, let's get started. I want you to know that each of you has been specially selected for this project. You each have a unique set of skills that will be absolutely imperative to the success of the project. You should be honored to be here."

Coleman caught Monroe's eye and jabbed a quick thumbs-up at him.

"I also am obligated to say," Henderson continued, "that this project is absolutely top secret. Each of you has been assigned temporary clearance simply to even be in this room today. You will keep that clearance for the duration of this project, and only in regards to the project. Not a word of this goes outside this room. A very limited number of people are aware of the project, so if there is a leak, it will be easily found, and definitively closed. Does everyone here understand?"

Monroe and Kendall nodded. Coleman gave an exuberant double thumbs-up. Westcott continued to look bored.

Henderson continued. "As Mr. Monroe here is aware, we're having a problem with surveillance at the Soviet Embassy Compound in D.C. Despite repeated efforts to conduct effective in-building surveillance, we've thus far been unsuccessful, wouldn't you say, Mr. Monroe?"

"Yes, that's right," Monroe said, suddenly concerned that he was about to be blamed for something.

"And why is that, Mr. Monroe?" Henderson asked. "I of course know the answer, but I'd prefer if you explained it for everyone's benefit."

Monroe coughed. "Well, I'm told that the Soviets aren't allowing anybody into the building unless they're full-time employees and native Russians. No contract workers of any kind. They have embassy employees perform maintenance, paint walls, everything. Our guys can't pose as undercover maintenance workers. And they host no diplomatic events there at all, so we can't get anyone in posing as a party guest. I'm told we simply can't get in there to plant a bug. I only know because I'd been asked to develop a bug that can either be somehow inserted into the building from a distance, or can pick up audio from outside the embassy. Which of course is impossible."

"Who's working on that mission for Ops?" Coleman barked.

"I don't know," Monroe shrugged. "I never meet the guys who use the bugs."

"I could get a bug in there. I once planted a bug in Stalin's bedpan."

"Yes, thank you, Agent Coleman," Henderson said. "We've all heard your Stalin's bedpan story enough times here."

"Not a story," Coleman said. "Glorious and true. And from what I could tell, he was a very ill man. Disturbing work."

"As Mr. Monroe was saying," Henderson said, "we seem to have run out of options for putting the Soviet Embassy under surveillance. And we don't dare to try any sort of break-in. The compound is too well guarded. However, there are some relatively new developments. The Russians have started getting sloppy, and it represents an opportunity for us. Our observation teams have recently noticed two very high ranking officials, Yevgeny Repin and Boris Sokolov, leaving the compound several times a week. They stroll through the park across the street from the facility and often sit on benches to chat. It's not unusual for them to spend an hour chatting on those park benches. But if anyone approaches, even within 50 feet or so, they simply stop talking. We can't get a microphone close enough to record whatever the hell it is they're saying."

"They're professionals," Coleman said, as if he were introducing the concept to the others at the table.

"Sir?" Monroe asked.

"Yes, Mr. Monroe?" Henderson replied.

"Why haven't we tried planting a bug on the bench? Or on all the benches in the park?"

"After the first couple times Repin and Sokolov started visiting the park, a full security detail started coming with them. They keep everyone else at a distance. They also started sweeping the benches every morning. If we had something planted, they'd find it, and Repin and Sokolov likely would never enter the park again. We can't risk losing this opportunity. We realized that we needed to find a way to monitor them that did not involve a fixed-location microphone or rely upon a miked agent to get close enough to pick up their conversations."

"Are we sure they're discussing sensitive information?" Monroe asked. "If I were them, I wouldn't discuss anything important in a public…"

"They're Russians, son," Henderson snapped. "These people don't care to talk about the weather, or their wives, or how the Redskins are playing. They only have one thing on their godless Soviet minds, and that is the total destruction of this fine nation."

"Fine nation," Coleman repeated.

Henderson glared at Coleman, who grinned broadly in return.

Monroe glanced at Kendall, who was staring at Henderson and Coleman like he'd just been struck in the head by a thrown rabbit.

Henderson continued. "As we continued observing the Soviets from a safe distance, we noticed something else. We noticed…cats."

"Cats," Coleman repeated, nodding his head.

"Cats, sir?" Kendall asked.

"Lots of them," Henderson said. "Wandering in the park. Strays. Filthy, and one of them walks in circles almost incessantly, but yes, cats. And we noticed that a couple of the cats would walk right past the bench where Repin and Sokolov often sit. Repin has even gotten into the habit of carrying small amounts of kibble in his pocket to feed the cats with. So now the cats seek them out."

"Kibble," Coleman said, almost to himself, as he continued nodding.

"So when I started reading about these cats in the reports," Henderson said, "a light bulb went off in my head. I thought, 'Why don't we plant surveillance devices on the cats?' But the field agents noted, rightly so, that there was no place to hide a bug on these cats. Since they're strays, they aren't wearing collars. The only option would be to hide it in the animal's fur. But fur is too short to truly conceal a bug, and there's a very good chance the cat would clean it off not long after we attached, if we were able to attach it at all. The idea of doing something with the cats seemed so perfect…but we couldn't figure out how to do it. We were stumped."

Monroe glanced at Coleman and Westcott, looking for signs that Henderson was goofing around. Apparently he wasn't.

"We realized that instead of focusing on how to get a bug *on* a cat," Henderson continued, "we needed to start thinking about how to get a bug *in* a cat."

"You're kidding," Monroe said before he could catch himself.

"The Central Intelligence Agency never kids," Henderson said with a glare. "The Constitution is not a joke book, son."

"No sir," Monroe said.

"The approach is simple," Henderson said. "The Russians feed the cats, encourage their presence. All our cat would have to do is walk up to them, enjoy a bit of kibble, and sit nearby. And we would be able to hear every word those filthy, atheist reds are saying."

"Kibble," Coleman said, nodding again.

"Of course, cats are not terribly easy to train," Henderson said, "but we don't expect that to be a problem. That's why we have you on the team, Mr. Kendall," he added, gesturing toward a very surprised-looking Jimmy.

"Me?" Jimmy said. He seemed to appear more ill by the moment.

"Absolutely. You're an expert in remote-control systems."

"Well, yes, I build remotes to control little cameras, but…"

"Excellent," Henderson interrupted. "I have complete faith in your ability to figure something out for our acoustic kitty."

"I'm sorry," Monroe said, a look of confusion creeping onto his face. "Our what?"

"Oh, my apologies," Henderson said. "I got a bit ahead of myself there, didn't I? That's the name of this project," Henderson continued. "Project Acoustic Kitty. Came up with it myself. Congratulations on being assigned to the team, gentlemen."

Monroe stared at the man, not realizing that his jaw was slightly open.

"Are you sure you have the right Jimmy Kendall?" Kendall blurted. "It's a fairly common name…"

"I'm fine with it if we happen to have the wrong Jimmy Kendall," Westcott said. "This one may be defective."

"I am not defective!" Kendall shouted.

"I'm afraid you'll just have to consider me skeptical about that," Westcott sniffed.

"Meanie," Kendall said.

"Imbecile," Westcott shot back.

"I'm armed," Coleman growled.

"Gentlemen!" Henderson shouted, staring everyone into silence.

"Fine," Coleman said, relaxing in his chair. "I never get to shoot anybody any more," he groused.

"You gentlemen are going to have to work this out," Henderson said. "If you're going to survive being sequestered together, you're going to have to find a way to work together. And nobody is allowed to shoot anybody," he added, looking at Coleman.

"Sequestered?" Monroe asked. He didn't like the sound of that word at all.

"Of course," Henderson said. "As you might imagine, a project of this nature needs to be kept under extremely tight wraps, even from others within the Agency. It would be difficult to maintain total secrecy here at Langley. People see cats here, they're going to wonder why. There are no cats in the intelligence industry. We're more of a dog culture."

"Dogs," Coleman said, seeming to have calmed back down.

"Besides," Henderson continued, "we don't have proper facilities here for all the work that will need to be done. No veterinary operating rooms, that's for certain. So, I've arranged for facilities in an offsite location. You'll stay in a nearby hotel for the entire time, until the project is finished."

"We won't get to go home?" Kendall asked.

"Not until the project is finished, no," Henderson said. "I'm sorry. The project must be completed outside the view of Langley. We don't need this leaking to the public. And it gives each of you extra motivation to be quick about your work. I want a prototype completed as soon as possible. The weather will only stay warm for five or six months at most. That's when Repin and Sokolov are most likely to spend lots of time in the park."

Monroe glanced at Kendall. The man looked like he was about to cry.

As for himself, the notion of leaving his apartment unattended for any length of time, much less an entire summer, was terrifying.

"How far away is the lab?" Monroe asked.

"Cape Girardeau, Missouri," Coleman said.

"Missouri?" Kendall shrieked. "Why Missouri? That's got to be a thousand miles away."

"There aren't many adequate facilities in out-of-the-way places in this country," Westcott said. "This particular lab also happens to be very close to a highly reputable animal-testing supply facility. And it has the benefit of being located very far away from curious eyes in Washington."

"Yes, you can thank Dr. Westcott here for the location of your project," Henderson said. "I was just going to send you to a site in West Virginia, but he convinced me that the site in Missouri was better. I'm sorry for the inconvenience, but there are very good reasons for it."

"But," Kendall said, "who's going to feed my birds? I can't trust my mom. She just switched back to Jim Beam."

"Suit yourself," Westcott said. "The fat one wants out."

"Hey!" Kendall shrieked. "I'm not fat. You are an angry, angry man."

"Mr. Kendall," Henderson interrupted, "don't worry about your birds. I'm sure they will be fine. If it will make you feel better, we'll make arrangements for them to be fed."

"Really?"

"Sure. Or we'll buy you new birds upon your return. One of the two."

Kendall whimpered.

"Don't worry about it, Chubbsy," Coleman said. "It's a nice town. Seen it. Very nice. Teacher's college nearby. Lots of college girls. None are attractive, though. Thought I saw an attractive one once. Turned out to be a shrubbery."

"My poor birds," Kendall said, mostly to himself. "Do you have birds?" he asked Monroe.

"No," Monroe said.

"There's nothing wrong with a grown man having birds, you know," Kendall said.

"I didn't say there was," Monroe said.

"I love birds," Coleman said.

"You do?" Kendall asked.

"Fun to shoot," Coleman replied. "Excellent when fried."

Kendall gasped in horror. "You're a bad, bad person."

"Not my fault birds are tasty," Coleman said.

Kendall ignored him, turning back to Monroe. "Who's going to feed my birds?"

"Why do you keep asking me?" Monroe said.

Henderson stood up. "Gentlemen," he shouted, catching everyone's attention. "If there aren't any questions, then this meeting is adjourned. Remember, none of this can be repeated outside these walls. Betraying the trust of this office will have dire consequences."

"Pow!" Coleman said with a gleeful grin, pointing finger guns at Westcott, Monroe and Kendall. "Pow pow!"

Westcott, Monroe and Kendall stared in stunned silence at Coleman as he blew on his fingers and pretended to holster them.

"I was thinking more along the lines of dismissal," Henderson said.

"Are you sure he should be licensed to carry weapons?" Westcott asked.

"He's passed all the tests," Henderson said. "At any rate, I'm very glad you're all on board. Your plane leaves at 8 a.m. Sunday from Dulles. I'm looking forward to seeing your first prototype, gentlemen. May God be with you."

Chapter 5

Monroe sat in his lab, trying to figure out the implications of what he'd just been told. He was going to be gone for months, maybe even longer than that, and he only had a few days to prepare. He didn't know what to do. He obviously would have to resign his job as the building super, but he worried about another super coming in and finding all his bugs. They wouldn't be easy to spot, and not everyone who found them would realize what they were, but the idea of leaving his bugs behind made him extremely nervous. Nobody in the building knew what he did for a living, but if they found any or all of the bugs and called the police about them, it wouldn't be long before the authorities traced Monroe's little friends back to him.

He considered trying to get back in to everyone's apartments and pulling the bugs. But getting into seven apartments in a couple days without arousing suspicion would be tricky. He considered faking some sort of infestation. He could say he found ants in his own apartment and wanted to make sure he kept them out of everyone else's. Of course, he'd never sprayed for bugs before, even after the numerous occasions when Mr. Corkels had claimed that roaches were living inside his television set and were the cause of his lousy reception. But the idea did hold some promise.

Being cooped up with the likes of Coleman, Kendall and Westcott for an indeterminate amount of time didn't sound like much fun to Monroe, either. One of the reasons he liked his job at the CIA was that it allowed him to work alone. He never liked working in teams. In high school and college, he was always the guy who did all the work while the other people half-assed things and assumed he would bail them out. Of course, he always did.

He could see this project going the same way. Coleman certainly wasn't going to be good for anything, except maybe shooting them all in the back every time one of them wanted to go down the road for a Coke.

Kendall might not be much help on the project, either. He seemed an odd choice for this project. He had a reputation in the Directorate for being competent but not particularly inventive. He'd probably reached his potential already. Then again, Monroe didn't work with Kendall's division very often. It was possible that Kendall had greatly improved his skills lately and that Monroe simply hadn't heard. Still, the man was downright odd. Friendly, sure, but more than a little eccentric.

Monroe had no idea what to think about Westcott. The man was obviously filthy rich and very accustomed to being the guy in charge. To an extent he'd be calling the shots on the project, but really, it wouldn't be his show. If it was anybody's, it was Coleman's.

As far as Monroe was concerned, it seemed likely that at some point during the project Coleman was going to shoot somebody. He hoped it would be Westcott.

~

The few days between the meeting in Henderson's office and the departure for Missouri were torturously long. Monroe had found himself removed from his previously urgent project – Kricks had assigned it to another lab tech almost immediately – and as a result, there was nothing for him to do.

Monroe spent a few hours cleaning up his lab, but since he cleaned it every day, even going so far as to polish the screen on his oscilloscope and dig particles out of his aging voltmeter with a toothbrush, there wasn't really all that much work to do.

On his first full day with nothing to do, Monroe brought a book to the lab. He felt silly going to work, what with there being no actual work to do, but he went anyway. He didn't want to waste his precious few vacation days, which he had been saving for a trip to Iceland. Monroe had heard that Icelandic girls were very pretty and easily impressed by American accents, and he was hoping that visiting there would help him put a bit more distance between himself and virginity. Deep in his heart, he was fairly sure that the trip would ultimately just provide him with the experience of masturbating in the Arctic Circle, but he wanted to go nonetheless.

He had been planning on taking his trip over the summer. Now he had no idea when he'd be able to go. He was a little relieved that he hadn't bought his tickets. He had a feeling that Henderson wouldn't sign off on any reimbursement for unused airline tickets.

The book Monroe brought to work was one that he'd pulled off his lone bookshelf at home. It was a rather tired-looking copy of an Oscar Wilde book called *A House of Pomegranates*. He'd bought it at a garage sale right after he moved into his apartment. He thought that girls who came over might be impressed if they saw a bookshelf full of classic literature...or even just old hardcover books that looked like they might once have been considered classic literature...and so he'd gone to a few garage sales, snapping up anything that looked remotely literary. In hindsight, the entire exercise was laughably pointless, but it had somehow seemed like a good idea at the time.

He'd heard of Oscar Wilde, but not *A House of Pomegranates*. It seemed like one of the single worst book titles in the history of the English language. He regretted not actually reading the spine of the book before snagging it off his bookshelf that morning. He started randomly flipping through it and could find no mention of pomegranates. He concluded that actually finding mention of pomegranates didn't really seem like it would be all that fulfilling, so he chucked the book back into his satchel and decided to roam the halls of Headquarters for a while.

After wandering aimlessly for about 20 minutes, Monroe realized that CIA Headquarters was obscenely boring. He knew for a fact that things like espionage, spy missions, and assassinations were plotted in the building, but it sure didn't seem that way. People walked around, wore ties, pushed their glasses on their nose, and in one instance, farted so explosively in a bathroom stall that Monroe had to suppress the urge to duck for cover.

Nearly distraught with boredom, and with another half-hour to kill before the cafeteria started serving lunch, Monroe decided to find Coleman's office. He could have looked up Kendall's office, but Kendall worked in the Directorate of Science and Technology, and Monroe knew all about that portion of the building.

Coleman worked for the Directorate of Operations. People in S&T always seemed to speak of Ops in tones of, for lack of a better word, awe. S&T was mostly research, the development of technology, work done in laboratories and office buildings. S&T did the work that nobody outside the CIA cared about.

Ops had people all over the world, even behind the Iron Curtain. Ops obtained information, planted false information, shot people, beat people up, shoved uncomfortable objects into people's noses, and, Monroe assumed, bedded every attractive woman east of the Danube, if there were any. Ops was exciting. Ops was where the action was.

Lab nerds from S&T, as a matter of practice, never dared to venture into Ops. Doing so would be like the high school spelling bee champion showing up at football practice and demanding to play defensive end. One simply doesn't do it unless one is in the mood to wear a jockstrap as an unsettlingly tight hat.

So, with a little bit of time to kill, Monroe headed over to Ops.

It turned out to be a little bit more interesting than the rest of the building. Monroe stumbled across one large room, occupied by a few dozen people, several teletype machines that never stopped printing, and three long, curved tables, all facing a giant world map that covered almost the entirety of the large wall on which it was hung. It was the biggest map Monroe had ever seen, at least 40 feet wide and 20 feet high, and it had a number of small red flags attached to it in various places. Several dozen little flags were in or right around Moscow. Another couple dozen in Berlin. Eight in Paris. Two in, of all places, Antarctica. And one, to his surprise, very near the Missouri bootheel. That was where Cape Girardeau was; he'd looked it up in his road atlas at home.

Monroe wondered if the flags marked the locations of Ops field agents. If so, maybe someone – Coleman? – was in Cape Girardeau that day. Maybe the flags just marked locations of clandestine offices. Before he had much time to consider it any further, he realized that a few of the people in the room were beginning to look at him with interest. Suddenly feeling like he was being sized up for the CIA version of a jockstrap hat, he left.

He was a tad concerned that someone might follow him into the hall, but nobody did. He was surprised to notice that his heart was beating fairly hard. His instincts told him he should either head back to the S&T area of the building or simply go take another long lunch. But the idea of finding Coleman's office was simply too tempting. The guy seemed...not all there. Weird. Like he had gone on one too many missions and had been forced to hold his breath for just a bit longer than he really should have while hiding out from some bad guy.

Monroe wandered away from the map room and found his way to the main lobby of the Ops section. He approached one of the several receptionists working the main desk, a burly woman who looked like she maybe used to wrestle professionally. With the practiced charm of a civil servant, she acknowledged his presence by looking up at him and changing her expression not a whit.

"I'm looking for Agent Coleman's office," Monroe said.

She flipped her directory book to the C section and slid her finger down a column of names and extensions.

"Which one?" she asked. "There are three Colemans."

"Uh...shoot, I forgot his first name. He's a little bit crazy, if that helps."

"You'll need to be more specific."

"He limps."

The woman sighed. "There are over 400 people in the Directorate," she said.

"Only three of them are named Coleman," he said.

The woman's expression became a vague glare.

"He likes to arm-wrestle," Monroe said.

"Ah," the woman said, sounding very much like a person who has just learned that her least favorite relative is about to move into her basement. "You're looking for Wyman Coleman."

"Yeah, that's him. Wyman."

"I'll let him know you're here," she said, lifting the handset of her phone.

"Oh no no," Monroe said, waving his hands. "Uhh, I'd like to surprise him."

The woman put the handset down, as if she were preparing to walk around her desk and shove her knee into Monroe's intestinal tract. "This is the Directorate of Operations, sir," she said grimly. "Nobody here enjoys a surprise. I *will* let him know that you are here." Her expression brooked no argument as she lifted the receiver and started dialing.

No wonder she got this job, Monroe thought, as he prayed for Coleman to be away from his desk. He wasn't sure how he was going to explain why he'd come to visit.

Monroe glanced at the directory. From where he was standing, it was upside down, but he could see Coleman's office number listed next to his name: 319NW. He quickly memorized the number.

"He's not answering," she said.

"Okay," Monroe said, trying to keep his sense of relief from being too obvious. "That's okay. I'll come back. Thanks."

The woman said nothing as Monroe walked away. He glanced back at her over his shoulder to see if he was being watched, but the woman was already chatting with another receptionist and had her back turned.

It didn't take him long to find 319NW. It wasn't an office. It was a cubicle, one of about 30 that filled a large bullpen-style area. Coleman wasn't in it. Monroe realized that he had no plan for the possibility of showing up and finding Coleman sitting at his desk. Not that he had anything to hide, but the idea of Coleman thinking that he was snooping on him seemed like something to avoid.

The cubicle was almost empty. On his desk blotter was a piece of typewriter paper with the words ON ASSINEMENT and BACK INDEFINATLEY written on it in a script so malformed that it appeared to have been written by a poorly trained primate. The CIA was no place for desks covered in knick-knacks, but Coleman seemed to have even fewer personal items than normal on his desk. A framed photo of President Johnson sat on one corner. A Snickers wrapper was tacked to the cubicle wall for reasons unfathomable to Monroe. Above the typewriter hung another framed photo, this one of Mount Rushmore. Monroe peered closer at it and saw that Coleman had scribbled a moustache on Thomas Jefferson.

Monroe had read somewhere that the Jefferson on Mount Rushmore wasn't the first one. The first Jefferson had been carved on the left side of Washington, but after two years worth of work, the sculptor realized that the granite on that part of the mountain was cracking. So the guy blew up two years of work, blasted Jefferson right off the mountain, and started over on Washington's right.

And Coleman had moustached it.

That was it. There was nothing else to indicate that the cubicle had ever been occupied. There were a few paper clips strewn across the desk, and the desk itself looked like it could stand to be Windexed, but nothing else of note.

Monroe looked around to make sure nobody had noticed him, then yanked the Snickers wrapper off the cubicle wall and crumpled it into his pocket.

His right arm still hurt from arm wrestling with Coleman.

~

Monroe made sure he was home early on Friday and Saturday night, just in case Marie had a date with Dick. If he only had two nights of listening before he was carted off to what sounded like the most remote outpost in all of middle America, he was going to make darn sure he missed nothing. He parked himself in front of his listening station at 5 p.m. each night and flipped open his copy of *A House of Pomegranates* to pass the time until something interesting happened at Marie's. Each of the short stories in the book was stranger than the last, and almost none of them seemed to have much of a point. It was like reading a children's book written by someone who hated children.

Friday night didn't disappoint. Marie got home from work around 6 p.m. and talked to one of her friends on the phone while she got ready to go out for the evening. She loudly complained to her friend that Dick was hinting far too much about his interest in wanting to engage in a sexual act that, to Monroe, sounded like it might be illegal.

Monroe gathered from Marie's conversation that she and Dick were meeting the friend and her boyfriend for dinner and drinks. Marie mentioned that she didn't want to get too drunk that night lest she "wake up with ligament damage."

Marie left soon afterward, and Monroe figured he had at least a few hours to kill. He read his book and occasionally flipped through the dials to listen to the other apartments but found little of interest. At around 10:15, Marie and Dick came home, and Marie was clearly under the influence of just about anything she'd been able to ingest in the previous few hours. Monroe listened intently while they had 20 minutes of extremely vocal sex, after which Marie gleefully consented to the precise act she had complained to her friend about earlier in the day. After listening to it, Monroe was even more certain that what he'd just heard was not only illegal, but also extremely unsanitary.

Saturday was a different story. Marie sent Dick home early in the morning and spent most of the day away from her apartment. Monroe filled the hours by packing. He packed up just about everything he could think to take on the trip, and it still only filled two suitcases. He wished he could somehow take his listening station, mostly because he was leery of leaving it in his apartment for so long. Thinking about the listening station reminded him again that he'd not done anything about the bugs in the various apartments, and he felt a twinge of...something. Not exactly fear. Concern, maybe. But not enough concern to bother with figuring out a way to get into people's places and remove the bugs.

Much to Monroe's disappointment, Marie didn't come home that night until close to midnight, and she immediately started getting ready for bed. He was fairly sure that he could hear her crying softly while she washed her face. He wondered why. But she didn't call anyone, just went to bed and cried a little more before falling asleep.

Monroe flipped off his listening station, puzzled. Marie never cried. It was annoying. His last night of listening, and it ended as a total dud.

Women.

Chapter 6

When Monroe approached the gate at Dulles, he saw that Kendall was already there, waiting. Monroe stopped walking and looked around for cover. If Kendall didn't see him, he might be able to kill some of the time before boarding hiding out at another gate or in a gift shop.

"Hey there, buddy!" Kendall shouted, waving his arms like Gilligan trying to flag down a passing plane. "Over here!"

Too late, Monroe thought. He waved back, mostly to get Kendall to stop waving his arms.

"So, you ready for this?" Kendall asked as Monroe settled into the chair next to him.

"I guess."

"I'm really worried about my birds. I asked my mom to check on them, but my mom's not very reliable now that she's switched back to Jim Beam."

"I'm sure the birds will be fine."

"Yeah," Kendall said. "I suppose you're right."

"If not, you can always get new birds."

Kendall's mouth fell open. "Good lord, don't say that! Bugs and Daffy are special to me. I could get new birds, but I could never replace them."

"Bugs and Daffy?"

"Yeah. So?"

"Nothing."

"Bugs Bunny and Daffy Duck are classic icons of early American cinema."

"Yeah."

"Anyway, I'd be devastated if anything happened to those two," Kendall said. "Maybe I should have asked Mrs. Albertson to look after them. Mom switched back to Jim Beam."

"They'll be fine."

"You think?"

"Sure."

"Okay." Kendall exhaled deeply. "Okay. I feel better. Thanks. Corn dog?"

"Um...no. Thanks. It's 8:45 in the morning."

"It's never too early for corn dogs, Art."

"Arthur."

Kendall looked at Monroe for a moment, sizing him up. "You're not an Arthur. An Artie, maybe."

"It's Arthur."

"Great. I'm going to go find a corn dog." Kendall stood and wandered off.

"Good luck with that," Monroe muttered, mostly to himself. He looked at his watch. He had 45 minutes left before boarding. He grabbed his satchel and headed for a newsstand.

Monroe always found newsstands a bit daunting. He was hardly an avid reader, so he found that he was a bit overwhelmed by the sheer number of options available to him. He stood at the magazine rack for several minutes, finding it difficult to even figure out which issue to pick up and flip through.

"Excuse me," a female voice said. Monroe looked; the woman who had spoken was pretty. Not dazzling, but pretty. She was trying to reach past Monroe to grab a copy of *Life*. Monroe stepped back.

"Thank you," the woman said. She picked up the copy and walked toward the checkout counter. Monroe noticed that she had a very nice butt. He grabbed a copy of *National Geographic* and pretended to leaf through it. He couldn't help but notice that her black slacks hugged the curves of her butt quite nicely.

The woman finished paying for her magazine and left the shop. She hadn't noticed him. Monroe sighed and shook his head. He looked down at the magazine and realized he hadn't picked up a *National Geographic* after all. He had grabbed *McCall's Needlework Patterns*. He quickly put it back on the rack.

The man behind the counter in the shop seemed to be glaring at him. "Already have that issue," Monroe said as he grabbed a copy of that day's *Washington Post* and flipped a quarter at the man.

Walking back to the gate with the *Post* tucked under his arm, Monroe saw that the woman with the nice butt was sitting, of all places, at the same gate.

She looked just as good from the front as she did from the back. Her shoulder-length brown hair was smooth and wavy. Her pale blue sweater featured a neckline that showed just a touch of what appeared to be very lovely cleavage. She was hardly the kind of girl who could make a living as a model, but she was definitely the kind to make a three-hour flight a little more enjoyable. Monroe hoped she would be sitting in his row.

He sat in a seat across from hers. She was buried in her copy of *Life* and once again didn't notice him in the least, which was just fine with Monroe. He could take nice long glances at her without her noticing.

"Hey, what did you move over there for?" Kendall practically shouted, having apparently returned from his corn dog hunt. The woman looked up and Monroe had to quickly avert his eyes to avoid detection.

Monroe looked over his shoulder, where Kendall was standing by the seats they'd been sitting in earlier. Kendall's carry-on bag was still in front of them. He was holding a hot dog and looking extremely put out.

"I forgot we were sitting over there," Monroe said.

"You forgot? It was ten minutes ago. Maybe less."

"Sorry."

"My bag is still here. You didn't see my bag?"

"No. I didn't see your bag. I'm sorry."

"Are you just going to sit over there?"

Monroe could feel his cheeks reddening. People were starting to stare. Kendall was loud. "I'd like to sit over here, yes."

"Why? I don't want to move my bag. My hands are full."

"Fine," Monroe said, standing up. "I'll come sit over there. Sheesh. Just keep your voice down."

"You don't have to sheesh me," Kendall said. "You sat in the wrong seats. Not my fault. Why did you want to sit over there so bad?"

"No reason," Monroe said, taking a seat next to where Kendall still stood, hot dog in one hand, oozing enough mustard to drown a small mammal. Kendall looked back over at the other side of the gate, where Monroe had been sitting, and took a huge bite of the hot dog. Half the dog disappeared into his mouth.

"Oooorrhrmmmm," Kendall exclaimed, his mouth full of hot dog. He turned to Monroe and smiled a gigantic grin. "You like that girl," he managed to say around the chunk of processed meat in his mouth.

Monroe turned bright red. "I do not."

Kendall's smile got bigger, to the point where small chunks of bun were falling out of the corners, and he pointed at his traveling companion. "Yes, you do," he said, finally swallowing. "Your face is all turning red."

"It is...I do not," Monroe stammered. He glanced over at the woman. She was looking in their direction, apparently trying to figure out what the commotion was all about. Monroe shot his eyes back toward the floor.

"Oh, come on, you can at least *look* at her," Kendall said. "She's not gonna bite."

"Just sit down and shut up, will you?"

"Boy, she's really pretty."

"Kendall, please…"

"You looooove her," Kendall said, pursing his lips into a smooching shape and aiming them at Monroe's cheek.

"Kendall, cut it out."

"You want to kiiiiiiss her."

"What are you, twelve years old?"

Kendall flopped into a chair, closed his eyes and repeatedly kissed the air between his lips and Monroe's face. Monroe could smell the mustard in the air.

"Dammit, Jimmy, cut it *out*."

"Mwah mwah mwah!" Kendall said, kissing the air more.

"Soldier, if that tongue comes out, I'm going to have to shoot it off," Coleman's voice said.

Kendall's eyes popped open and he jerked upright, looking up at Coleman, who was standing over them and scowling. "Sorry, uh, sir," he said, wiping mustard off his mouth.

"No glory in kissing a man on the face," Coleman said.

"No sir," Kendall replied.

Coleman stared at Kendall and Monroe for a moment. "You two aren't manly lovers, are you?"

"No!" Monroe and Kendall shouted in unison. Monroe peripherally saw the woman look at them again.

"I'll have none of it on this mission," Coleman said. "You two want to fiddle faddle, it'll have to wait until the project is over."

"Really, we're not…we don't even know each other very well," Monroe said.

"I've never even been to a bath house," Kendall said.

"I'll let this slide this time," Coleman said. "Next time, blam, I staple your tongue to a solid object."

"I think I already need an antacid," Kendall said.

"Concerns," Coleman said, scowling.

"What do you mean, concerns?" Monroe asked.

Coleman leaned down until his face was just a few inches away from Monroe's. "Concerns," he said. He held Monroe's gaze for a moment, then stood up again, and his face brightened as if he'd not had a single concern since the day he was born. "Hope the flight departs on time and that we don't come under fire," he said.

"Are you expecting us to come under fire?" Monroe asked, somewhat alarmed.

"Never hurts to be prepared," Coleman said.

"Okay," Monroe said. He glanced over at the girl, whose gaze jumped down to her magazine. Had she been watching? She was looking at her magazine, so he took a nice long look at her sweater.

"You boys seen Westcott?" Coleman said, making some kind of disturbing snorting noise, as if he were attempting to suck a glob of deeply wedged snot even further into his nasal cavities.

The woman's gaze lifted from her magazine again. Monroe had to jerk his eyes away from her chest. His cheeks reddened again.

"Nope," Kendall said, having just stuffed the second half of his hot dog into his mouth. "We've been here for a little while. He likth to live dangerouthly, huh? Me, if I'm afraid I'm going to be late for a plane, I thtart breaking out in a rasth, really bad. All over." He looked meaningfully at Monroe. "*All* over. You know? All."

"Okay, yeah, I get it," Monroe said.

"Concerns," Coleman repeated, to nobody in particular. He snorted again.

Monroe glanced over at the woman. She seemed to be staring at Coleman. At Coleman? Monroe looked at the man. His buzzcut was so perfectly square that it made his head look like a flesh-colored cube. She was staring at him? Figures, he thought. Girls always go for the blockheads.

"Hey, here he comth," Kendall said, swallowing and gesturing toward the walkway.

Westcott was dressed in what appeared to be a very expensive suit. He looked like he was in a terrible mood.

"Good morning, gentlemen," he said to the three of them, straightening the collar on his jacket. "Oh, good," he said to Kendall, "you're already eating. I was afraid you might actually experience a hunger pang on the plane."

"I don't like flying," Kendall said. "Eating calms me down. My doctor says it's okay."

"I think your doctor is simply trying to cut his losses," Westcott said. He looked over at the woman. "Have any of you introduced yourselves to my assistant?" He said, gesturing toward her.

Monroe fought the urge to let his jaw drop.

"We didn't realize she was your assistant," Kendall said, elbowing Monroe in the ribs so hard that he involuntarily yelped.

"What's wrong with you?" Coleman said.

"I'm not," Monroe blurted.

"You're not what?"

"Um…nothing," Monroe said.

"Morning, Ava," Westcott said to the woman, who was gathering her things and smiling, not a real smile, but the kind people use when they're meeting strangers in a professional setting.

"Hello, Dr. Westcott," Ava said.

"Gentlemen, this is Ava Moriarty, one of my veterinary assistants," Westcott said to the others.

"Your best veterinary assistant, as I recall," Ava said without smiling.

Westcott seemed to blanch just a bit. "Yes," he said, "my best veterinary assistant."

"Special Agent Coleman," Coleman said, thrusting his beefy hand at Ava. "I admire your ample hips."

"Agent Coleman," Westcott said, "Ava is on this trip because I need her here. She is not here for you to ogle."

"Central Intelligence Agency," Coleman said, tapping himself on the chest.

"What is that supposed to mean?" Westcott asked.

"Can't tell you that. Classified."

Before Westcott could reply, Ava grabbed Coleman's hand and shook it. "It's nice to meet you, Agent Coleman," she said. "And don't worry, Dr. Westcott. I grew up with three brothers. I think I can handle a little boorish behavior."

"Hoo hoo!" Kendall said. Coleman glared at him, and he fell silent again.

Westcott continued with the introductions. "These two," he said, "are the alleged technical wizards assigned to this abomination of a project. They have names, but I haven't bothered to remember them."

"I'm Jimmy Kendall," Kendall said, "and this is Artie Monroe. We're with the Directorate of Science and Technology."

"It's Arthur, actually," Monroe said.

"How do you do," she said to them, shaking each man's hand.

"Just fine, ma'am," Kendall said. "A little worried about Mom switching back to Jim Beam, but otherwise just fine."

Monroe said nothing. He was finding it difficult to look Ava in the eye.

"What did your mom drink before?" Ava asked Kendall.

"Lemonade," he replied.

"Oh."

The attendant at the gate began making announcements. She was saying that the flight to St. Louis was not very full, and that everyone was welcome to board.

"Say goodbye to D.C. for a while, team," Coleman said. "It's off to the sticks for us. Time for glory."

"It amazes me that you see the creation of surgically altered cats as glory," Westcott said as they gathered their things and made their way to the boarding line.

"There's glory in every assignment," Coleman said. "Just have to sniff it out."

"And what does our glory smell like?" Westcott sneered.

Coleman breathed deeply. So deeply that it appeared for a moment that the man might injure himself doing so.

He exhaled. "Mustard," he said, and marched aboard the plane.

~

A three-hour flight and two-hour drive later, Coleman steered the rental van off the highway and onto a side road.

"Are we there yet?" Kendall said.

"Not yet," Coleman said. "But close. Good diner about a mile down the road. Cheeseburgers better than the inside of a Turkish woman's thigh."

"Turkish women have good thighs?" Kendall asked.

"Not particularly," Coleman said.

A short drive later, he steered the van into the parking lot of a small diner. Monroe peered at it through the window. The place looked like it hadn't had its windows washed since sometime during the Roosevelt administration. He tried to set his concerns about beef quality aside; he hadn't eaten since they took off from Dulles, and he was starving.

"Everybody out of the pool," Coleman said, shoving the gear shift into park and jumping out his door.

"I don't know about you guys," Ava said, "but it seems to me that this is going to be a very long month." Monroe and Kendall were seated on the bench in front of her, but she didn't wait for them to leave first, pushing open the van door and hopping out. Monroe didn't mind, since it offered another opportunity to get a long look at her butt.

"Oh man," Kendall said behind Monroe as the two of them got out, "do you really think we might be done in a month?"

Ava waved the dust of the parking lot out of her eyes. "Yeah," she said. "Why wouldn't we be?"

Kendall shrugged. "I didn't think we'd be able to finish in a month, that's all. Heck, I figured we'd be lucky to finish in six months, before it gets too cold in the fall. That's why I'm so worried about my birds. Mom switched back…"

"Wait, wait," Ava interrupted, waving her hand in front of her. "What are you talking about? I thought this was just a one-month assignment. We're going to be done in a month. Right?"

Kendall and Monroe looked at each other. "Uhh, are you sure you're on the right assignment?" Kendall asked.

"I don't know," Ava said. Her expression was quickly turning into one of deep concern. "Dr. Westcott and I are here to help you guys test some new chemical agent on feline subjects. Right?"

Kendall chuckled. "Nope. Who told you that?"

"Dr. Westcott."

Monroe was the first to connect the dots. "Uh oh," he mumbled.

"Well, that doesn't make any sense," Kendall said. "Dr. Westcott's been in on this whole thing for a while. Longer than either of us have been. He already knew what was going on when Henderson explained it to us."

Ava's expression dropped from one of concern to one of growing distress. "What exactly are you here to do?" she asked.

"We're making an acoustic kitty," Kendall said pleasantly, as if the phrase made perfect sense. "That's not what you're here to do? I'm really confused."

Ava's voice dropped an entire octave. "What…exactly…is an…acoustic kitty?"

"You mean you really don't know?" Kendall asked. "Are you sure you're on the right project?" He looked at Monroe. "I'm really confused."

"Don't look at me," Monroe said. "I'm not in charge here."

"Someone please tell me what's going on here," Ava said. "Tell me what an acoustic kitty is."

"Well…" Kendall replied, "it's a cat that's wired up to be used as a surveillance device."

Ava continued to stare at Kendall. He kept talking. "We're supposed to figure out a way to, you know, put wires and microphones and remote-control functions into it, and keep it alive, and be able to send it into some park in D.C. so it can eavesdrop on the Russians for us."

Ava's eyes, which were starting to look like they belonged to a Titanic crew member, shifted to Monroe. "No, really," he said.

"How far along is the project?" she asked.

Kendall was getting increasingly nervous. "Look, Miss Moriarty, maybe you should go talk to…"

"No, I need *you* to tell me. How far along is the project?"

"We start tomorrow," Kendall squeaked.

Ava's jaw dropped open and her face went pale. "Oh…my…God…" she said, pushing all ten of her fingers into her hair.

"I'm really sorry," Kendall said. "I have no idea what's going on here, but I really have to pee and you're almost completely freaking me out. I swear none of this was my idea."

Ava took several aimless steps around the parking lot. "Oh my God," she said. "That son of a…," she muttered. Monroe saw tears welling in her eyes. He and Kendall glanced at each other. Kendall shrugged, clearly just as confused as Monroe was.

Ava turned again, toward the diner, and scanned the interior until she saw Westcott sitting at a table with Coleman. Before Westcott happened to see her looking in at him, she turned again, facing directly away from the windows, and leaned on the van hood. She cried softly, shaking her head.

Monroe and Kendall stood in the lot for a few moments, watching Ava shake her head and run her hands through her hair. Monroe wondered if he should console her. He thought that definitely someone should console her.

Suddenly Ava straightened, sniffed deeply, and pushed tears out of her eyes with her hands. She took a deep breath, exhaled, then looked at the bewildered Monroe and Kendall. "Let's eat," she said, turning and heading into the diner.

Monroe and Kendall stood in the parking lot and watched her go inside. "What was that all about?" Kendall asked. "This project just keeps getting weirder and weirder, and we haven't even started the really weird stuff yet."

"Yeah, no kidding. I guess Westcott lied to her for some reason."

"Yeah," Kendall said. "You should have made your move. Best time to pick up women is when they're crying."

"Jimmy," Monroe said, "stop."

"Hey, you're the one who likes her."

"I do not."

"Yes, you do," Kendall said, making kisses into the air. "You loooove her."

Monroe elbowed Kendall in the ribs.

"Oww! Hey! What was…"

Monroe jerked his head toward the window. Coleman was staring straight at the two of them and scowling.

"He's going to shoot me, isn't he?" Kendall said.

"Probably. Let's eat."

~

Much to Monroe's surprise, Ava didn't say anything to Westcott during the meal. She had clearly been duped into coming. Why wouldn't she tell Westcott to take a hike? But she didn't say a word. She barely spoke to anyone, just focused on her cheeseburger when it arrived. But Monroe saw that she spent long stretches of time deep in thought, with her gaze shifted out the window.

Westcott didn't seem to notice a thing. He complained about the food, complained about how everyone smelled after traveling for nearly six hours, complained about the service, complained that the diner didn't serve alcohol, and demanded that they leave nothing more than a five percent tip. Nobody seemed to argue the point, so Monroe made sure he was the last one to leave the table and tossed an extra $5 from his own pocket under his plate.

Once everyone was back in the van, Coleman put it into gear and said, "Chow's over. It's go time."

"What's go time?" Kendall asked.

"To the lab, Chubbsy."

"I'm not chubby!"

"Why are we going to the lab?" Westcott asked.

"Only 2:30, doc," Coleman responded. "Plenty of work left in the day."

Westcott chortled. "You're welcome to go, but I'm not working today. It's Sunday. I don't work on Sunday."

"Suit yourself," Coleman said.

Coleman steered the van through a series of two-lane streets that were increasingly populated with houses and buildings. Nothing was higher than two stories. After less than ten minutes of driving, they turned onto what appeared to be the main downtown artery. Monroe could see a wide brown river flowing behind the buildings on their left.

"The Mississippi," Kendall said. "Haven't seen it in years, not since visiting my grandma in the Quad Cities before she died."

"I've never seen it," Monroe said. He stared at the wide brown river for a few moments. "I haven't missed much," he concluded.

"Hey," Kendall said, craning his neck around, "was that a bowling alley we just passed?"

"I didn't notice," Monroe said.

"No glory in bowling," Coleman said.

"No glory?" Kendall replied. "No glory? You try bowling a 270. It isn't easy. Trust me, you bowl a game like that, you'll get glory, mister."

"No opponent in bowling," Coleman said. "No defeat of an opponent, no glory."

"Have you ever *been* bowling?" Kendall asked. "The whole point is to beat your opponent."

"Negative," Coleman said. "You bowl against the pins, not an opponent. If your opponent had to stand halfway down the lane and try blocking your throw, then maybe there's glory. But those pins, they just sit there waiting for you to knock them down. Defenseless. No glory."

"Ahh, you're nuts," Kendall said to Coleman.

Coleman slowly pulled the van over to the shoulder.

"Are we here?" Kendall asked. They seemed to be parked in front of a dentist's office.

Coleman turned around in his seat so that he was directly facing Kendall. Before anyone could realize it was happening, Coleman pulled his gun out of his shoulder holster, held it by the barrel, and began lightly thumping a rather startled Kendall on the forehead with it.

"Agent...Coleman...not...crazy," he said, punctuating each word with another thump of the gun butt against Kendall's forehead. Kendall's eyes went as wide as bloodshot Frisbees.

"Agent...Coleman...not...crazy," Coleman repeated. Thump, thump, thump, thump. "Understand?" he asked, holding the butt over Kendall's head.

Kendall nodded and whined unintelligibly.

"Super," Coleman said, suddenly as cheery as a cartoon deer in a meadow of sunshine. He whipped back around in the driver's seat, put the van into gear, and pulled out onto the road. He turned on the radio and immediately began singing along with "Love Me Do."

"I don't think any of us saw that coming," Westcott said, sounding almost bored.

Kendall was visibly shaking as he slowly turned his head to look at Monroe. "What did I do?" Kendall whispered.

"I don't know," Monroe whispered back. "Maybe don't do it again."

Ava leaned forward from her seat on the rear bench. "Is he always like that?" she asked.

"We only met him a few days ago," Monroe said, "but yeah, I'd say this is pretty much on par for the course."

"He whacked my head with a gun," Kendall said, still shaking.

"Look on the bright side," Monroe said, slapping Kendall on the back, "at least he didn't whack your head with the bullets."

Kendall whimpered.

"Could you guys do me a favor?" Ava whispered.

"Sure," Monroe replied.

"Don't leave me alone in a room with him."

"Same here," Kendall whispered. "Don't leave me alone with him either, Artie."

"It's Arthur," Monroe corrected.

Coleman drove the van past a series of small storefronts – a hardware store, barber shop, candy store – before spinning the wheel to the left and driving into an alley between two buildings.

"You're not an Arthur," Kendall replied. "You just need to take my word for it. You can't be something you're not, Artie."

"Kendall…"

Coleman threw the van into park. "Okay, we're here!" he said like a father pulling the family wagon into the parking lot at Disney World.

Monroe looked around. The van was parked about two-thirds of the way down the alley. All he saw on both sides were solid brick walls, and a fire escape ladder.

"We are?" Ava said, looking around. "I don't see anything."

"Of course you don't," Coleman said, throwing his door open. "They don't call us the CIA for nothing." He got out and slammed the door behind him.

"Where exactly are we?" Westcott asked, peering through the windshield.

"Lab," Coleman replied. "Come on, everybody out. Work time." He climbed out of the van.

"This isn't the lab," Westcott said. "The lab is on the west end of town."

"That lab was inappropriate," Coleman said. "Got us a better one."

Westcott opened his door. "What do you mean, you got us a better one? That lab was state of the art! I spent a lot of time bringing that facility up to snuff. The yokels who own it clearly don't know what they're doing, but I spent weeks telling them how to make it better. I suffered through countless conversations with those people. And now you're telling me we aren't even using that facility?"

"Affirmative. Don't worry, doc. I brought all your crap over. It's up there."

"Up?" Westcott yelped, looking up at the buildings on either side of the alley. "What up? There is no up. There are no fucking stairs anywhere to be seen, no doors, nothing. I had a perfectly good, state of the art facility completely ready. I checked in on those morons running the place just last week!"

"Figured you'd be upset. I had everything brought over on Friday. Simpler that way."

"You...you..." Westcott stammered. "How dare you go behind my back on this? What possible reason could you have had for ripping everything out of a perfectly good facility and bringing it to some...*building*...down by the god damned *river*?"

"Other place wasn't secret enough," Coleman said, pulling down the fire escape ladder. "Right out in the open. Might as well have posted a sign. This place, nobody will know about."

Coleman jutted a thumb toward his chest and winked at Westcott. "Central Intelligence Agency," he said, before shoving his cane through a belt loop and beginning to climb the ladder. As he climbed, he made sure that he never put his weight on his bad leg. Instead, he pulled himself up with his arms and hopped up each rung on his good leg.

Westcott's entire head was purple. "Who gave you the authority to do this without my permission? I'll have you knocked down to...well, to whatever the lowest rank in your pathetic organization is!"

"Henderson gave the authority," Coleman said without looking down.

Westcott's jaw moved a couple times, but no words came out. He glanced over to where Monroe, Kendall and Ava all stood watching him. He seemed to consider saying something to them, but didn't. Instead, he looked up at Coleman, who had reached the first landing on the fire escape and was preparing to climb to the second.

"Coleman," Westcott said, "what are you doing up there? Where is the damn lab?"

"Up here," Coleman replied. "Think I'm climbing for fun? CIA doesn't have fun, doc."

"Oh, I don't know," Ava said, watching Coleman and shielding her eyes from the sky. "I'm having fun."

"He's actually right," Monroe said. "I've never had any fun at the Agency."

"Yeah," Kendall said, nodding. "I was once reprimanded for wearing a shirt that was considered inappropriately vivid."

"You mean to tell me," Westcott shouted, "that I have to climb a fire escape to get into my own lab? Where's the front door?"

"Isn't one," Coleman said. "Quit your bitching and climb."

"You're kidding," Ava said. "That's the way to the lab?"

"To the *secret* lab," Coleman shouted down from the second landing. He held his index finger in front of his lips. "Shhhh." He looked around, as if to make certain that nobody was watching, then began climbing the ladder.

Monroe glanced toward the end of the alley, where the street was, and saw a middle-aged couple walking past. The woman stopped and pointed at Coleman. The man appeared to say something and shook his head. They moved on.

Coleman pushed open a window. He swung a leg over the sash and paused as he was halfway in. "Move out, soldiers!" he shouted down to them.

"Somebody shoot me," Westcott muttered. "Coleman, where is the god damned *door*?" he shouted upwards.

"Poor listening skills," Coleman shouted back down. "Unfortunate trait. *Secret* lab, remember? No door. Just the window. Climb."

"You really expect me to climb up that creaky damn ladder every single day?" Westcott said.

"No," Coleman said. "Henderson does."

Westcott sighed. "We're going to see about that," he grumbled, reaching for the ladder. He started to climb up.

"Guess I won't be wearing any skirts anytime soon," Ava said, peering at the fire escape. She looked at Kendall and Monroe. "Tell you what, why don't you boys go on up first? I think I'm fine being the last one up."

"Okay," Kendall said, stepping forward and climbing. "Looks kinda fun, actually."

Monroe said nothing as he followed Kendall. Ava brought up the rear.

Kendall showed surprising agility, reaching the second platform in just a few moments. "Whoa," he said as he peered into the window through which Westcott had just crawled. He looked down at Monroe. "Well Artie, it's certainly...interesting," he said, before climbing through the window.

"Don't call me Artie," Monroe said, continuing to climb. "And what do you mean by interesting?"

Kendall, having disappeared into the building, didn't respond. "I don't think he heard you," Ava said.

Monroe was breathing hard as he reached the second platform. "Whew, I need to get in better shape if I'm going to do this every day."

"You should run," Ava said from below as she came up the second ladder. "I run three miles every other day. Keeps the pounds off."

"You mean you just run?" Monroe asked. "For no reason?"

"Not for no reason, silly," Ava said, reaching the platform herself. "For fitness. You should try it. I think it's something that's really going to catch on."

"That's crazy. Nobody's going to just run for the fun of it. Lunatics, maybe."

"Suit yourself," Ava said.

"Artie," Kendall said from inside the window, "you're going to want to see this."

"Okay, keep your shorts on," Monroe said. He peered inside the window. "Oh," he said.

What he saw inside was, for all intents and purposes, a warehouse. An old one. With cobwebs in the ceiling. And little piles of what appeared to be mouse droppings in the corners. Off to the left sat a row of four folding tables, on which were scattered piles of very worn-looking electronics equipment. The walls were exposed brick, and more than a few of the bricks looked as if they were about to finally give up and crumble into dust at any moment.

A wall ran along the right side of the space, and it looked like it had been erected very recently. The drywall had not even been primed, much less painted. The wall had one lone door, which stood open. From where he stood, Monroe couldn't see what was on the other side of the wall.

"Should have everything you need," Coleman said. He was sitting on a plain wooden chair near the door to a small bathroom in the far corner. "If not, let me know. I'll see what I can do. No promises."

"No kidding," Monroe said as he crossed the room toward the workstations, where Kendall was already picking through the instruments like a plumber sifting through sewage for a lost wedding ring. "Coleman, the stuff I had back at Langley was crap," Monroe said, "but it was better than this. We're supposed to save the world from the red menace with this junk?"

"Can't always choose your weapons in the field," Coleman said. "Sometimes you have to go to battle with a fork in one hand and a prostitute in the other."

Behind them, Ava had climbed through the window and was trying to get her bearings. "This is…interesting," she said.

"That's what I said!" Kendall said.

"Where's the medical area?" she asked.

"Agent Coleman!" Westcott bellowed from somewhere on the other side of the brand-new wall.

"Hear that?" Coleman said, pointing to the doorway. "That's coming from the medical area."

A moment later, Westcott burst out of the section in question. His head was once again purple. "Agent Coleman!" he shouted.

"Present," Coleman said, tilting back in his chair.

"I had everything set up in the other facility exactly as it needed to be set up," Westcott shouted. "What did you do, just throw everything into boxes and have it carted over here willy nilly?"

"Willy nilly?" Coleman said. "Willy nilly," he repeated, contemplating the term. "Yep. Fairly accurate description there, willy nilly."

"Everything is all mixed up. Nothing was packed properly. It will take us a week just to get everything set up again! Not to mention the fact that this entire floor is covered in an inch of dust! We'll have to clean everything from top to bottom before we can even take a temperature! I have never encountered such utter incompetence in my life! I don't know about you, but where I come from, standards are high. One does not simply do a job half-assed and expect it to be acceptable. What do you have to say for yourself?"

"You're welcome," Coleman said, tipping farther back on the chair, until his body was at a 45-degree angle to the floor.

"'You're welcome?'" Westcott bellowed. "That's it? *You're welcome?*"

"Did the best I could, doc," Coleman said. "Gives you stuff to do for a while. Not the worst thing."

"Not the worst thing? *Not the worst thing?* That's it! I'm reporting you! Walter is going to hear about this!"

"Already knows," Coleman said.

"What the hell do you mean, he already knows?"

"He knows. I told him. He said you'd be mad. Said you'd get over it. Your place was too expensive and too insecure. Here is budget-conscious. And they'll never suspect the CIA would operate in this shabby of a facility." He winked and tapped his temple with his finger. "Central Intelligence Agency," he said.

"He...I...you..." Westcott said, seeming to shake with rage. Instead of saying anything further, he glared at Monroe, Kendall, and Ava, then wheeled around and went back into the medical area, slamming the door behind him.

"I think I'll just hang out in here for a little while," Ava said.

"Ava!" Westcott shouted through the door. "Get in here. Now!"

Ava sighed deeply. "On second thought, I guess I'd rather be treated like dirt for a while," she said, heading toward the door.

"Happy to offer you a sidearm," Coleman said.

"No thanks," Ava said. "Do you have a broom, by any chance?"

"Broom is a questionable weapon. I recommend the sidearm."

"I meant that I need something to clean with."

"Ah. Supply closet's in there. Broom, mop, bucket. Everything you need. In the CIA, cleanliness is next to shooting important foreigners."

"Thanks."

"Good luck," Monroe said.

"I think I'll need it," Ave said as she closed the door behind her.

"Eww," Kendall said as yanked his hand away from a microscope. "This one's sticky."

"Hey Coleman," Monroe said. "Tell Henderson we said thanks."

"Ten-four," Coleman replied. "I'll pretend I didn't hear the sarcasm. No room in this army for sarcasm, soldier. Keep unpacking. Work to do."

"Hey," Kendall said. "There's no door."

"Sure there is," Coleman said. "Right there." He pointed to the door leading to the medical area.

"No," Kendall said. "I mean there's no door out of here. We're in a big room with no door."

"I told you," Coleman said, "secret lab. Can't be secret if any Tom, Dick and Harry can walk right in off the street."

"Couldn't you have just kept the door locked?" Monroe asked.

Coleman thought for a moment. "Valid point," he said. "But moot. Door's bricked over. Window's the door. You'll adjust. Secret lab."

"What if the place catches on fire?" Kendall asked. He seemed very worried.

"Fire escape, Chubbs!" Coleman barked, pointing out the window. "You act like I haven't considered all scenarios. *Secret. Lab.*"

"I'm not chubby," Kendall said, but without much conviction. "And this voltmeter smells like old cheese."

"Cheese," Coleman said. "Good for the bones."

"You going to help us clean any of this up?" Monroe asked.

"Bad leg," Coleman said. "Not much help. Plus, I'm on security detail. You boys go right on ahead." He leaned back on his chair until his head and shoulders were leaning against the brick wall behind him, and his feet were off the ground. Within seconds, he was snoring loudly.

"Why do I get the feeling we're going to be here for a long time?" Monroe asked Kendall.

"I think I just found a dead frog," Kendall said.

~

As it turned out, the motel where the team was staying, the Coral Motel, was across the street from the "secret lab." Monroe assumed the only reason for giving the place such a name was that the entire exterior was painted a seafaring coral color. Geography was not his strong suit, but Monroe was fairly certain there was no actual coral within a thousand miles of the Coral Motel.

It was a true motor lodge, with doors that opened directly to the parking lot. The pool around back was empty and filled with leaves. It looked as though it hadn't been used in years. When Monroe approached it, something in the leaves rustled and hissed at him.

Coleman had rented a block of rooms, five in a row, as far away from the rental office as possible. He put Westcott on one end, with Ava next to him, Coleman in the middle, then Kendall, and finally Monroe. Westcott had thrown a fit, saying that he did not want a room facing the street. Possibly because he wanted to put some distance between his room and Westcott's, Coleman allowed him to switch rooms. Westcott ended up in a room on the opposite side of the building, facing the not-really-a-pool.

Monroe realized that it was highly unlikely that any of the others would walk past his room on the way to his or her own. His happened to be the farthest away from the parking spaces. He couldn't have set it up any better if he had made the arrangements himself. He would have preferred a buffer zone of a few rooms, but asking for something like that would have been an odd request, and considering the fit Westcott had thrown, he didn't want to cause any further commotion.

That first night, they had dinner at a steak house that sat conveniently next door to the motel. As usual, Coleman paid. None of them said much; after traveling all day and spending several hours cleaning up the lab, they were all tired.

Monroe tried to drink as much Coke as he could during dinner. He was going to be up late. As it turned out, he'd finished what he needed to do by 2 a.m. and was therefore able to get a solid four hours of sleep.

Chapter 7

Everyone woke up early the next morning, and by 7:30 the group had gathered to walk across the street to the lab. Before they did, though, Coleman tossed the van keys to Kendall.

"What are these for?" Kendall asked.

"Cat run," Coleman replied.

"Cat run?" Kendall asked.

"You're picking up the first batch of cats."

"Whoa," Kendall replied, waving his hands in front of him. "No no. Why me? Shouldn't the vets do that?"

"No," Coleman said. "Address and directions are on the front seat. Take him with you if you want," he added, gesturing toward Monroe.

"I can pick up the cats," Ava said.

"No," Westcott said. "I need your help this morning. The engineers can handle it." He said the word "engineers" with the kind of disdain most people reserve for words like "molesters."

"See? It's fine," Coleman said. "Cat run. Scoot along."

"Don't worry about it," Ava said. "I've been to these kind of places all the time. It's like picking up groceries."

"Groceries don't have claws," Kendall muttered.

"You'll be fine," Ava said. "Just load them into the van and honk when you get back. I'll sneak out of the secret lab and help you bring them up."

"How many cats are we talking about?" Monroe asked.

"Plenty," Coleman said. "See you when you get back." He started to cross the street.

Westcott and Ava followed. "Try not to screw anything up," Westcott said as he walked away. "And don't get too attached to any of them."

Kendall waited until Westcott was out of earshot. "For a vet, he doesn't seem to like animals much," he said.

"I think the only animals he likes are the ones cooked medium rare," Monroe said. "Come on, let's get going."

~

"Hello?" Kendall said through the small hole cut into the middle of the thick glass. The window was the only thing in the building's surprisingly small lobby, other than a heavy (and very obviously locked) door directly across from the one they'd come in. Neither door had any kind of window on it; both appeared to be built to withstand a direct hit from a hydrogen bomb. Everything in the lobby, which was about as wide and deep as a large refrigerator, was painted beige. Kendall and Monroe could barely fit in it.

The drive had taken them three hours. The directions had essentially instructed them to drive to St. Louis and turn left, leading them to a town called Bonne Terre.

Bonne Terre, they discovered, was even smaller and more remote than Cape Girardeau. A single street ran through the center of town; the directions led them to a warehouse-like building on the far side of it, several miles away from anything else.

As they stood in the lobby, Monroe and Kendall peered through the window. On the other side of it was a small plain reception desk with nothing on it but a phone, a typewriter, a notepad, and an enormous pineapple. The walls of the room were bare except for a postcard tacked to the middle of the wall directly opposite the window. It showed a closeup of a bikini-clad female behind in some kind of tropical setting. The words WISH YOU WERE HERE! were printed squarely between her cheeks.

"Hello?" Kendall repeated. He looked on the little counter in front of him for a bell but found none. "Do you think they're closed?"

"I don't know," Monroe said. "The front door was open. Maybe talk louder."

"Hello?" Kendall said more loudly.

"Hold yer fuckin britches!" a voice, laden with a heavy Southern accent, boomed from somewhere deeper in the building. "I'm comin'!"

"Holy buckets," Monroe muttered.

"I don't think I like this place," Kendall said, eyeballing the front door.

"Oh no," Monroe said. "You are not leaving me here alone with whatever is about to come through that door."

Kendall eyed the door a moment longer, then seemed to change his mind. "You're right," Kendall said. "Friends don't do that kind of thing."

"We're friends?"

"Well...yeah. I mean, I guess so. Right?"

"Uh, yeah," Monroe said. He looked away from Kendall, into the empty room, and tapped his fingers on the counter. "Sure."

The two men stood in silence for several moments as they waited for the owner of the deeply accented voice to make her appearance.

"Gonna rain today," Kendall said.

"You think?" Monroe replied.

Kendall thought for a moment. "Yeah," he said. "I think so."

"Hm."

An unseen door swung violently on its hinge and crashed against a wall. Monroe heard the sound of feet slowly shuffling through it. Finally, the loud woman came into view. She was more obese than Monroe thought was humanly possible. Her enormous round face was flushed red. The deeper red around her cheeks and nose appeared more permanent and made her wiry reddish-blond hair even more orangeish by comparison. She was breathing heavily, as if the task of returning from wherever she'd been in the building was all the physical exercise she could handle for the week.

She spotted Monroe and Kendall and took a moment to squint at them as if she suspected they were about to steal her pineapple.

"What do you two want?" she demanded, her beady eyes darting from Monroe to Kendall and back again.

"Mr. Coleman sent us," Kendall said.

"Well, yip-dee-fuckin-doo for you," the woman said, leaning on the desk. "Am I supposed to know who Mr. Coleman is?"

"I...I don't know," Kendall stammered.

"I'm sorry," Monroe said. "We're here to pick up some cats. Mr. Coleman is, uh, our boss."

"He, *uhhh*, is, huh?" the woman spat. "Sure about that, Tonto?"

Monroe looked sideways at Kendall, who was staring at the woman in sheer terror. No help.

He decided to try again. "What we're wondering is, did Mr. Coleman place some kind of order for us?" Monroe asked. "We were under the impression that he'd already made the arrangements."

"Ain't a fuckin McDonalds," the woman said, exhaling heavily and filling the tiny vestibule with the smells of cigarette smoke and a vague sense of peanut butter. "You don't just 'place an order.' God damn city folk. Hang on, let me look at the books here." She reached to her left, and when her beefy hand reappeared, it was holding a ledger. She dropped the ledger to the counter and used one arm to prop her considerable weight while the other hand flipped through the book.

Monroe almost thanked the woman, then thought better of it. He looked at Kendall, who appeared to be sweating profusely. Kendall mouthed the word "Tonto?" at Monroe, who shrugged.

"Okay," the woman said. "Here it is. No wonder I didn't remember it. My idiot brother wrote it down. Can barely fuckin read it." She held up the ledger so that Monroe and Kendall could see it. "Don't this shit look like it was written by a retarded four-year-old? I'm surprised he didn't write it in fuckin crayon. Is that the worst shit you ever seen or what?"

The woman appeared to be waiting for a response. Monroe looked at the handwriting. It actually was very bad. The name "Coleman" was written as "Colnan."

"Um, yes," Monroe said, attempting a smile.

"Damn right it is. The boy's a total moron. You know he once managed to staple his own nose? I said to him, 'Boy, that is the dumbest fuckin thing I have ever heard of.' And I've heard of a lot of dumb fuckin things. How in the fuck can a grown man staple his own god damned nose?"

"I don't know," Monroe said.

The woman stared at them for a moment. "Y'all don't say much, do ya?"

"No, ma'am," Monroe said.

The woman grunted in contempt. "Y'all got twenty on order. There's a loading dock around back. Drive on back and my idiot brother'll load 'em up for you." She started to shuffle back out of the office, but paused after a step and looked back at Monroe and Kendall. "You geniuses do have carriers for these animals, right?"

~

"Keep this one off of me," Monroe said, scooping a dark gray cat off of his lap and attempting to toss it toward the back of the van. "He keeps climbing into my lap, and it's driving me nuts."

"That red one keeps staring at me," Kendall said, peering over his left shoulder for the fifth time in a minute. Monroe glanced back. Sure enough, there was an orangeish-red cat sitting squarely in the middle of the first bench and staring directly at Kendall.

"I don't think it's going to eat you, Jimmy," Monroe said.

"You sure they've all been declawed?" Kendall asked.

"That's what the kid said."

"Why didn't Coleman tell us we'd need carriers?" Kendall said. "I thought we were never going to catch that black one."

"This was all probably some big joke on Coleman's part," Monroe said. "That's why he didn't want Ava coming with us. He knew what he was doing."

"Maybe he thought there was glory in fetching cats," Kendall said.

"Don't start," Monroe said. "Only our second day here and I'm already wanting to go home."

"Can't think negative like that, Artie," Kendall said. "You're just going to make yourself miserable. We're stuck here, so we might as well try to enjoy it."

"Yeah, right," Monroe said. "I can't help but get this feeling that this whole thing is an enormous waste of time."

"See, that's what I mean by being negative. That was a very negative thing to say."

"I don't know. I just get the feeling nobody at Langley even cares about this project?"

"What do you mean? Henderson cares. Otherwise he wouldn't have sent us here."

"I guess. But look at where we're working. The equipment we got is all beat up. It took me an hour last night to scrape that yellow gunk off the soldering iron."

"Did you ever figure out what that stuff was?"

"No. I decided I was better off not knowing."

"I'm going to guess that it was some form of pus."

"Jimmy. Stop. That's disgusting. My point is, the agency doesn't seem to be putting a lot of budget into this program."

"Well…if that's the case…what does that say about their opinions of us?"

"That's what I keep asking myself," Monroe said.

They drove in silence for a few moments.

"Do you remember how I was after my dog got caught in the street sweeper and ended up thrown into the back of a pickup truck and we never saw him again?" Kendall asked.

"Jimmy," Monroe said, "I've only known you for about a week."

"Oh yeah," Kendall said. "Well, anyway, this kinda reminds me of that."

"Yeah."

~

Monroe steered the van into the alley and threw it into park. The gray cat was sleeping on his lap. "God, I never thought we'd get here," he said. "I think my entire lower body is asleep."

"Dammit, he's still looking at me," Kendall said, peering back at the orange tabby on the bench behind him. "Three hours of driving, and he stared at me the entire time."

"Jimmy, it's a cat."

"It's creeping me out!"

"Okay, just grab one and let's start taking them up to the lab."

"I'm not taking the orange one."

"Fine. Take that white one." Monroe scooped up the gray cat from his lap – causing the cat to meow its displeasure at being disturbed – and tried getting out of the van. As soon as he tried to stand up, the cat slithered out of his grasp and dropped to the alley floor.

"These things are hard to pick up," Kendall said, still inside the van.

"Tell me about it," Monroe said, scooping the gray cat again. The cat immediately began trying to wriggle out of Monroe's arms.

"How the hell are we going to climb a fire escape with these things?" Monroe said, struggling to control the gray cat. "I can wrap him up if I use both arms, but I'll need one arm to get up the ladder. There's no way."

"This is Coleman's fault," Kendall said. "He did this on purpose. To make us look stupid. That's why he didn't send carriers with us."

"Either that or he didn't know what he was doing."

"Sit still, you stupid cat! I'm not afraid to kick you!"

"Listen," Monroe said, "we're not going to let Coleman get the last laugh. I have an idea for how we're going to get the cats in the lab. Leave the white one alone. We need to find a hardware store."

~

Monroe wiped sweat off of his forehead as he climbed through the window into the lab. Coleman was there, sitting in the folding chair that he apparently had claimed as his domain in the lab. He was slumped in the chair with his head thrown straight back, his jaw slack and hanging open. As Monroe finished climbing through the window, Coleman half-snored, snorted, and jerked in the chair, but did not wake up.

Ava emerged from the "medical section" of the lab. "You're back," she said.

"Oh," Monroe said, practically jumping. "Uh, hi."

"I was worried about you guys. You've been gone all day."

"Yeah," Monroe said. "Well, the place was really far away."

"You're kidding."

"Nope. You can go back to the lab, or whatever. We'll bring the cats up."

"Oh, I'm good. I could use a break from the lab, anyway."

"Oh. Uh, you sure? Really, we have things under control."

"Stop. I really don't mind. Where are the cats?"

"Down there," Monroe said. "We're about to, um, bring them up."

"Great. I'll help. Let's go."

"No," Monroe said, more abruptly than he would have liked. "Really, you can go back to what you were doing."

Ava gave Monroe a sideways look. "Okay," she said. "If you really don't want my help, I can take a hint." She furrowed her brow at him, but said nothing further as she went back through the doorway.

Monroe waited a few seconds before going back to the window and leaning out of it. "You ready, Jimmy?" he yelled down.

"I think so," Jimmy's faint voice returned. "This one just urinated in the sling, though."

"Understandable," Monroe said. "Okay, let 'er rip."

"You sure this is going to work?" Jimmy called up.

"No," Monroe yelled. "Just try it."

Behind him, Ava came back out. "I'm sorry, I couldn't help but overhear some of that," she said. "What exactly *are* you guys doing?"

"Whoa," Monroe said, his body jerking as he suddenly leaned way out of the window. His feet started to lift off the floor. "Oh *shit!*" he said.

Ava sprung into action, jumping toward Monroe, grabbing his ankles and weighing them down before he could flip all the way out of the window. A moment later, Monroe's weight shifted, and he fell back inside the window, collapsing on the floor.

"Oh my God," Monroe said, out of breath. "I thought I was about to fall all the way back down to the alley."

"Good thing I came back out here," Ava said. She looked up at Monroe. "Are you..." The sentence froze in her throat. Monroe was carrying a large blanket that appeared to be violently shaking. He was wrestling with it, his face a mask of effort. "What the hell is that?"

"Um...nothing."

"Arthur, it's moving. What do you have in there?"

Before he could answer, the blanket flipped open and a dark gray cat jumped out of it, landing lightly on the floor. It ran in two circles at full speed before darting over to Monroe's workstation and hiding under it. It meowed twice in an expression of clear disgruntlement.

"What in the *hell* are you two *doing?*" Ava asked.

"We had to figure out a way to get the cats up here," Monroe said. He shrugged. "We didn't have any carriers, so we had to improvise." He stood and held the blanket out the window. "Here, Jimmy, catch!" he shouted downward, before releasing the blanket so that it could float back down to the alley.

"Did you actually catch that?" Jimmy shouted from below. "I can't see anything. Did you get it?"

Monroe leaned out of the window. "Yeah! It's in here! Nice shot! I think it's pretty pissed off, but it's up here."

Ava shouldered Monroe out of the way so she could look at the alley. She spotted Jimmy, who was shielding his eyes from the sun and looking up at the window. The van was parked as closely to the side of the building as possible. Rubber tubing was protruding from the driver's side door; the door had been closed over it. The other end of the tubing was tied to the handle of a large colander. Another piece of tubing led from the colander's other handle to the lowest platform of the fire escape. The colander was suspended in mid-air, pulled tight by the two lines of tubing.

"Hi, Ava!" Jimmy said from below, waving.

"Hi, Jimmy," Ava said slowly. She turned to Monroe. "What did you boys just do? Is that contraption what I think it is?"

"We didn't have any carriers," Monroe said. He shrugged.

"Please tell me that you did not build a *slingshot* to get them up here. Tell me that isn't what I'm seeing down there."

Monroe hesitated, glanced downward at the contraption that was most definitely a slingshot. "I'm open to other suggestions," he said to Ava.

"Oh my God, Arthur, what if Jimmy had missed the window? Did it not occur to you to just carry them up the fire escape?"

"Of course it did. We couldn't climb up the ladders with wriggling cats in our arms."

"Okay, so let's put them in carriers and use some rope to pull the carriers up here."

"We have carriers?"

"Yes. Twenty of them. All stacked up in the medical area. You didn't know we had carriers?"

"Nobody told me," Monroe said.

"I wondered why you didn't take them with you."

"Are you ready for me to send up another one?" Jimmy shouted from below.

"No!" Ava shouted back down.

The noise of Ava's reply woke up Coleman, who shot up from his chair with a start. "What? What? I'm awake," he said, blinking his eyes in disorientation. He finally focused and spotted Monroe and Ava by the window. "What's your status?" he asked with suspicion.

"Your engineers decided to *slingshot* the cats up here because you didn't give them the carriers," Ava said.

Coleman grunted. He grabbed his cane and as he stood, he spotted the gray cat cowering under Monroe's table. "How did that one get up here?"

"The, um, the slingshot," Monroe said.

Coleman's eyebrows shot up. "It worked?"

"Yeah," Monroe said, feeling like a schoolboy who'd been caught convincing a friend to lick a frozen flagpole.

"Outstanding," Coleman said with genuine awe. "Do it again," he added, hobbling quickly toward the window. "Let me see."

"No!" Ava said. "You guys are going to end up hurting one of the cats."

"No harm one more," Coleman said.

Ava looked at him, incredulous.

"I was asleep," Coleman said. He turned to Monroe. "Let 'er rip, pipsqueak."

"I don't believe you guys," Ava said, stepping aside and throwing up her hands in resignation. "Just a bunch of overgrown little boys."

"It'll be fine, toots," Coleman said. "Look at that one over there," he said, stabbing his cane toward the gray cat, which seemed to be so intent on keeping an eye on Monroe that it wasn't blinking. "He's fine."

"One more," Ava said. "Then we do it my way. And next time make sure you send the carriers with them."

"Not sending carriers turned out to be a good thing," Coleman said. "Required teamwork to solve a problem. Resourcefulness. That's how we do things in the agency."

"You intentionally sent us without any carriers?" Monroe asked.

"Negative," Coleman said. "Just forgot. Positive outcome, though, don't you think?" He leaned out the window, not bothering to wait for a response to his question. "Send one up, Bird Boy," he shouted.

"Don't call me that!" Kendall shouted back up.

"Send one up, Chubbs!"

"Don't call me that either, you big fathead!"

"Go ahead, Jimmy," Monroe said, leaning out. "I'm ready."

"Okay, here goes!" Kendall shouted.

Ava stood back and shook her head. She heard Jimmy grunt with effort down below, followed by the sound of the rubber tubing snapping and a cat shrieking.

The shrieking stopped at the exact same moment that Ava heard a heavy thud on the other side of the wall, well to the left of the window.

"Oooooh," Coleman and Monroe said simultaneously, both of them wincing. Ava gasped, holding a hand in front of her open mouth.

A moment later, she heard a second thud from the alley below.

Coleman and Monroe both looked down at the alley for a moment.

"Unfortunate," Coleman said.

"Yeah," Monroe said.

"Glorious idea, though," Coleman mumbled, slapping Monroe on the back.

"Gross!" Jimmy shouted from the alley.

Chapter 8

By the next day, the cats had become part of the lab's scenery. Ava persuaded Westcott to allow the cats to roam the lab during the day by arguing that the cats were more likely to stay healthy if they were allowed to be active than if they were stuck in the smallish carriers 24 hours a day. The only time they were forced back into the carriers was at night when the team returned to the motel.

Ava tended to the cats, brushing them frequently to keep the amount of dander and shedding at a minimum in the lab, and making sure they all were fed.

Kendall took to the cats immediately. If one hopped up on his table – and with 19 cats in the lab, there was at least one on his table almost all the time – he would stop working to pet it for a moment. At first this habit elicited responses from Westcott, who warned Kendall not to befriend them, but Kendall kept on doing it anyway, and after a few more warnings, Westcott gave up.

Coleman seemed to almost not be aware that the cats even existed. If one were perched on his three-day-old copy of *The Washington Post*, which he had delivered by mail to the lab every day and he habitually kept on the floor near his folding chair, he wouldn't bother shooing the animal off the paper before picking it up. He would simply yank the paper out from under the unwitting victim, usually sending it flying. On another memorable occasion, Coleman sat down in his chair despite the fact that a chunky orange cat was sleeping on it. The cat's quick reflexes saved it from a rather grisly demise, but not from having Coleman's full weight on its tail for several seconds, until the panicked (and loudly screeching) animal managed to yank it free.

It wasn't long before all the cats started giving Coleman and his folding chair a wide berth.

Monroe didn't dislike the cats, but he didn't befriend them, either. Mostly he thought of them as minor annoyances. He didn't like them on his table and had to spend a few days shooing them away every time one of them hopped up to perch. Soon most of them learned not to bother jumping up on Monroe's table, especially when Jimmy's clearly came with an open invitation.

One cat in particular, however, refused to learn the lesson. It was a skinny black cat with one white paw. No matter how many times Monroe pushed it off the table, eventually it tried again. It became apparent that Monroe was locked in a battle of wills against the cat, which he had come to think of as being named Whitey, although he never spoke the name aloud. He agreed with Westcott's suggestion not to become too attached to the animals, whose life expectancy likely became much shorter the moment they were loaded into the van.

Before long, Monroe stopped pushing Whitey off the table. Instead, he pushed the cat to the far end, away from where he preferred to work. Whitey seemed to accept this, staying at his end of the table as long as Monroe didn't try to push him off again.

Meanwhile, the work at hand progressed. Monroe and Kendall faced the most pressure, as there wasn't a lot the medical team could do, other than continuing to clean and disinfect the lab, until the electronics were ready to be implanted.

Under normal circumstances, Monroe enjoyed his work and typically stayed in his lab 10 to 12 hours a day, even with plenty of Marie-related entertainment at home. With the temptations of home removed, work was all that was left.. He quickly got in the habit of working until 6 or 7 p.m., eating dinner with the others, then returning to the lab for a few more hours.

Kendall seemed to be burdened by no such addictions to work. He spent half his day petting and talking to the cats, and the other half trying to talk everyone else into going bowling. He was often lethargic after lunch, during which he typically ate enormous amounts of fried foods; on several occasions Monroe spotted him asleep at his workstation, even though he was sitting upright.

Despite his poor work habits, Kendall made remarkable progress. Within a matter of days, he'd designed the array that he intended to be his prototype remote-control system. It was surprisingly simple, with four electrodes connected by two wires, forming a cross with a fifth electrode in the middle, where the wires met. Kendall's idea was to implant the array into a cat and teach it to respond to electrical stimulation delivered through the electrodes. A zap with the electrode closest to its head would mean to move forward, a mild shock from the electrode in its lower back would mean to back up, and so forth. The challenge, Kendall explained to anyone who would listen, was to create enough of an electrical impulse to goose the cat, but not enough to cause it serious pain or, worse, electrocute it.

For Monroe, progress was less apparent. Building the bug was simple enough. The hard part was building one that could function inside a cat. He knew little about which of his electronics might or might not work when shoved inside a living thing, so he asked questions of Ava and Westcott constantly. It wasn't long before Westcott became obviously impatient with Monroe's inquiries, so eventually Monroe only asked Ava.

Still, as the days progressed, Monroe felt that he was getting closer to having a prototype that was ready to be implanted into whichever cat drew the short straw and earned the first spot on the operating table.

It helped that it had only taken him a little over a week to complete his side project. He'd crafted his first round of bugs at night, after the rest of the team had retired to the motel for the evening, ranked among the finest he'd ever built. Sleek and flat. Very low-profile. They'd have to be to avoid being noticed by a seasoned pro like Coleman.

Building a new, smaller listening station – small enough to fit under the bed in his room – had been more of a challenge than he anticipated. Monroe was proud of himself for the new design. He liked it so much that he already planned on building one just like it for his apartment once he was back at home.

All that remained was to find an opportunity to put all the bugs in place. Monroe was anxious to get to know his new coworkers better. Especially Ava.

Life in Cape Girardeau was looking up.

Chapter 9

"So what do you think we should name them?" Kendall asked Monroe on their second Thursday in Missouri.

"The cats, you mean?" Monroe asked.

"Yeah."

"I don't think we should."

Kendall paused. "I do."

"Jimmy," Monroe said, "we don't want to start thinking of them as pets. We're going to be experimenting on them in very creepy ways. Some or all of them are going to die relatively soon. And not from happiness."

"They should at least have names," Kendall said. "Soldiers are sent off to get shot. They have names."

Monroe thought of about a thousand different and very valid ways to argue Kendall's point. He also realized that not one of them was going to work.

Monroe sighed deeply in resignation. "Okay," he said. He pointed to one. "Fred." He pointed to a light gray one. "Max." He pointed to a third. "Earl. Hey, this is fun."

"No no," Kendall said. "We can't just give them random names."

"Nanook," Monroe said, pointing to a mottled gray and black cat.

"Stop stop," Kendall said, waving his hands.

"Hey, I know," Monroe said. "We should name them after Senators. Walter," he said, pointing to another. "Roger. Bucky," he said, pointing to two more.

"There's no Senator named Bucky."

"Sure there was. Bucky Harris. Second base. Player-manager."

"Huh?"

"I meant the Washington Senators. The baseball team. The old one."

"Oh," Kendall said. "Geez, that's way too obscure. Besides, the Senators sucked. And they moved. To Minnesota. I can't even stand to follow the new version. Bad idea."

"Okay," Monroe said, "what's your suggestion?"

"Well, talking about Senators gave me an idea. We could name them after Presidents. The first one to be operated on could be Washington.

The second would be Adams. The third…uh, whoever the third President was."

"Taft."

"Taft?"

"Hm, no, that can't be right. The other Adams, maybe?"

"Jefferson!" Coleman bellowed from his chair, causing both of them to jump. He'd been sleeping, head back, slack-jawed, just moments before. "Thomas Goddamned Jefferson! Jesus H Tapdancing Christ, the third President was *Jefferson!*" He glowered in their direction for several seconds, then yelled, "Turd-bags!" He glared again, then allowed his neck to go slack as his head dropped back again. His jaw fell open and he almost immediately resumed snoring.

"If I didn't see him do that I wouldn't believe it was possible," Kendall said.

"CIA training," Monroe said, quietly.

"Yeah," Kendall mumbled, keeping a wary eye on Coleman. "So. What do you think? Name them after Presidents?"

"I guess so," Monroe said. "I still want to officially object to the idea of giving them names at all. Numbers would have been fine."

"Nobody honored a number," Kendall said. His eyes widened. "Oh my God."

"What?"

"I'm starting to talk like…*him*," Kendall said, jerking his head toward Coleman.

"Great. So do we know who's going to be Washington?"

"Hey, doc!" Kendall shouted toward the medical room.

"What?" Westcott shouted back.

"Which cat is going to be first?" Kendall asked.

"I don't care!" Westcott bellowed back. "Leave me alone! I'm working!"

"But we need to know which one will be Washington!"

They heard the sound of a chair being pushed back, followed by footsteps. Westcott appeared at the door, glared at the two of them for a moment, then slammed the door shut.

"Cool, we get to pick," Kendall said.

"Seems that way. So who gets the first death sentence?"

"Hey hey hey, mister," Kendall said. "Don't say that. We might get everything right on the first try. Has that ever occurred to you? Being picked first is not a death sentence. Gosh. Meanie."

"Whatever you say, Jimmy. Who's first?"

"Geez, I don't know. Maybe we could do eenie-meenie-minie-moe."

"How do you do eenie-meenie-minie-moe with nineteen cats?"

"We'll have to do it as a tournament," Kendall said, grabbing a pad of graph paper. "Don't worry. I've done this before. Mom once needed me to decide which one of her fish she should swallow. My one regret was that I didn't do it in a double-elimination format, but now I can make up for that."

"No offense, Jimmy, but I hope I never meet your Mom."

"You'd be surprised how often I hear that," Kendall said as he began sketching out a tournament bracket on the graph paper.

"No, you know," Monroe replied, "I don't think I would be."

Chapter 10

"This was more fun when *they* did not come with us," Boris grumbled, nodding his head toward the four-man security detail that had accompanied them to the park.

"We were lucky to be able to come to the park by ourselves even once," Yevgeny replied, unwrapping his pastrami sandwich. "At least they do not bother us with conversation."

"True," Boris said. "What did you bring today?"

"I am not sharing it with you. We have discussed this."

"So sensitive you are these days! I only asked what you brought."

"Pastrami."

"You have offended me. I do not want to know about your sandwich."

Yevgeny sighed. "I am telling you anyway. It is pastrami. With mustard."

"Mustard on pastrami? That is disgusting. You have brought with you a disgusting sandwich."

"Good. Then I do not need to expect that you will ask to help me eat it."

Boris loosened his tie. A nice breeze was blowing, but the day was still warm. "I had my hair cut this morning," he said.

"Is that so?"

"Yes."

Yevgeny glanced at Boris. "It looks good," he said, taking a bite of his sandwich.

"You barely looked. How can you tell if it is good or not?"

"Are you not happy with it?"

"Of course I am," Boris said. "But you cannot tell if it is good or not by only looking at one side of it for half of a second. Your disgusting sandwich is so important?"

"You are impossible."

"And you are selfish."

Yevgeny sighed again. "Would you like a bite of my sandwich, Boris?" He held the sandwich out.

"Is there a part with less mustard?" Boris said, taking the sandwich. "I do not like mustard."

Chapter 11

That evening, Coleman suggested that they all go out for steak. Normally, Monroe would be fine with going out for steak. But when Coleman knocked on the door to his motel room, Monroe told him that he wasn't feeling very good and that he wanted to stay behind and rest.

"Don't get all namby pamby on me now, son," Coleman had said. "A good steak will cure whatever ails you."

"Not if I can't eat it because I'm in the can for twenty minutes," Monroe said.

"No need to get graphic, son," Coleman said. "I'll bring one back for you. A good field agent eats his meat."

"I'm not a field agent," Monroe replied.

"Was trying to be nice. We return around 1930 hours. My condolences to the person on latrine duty." And with that, Coleman left.

Monroe closed the door and went to his window. He peeked out through the curtains until he saw the van pull away. He waited a full ten minutes before gathering up his paper sack of bugs and the master key that he'd stolen from the housekeeping closet.

Stealing the key had been far easier than he had hoped. A few days earlier, he had walked back to the motel to retrieve an important notebook he'd forgotten in his room, and he happened to see the housekeeper loading toilet paper into her cart from the supply closet. Realizing an opportunity when he saw one, Monroe had approached and asked for a few more rolls of toilet paper. The housekeeper had bent down to grab some from the bottom of her cart, and as she did, he scanned the inside of the housekeeping closet. Sure enough, two extra master keys hung inside the supply room on a hook next to the door. After the maid had given him his rolls, he made a show of tripping on the cart and dropping them all. When she bent down to pick one of them up, he snatched one of the keys.

The next day, he went for a walk during lunchtime and stopped in at the hardware store down the street, where he'd had a copy of the key made. Later he'd slipped the original back under the door, so that if the maid spotted it she'd simply think it had been knocked off the hook somehow.

Easy.

Armed with his illicit master key, Monroe went to Westcott's room first. It was remarkably neat, with toiletries lined up in perfect order on the bathroom sink. Westcott even kept his slippers perfectly lined up on the floor next to the sink. Wandering back into the room, Monroe attached the bug to the underside of Westcott's bed, near the edge but not so close that it would be accidentally discovered by the housekeeper.

Something under the bed caught his attention. He pulled the bedspread up a little higher so he could get a better look. It was another pair of slippers. He almost ignored them, but something about them didn't seem right. He grabbed one and went back to the bathroom with it. Sure enough, it was different from the pair on the floor. Not just different in style, but different in size. Monroe checked the tags inside each slipper. The pair on the floor was a size 11. The slipper in his hand was a 9.

Monroe suddenly wondered if he was in the right room. He checked the dresser to see if he recognized any of the clothes in it. But when he pulled open a drawer, he stopped short.

The drawer was full of bottles of Glenlivet scotch. Four of them. One was nearly empty.

Trying to hurry, Monroe slammed that drawer shut and pulled open another. He spotted a sweater that he immediately recognized. Westcott had been wearing it only the day before. He breathed a sigh of relief; if he was going to end up getting arrested for breaking and entering, he could at least claim that he had broken into the right room. The slippers must have been left by a previous guest in the room.

Monroe hurried to put the rogue slipper back under the bed, exactly as he had found it. He had three more rooms to visit, and the rest of the team wouldn't be gone for very long. He snuck out the door, making sure nobody saw him.

Kendall's room was next. It was a total disaster, the kind of room one would expect to see from someone who'd had his mother around to pick up after him his entire life. Underwear on the floor, socks tossed onto a chair, towels on the bed, crap strewn everywhere in the bathroom. Several issues of *Popular Mechanics* sat in a loose pile on one of the nightstands.

Monroe almost didn't bother leaving a bug in Kendall's room. He didn't think his chubby friend was likely to do anything remotely interesting. What the heck, he thought, and attached the bug to the bottom of Kendall's bed. He also made a note to himself to turn down any invitations Kendall may extend to hang out in his room.

Coleman's room was a lot like his cubicle back in Langley – nearly empty. The man kept only the barest of essentials in his room. Monroe thought for a moment that he'd gone into an unoccupied room. Nothing sat on the nightstands except for a small round alarm clock. No books anywhere, no magazines, no clothes anywhere in sight, nothing. Out of curiosity, Monroe pulled open the drawers of the room's dresser. Six shirts, six undershirts, six pair of underwear, six pairs of socks, six pairs of slacks. Including the outfit that he was wearing that morning, Coleman kept exactly one of every item for each day of the week, nothing more. The bathroom was much the same; a small tube of Crest, a toothbrush, and a razor. Not even shaving cream.

Monroe hesitated before attaching the bug to Coleman's bed. If anyone were likely to find a bug, it was Coleman. Monroe could even imagine him doing periodic sweeps of his room. He looked around the room, trying to find a viable spot that Coleman would never check. Under the bed seemed too obvious.

Eventually he decided to take a risk, though in a way it didn't seem like a risk at all. He popped open the front panel on the room's TV, the little door that opened to reveal knobs to control the brightness and contrast. He attached the bug to the inside of the door. When he closed it again, the bug fit perfectly inside.

Monroe saved Ava's room for last. He wasn't surprised to find that she had given it a small bit of femininity. She kept things neat but not sterile. She had strewn a few framed photos on the nightstands, on top of the TV, and on her dresser. The same person appeared in each photo. It was a little boy.

He looked to be about five or six years old. A couple of the pictures showed him smiling and hugging Ava. In the picture on the dresser, apparently taken in a park somewhere, Monroe could see that the little boy had dark, sunken eyes, and he looked too thin. His skin was too pale.

Ava had never mentioned having a son. He'd never met a mother who didn't spend half of her time talking about her children in some way.

Come to think of it, Monroe thought, Ava never mentioned a husband, either. There was no husband in any of the photos, though. Just Ava and the boy. Interesting.

Ava's room smelled good. She kept candles on the nightstands, and the aroma of her perfume lingered in the bathroom. She'd left the cap off of her perfume. Chanel. Monroe looked at it for a moment, then went ahead and screwed the cap back on. He didn't know a lot about perfume, but he knew that it evaporated easily, and that it was expensive.

Monroe found himself lingering in her room for longer than he knew he should. The van could come back at any moment. He lingered anyway, but just for a few extra seconds. Her room was calming.

Before he left, he made extra sure that the bug under Ava's bed was very securely attached and working properly.

~

About 45 minutes later, Monroe was relaxing on his bed, watching a repeat of "Gunsmoke" when someone banged on his door so hard that he thought for a moment he might be under attack.

It was Kendall. He was clearly very excited about something. "Guess what?" he asked.

"What?"

"We found a bowling alley!"

"Congratulations."

Kendall stood there grinning.

"Good night, Jimmy," Monroe said, reaching to close his door.

"Whoa, no no," Kendall said, putting his hand out to stop the door from closing. "Come on. We're going."

"Bowling?"

"Yeah. They wanna go."

"Who?"

"Coleman and Ava. I talked them into it. Coleman kept talking about how there's no glory in bowling, and I told him that if he can beat me, I'll wear my underwear outside my pants tomorrow at the lab."

"Kendall, I don't want to have to look at your underwear all day tomorrow."

"Oh, don't worry," Kendall replied. "I won't lose. Coleman says he hasn't bowled ever. I'm gonna smoke him. It's gonna be *great!*"

"Well, you guys have fun," Monroe said.

Kendall's face fell. "Wait, wait," he said. "You gotta go. We need four. It's not right to bowl with just three. Westcott refused to go, said something about infections. Actually, now that I think about it, his exact words were, 'Bowling is an infection.' That guy, most of the time I have no idea what he's talking about. Anyway, you gotta go. Come on."

"I don't know," Monroe replied. He was about to give his upset-stomach excuse again, but stopped himself. "Um, did you say Ava was going?"

"Yeah, Ava and Coleman."

"Give me ten minutes."

~

The bowling alley was hung so thick with smoke that it burned their eyes and made everyone but Coleman cough incessantly. It was late, and the weeknight leagues were finishing up. Fat men in loud shirts walked everywhere and leered at fat women in equally loud stretch pants. Kendall seemed enthralled.

"This place is an absolute dump," Ava said.

"It's not that bad," Kendall protested.

"I mean it as a compliment," Ava replied. "The only thing that would make me like it better is if it had a pool table."

"You mean like those?" Kendall asked, pointing toward the alley's bar. Inside, behind a set of swinging saloon doors, they could see a pair of pool tables, both of them sporting dingy pink felt.

"Pink tables," Coleman grunted. "Un-American."

"It's certainly not my favorite color," Ava said, "but it'll do."

"You like this place?" Monroe asked.

"Sure," Ava said. "Why not?"

"It doesn't seem like you."

"I'm full of surprises, Arthur. Everybody is, if you ask me. My dad used to take me to a place like this all the time when I was a kid. Used to make Mom really mad."

"This place is crawling with malfeasance," Coleman said.

"I don't know about you boys," Ava said, "but this place has me in the mood for a drink. Anyone else want one?"

"Why not?" Kendall said. "Drinking and bowling at the same time, it could be fun!"

"Can't drink on duty," Coleman said.

"You aren't on duty, Coleman," Ava said.

"Always on duty. CIA," he said, pointing his thumb at his chest.

"Suit yourself. Monroe?" she asked.

"Um, okay," Monroe replied. "I'll take a beer."

"Be right back," she said. "Get me some shoes. Size 7. *Clean* ones."

"Okay," Monroe said.

Ten minutes later, they were at their assigned lane with shoes and balls. Ava returned with two Budweiser bottles and a large plastic cup full of white wine. "What they seem to lack in general hygiene around here they make up for in portion size," she said. "Who's up?"

"Monroe," Kendall said.

"I don't want to go first," Monroe said.

"I put everybody down in alphabetical order," Kendall said. "That makes you first."

Monroe glanced at the scoresheet, where Kendall had scribbled ARTIE. He to himself as he stood wearily and grabbed his ball.

"Let's see what you got, Arthur," Ava said. Arthur lined up his throw, walked forward, tossed his ball...and fired it straight into the gutter.

"You bowl like you arm-wrestle," Coleman said.

"Arthur," Ava said, "swing your arm in a straight line with the lane. You're throwing across your body."

"Okay," Monroe said, even though he had no idea what she was talking about. His second ball at least made it more than two-thirds of the way down the lane before nestling in the gutter. He shrugged and sat back down, grabbing his beer.

"Son," Coleman said, "that was an embarrassment to the American intelligence community. Shape it up."

"Sorry," Monroe said.

"Have your fun now, Coleman," Kendall said. "I'm gonna wipe the floor with you."

"I know twelve different ways to kill a man with a cracked fingernail," Coleman said.

"My turn," Ava said, hopping up from her seat. As she gathered her ball and started focusing on the lane, the three men fell silent. She was wearing a simple white t-shirt and khaki Capri pants, but both were snug and gave away the fact that she had a rather curvy figure.

Eventually she tossed her ball. She exhibited the form of a pro, planting her forward foot, lifting the off-leg for balance, and turning her body slightly to the side in order to generate the proper spin. Her ball hugged the right side of the lane, barely avoiding the gutter, before curving back toward the center and crashing into the pins with authority, knocking them all down.

"Strike!" Kendall shouted.

Ava dusted her hands and sashayed back to the table. "Better bring your 'A' game tonight, gentlemen," she said as she took a sip of her wine. "I appear to be on fire."

"Ahh, starting to make sense," Coleman said.

"What's starting to make sense?" Ava asked.

"Attractive woman like yourself, early thirties, unmarried, one wonders why," Coleman said. "A man doesn't want to lose to his woman in competition."

"Agent Coleman, why I am still single is none of your business," Ava replied. "And I'm sorry, but your views on the male-female dynamic are Neanderthal."

"Just stating the facts, Miss Moriarty," Coleman said. "No need to be unpleasant. Though the unpleasantness is likely another reason."

"It's my turn to bowl," Kendall said, practically leaping out of his chair. He grabbed the ball that he'd so carefully selected, a bright lime green 12-pounder.

"Sissy ball," Coleman said.

"It is not!" Kendall said. "Besides, it's not mine. I just picked it out. It happens to fit my fingers."

"Even the girl picked a black ball," Coleman said, gesturing toward the three black balls sitting on the return rack.

"Jimmy," Ava said, "please use the sissy ball to kick his butt."

Kendall left only two pins standing after his first roll and picked up a spare with his second. "Ha hoo!" Kendall shouted when the last pin fell. He whirled around and pointed both index fingers at Coleman. "I can't wait to see your underwear tomorrow," he said.

"Concerns," Coleman said, shaking his head. He left his cane behind as he stood to take his turn, preferring to limp. He bowled like a caveman. His strategy seemed to be simply to throw the ball as hard as possible and hope that the explosion at the end of the lane was sufficient enough to knock all the pins down, and possibly to shatter one or two in the process. The sound of his hypersonic ball crashing into the pins was loud enough to attract attention from bowlers ten lanes away. And on-target enough to score a strike.

Coleman cocked his head, like a boxer coming out of his corner, as he walked back to the table. "It's on, bird-boy," he said to Kendall.

"Stop calling me that!"

~

The game seemed to fly by. Monroe was having so much fun listening to Ava spar with Coleman that he almost didn't mind the fact that he had scored just a 38 after eight frames. Normally such exposure of his athletic ineptitude would practically make him want to run from the alley. Not tonight.

Tonight was different. He was enjoying himself. With people. Ava seemed to be having fun beating Coleman's score, and she was doing so by a wide margin. Coleman took it in stride for a few frames, but when it started to become clear that Ava was going to win hands-down, he started to become even more surly than usual.

Kendall, for his part, only cared about how he was doing against Coleman. At the end of nine frames, Kendall had a 151 score; Coleman had 153. Both had finished the ninth frame with spares. Monroe had 40 points and was mostly concerned with sneaking glances at Ava's body when he hoped she wouldn't notice. As impressed as he was with her figure, he was more impressed with the 255 score she was touting after nine frames, having bowled a strike with her last ball.

Making it all the more amazing was that Ava had gotten herself fairly drunk over the course of the game. She was working on her fourth cup of wine. Kendall had put away four or five beers himself. As for himself, Monroe had stopped drinking his first beer about halfway through it.

"Arthur!" Ava yelled, slapping him squarely between the shoulder blades. "You're up. And darn it, quit swinging your arm out wide when you wind up to throw. I swear, it's like you aren't even listening." Her breath practically reeked of wine.

Monroe approached the lane. At least the game was nearly over. He started toward the line to throw, then caught himself. He backed up and started over, but this time, he focused on trying to bring his arm straight back. He visualized the ball going down the center of the lane, crashing into the pins for a strike.

He threw.

The ball shot like a laser, straight into the gutter.

Monroe sighed. He turned to Ava and shrugged. "I tried that time, I swear," he said.

"At least you gutter-balled it with gusto," she replied. She set her wine down and got up, grabbing his ball as it came back out of the return. "Okay, mister," she said, "I'm going to show you how to bowl."

"You don't have to do that."

"Yes, actually, I do. It is driving me *nuts* that you can't throw a damn bowling ball straight. It's painful to watch."

"Uh…"

"Come on, I'm not going to bite. Here," she said, handing him the ball. "Stand like this." She pushed him into position, with his hips square to the lane. He felt himself turn bright red as her hands pushed on his body.

"See those arrows on the floor?" Ava asked, pointing to the marks at the front of the lane.

"Oh," Monroe said. "Yeah."

"Yeah," Ava said. "They show you where to aim. Look at those, not at the pins."

"I never noticed those before."

"Obviously. Now when you approach, bring the ball straight back…" As Ava said this, she grabbed Monroe's wrist and pulled his arm straight back. He felt the difference in the motion and realized that his natural motion was all wrong, taking the ball away from his body.

"…then straight forward," Ava finished, pushing his arm in an arc, straight ahead. "And throw like you're just trying to set the ball down on the lane. Don't try to heave it. Okay?"

"Yeah. I think so."

"Arm straight back, straight forward, set the ball on the lane."

"Check."

She patted him on the back. "Make me proud."

He watched her walk back to the table. Mostly, he watched her butt walk back to the table. He turned and looked down the lane at the ten pins.

He averted his gaze and focused on the arrows. He picked out the middle one, positioned his body, approached, pulled his arm back, being careful to keep it in close to his body, brought his arm forward…

…and drove the ball squarely into the back of his knee, striking it with such force that it gave, causing him to collapse in a confused heap on the lane. He fell straight forward, crashing his forehead hard on the floor. He heard a loud buzzing noise just as the ball somehow rolled up his spine and over his head. Dazed with pain and still unclear as to exactly what had just happened, Monroe's eye managed to spot the ball rolling down the lane with surprising velocity. It knocked down nine pins.

"Man down!" Coleman shouted. "Man down! Medic!"

Before he could move, Ava and Kendall were there, crowding him, trying to help him sit up. As they righted him, he realized there was a sharp pain on the right side of his forehead. He touched it, and his fingertip came away slightly bloody.

"Oh my God, are you okay?" Ava asked.

"I'm bleeding," was all Monroe could say.

"It's not bad," Kendall said. "I think you're going to have a good lump there in the morning." He looked at Monroe's forehead and winced. "Or maybe in about five minutes."

"I have to say," Ava said, suppressing a grin, "I have never seen anything like that in a bowling alley, and I've been bowling since I was six."

"Thanks," Monroe said. His forehead really hurt. He could feel it throbbing. "Hey, at least I got a nine."

"No, you didn't," Kendall said, grimacing. "You fouled."

"Huh?"

"The buzzing sound. You went over the line." Kendall was pointing to the line just in front of the arrows. "You can't put any of your body across the line. Um, including your head."

"Great," Monroe said.

"Come on, let's get you up," Ava said, as she and Kendall hoisted Monroe upright. He wobbled for a second, then righted himself.

"I'm okay," Monroe said. "I think I'm done bowling for the night."

"We should get you back to the motel so you can lie down," Ava said.

"Now?" Kendall said. "But Coleman and I haven't bowled. I'm down two pins!"

"You boys will have to settle things another night," Ava said.

"But...but...awwwww!" Kendall cried.

"Relax, toots," Coleman said to Ava. "That soldier's going to be just fine. I've taken much worse shots than that to the head."

"No kidding," Ava said.

"A shot of whiskey and a night in a Turkish sauna and he'll be fine," Coleman said. "He can wait five more minutes while I finish beating Chubbsy."

"Don't call me that," Kendall said with no small amount of resignation.

"Men need to compete," Coleman said. "A good woman would not interfere with that. You probably wouldn't understand. You finishing your last frame?"

She seemed hesitant to stay, even for a few minutes, then relented. "Yes," she said. "On one condition. If I bowl three straight strikes, the game's over and you both lose. Underwear outside your pants for both of you tomorrow."

"My head definitely can wait for that," Monroe said, feeling another throb of pain.

Coleman cocked an eyebrow. "Offensive. And yet, alluring. What if you lose?"

"If I lose, then nothing," she said. "Then you two just finish your game and whoever wins, wins."

"Doesn't work like that," Coleman replied. "No glory in a bet without consequence. You lose, no undergarments tomorrow."

"Ha," Ava snorted. "I don't think so. But nice try. Look, bowling three strikes in a row is very difficult. If I don't do it, I should only lose something small."

"You have to tell us why you got so upset in the parking lot of that diner the day we arrived," Monroe said. As soon as the words came out, he regretted saying them.

Everyone stopped for a moment and stared at Monroe. The look on Ava's face showed that it was a topic she clearly did not feel like discussing.

"Okay, maybe not," Monroe said. "I'm fine with the undergarment thing."

"What happened at the diner?" Coleman said. "I missed something? I never miss anything. The Central Intelligence Agency misses nothing."

"Look," she said, "it's not that big of a deal, but I really don't want to get into all that."

"That settles it," Coleman said. "That's your bet. You lose, you talk. Must be worth knowing if you're so interested in hiding it."

"I never agreed to that bet!" Ava said.

"Don't need to," Coleman replied. "I said it for you. Underwear vs. spilling beans. Fair bet. It's that or the bra."

Ava shot a harsh look at Monroe. He couldn't take it, looked down at his shoes. His face was so hot that he wondered if it might actually catch fire.

"You're on," she said to Coleman, grabbing her ball.

"Your backside is delightful," Coleman said loudly.

"I'm sorry?" Ava said with a mixture of surprise and anger.

"Your backside," Coleman said. "It's delightful."

"Hey," muttered Monroe.

"You're trying to distract me," Ava said.

"Yes," Coleman replied. "Standard CIA tactic. Confuse your enemy."

"That's pathetic. What's the matter, afraid of losing to a woman?"

"An Agency man fears nothing. Except perhaps spoiled meat. And occasionally polio."

Ava rolled her eyes as she turned toward the lane and lined up her shot. She lined up her throw, approached, released…and threw a perfect strike.

"Woo hoo!" Kendall shouted, pumping his fists into the air.

"Jimmy," Monroe said, "if she makes these, you lose."

"That's okay. It would be worth it."

"That's one," Coleman said. "Two more to go. Won't happen."

Ava said nothing, choosing simply to smile at Coleman.

She retrieved her ball and lined up the second shot. She approached, and just before she released her ball, Coleman let loose with an enormous fake sneeze.

Ava threw a second straight strike.

"Holy cow," Monroe said.

"Wow," Kendall said. "She's good."

"At ease, boys," Coleman said. "America always wins. Toughest shot is coming up. She won't make it."

Ava said nothing, grinning at Coleman again as she retrieved her ball and lined up her throw.

"No chance," Coleman said. He appeared to have lost his sense of humor. The mocking tone was gone from his voice. "America always wins. CIA always wins."

"What about the Bay of Pigs?" Monroe asked.

"Doesn't count."

"Why not?"

"Just doesn't," Coleman said. "The CIA will not lose this bet."

Chapter 12

"That's just plain unsanitary," Westcott said the next morning as the men gathered in front of the motel.

"Shut up," Coleman said, adjusting his boxers in another attempt to make them feel at least somewhat comfortable.

"Hey, I just noticed you have pinstripes on yours," Kendall said, adjusting his own plain white boxers, which were, just like Coleman's, on the outside of his slacks. "Where did you get them?"

"No questions about the gear, son," Coleman growled. He had been in a foul mood since the moment Ava's final throw of the night had resulted in a third consecutive strike. "I'm in the mood to shoot people today."

"Sore loser," Kendall said, slurping from a paper cup filled with steaming coffee.

Ava's door opened. She looked Coleman and Kendall over and began chuckling. "Well, aren't you gents all dressed to the nines this morning?" she asked. "Better hustle when you cross the street this morning, Agent Coleman. Wouldn't want to have to explain your fashion statement to a burly police officer."

"I'm walking," Coleman said as he headed toward the street. "You people can follow if you want."

"Somebody woke up on the wrong side of bed," Ava said. As the rest of them started walking, she spotted Monroe, who was, as usual, simply trying to stay out of everyone else's way. She winced when she saw the large, dark welt that had raised on Monroe's forehead overnight. "Ouch," she said. "Does it hurt?"

"Not really," he lied.

"It looks like it hurts," she said.

"I'm fine," Monroe insisted.

"I'm not so sure."

A few steps ahead of them, Coleman stopped walking. He turned, took a step toward Monroe, and whacked him squarely on his welt with an open palm.

"Owwwww!" Monroe shrieked, recoiling. "What was that for?"

"It hurts," Coleman said to Ava as he turned back around and continued walking.

"You big bully," Ava said. "How would you like it if somebody did that to you?"

"Boris Bern," Coleman said.

"Boris Bern?" Ava said. "Did you even hear what I said?"

"Boris Bern," Coleman said. "Last person to take a swing at me. Dead now."

"You killed him?" Ava said with alarm.

"No. Was sad. He hid from me by jumping in a bear pit in a zoo in Calcutta. Bears ate him."

"That's not sad, that's horrible," Ava said.

"Sad because I didn't get to shoot him first."

"They really should not issue you weaponry," Ava said.

"Too late," Coleman said as he finished crossing the street. "Already armed. Fifth Amendment."

"The Fifth Amendment is the right to not incriminate yourself," Ava said. "I think you mean the Second Amendment."

"The important thing is that one of the Amendments grants me the right to shoot people," Coleman grunted.

"You're crazy," Ava said.

"Wanting to shoot people isn't crazy," Coleman said, yanking down the ladder to the fire escape. "Not wanting to shoot people is crazy."

~

To Monroe, the day seemed to last twenty hours. He was anxious to get back to the motel and try out his equipment. He would have done some test-listens the night before, but he could barely focus his eyes and his head felt like it wanted to split open and give birth to bunnies. Having to wait the extra day was driving him crazy.

Kendall wasn't helping Monroe's mood. He spent the entire day obsessing over which cat would be Washington. Since Washington would be the first on the operating table, Kendall found himself unable to choose. He kept asking Monroe which one he would pick, and each time, Monroe would pick one of them, any one, and each time, Kendall would say, "Oh good lord not *that one*," or "Oh no no, he's the only one who looks after the little black cat," or "I just can't pick that one; he smells too good."

By mid-afternoon, Kendall had essentially cracked under the pressure. He sat in his chair, shoulders slumped, and said to Monroe, "I just can't decide. I just can't do it. It's too hard."

Monroe pointed to one. "That one."

"No."

"Fine. That one."

"No."

"That one."

Kendall seemed to brighten for just a moment. "Maybe," he said. "Wait. No."

The door to the medical room opened. Westcott stuck out his head and peered around. He pointed toward a gray cat slinking around near Monroe's table. "I want that one prepped for surgery by tomorrow," he said.

"You do?" Kendall asked.

"I'm sorry, did I speak too quickly for you, Kendall?" Westcott said. "Yes. I. Want. Him. Prepped. I'm telling you because one of you will need to help Ava when she gets back from buying the supplies we need. Tell her I picked that one, and try not to fuck that up." He disappeared back into the medical area and shut the door.

Monroe looked at Kendall. "Okay," Monroe said. "There's your Washington."

"I'm not very happy with his choice," Kendall said. "That one has a highly developed palate. I got him to drink grape soda a couple days ago."

"I'm not sure what to say to that, Jimmy."

"It's not easy to find a cat that will drink grape soda."

"I'm sure it's not. Well, um, I'm sorry."

"Thanks. I'll be okay. But if Washington doesn't make it, I don't know if I'll be able to drink grape soda any more."

"Who's Washington?" Ava said, climbing through the window. "And what might he not make?"

"Hi Ava," Kendall said. "Washington is that little guy right there," he added, pointing to the gray cat in question. "Westcott picked him to be Washington."

Ava shot a confused look at Monroe.

"Dr. Westcott picked this cat to be the first one to be tested," Monroe offered as an interpretation.

"You named it?" Ava asked.

"We're naming them after the Presidents," Kendall said. "Washington was the first President, so Washington here is our first acoustic kitty."

"I don't think it's a good idea to name these cats," Ava said.

Kendall waved dismissively. "I'm sure Dr. Westcott is good at what he does," he said. "Ol' Washington here is going to go down in history. Just like the real Washington. Hey, how about that for a coincidence, huh?"

Ava sighed and rubbed her temples.

"He gets excited about stuff," Monroe said.

"Okay, well, if one of you could give me a hand with Washington, I'd appreciate it," Ava said.

"I'll help," Monroe said.

"Aw, I wanted to help," Kendall said.

"Don't worry, Jimmy," Ava replied. "There'll be plenty of opportunities to prep cats. Besides, I just came back with a bunch of bags of cat food and litter. Maybe you could help me out by bringing them up here?"

"Okay, but don't say that about having to prep lots of cats," Kendall said. "You'll jinx it. Don't listen to her, Washington," he said to the cat, which had begun staring in fear at a trashcan.

"Come on, uh, Washington," Ava said, scooping up the cat. "Jimmy, really, I don't think you should get too attached to these cats."

Kendall shoved his index fingers into his ears. "La la la la laaaaa, I can't hear you, la la la laaaa."

"Yeah, that's healthy," Ava said to nobody in particular. "Come on, Monroe," she said, heading into the medical room. As Monroe followed her in, he realized he was finally going to see the inside of the medical section. He and Kendall had come to regard it with a mild sense of awe, since Westcott seemed determined to keep the Agency men out of his domain as much as possible.

The majority of the space was occupied by what looked like an operating room. A small table sat in the middle, surrounded by a wide variety of machines that Monroe didn't recognize. They looked vaguely like the life-support machines he saw on TV medical dramas. The walls of the room were lined with supply cabinets. To his left, between a pair of cabinets, was another door.

"What's in there?" Monroe asked.

"Westcott's office."

"He has an office? None of us have offices."

"I guess it was one of his conditions for taking on the project. He wanted an office. He's in there most of the day."

"Sounds like he's on the phone."

"He's on the phone most of the time in there," Ava said as she set Washington down on the table.

"Who's he talking to?"

"No idea. With him, the rule of thumb is that the less I know, the less work I end up doing. I stay out of whatever he's doing in there."

"So we're doing all the work and he's talking on the phone."

"He's my boss," Ava said. "I just work here. Can you help me hold the cat in place?"

"Sure," Monroe said. Washington was busily peering over the edge, preparing to jump down. Monroe yanked his hands out of his pockets and tried his best to keep the cat still, but it continued to squirm.

"Cats don't like operating tables," Ava said. "Kind of an oddity about them. Doesn't matter if they've never been on one. They know it's a place they really don't want to be. Keep a good hold on him."

"I'm trying."

Ava turned toward a side table and began looking through its drawers for her electric clipper. Monroe put his hands around the cat and pushed on its lower back, attempting to make it sit. Washington arched his back instead, then managed to slither out of Monroe's grip entirely. He took advantage of the opening to leap off the table and skitter back out of the medical room.

"Shit," Monroe said.

Ava laughed. "I thought I told you to hold on to him."

"Sorry. He's slippery. I'll go get him."

"Just be firm. He'll sit still once he realizes you're in charge."

"Okay." The idea of Monroe being in charge of anything, much less an entire cat, seemed to him to be outside his area of personal expertise. He found Washington hiding near Kendall's trashcan and scooped him up. The cat meowed its dissatisfaction.

"You tell him, Washington," Kendall said. "Is it going okay in there?"

"We haven't started yet," Monroe said. He held Washington up a bit. "See? Still furry."

"Poor little guy."

Monroe rolled his eyes and went back to the medical room. He made sure he closed the door behind him this time. "Jimmy's not going to handle this very well," he said.

"That's why I'm glad you volunteered first," she replied. She was holding a needle. "Okay, hold him down on the table. I need to sedate him before we start shaving. Otherwise he'll squirm all over the place."

Monroe put Washington on the table. Ava was right; the cat somehow knew this was a place it didn't want to be. His head bobbed and weaved as he looked for an escape route. But this time Monroe was ready for him and held him in place. Washington continued to squirm, meowing incessantly.

"Here we go," Ava said, pushing the needle into Washington's rear hip. Within about 20 seconds, the cat was fast asleep.

"We should give some of that to Coleman," Monroe said.

"I would if I didn't think he would arrest me the moment he woke up," Ava replied. She positioned Washington on his belly and flipped on the shaver. "How's the head?"

"I don't know. Furry?"

"I meant yours."

"Oh. It's fine."

Ava shot him a look.

"It hurts a little," Monroe admitted. "But I'll be okay."

"No blurred vision or anything?"

"No. Really, I'm fine. But...thanks."

"It's my job," Ava said. "I take care of things." She began clipping Washington's fur in long strokes, leaving strips of disturbingly pale skin behind.

Monroe watched for a moment, fascinated by how the cat started to take on a bit of an alien appearance once large chunks of its hair were shaved clean off. "I haven't seen skin that pink since my Uncle Joe mooned me on Christmas morning," he said.

"Every time I start to think one of the men on this project is normal, something like that is said," Ava said, shaking her head as she worked.

"Sorry. You don't forget a thing like that."

"I was only joking. Mostly. It's just...well, based on my admittedly limited experience thus far, the CIA seems to employ the highly unusual."

"I never really thought about it," Monroe said. He wasn't sure where to put his hands now that his duties as cat-pinner-downer were done, so he shoved them back into the pockets of his slacks.

"So is everyone at the CIA as unique as you and Jimmy and Coleman?" Ava asked as she continued to work.

Monroe shrugged. "Maybe. I really don't know that many people at the agency."

"Oh. Are you new?"

"No. Not really. Been there about, oh, 11 years."

Ava stopped shaving and looked up at Monroe. "You've been there for 11 years and you don't know anyone?"

"Well, I know my supervisor a little. He's…okay. Actually, he's kind of a dick. To me, anyway." Monroe stopped. "I'm sorry. I shouldn't say dick in mixed company."

"I grew up with a bunch of brothers. Don't worry about it."

"Oh. Okay. Well, anyway, I'd met Jimmy a few times, but only in passing. Never met Coleman until I started on this project. I don't mix with the field agents very often. There are a couple other guys that I work with once in a while. That's about it."

"I guess you don't see them socially very often, then, huh?"

"No."

"Hm," Ava said. She gave Monroe an odd look for a moment. "Guess we better finish what we came here for, huh?" She went back to shaving Washington's back. Watching her render his back hairless was like watching somebody peeling off a toupee and finding a small pig underneath.

"Um…if you don't need me…" Monroe started.

"Oh," Ava said, as if she were expecting him to stay longer. "Okay. I'm sure you're busy."

Monroe shrugged. "Kendall and I were going to start working on building out the equipment in the van this afternoon," he said. "But…uh, I can stay if you need more help."

"You sure? I don't want to keep you."

"It's okay. Plenty of afternoon left."

"Okay," she said with a small smile. "Good. Thanks. I just need you to stick around for a few minutes. To keep an eye on him while I clean up."

As Ava walked to the sink and began cleaning the clippers, Monroe looked at Washington. His back, from the base of his neck to the beginning of his tail, was shaved clean. He looked like a member of one of the obscure South American pygmy tribes he saw pictures of in *National Geographic*. Washington was sound asleep. Not wanting to touch the cat's bare skin, Monroe scratched its head while it slept.

Ava noticed out of the corner of her eye. "I wouldn't if I were you."

Monroe withdrew his hand. "Sorry."

"No need to apologize. Just a suggestion. He won't be the same cat by tomorrow afternoon."

"Oh. Yeah, I guess not."

Ava smiled. "You don't say much, do you?"

Monroe started to open his mouth, but then closed it and simply shrugged.

"I suppose it was a rhetorical question," Ava said. She walked past him and put the clippers away in a drawer in the prep table. "So you want to know why I was so upset that day at the diner, huh?"

"I didn't mean to pry. It's really none of my business."

"It's okay. I don't mind. I'm just...accustomed to keeping my problems to myself. Not to sound cynical, but in my experience people love to hear about your problems but don't have much interest in helping solve them. I prefer not to feel like my life is someone else's entertainment."

"Yeah."

"You've got to have problems, right?"

Monroe shrugged. "I guess."

"You guess, huh? I'll take that as a yes. I suppose everyone has problems. Even John Lennon has problems."

"John Lennon?" Monroe considered this. "No, I don't believe he has problems."

"Trust me. Everyone does."

"Okay."

Ava leaned against the prep table and ran her fingers through the hair at the base of her head. She sighed heavily. "I have a son," she said. "He's 6. We have a small townhouse in Fairfax. His father..." She sighed again. "He's not in the picture."

"Oh."

"I dated him for a while, I really liked him, but after a few months of dating, he decided to start smacking me around. I waited for him to go to work one night, and I took all my things and left. Found out about two weeks later that I was pregnant. By then I was seven states away, in Virginia."

"Wow. So where were you before that?"

"Oklahoma."

"No kidding?"

"No kidding."

"I hear there's lots of Indians there."

"There's a bunch of big reservations there, yes."

"Are they cool? The Indians?"

"Not really," Ava said. "You do realize they don't still run around in buckskins and headdresses, don't you?"

"I would if I were an Indian," Monroe said, trying to hide his disappointment.

"A lot of them are like truck drivers. Can't read, don't brush their teeth much, wear clothes that look like they haven't been washed in months. I learned to avoid them. I learned to avoid Oklahoma entirely. Being a single mother is difficult anywhere, but it's even more difficult in Oklahoma. A friend of mine got pregnant when we were in high school. She had to go stay in a home for single mothers. Her mother forced her to do it. And the things all of our friends – her friends – said about her afterward. It was awful. Like she'd shot the Pope or something."

"What's your son's name?"

"Robert. Well, Robbie. Only my mother calls him Robert."

"Who's watching him while you're here?"

"She is," Ava said. As quickly as she said it, her eyes welled up. She looked down and sniffed wetly, rubbing her eyes. "She's probably letting him eat nothing but McDonald's," she said, trying to laugh. "Mom loves their cheeseburgers."

Monroe gave her a moment. "Westcott didn't tell you that you might be here for a long time, did he?" he asked.

Ava wiped her eyes again. "No," she said quietly. "He said we'd be here for two weeks to a month. He flat-out lied to me."

"So…" Monroe looked over his shoulder, making sure Westcott wasn't within earshot, "…why don't you just quit? Go home?"

"I can't. And he knows it." She sniffed, trying to compose herself. "Robbie has lots of problems. Doctors found a tumor on one of his kidneys a couple years ago and had to take it out. Since then he's not the same. Gets sick a lot. He also now has asthma, which the doctors assure me has nothing to do with his having only one kidney, but you know, he didn't have trouble with breathing before the operation." She sighed. "Sorry. I get…frustrated. Anyway, he's fine, he'll be fine, but he goes to the doctor a lot. And it's expensive. Insurance covers a lot of it, but not all, and it adds up. Westcott pays really well. The things we do at work there, lots of people wouldn't do it, no matter what the pay. I don't have much choice. I make double what I used to. I need to. I have to work for Westcott."

"He doesn't have other assistants he could bring instead?"

"Of course he does. He insisted on bringing me. I've worked with him for almost seven years now. Nobody else has worked there for more than two or three years. People can't do it for long. As you have probably gathered, he is not an easy man to work for."

"What exactly do you *do* for Westcott? I thought you guys were veterinarians. What's so bad about that?"

"You don't know? I thought somebody would have told you by now."

"Tell me what?"

"We're not a veterinary practice. We...ugh, I hate telling people this. I usually lie about it."

"You could lie now if you want."

"You're sweet. But you seem like one of the few people who won't react badly to the truth, so I'll tell you." Ava paused and took a deep breath. "We do animal testing."

"What, like, math and stuff?"

"Huh? No. Like, big companies develop a new kind of hairspray and want to make sure it won't cause people's skin to slough off or turn orange. So they send it to us, and we spray it on different kinds of animals, and take notes about what happens next."

"Oh," Monroe said. "Ew."

"Yeah."

"So do you get, like, bunnies that turn purple and dogs that go bald and stuff like that?"

"I'd say those would be among the luckier animals, yes. We once managed to grow horns on a Labrador."

"You're kidding."

"Not really. Turned out the horns were pointy tumors. The dog died."

"Oh. That's not very funny."

"It wasn't supposed to be."

"Yeah. Hey, do you have monkeys?"

"Yep. Well, chimps. Monkeys are harder to control and aren't as smart."

"Nobody likes a mean monkey. You have to shoot hairspray on monkeys?"

"Chimps," Ava corrected. "And among other things, yes. We also do medical testing, so sometimes we inject them with things, or give them oral medications."

"And then they freak out?"

"Sometimes. This doesn't bother you?"

"I'm not much of an animal person. I had a dog for a little while when I was growing up. His name was Fucker. His real name was Ralph, but my Dad mostly called him Little Fucker, so after a while, that's what we all called him. Mostly we left off the Little part and just called him Fucker. Anyway, Dad shot him."

"Oh my God," Ava said. "He *shot* him?"

"You kinda have to know Dad," Monroe said. "It seemed to make sense at the time."

"I'm starting to understand why my job doesn't bother you."

Monroe shrugged. "We all have our stuff that we don't want to talk about."

"I suppose so. So, now you know my story." She smiled. "Thanks for letting me ramble. And I'm sorry for forcing you to watch me cry and carry on."

"It's okay. I really didn't mean to pry. It's not my nature to stick my nose in other people's business."

"I noticed that. So what's your story?"

Monroe shrugged again. "Not much to tell. Grew up out west, further west than you, went to college out there, heard about an opening in Langley through one of my professors, been with the Agency ever since."

"Where in the west did you grow up?"

"Oregon."

"Wow. That's a lot farther west than me. You don't miss it? Do you go home very often?"

"No."

"Why not?"

"I don't know," Monroe said. "I don't really have a good relationship with my family."

"Dad shooting dogs was just the tip of the iceberg, huh?"

"You could say that."

"Any girlfriends?" Ava asked, teasing a small smile.

Monroe snorted. "No."

"Ever?"

Monroe shrugged again. He felt like his shoulders were shrugging of their own accord in some kind of self-conscious nerd-spasm. "I've never really had any takers."

"Oh," Ava said. "I'm sorry. Now I'm prying. It's really none of my business."

"It's okay," Monroe said, even though he could feel his face turning bright red. "I don't mind. I've just...never been lucky with women. Maybe someday. Been kinda busy, though."

"Busy," Ava repeated, with a tone of doubt.

A knock on the frame of the door to the operating room caught their attention. It was Kendall. "Hey, what's taking you guys so..." He saw the sleeping, half-shaven Washington asleep on the table. "Oh my gravy," he said with a horrified expression. "He looks terrible!"

"He's fine, Jimmy," Ava said. "But this is why I keep telling you guys not to get too attached to the animals."

Kendall stared at Washington. "I didn't realize how gross cat skin is with no fur on it," he said. "I mean, what are those spots? Are those giant freckles or something?"

"Okay, you boys go on back to work," Ava said, sweeping her arms at Kendall and Monroe in an effort to clear them from the room. "I'll keep an eye on the cat."

"Washington," Kendall said.

"Okay, yes, I'll keep an eye on Washington. Arthur, thank you for the assistance," she added, smiling at Monroe. It was a deep, warm smile, and despite himself, Monroe smiled back.

He was still smiling as he and Kendall sat back down at their workstations.

"I don't think I like Washington as much now," Kendall said. "He's creepy."

"Probably for the best," Monroe replied, still smiling.

Chapter 13

It took Monroe just a few minutes to set up his listening station once he got back to his room after dinner. He stared at it for a few moments. He'd been so excited all during dinner. It had been weeks since he had been able to do any listening. But now that he had his station in front of him, the little homemade version, he found himself hesitating. He normally didn't know the people he listened to very well.

He decided to start with Westcott. Of the four other people on the team, Monroe knew him the least.

"No, Ethel," he heard Westcott say. "No. I said no goddamned flowers. I'm not going to sleep under a bedspread with goddamned *flowers* on it." He paused. He was on the phone, Monroe realized. "You paid how much for it? Oh. Well, it must be really nice then. Why is it…oh, gold leaf? I do like gold leaf. But, no. I don't want anything with flowers on it. Take it back." Pause. "No, I said take it back. Yes, I realize returning things is embarrassing, but that's what you get for not checking with me first. If it bothers you that much, have Lupe do it. That's what I pay her for….No, I said we are *not* keeping it…Ethel, now you're just being ridiculous. This is a ridiculous conversation. Take the bedspread back and get something normal and not *floral*. Okay? Okay. Bye. Yeah, whatever. Okay. Bye."

Click.

Westcott sighed heavily. "Cow," he said. Monroe reached for the dial to flip over to a different room.

"What's her fucking problem now?" an unfamiliar man's voice said. The speaker clearly was inside Westcott's room. Monroe pulled his hand back from the dial.

"Ever since I got here, she's been spending my money like it's water," Westcott growled. Monroe heard ice clinking into a glass. "It's her way of getting back at me for taking this trip."

"So let her spend some of your money," the other voice said. "It's not like you don't have plenty more where it came from."

"I won't if she keeps this up," Westcott said. "She bought some five-hundred-dollar bedspread. Five hundred dollars! I could buy a car for five hundred dollars. Bitch."

"Sure, a shitty car," the other voice said. "Not the kind of car I'd be caught dead in, that's for sure. Look, as long as her lard ass isn't making you go back home, it's fine with me. I'd rather have you here."

"God, talking to her puts me in a bad mood," Westcott grumbled.

"So have another drink," the other man said, "and quit your bitching. How many have you had tonight?"

"Shit if I know. Six?"

"That's it? Baby, you're slacking. Here, top that glass off. Last night you ended up all pissy, and when you're pissy, I don't get laid. I want to get laid tonight. So drink up."

Monroe heard the sound of glass clinking, presumably as Westcott refilled his glass, probably with Glenlivet. "So that's all I am to you?" Westcott said with mock indignation. "Just a stud?"

"Of course not, you dumbass. You also keep me in the finest clothes. I mean, look at this robe. It's divine."

Westcott laughed. Monroe thought his laugh was downright creepy. Especially under the current circumstances.

"You realize," Westcott said, "that your robe is hanging open?"

"Oh, is it? And darn, I forgot to wear anything underneath."

"Get over here," Westcott said.

"Oh God," Monroe blurted as he punched the power switch on his listening station. What in the hell was that? he wondered. Westcott had a man in his room? And he was…they were…

"Ewwww," Monroe shouted as he jumped up off of his bed, shaking his limbs as though they were covered with gay cooties. "Gross," he said. "Gross gross gross." He walked a few more laps around his room, trying to shake off the willies, but it wasn't working.

He grabbed the phone and dialed Kendall's room.

"Hewwo?" Kendall said.

"Hello? Jimmy? Is that you?"

"Hann on." Monroe heard Kendall setting down his handset, followed by the distant sound of water running. A moment later, Kendall was back.

"Artie? Is that you? Sorry, I was brushing my teeth. Is everything okay? You sound funny. What's wrong?"

"You will not believe what I just heard!"

"What happened? Is something wrong?"

"I…" Monroe glanced at his listening station and realized the enormous mistake he was about to make. "Ohh, shit," he muttered.

"Shit? What is it? You heard shit? I don't understand."

"Ahh, I mean, I just got out of the shower. And, uh, when I was in there, I…I heard sex."

"You heard sex? In your shower?"

"Through the wall."

"From Coleman's room? I don't think Coleman has sex."

"No," Monroe said. He was getting flustered and needed to get out of this conversation before he really screwed things up. "It must have been from some other room. Never mind. I'm making it into a bigger deal than it is. I'll talk to you tomorrow."

"Well, hang on," Kendall said. "How did you know it was sex?"

"The walls were banging," Monroe stammered. "You know, like, the headboard. And I heard the woman. She was loud."

"Oh yeah? Are they still doing it? Can I come hear?"

"No! I mean, no. No, they finished. It's quiet now."

"They might start up again, though. Let me come over."

"No. No no. I'm sure they're done. I think they left."

"Already? You said they just finished."

"I heard a door slam. Sounded like them. Look, I need to go dry my hair. I'll see you tomorrow."

"Aww, okay. I never get to have any fun. Maybe I should listen to my walls, huh?"

"I'd recommend that. The trick is to stay in your room and listen for a very long time, to see if you hear anything good. Maybe use a glass, you know, to put up against the wall."

"Ooooh, or maybe I could use one of your bugs. I could put it against the wall. Those things pick up sounds through walls, don't you think?"

"Jimmy," Monroe said. "That's not what the bugs are for."

"Oh, yeah, right," Kendall said. "I'll just use a glass."

"There you go. See you tomorrow."

"Bye." He hung up.

Monroe breathed a sigh of relief as he hung up. He shook his head as he ran his fingers through his hair. "Idiot," he muttered to himself.

Just to be safe, he hid the listening station and headphones for a half hour. No telling if or when Kendall would come knocking on his door.

~

The 30 minutes came and went with no further word from Kendall. Monroe dragged the console back out and powered it on. He flipped the toggle from Westcott's room to Coleman's before putting on the headphones.

He heard total silence in Coleman's room. It was so silent, in fact, that Monroe had to check to make sure everything was working. No snoring, no television, nothing. Monroe would have thought that Coleman wasn't in his room, but then he heard him clear his throat. Boring, yet somehow fascinating, since it seemed nearly impossible for a human being to be so completely silent. Nonetheless, Monroe quickly tired of the silence and flipped over to Ava's room.

He caught her in mid-sentence. "...no idea," she said, followed by a short pause. She was on the phone. "Nope," she continued. "We're reaching a critical point, though. Tomorrow should tell us a lot about how close we are to being done. No, I can't really say, Mom." Pause. "Right. Not that I think you're a Russian spy. I just wouldn't want to risk my job. And there's this one guy from the CIA here who is...I don't think he would handle a perceived security leak very well." Pause. "I know, Mom. Yes, I'm being careful. And I wish I had better news for you. This whole thing was really unexpected. I promise, I'll do something really nice for you when I get back. Like I said, I'll know a lot more after tomorrow. If things go well, I might be back home inside a few more weeks. If not...you know, I'll just cross that bridge if I come to it. I should be able to at least get some kind of big bonus out of this. Maybe I can take the three of us to Mexico or something. I hear Cancun is nice." Pause. "No, Mom, I said Cancun. What did you think I said? No, you know, never mind." She laughed. "Can I talk to Robby? Okay."

She fell silent for a few seconds. Monroe could hear her shifting around on her bed. When she spoke again, her voice was different than he'd ever heard it. She spoke almost like a cartoon character, as if she'd just sucked on a helium balloon.

The brief mental image of Ava sucking on a helium balloon was strangely arousing for Monroe. Sometimes he was amazed at the random things that would turn him on. It reminded him of just how pathetic his sex life truly was.

"Hey there, big guy," Ava said. "How was your day? ...Oh, you did? Aww, did it hurt? Grandma didn't say anything to me about that. Did she put a Band-Aid on it? ...Oh, I'm sorry, baby. Sounds like you were a very brave little man about it, though. ...Good. Hey, I...what's that? ...Oh, honey, I don't know. Probably not for at least a few more weeks.

…That's, well, it could be a lot of days. Probably at least 21. Maybe 28. But I really don't know. …I know. I wish I could come home, too. Believe me, you have no idea how much I want to come home. But Mommy has to work, and they won't let me come home until this job is over. You remember me telling you that, right? …Oh, I know. I…I know, baby, but I can't. I would if I could…oh, Robby, don't cry. Please…" Ava sighed deeply. It sounded like she was starting to cry herself. "Sweetie, please don't cry. There's really not anything I can…Robby, I'm so sorry, but I can't. …Robby, please, don't cry. …Okay, listen, let me talk to Grandma again, okay? I'll talk to you again tomorrow. …Okay. Bye, honey."

Ava hesitated a moment, then fell apart. She sobbed hard.

"Hey, Mom," she said after a moment with a sniff. "Yeah, I can tell he's just really upset. He sounds tired. I'll try to call earlier tomorrow when he's not so tired. Maybe that will go better. I probably can't take more conversations like that one. …I know. I'm doing everything I can. I just hope tomorrow goes well. I need to go, Mom. …Okay. Bye."

She hung up.

Monroe listened for a few moments as Ava cried softly. He clicked off his listening station and decided that he should call it a night.

Chapter 14

Kendall was beside himself for most of the morning, pacing around his workstation, and even climbing down the fire escape twice to work off his nervous energy. As a result, by 11 a.m. he smelled like sweat, and his shirt clung to his rounded belly in a way that Monroe found particularly disturbing.

"Kendall, just sit down," Monroe finally said. "You're driving me nuts. It's not like you have to do anything during the operation."

"I know," Kendall said, continuing to pace slowly. "I'm worried about Washington, that's all. He doesn't know what kind of risk he's facing. The poor guy's just wondering why he hasn't had any kibble since last night. He might not ever get another bowl of kibble. Do you realize how sad that is?"

"No."

"I could really use a corn dog."

"I'm sure Washington would want you to have one," Monroe said with mock seriousness.

"Don't say that," Kendall said. "That's the kind of thing people say about dead people. 'Oh, Aunt Maisy would want you to have her undergarment collection.' Well, some of us don't want our dead aunt's undergarments, you know? Some of us find that sick. What kind of woman wills her undergarments to her nephew? It's a sick, sick joke, I tell you."

"Son, every time I think you can't get pansier," said Coleman, who for once was not sleeping in his chair, "you get pansier."

"It was a hypothetical example," Kendall said, in less-than-convincing fashion. "I meant, *if* my aunt had done that, it would be weird."

"I'd want you to have a corn dog," Monroe said. "Is that better?"

Kendall thought for a moment. "No," he said. "I'd throw up all over this place if I had a corn dog right now."

Ava came out of the operating room. Kendall practically pounced on her. "Is he okay? Is it over?" he asked.

"Calm down, Jimmy," Ava replied. "We haven't even started yet. I'm just getting a little air. This procedure might take a while."

"Need a mask," Coleman said from his chair.

"No," Ava said, slightly confused. "I have one."

"Meant that *I* need a mask."

"For what?"

"Watching."

"I'm sorry," Ava replied. "Dr. Westcott doesn't want a bunch of people in the operating room."

"Not a request," Coleman said, standing up. "Need to see the operation for myself."

"Why?"

"Not a question the CIA answers," Coleman said. "Need a mask."

Ava shook her head in exasperation. "I don't have the energy to argue with you, Agent Coleman," she said. "If you want a mask, I'll get you a damned mask."

"Whoa," Kendall said softly.

Coleman's eyebrows shot up. "A woman with fire. Unexpected. And mildly arousing."

Ava rolled her eyes. "I suppose you two want to watch, too?" she said to Kendall and Monroe.

"No," Monroe said.

"Yes," Kendall shrieked. He looked at Monroe and grabbed his sleeve. "It's Washington," he said. "Somebody needs to watch out for him."

Monroe very much wanted to not watch the operation, but he realized that any resistance would ultimately prove futile. "Okay," Monroe said, "give me a mask, I guess. Somebody needs to keep an eye on Kendall."

"Suit yourselves," Ava said. She led them into the operating room, where they saw Westcott washing his hands and forearms over a large stainless steel sink. He turned when he heard everyone enter.

"Sorry, people, but this isn't a peepshow," he said. "Wait outside. We're just getting ready to start."

"No can do, doc," Coleman said. "Have my orders. Happy to escort Laurel and Hardy out," he added, jerking a thumb at Monroe and Kendall.

"Am I Laurel or Hardy?" Kendall asked.

"It doesn't matter," Monroe said.

"Sure it does. Hardy is fat. I'm not fat. I don't want people calling me fat when I'm not."

"You're fat," Coleman said.

"You're unfriendly!" Kendall shot back.

"Supposed to be," Coleman said. "CIA."

"Gentlemen!" Westcott shouted, getting everyone's attention. "You are not going to watch this operation. Get out."

"Nope," Coleman said.

"If you are standing in here, I am not going to operate. I do not work under those kinds of conditions. In the operating room, I am in charge. You need to go and let me do my job."

"Not leaving," Coleman said. He reached into one of his pockets and produced a slip of paper. "Know what this is?"

"Should I?"

"Phone numbers."

"What?"

"On the paper. Phone numbers. *Washington Post. New York Times. CBS Evening News.* People who would love to know what you do at that company of yours."

Westcott laughed. "You will do no such thing," he said. "And I will not be spoken to in that manner. Certainly not from the likes of you."

"Suit yourself. Chubby, fetch me a phone."

"I'm not chubby!" Kendall shrieked.

"Agent Coleman," Westcott said, "if you report on me to the media, I will of course be more than happy to tell them about this disgusting little experiment we're doing here. I'm sure the public would want to know all about how their government is trying to turn cats into something out of a science-fiction movie. And a bad one at that."

"This project is classified as top secret," Coleman said. "Talking about it in public, that's treason. Pretty sure they still hang folks for that."

"I will not be threatened, Agent Coleman! You had better believe that Walter is going to hear about this. I wouldn't be surprised if he fired you, to be frank. I would."

"Chubby, fetch Doc a phone."

"Stop calling me that!" Kendall cried.

"The man wants to make a call," Coleman said. "Don't think he's going to get the answer he wants, though." He paused and stared hard at Westcott. "Sure you want that phone?"

Westcott met his gaze, staring back at Coleman for a long time. "Civil servants," he finally said with distaste. "Find a chair, sit in it, and stay sitting. You are not allowed to touch the patient, interfere with the procedure in any way, or shoot anything. Am I making myself clear?"

"Pleasure working with you, doc," Coleman said.

Westcott turned to Monroe and Kendall. "You two, out. One idiot from the Agency in my operating room is enough."

"They can stay," Coleman said.

"Excuse me?" Westcott said.

"They can stay."

"And why is that?"

"Because you want them to leave."

Westcott glared at Coleman, then at Monroe and Kendall, before turning his back on them to face the operating table.

"Might want to watch the civil servant cracks in the future, doc," Coleman said.

"If you guys are going to be in here, you need to wear masks and gowns," Ava said. "They're in that cabinet."

"One more thing," Westcott said, wheeling back around. "If any of you think you're going to be sick, get the hell out of my operating room immediately. If you throw up in here, you contaminate everything. I don't care if you repaint all the walls in your lab, just don't throw up in here."

"I can't believe I'm going to do this," Monroe said quietly to Kendall. "I'm not very good with blood."

"Just think of it as bright red cough syrup," Kendall said. "That's what Mom used to tell me. It actually works. You should try it. Although I should say that if the blood is actually gushing, the cough syrup thing doesn't work as well. Cough syrup really doesn't gush."

"We need to make sure that your Mom never ever meets my Dad," Monroe said.

"Why? Does your Dad throw warm cough syrup on the neighbors?"

"Just take my word for it. And grab me a mask."

~

A half hour later, Washington was on the table, knocked out cold by anesthetics. He was on his belly, with his shaved back exposed. Ava had set up a complex series of blue sheets that covered all of the cat except for his back. That made Monroe feel better. It was somehow worse when he could see the entire cat. Seeing just its back made it somehow seem less like a living thing.

Westcott stood over the cat and asked for his scalpel. Ava handed one to him. Much to Monroe's disappointment, her scrubs were very loose-fitting. He couldn't really see anything good under them. They made her look lumpy.

Westcott held the scalpel over Washington. He lowered it, made an imaginary incision in the air a few inches above the cat's skin, then lifted the scalpel again. Monroe thought for a moment that the man looked like he was leaning to the left more than someone should while performing surgery.

"Hmm," Westcott said. He tilted his head left and right, as if he were trying to think of something.

"Do you need something, doctor?" Ava asked.

"No," Westcott growled. He dabbed at a small bit of sweat on his forehead with his sleeve.

"Slice it open, doc," Coleman said. "You can do it."

"Gross," Kendall said.

"I've heard enough orders from you today, Agent Coleman," Westcott said. "Perhaps you don't realize how fortunate you are to have a skilled surgeon on board for this project."

"So far it's just you waving things around. Chop it up already."

"Cro-Magnon," Westcott said as he lowered the blade again. After another hesitation, he began making a long incision down Washington's spine. Blood oozed from the cut.

"Cough syrup, cough syrup, oh tasty cough syrup," Kendall sang softly to the tune of "Lollipop." "Cough syrup, cough syrup, oh tasty cough syrup…"

Monroe looked over at Kendall. He was sweating profusely. He kept repeating the one line of his "song" as a mantra.

Coleman pulled his gun half way out of its holster and glared at Kendall.

Kendall stopped singing.

Monroe found it a bit hard to see what was going on with the operation. The sheets blocked his view; he could see the opening on Washington's back, but nothing of what was happening below the surface. He didn't mind, exactly, but he was curious as to what Westcott was up to. He wondered if anyone else thought, as he did, that Westcott seemed to be struggling, like he was fighting off a bit of flu.

Westcott and Ava worked in silence for a little while, with Westcott occasionally asking for a sponge or more suction or an adjustment to the light.

At one point, Westcott stopped for a moment. "Hmm," he said, dabbing his brow with his sleeve again. Ava looked up at Westcott, appearing concerned.

"Oh, right," Westcott almost whispered. Monroe glanced at Coleman to see if he had noticed. Coleman's eyes were closed and he seemed to be using his cane to prop himself up. Monroe nudged Kendall, who had started humming softly on the other side of him.

"Hey," Monroe whispered.

Kendall stopped humming. "What?"

"Check it out. I think Coleman's sleeping."

Kendall leaned forward and peered around Monroe. "How can he sleep through this? It's taking every ounce of willpower I have just to keep my bowels closed."

"Oops," Westcott said. Out of nowhere, blood began spurting out of Washington's back. "Ahh, here we go," he said. The spurting stopped for a moment, then started again, heavier than before. "Shit."

"Cough syrup, cough syrup, ohhhh tasty cough syrup," Kendall began singing in a tone so manic that it almost seemed like shouting.

Westcott looked at Ava. "Uhh, can you…?"

"Yes, sir," Ava said, sounding slightly aggravated as she reached for a handful of gauze. She wadded it up and shoved it in its entirety into the incision.

"What are you doing?" Kendall half asked, half shouted. "That doesn't look healthy."

"We need a fresh cat," Westcott said.

"What does that mean?" Kendall shouted. He was drenched with sweat and looked like he was about to fall over at any moment. He turned to Monroe. "What did he mean by that?"

Monroe shrugged. "Don't ask me. I'm not the guy with the knife."

Ava looked at Westcott again, but he didn't meet her gaze.

"It appears this subject was not a good choice," Westcott said. "Weak aorta. It appears to have burst."

"Burst?" Kendall said, walking toward the table. "What do you…" He looked down at Washington. "Oh. Ohh, that is so gross."

Ava shook her head, almost imperceptibly, but Monroe noticed. Her movements were jerky and agitated as she stuffed more gauze into the surgical opening.

"Bulgarian sandwich!" Coleman suddenly shouted, jerking awake. He looked around and realized he'd made himself the center of attention. "What's going on? Why aren't you chopping up the cat?" Coleman looked at the bloody mess that used to be Washington. "What's with him? He looks dead."

"He is dead," Ava said. "Or at least, he will be once he finishes bleeding out in another 30 seconds or so." She tossed a bloody hunk of gauze into a nearby bin with disgust.

Westcott yanked off his gloves and tossed them into a bin. "Unfortunate. We discovered the subject had a weak aorta. Bad luck."

"Bad luck?" Ava said. "Bad *luck*?"

Westcott glared at her. "Yes, bad luck," he said. "If your opinion differs, I would remind you that you are a veterinary assistant and I am your employer."

"You are unbelievable!" Ava said, her voice rising.

"There is no need for that kind of tone, Ava," Westcott said.

"Of course there's a need for it, you pompous jerk!" Ava shouted.

The six eyebrows above Coleman's, Monroe's and Kendall's eyes all shot up at once.

"I kept wondering what you thought you were doing," Ava said, "especially since all you've done since we got here was to act like you're some hotshot ..."

"Ava, keep yourself under control here," Westcott said, shooting a quick glance at Coleman.

"No, darn it, I'm *tired* of keeping myself under control! You lie to me to get me out here on this godforsaken project, you tell me we're only going to be here for a month, and here I'm thinking maybe we're getting close to being finished so we can all go home, and you cut the cat's aorta! The *aorta*! Why didn't you just drop an anvil on its head?"

"People actually do that?" Kendall asked.

"Just in cartoons," Monroe said.

"Ava," Westcott said, trying to sound authoritative, "mind your place."

"When was the last time you actually performed an operation?" Ava shouted. "You're the one who wants to be Mr. In Charge Here. How long has it been, huh? Ten years? Fifteen?"

"I have had just about enough of all this insubordination today," Westcott commanded. "Mistakes happen. You know that. I will not hear another word of this. Exactly how many surgeries have you performed, Miss Moriarty?"

"That is not that point, and you know it!"

"I will presume, then, that your answer is none. I therefore think it's safe to say that you have no idea what you're talking about. Now mind your place and prep another cat for surgery tomorrow! And that is final!"

"Answer the question," Coleman said.

"What?" Westcott said.

"Answer the question. How long since your last surgery?"

"I will not stand here and have my reputation impugned," Westcott said, yanking off his mask.

"Still haven't shot anybody today," Coleman said. "Answer the question."

Westcott's jaw dropped open, snapped shut again. He shot a long glare at Ava, but she didn't back down. She glared right back. Monroe was beginning to wonder if somebody really was about to be shot, and for the first time, he wondered if the shooter might be someone other than Coleman.

Westcott looked at Coleman. "Twenty-one years," he said. "But I am just as qualified now as I ever was. One does not unlearn the skill of surgery."

For a moment, Westcott and Coleman stared each other down.

"That's it," Coleman said, yanking his service revolver out of its holster. "I'm shooting you."

For a split second, Westcott merely looked at the gun, as if he assumed Coleman were bluffing.

But only for a split second.

Westcott shrieked as he dove under the surgical table. Coleman's shooting turned out to be as rusty as Westcott's surgical abilities; his first shot blew Washington's bloody corpse off the table and against the wall, where it left a wide red stain before falling to the floor with a wet plop.

Kendall screamed, a high, wailing scream that likely would have caused any dog unfortunate enough to hear it to suffer a burst aneurysm. He threw Monroe out of the way, tossing him to the floor, and charged Coleman. The charge was so slow and clumsy that had Coleman even slightly suspected that it might be coming, he could have easily dodged it. But as it was, Kendall plowed into the extremely startled agent with his full weight, knocking Coleman off his feet and sending his cane flying across the floor. Coleman's head slammed against the hard tiles on the floor, knocking him out cold instantly. Kendall scrambled to his feet and whirled around in total disorientation, his eyes bulging with terror.

"I'm going to barf!" he shouted.

"That way!" Ava and Monroe both shouted, simultaneously pointing toward the door. Kendall spotted it and charged out of the room. A moment later, they could hear him retching out the window.

"Holy crap," Monroe said, surveying the room. It looked like someone had decided to play volleyball in the middle of the O.R., but with a bloody cat instead of a volleyball.

"Is he out?" Westcott said, peering over the operating table at Coleman. "Where's his gun? Ava, get his gun!"

Ava went to Coleman, felt his wrist. "He's alive. Probably going to have a wicked headache when he wakes up. We better make sure Kendall's far away when he does." She noticed Coleman's gun, which was lying on the floor near his hand. She pushed it as if it were a dead rat, sending it skittering across the floor. "Better keep that away from him, too," she said.

"Son of a bitch actually *shot* at me!" Westcott said. "He's fucking *crazy*! This is insane!" He came out from behind the table. "I'll make sure you lose your job for this!" he shouted at the unconscious Coleman. "I'll be surprised if you don't end up in jail over this, you insane lunatic!"

"You're both insane!" Ava shouted back. "You haven't performed a surgery in twenty-one years. I might have shot at you, too."

"I had a business to run! A business that, I might remind you, provides very well for you and your family. I couldn't have built the business into what it is today if I were still taking care of people's sick poodles. People are willing to pay a lot more for animal testing than they'll pay to get Fido's tumor removed. Besides, this is all beside the point. I still know what I'm doing, dammit!"

"It's been twenty-one years!" Ava said. "You just cut open the cat's aorta! It sure looked to me like you most certainly did not know what you were doing! This is experimental surgery! What on earth made you think you could do this? You dragged both of us halfway across the country, and you *knew* you weren't qualified to perform these surgeries. I just don't understand what you were *thinking*! You uprooted me, took me away from my son, for what?"

"You will mind your place, Miss Moriarty!" Westcott shouted, stomping his foot. It made him stumble just a bit for no apparent reason. "I know what I'm doing, and that should be a good enough answer for you."

"You have no right…"

"Another word out of you and you're fired!" Westcott shouted. "Do you want to pay your own way back to Virginia to find yourself another job?"

Ava blinked in surprise. She fell silent for a moment, her anger draining away like it had a slow leak in it. "No," she said softly.

"It's good to see you haven't completely lost track of your faculties," Westcott said. "When I did perform surgeries, I was one of the best. I still am. One can never know how a patient will respond to surgery. Now clean up this mess and prepare another subject for surgery tomorrow. I'm leaving."

Westcott picked up Coleman's gun. "I'm going to assume that when Agent Coleman wakes up, he is going to be more angry with Kendall than he will be with me, but just in case, I'm going to hide this. I assume neither of you will object." He didn't wait for a response before storming from the operating room. A moment later, they heard him climbing down the fire escape.

"Your boss is a dick," Monroe said, finally standing up.

Ava's shoulders slumped as the surveyed the damage to the room. She picked up a sheet and wrapped it around Washington's body.

"Need some help?" Monroe asked.

"Yeah," she said. She seemed almost dazed. "Take this and go find someplace woodsy to dump it in."

"We're not burying him?" Monroe asked, taking the grisly package from her.

"Do whatever you want with it. Just don't throw it away in a Dumpster where anyone can find it. National security, you know," she said with a grin she clearly didn't feel.

"Okay."

"When you get back, I could use a hand prepping the next cat."

"Okay."

"And tonight somebody needs to take me to the bowling alley so I can get stinking drunk."

"Okay."

"Stop saying 'okay' and just get rid of that thing. Take Kendall with you. I don't want to clean up puke, and I certainly don't want him around when Coleman wakes up."

"What are we going to do about him?" Monroe asked, gesturing toward Coleman. "He's going to be steaming mad. And he won't be happy about missing his gun."

"Just leave him. If he wakes up, I'll deal with him."

"You sure?"

"Yeah. I think I'm the one person in this outfit he won't shoot. Besides, now he's unarmed."

"Fair enough." Monroe started to leave, but stopped halfway out the door and turned back. "Ava?"

"Yes?"

"For what it's worth...I'm sorry."

"For what?"

"For your boss. If he won't apologize to you, I will."

"I appreciate that," Ava said with a shrug. "You better get going before that sheet starts leaking on you."

"Ew. Okay. Back in a bit."

"Monroe?"

"Yeah?"

"Thanks."

Monroe smiled. "You're welcome."

~

Monroe decided to simply dump Washington's body, rather than burying it. A burial seemed like too much work. On top of that, he and Kendall were both tired and hot from cleaning Kendall's former lunch off of the fire escape.

They'd driven out of town a bit, and it didn't take long for the road they were on to turn into a rural two-laner. Monroe pulled off at a small clearing.

"At least he didn't suffer," Kendall said as he got out of the van with the body, which by that time was wrapped in no fewer than five sheets, as Washington's innards kept soaking through the first few.

"True," Monroe replied. "He probably was already dead by the time he got shot."

"We can at least be thankful for that."

"Yep."

"I still could use a corn dog."

"Jimmy, you just heaved all over the fire escape less than an hour ago."

"Which is why I'm hungry again. I can't help it if I have a high metabolism. I require a lot of food."

"Okay, whatever. You can get one at the bowling alley."

Kendall's face brightened. "We're going bowling?"

"Well, I'm not sure if we're actually bowling," Monroe replied. "Ava wanted to go get drunk."

"We should bring Coleman."

"Are you nuts? You tackled him. Knocked him out cold. And, let's not forget, prevented him from shooting someone. He's going to want to kill you when he comes to."

"Maybe. But I think he won't. I think, deep down, he isn't a man of violence. He won't shoot me," he said, shifting the bundle of dead cat in his arms.

"Your funeral. Speaking of which, I guess we should do what we came here for. I'm thinking we can heave him into the trees here."

"Should we say something?"

Monroe shrugged. "If you want."

"I feel like we should say something."

"So say something."

Kendall cleared his throat. "Oh dear Washington, we didn't know you well, but we knew you well enough to mourn your getting your aorta cut and getting shot after you were dead. You deserved better, and I hope Kitty Heaven is filled with all kinds of mice who don't run well and cats in heat. Girl cats, I mean. Um, Amen."

"Amen."

Monroe grabbed one end of the sheet, and Kendall moved his hands to the other. Together, they heaved the body into the woods. It landed with a sickening thud. The two of them looked at it for a second.

"That was gross," Kendall said.

"Yeah. Let's go to the bowling alley."

"Okay."

~

"You guys," Kendall said, "he's still out of it."

"Still?" Monroe said, coming out of the operating room, where he and Ava had just finished prepping a smallish gray cat, who had since been dubbed Adams. Still groggy from the anesthetics, the newly barebacked cat was lazily bumping into walls at Monroe's feet.

Coleman was laying on the floor in the lab, between the two workstations. Ava had found a few small blankets and propped his head on them.

Ava followed Monroe out of the operating room. "I didn't think he took that hard of a shot to his head," she said.

"Think we need to get him to a hospital?" Kendall asked.

"Under normal circumstances, I'd say yes. But then everyone at the hospital would find out he was CIA. I don't think he would want that. And his vitals have been consistently good. Unless he begins deteriorating, I think we may as well just keep him with us."

"Are you guys sure you want to take him to the bowling alley?" Monroe asked.

"We can't leave him here," Kendall said.

"What I mean is, we could just not go to the alley tonight," Monroe said.

"Arthur," Ava said, "I don't care if we have to drag him by his hair the entire way. I need to drink. And since we can't leave him here, he's coming with us."

"I like her," Kendall said. "She's fun."

"Besides," Ava said, "if he doesn't like the idea, he's welcome to wake up and say so."

Chapter 15

"I can't believe he's still not awake," Kendall said as he dropped Coleman into a chair in the bowling alley's bar. "I thought for sure he'd come to when we dropped him off the fire escape. Or maybe after he fell out of the van in the parking lot."

"I know," Monroe said. "The water in that puddle he fell in was really cold. And something in that water was squishy."

"That water made my fingers smell funny," Kendall said, sniffing the digits in question.

"You guys complain a lot," Ava said. "Don't worry about Coleman. He'll wake up when he's ready."

The bar's lone waitress, a pudgy woman in a sleeveless denim shirt and rhinestone-encrusted jeans, wandered over to the table. "Y'all need somethin'?" she asked with the enthusiasm of an addict in rehab.

"I want a glass of white wine," Ava said. "Whatever you have. You know, make that two glasses. No, just bring the whole bottle."

"Let the good times roll," the waitress said, jotting on a small notebook.

"I'll have a beer," Kendall said. "Something frothy."

"We have Bud," the waitress said.

"And?"

"We have Bud."

"Is Bud frothy?"

The waitress stared at him and said nothing. Her expression was vaguely threatening.

"Bud sounds fine," Kendall said.

The waitress jotted. "You?" she said to Monroe.

"A Bud's fine," he said.

"What's wrong with him?" the waitress said, jabbing the eraser end of her pencil at Coleman, who was slumped back on his chair, head tilted so far back that his mouth could have been used as a nightstand.

The three of them glanced at each other for a brief moment.

Kendall volunteered. "Nothing," he said.

The waitress glared at each of them. "He ain't movin'," she noted.

"He'll take a Bud," Kendall said.

The waitress stared at Kendall for a moment, then jotted on her notebook again. "Three Buds and two wines," she said. "And if that one pisses on himself, I'm not cleanin' it up, y'all hear me?"

"Yes ma'am," Kendall said. "Thank you. And if I may say so, I really like your jeans. Very sparkly."

"Well, ain't you a fuckin' charmer," she said as she walked away.

"I sure do like the people in this town," Kendall said.

"I don't care what kind of people they have here," Ava said, "as long as they keep the drinks coming."

"You know, he doesn't look all that different than he does when he's sleeping in the lab," Kendall said, looking Coleman over. "Except for the bloody cheek and the muck on his shirt, that is."

"I think I like him better like this," Monroe said. "You're really not worried about him trying to shoot you once he wakes up?"

"Westcott has his gun."

"I don't think that would really slow him down much."

"He won't hurt me."

"You have more faith in that than I do."

"He's just a big old teddy bear. I'm sure of it."

The waitress returned and set three bottles of Bud and a bottle of wine, along with a single plastic cup, on the table. "Knock yourselves out," she said, leaving again.

"I think she's a little sweet on me," Kendall said.

Ava filled the plastic cup to the top with wine. "Cheers," she said, hoisting it. She looked at the Bud bottles on the table. "Come on, guys, I'm not drinking alone."

Monroe and Kendall hoisted their beers in the air and tapped them against Ava's cup. "Cheers," Kendall said.

"Cheers," Monroe added.

"Here's to drinking for all the wrong reasons," Ava said before putting the cup to her lips and downing half the contents in a single pull.

"Whoa," Kendall said. "I thought I was the only one in mourning."

"I'm not mourning the cat," Ava said. "Actually, come to think of it, in a way I guess I am. To Washington," she said, raising her cup again.

"To Washington!" Kendall said. "May he come back as something that does not get operated on."

"To Washington," Monroe said. They all drank. Ava finished her cup and poured herself a second, though she did it without any of her usual composure. She drank half of that cup in a single pull.

"Uh, you might want to slow down just a bit there, Ava," Monroe said.

"I don't think so, Arthur," she said. "Either I get drunk, or I go back to that lab, chop Dr. Westcott into small pieces and feed them to the crows on the roof."

Monroe and Kendall shared a look.

"Drink up," Kendall said.

"Thank you, Jimmy, I think I will," Ava replied, taking another long drink from her cup. She looked over her shoulder at the pool table and saw that it was open. "Come on. We're playing pool. We can play Cutthroat until Coleman wakes up."

"What's Cutthroat?" Kendall asked.

"It's easy," Ava said, digging in her purse and fishing out a quarter. "Each person has five balls. The first person has 1 through 5, second person has 6 through 10, third person has 11 through 15. The goal is to knock your opponents' balls off the table. Last man standing wins."

She shoved the quarter into a slot on the side of the pool table. The balls crashed into the holding area next to the slot. "Rack 'em, Jimmy," she said.

"Sure!" Kendall said as he bounded to the triangle hanging on the wall.

"Jimmy?" Ava asked.

"Yeah?"

"Just so you know, racking 'em isn't supposed to be a treat. Usually the winner gets to order the loser to rack 'em up. At least, that's what my dad always said to me when he beat me."

"But I haven't lost yet," Kendall said. "And I like putting the balls in the triangle-thingy. It's fun."

"Sometimes I wish I could be you," Ava said.

"Really?"

"Sure. But only sometimes."

"Oh."

"So, Ava," Monroe said, "do you play a lot?"

"Maybe," Ava said with a grin. "I will say, though, that my dad beat me every time we played until I was 13." She chugged the rest of the wine in her cup. "You break, Arthur. You're 1 through 5. Jimmy can be 6 through 10. I'll be 11 through 15."

"Shouldn't there be more than one stick?" Kendall asked. "I only see this one." The cue in Kendall's hand looked like it had been dragged by a moose every day since the beginning of the Eisenhower

Administration. The three of them looked around but saw no other cues anywhere in the bar.

"Looks like it'll be a bit of a challenge tonight," Ava said. "At least we all shoot with the same stick, so it's fair."

"Okay," Monroe said, grabbing the cue. He set down the cue ball, lined up his shot, and fired. He sank the 4.

"Great," Monroe said, handing the cue to Kendall.

"You sank one of your own," Kendall said with a laugh. "I like this game."

"Very funny."

Kendall carefully lined up his shot. He bent over the table and stared at his shot for what seemed like an eternity.

"Come on, Kendall," Monroe said. "Shoot."

"Don't rush me," Kendall said. He pulled back the cue, thrust it forward...and almost missed the cue ball entirely. He only grazed it, sending it about a foot to the left of where it started.

"Shit," Kendall said.

"I like this game," Monroe said.

"That's not very nice," Kendall said.

"Okay, my turn," Ava said, taking a long drink from her third cup of wine. Her bottle was nearly gone. Monroe's bottle of Bud sat untouched on the table.

Ava bent over the table to line up her first shot. From where he was standing, Monroe could see straight down her blouse. She was better endowed than her loose shirts implied.

Ava shot. The cue ball rocketed across the table, sank Monroe's 1 ball, then ricocheted just enough to nick Kendall's 9 ball, sinking it as well.

"Holy crap," Monroe said.

"Did you do that on purpose?" Kendall asked.

Ava merely smiled. "Three ball, corner pocket," she said. A moment later, Monroe only had two balls left on the table.

"And when was the last time your father beat you at pool?" Monroe asked.

"When I was 13," Ava said. "Seven ball, side pocket." Crack. Another ball down.

Within five minutes, the game was over. Neither Monroe nor Kendall touched the cue again.

"Wow," Kendall said.

"I'm actually not *that* good," Ava said. "I got a little lucky there."

"Not from where I was standing. Jeez. That was like watching Paul Newman."

"Please," Ava said. "Newman's an actor, not a pool player. Anyone who plays real pool at all can tell the difference."

"I stand corrected."

A large man wearing a sleeveless t-shirt and mesh baseball cap approached the table. He had the haggard, somewhat unwashed look of a professional truck driver. "That was some impressive work, ma'am," the man said. "I'm not so bad myself. Care to play a little nine ball?" He smiled, exposing a large set of very yellow teeth. "I'm George."

"Thanks, George," Ava replied, "but no thanks."

"Oh, now come on there, miss," George continued, looking at the nearly empty cup of wine in her hand. "I could make it interesting. Say, twenty bucks a game?" Monroe could smell beer on the man's breath from where he was standing, a good six feet away.

Ava finished her wine as she considered the offer. "Twenty bucks, huh?"

"Yep," George replied. He reached into his pocket and produced three twenty-dollar bills. "Lucky me, it's payday," he said, waving them in the air.

"I wouldn't want to take a hard working man's pay away from him," Ava said. "You look like you need it more than me."

"Come on," George said. Whether he deliberately ignored the insult or simply hadn't noticed it was unclear. "Afraid you'll lose? It's my money. I'll be the one who worries about losing it."

"Okay, you're on," Ava said. She caught Monroe's eye, saw the slight concern in his face, and shrugged. "Shoot to see who breaks?" she asked George.

"You bet. Ladies first."

Ava grabbed the cue ball, lined up a shot on the empty table, and shot it off the far bumper. It rolled back toward her, stopping less than two inches from the near bumper.

"Ha," Ava said to nobody in particular. Monroe realized that she was starting to show the effects of three cups of wine in less than 20 minutes.

"What are they doing?" Kendall asked.

"Whoever gets the ball closest to the near bumper gets to break," Monroe replied.

George's smile faded a bit as he lined up his shot. He leaned his tremendous bulk over, shot, and saw his ball stop several inches behind where Ava's had rested.

He grunted. "Your table," he said, handing her the cue. He silently went about the task of pumping a quarter into the table and racking nine balls in a diamond pattern.

Ava broke, scattering the balls around the table and sinking the 7. She studied the table, then sank the 1 by ricocheting it off a side rail. On her third shot, she struck the 2, which in turn hit the 9, which dropped straight into a corner pocket.

"Holy *shit*," Monroe said.

"Son of a bitch," George mumbled. He shook his head as he dug out his twenties and tossed one on the table in Ava's general direction. "Hell of a start, lady," he said, "but my money says you can't do that twice. Got a little lucky with that break, you know."

"Wasn't luck, my friend," Ava said, collecting the bill and sliding it into a hip pocket. "But you can break this time."

"Bet your sweet ass I will," George grumbled.

Monroe thought about telling George to watch his mouth, regardless of how sweet Ava's ass might be, but he didn't. George was a fairly big guy. He didn't appear to be in great shape, but his arms were almost twice the size of Monroe's spindly limbs. In fact, they appeared to be larger than Monroe's legs as well.

George waited for Ava to rack. As the winner of the previous game, she wasn't required to do so, but Monroe noticed that she did anyway. He broke and sunk the 3. On his second shot, he sank the 1. Three more shots, and the 2, 4 and 5 balls were gone. The 6 was a tricky shot, forcing George to bounce the cue off a rail, but he pulled it off. The 7 was a much simpler shot, but George rushed it a bit, and it missed the corner pocket.

"Shit," he mumbled.

Ava took the stick from him. She stared at the table for several minutes, walking around it and considering her options.

"I ain't getting any fuckin younger here," George said.

Ava said nothing in return, but his comment seemed to help her decide what to do. She lined up a shot at the 7 ball and struck it so that it careened off an end bumper, came almost all the way back to the other end, and grazed the 9, which drifted toward a corner pocket, hung on the lip for a moment, then dropped in.

"Ha!" Ava shouted.

Kendall whooped and pumped his arms in the air. George glared at him, and Kendall immediately shot his arms back down to his sides. "Sorry," he said.

Ava bounced over to the table and emptied the last of the wine into her cup. She took a celebratory drink.

George dug a second twenty out of his pocket and tossed it on the table. "You seem to be making an awful lot of shots," he grumbled.

"I seem to be kicking your butt," Ava said, finishing her fourth cup of wine.

"No woman's gonna beat me three times in a row," George replied. "I'll rack 'em this time, and I break."

"Whatever you say, Sarge," Ava said, mock-saluting him while his back was turned.

Monroe sidled up to her. "You okay? You aren't really acting like yourself."

"I'm not drunk, if that's what you mean," Ava said. "Tipsy, maybe, but not drunk. And you don't really know what I'm like. There was a time when I did this to help pay my way through school. You'd be amazed how bad the pool players are in Oklahoma. Besides, I'm having fun for once, so don't worry about it."

"I'm not sure George is having fun," Monroe said. "You're kind of egging him on. He seems…cranky."

"I am not egging him on," Ava said. "Look, if the guy wants to lose his money, that's his problem. He said so himself. Relax. We're just playing a game."

"I think you should be careful. Maybe let him win, then we'll go home."

"Are you kidding?" Ava said, recoiling. "I am not letting him win. I have had enough of losing today. I'm not losing if I can help it. Go on."

"Just be careful," Monroe said. He went back to standing next to Kendall.

"He's getting really mad," Kendall said, almost whimpering.

"I know."

"He's really big."

"I know."

"I haven't been in a fight since I kicked Willy Haines in the wing-ding in third grade."

"Geez," Monroe said, covering his eyes with his hand.

"What?"

"If this ends up in a big fight, I'll end up with a guy who uses the word 'wing-ding' on my side."

The sound of George breaking interrupted them. He sank two balls on the break, the 4 and the 8. After four more shots, he had just two balls left on the table, the 7 and the 9. "I got you now," he said. "Tell you what, if I sink both balls on this shot, you let me grab one o' them nice titties of yours."

"Hey," Monroe said, but so inaudibly that Kendall barely heard him.

"I don't think so," Ava said. "You could be Elvis Presley's uglier older brother and I wouldn't let you touch me. Just play."

"Oh God," Kendall whined. "Why is she talking to him like that? We should go. We should go."

"What the hell are we going to do?" Monroe replied. "We can't go without Ava, and I can't get her to leave."

"You got a smart mouth on you, girlie," George said. "Tell you what. Double or nothing says I sink these two balls and run the table on your tiny ass."

"You don't have double," Ava said. "You only have twenty left."

"I got double," George said. "I just didn't flash it."

"Let's see it."

George paused for a moment and glared at Ava. "I said I got it," he said.

"And I said, let's see it. Where I come from, if it's not on the table, it's not on the table."

"Ava..." Monroe said.

Ava didn't respond. "Look," she said to George, "I don't need to keep playing. Why don't we just finish this game and be done with it. You're kind of a jerk anyway."

"Cough syrup, cough syrup, ohhh tasty cough syrup," Kendall began to sing.

"Fine," George said. He dug into his pocket and produced two twenties, which he planted on the edge of the table. "I got it. Okay? I sink these two, I get my first forty back. I blow it, you get this forty."

"Okay," Ava said. "Shoot."

George scowled as he lined up his shot. He studied it for a long time before finally taking it. The 7 went down.

Only the 9 remained. George paced around the table until he found an angle he liked. It was a long shot, requiring the 9 to go three quarters of the way across the table to a corner pocket. He lined it up and shot.

The 9 bounced against the bumper near the corner pocket and rolled away.

"Whooooooo!" Ava shouted. She scooped George's last $40 off the table. "Whoooo, boys!" she shouted, waving the $40 at Monroe and Kendall. "Looks like dinner's on me tonight!" She turned to George. "Hey, look, no hard feelings, huh? I caught a few breaks tonight, that's all. Maybe we can play again soon, huh? Might be able to get back at me a little."

George's face was a deep red. "Lady, you ain't leaving here with my money," he said slowly.

Ava's celebration slowed. "Look, I'm sorry, but you lost fair and square. We used the same cue and everything. A bet's a bet."

"You ain't walking out of here with my money," George repeated. "Hand it over."

"No way," Ava said. She turned to Monroe and Kendall. "Look, I realize I got a little carried away with the table talk. Sorry. Where I'm from, it's what you do when you play pool. But a bet is a bet."

"You got my entire paycheck, lady. Give it back."

Ava rolled her eyes and turned to Monroe and Kendall. "You can't reason with some people," she said. "Come on, let's get going before he starts crying."

Behind her, George raised the pool cue, holding it at the thin end. He pulled it back like a baseball player about to swing at a fastball.

"Ava, *get down!*" Monroe shouted.

Ava turned just as George swung. She instinctively ducked her head and raised her arm, bracing for impact.

A large hand caught the fat end of the pool cue a split second before it could collide with Ava's arm. George's face went from fury to surprise as Coleman wrapped his other hand around the cue and yanked forward hard. The cue came flying out of George's beefy hands. With surprising speed, Coleman shifted his grip to the thin of the stick, and in a single fluid motion, swung hard and fast, shattering the heavy end of the stick on George's shoulder, causing him to yelp in pain.

Coleman was on him before he could recover, grabbing George by his t-shirt, yanking him upright, and head-butting him with such force that George's hat flew across the room. The large man crumpled to the floor before the hat had a chance to land on the bar.

"God bless America and its hand-to-hand combat techniques!" Coleman screamed at George. He looked at the few other patrons in the bar, all of whom had scattered when the fight broke out. "Anyone else care to behave like an enemy of the state?"

The other patrons all shook their heads in unison as quickly as they could without popping a vertebrae.

Coleman tugged on the sleeves of his soiled shirt as he looked down at George. "Disappointing," he said. "Not nearly enough glory."

Ava, Monroe and Kendall stared at him in shock as he limped back to the table to retrieve his cane. "Who's driving?" he said to them. "I have a headache. Why is my shirt dirty?"

"Uh, I think I'm driving," Monroe said, trying not to make any sudden movements.

"We're bugging out then," Coleman replied. "Grab your gear. And where's my goddamned gun? Finally have a need to shoot somebody and I don't have my damn gun."

"Westcott has it," Kendall squeaked.

Coleman's eyebrows shot up and he looked at Monroe. "No, really," Monroe said.

Coleman grunted. "Interesting," he said. "Unexpected. Somewhat infuriating." He grunted a second time. "Better be clean when I get it back," he said, ambling toward the exit. His limp seemed to be more pronounced than before. He waved to the bartender as he walked. "America thanks you for the sacrifice of your mighty pool stick," he announced. "It served your country well tonight."

"Thanks," replied the rather stunned-looking bartender.

"I guess we better go with him," Ava said, scooping up her purse. She paused, then threw one of George's twenties on him. "Might help with the hospital bill," she said, wincing. Monroe and Kendall followed her toward the door.

Coleman turned to Kendall as they headed out the door. "I just remembered what happened," he said. "You and I need to talk after I get my gun back."

Chapter 16

About ten minutes after getting into his room, while he had a mouth full of toothpaste, Monroe heard a knock at his door. He walked to it and tried to talk around the toothpaste. "Hewwo?" he asked.

The knocking stopped. After a moment, he heard Ava's voice on the other side of the door. "Monroe? Do I have the right room?"

Monroe quickly scanned his room and spotted at least two dirty pairs of underwear laying on the floor. "Juff a minute," he yelled, shoving underwear under the bed, next to where he stowed his listening station. He ran back to the door and pulled it open.

Ava saw the toothpaste. "Oh," she said. "I thought I had the wrong room."

Monroe held up a "just a minute" finger and returned to the bathroom. After he rinsed, he found her still standing at the front door. He realized she was holding a full bottle of wine in one hand and two cups in the other. She held them up. "I still don't feel like drinking alone," she said.

"Come on in," he said. His mind was racing, wondering if he'd left anything else out that he'd rather she not see.

"Thanks," she said. She headed for the only chair in the room and saw Monroe's headphones laying on it. He felt his face go red; those were the cans he used to listen to the other rooms. "Bringing your work home, huh?" she said, tossing them on the bed. She kicked off her shoes and put her bare feet on his bed. "You mind?"

"No."

"Hope you like wine," she said, pouring two cups. "Relax, I'm not going to bite. Sit." She held out one of the cups.

"Thanks," he said, taking the cup and sitting on the edge of the bed. He hated wine but wasn't about to say so. He stole a quick glance at her bare feet. He wasn't really into feet, but hers were nice and her nails were painted.

"I hope I'm not intruding too much," she said. "I'm a little keyed up after what happened at the bowling alley. And frankly, I'm not drunk enough to be able to sleep yet."

"I don't mind," Monroe replied. "It was kind of a crazy night. I thought that guy was going to take your head off."

"Ahh, he wasn't so tough. Fat bastard. At least I took him for $60."

"You're really different when you drink."

"I hope I didn't get Coleman in any trouble."

"I have a feeling it's not the first bar fight that place has seen. Besides, almost nobody knows we're even here."

"That's true. Thank God Coleman woke up in time."

"Yeah. Although I get the feeling he'd been awake for quite a while and was just waiting until he felt like letting us know."

"Probably."

They fell silent. Ava took a sip of her wine. Then she drank almost the rest of the cup.

"What's with all the drinking tonight?" Monroe asked. "If you don't mind my asking."

"What, a girl can't have a few drinks when she feels like it?"

"Sure. I guess. You just seem...driven."

She looked back at Monroe for a moment, then sighed and rubbed her eyes. The gesture made her look very tired. "I'm mad at stupid, goddamned Westcott. I thought maybe, just maybe, we'd make major progress today, even though it was just the first attempted operation. That we would be closer to going home. Instead, we didn't even get a chance to put any of the electronics inside at all. He cut the damn cat's aorta in half. This is going to take forever, even if he gets his skills back relatively quickly. I'm not going to get to see my son for...months..." She stopped, suddenly fighting the urge to cry.

"Uhh...I'm sorry," Monroe said.

"It's okay," Ava said, sniffing. "Not your fault. God, I'm sick of crying. I'm sick of being upset. I'm sick of Westcott, I'm sick of Coleman, I'm sick of cats, I'm sick of my life."

"Wow."

"Yeah, wow. So, that's why I'm drinking tonight. Because if I don't, I'm probably going to kill either myself or someone else."

"Okay. So you're still sick of Coleman, even though he saved you tonight?"

"I'm grateful for what he did. Doesn't mean I have to like the guy. All the talk of weaponry is a little much for me. He reminds me a little too much of some of the guys back home. And I keep catching him looking at my chest."

"Oh. Really?"

"I wouldn't mind, I guess, if he weren't such a freak. He's not bad-looking, you know."

"Um...I wouldn't know. But okay."

"I could use a man in my life," she said, refilling her cup. "It's been...geez, a long time. Let me think..." She fell silent for nearly a minute, appearing to calculate something in her head.

Monroe looked at his almost-full cup of wine. He took a sip and tried not to wince. It was like the cheap communion wine he was forced to drink as a kid, but white. It reminded him of Father Kramer, who smelled like that wine even when there was no wine around, and who had enormous amounts of ear hair. Monroe had always wondered how he could see all that hair in the mirror every morning and not feel the need to eradicate it.

"Oh my God," Ava suddenly said. "It's been over a year! Christ. I think I'm even more depressed now."

"Over a year for what? Oh...never mind. I think I know."

"God," Ava said. "If I get hit by a bus tomorrow, my last time would have been with Chuck. That's so horrible." She looked at Monroe. "You know what that jerk did?"

"Who? Chuck?"

"Yeah. Chuck. He dumped me. *He* dumped *me*. A man who never wore socks that matched. Who couldn't bother laundering his clothes. Who drank maple syrup straight from the bottle. Who read Green Lantern comic books and screamed at you if, God forbid, you pointed out to him that it is patently ridiculous for any kind of grown man to run around in decorative tights and still claim he's straight. Who cried when his Mommy was mad at him for not coming to dinner often enough. Whose name, for God's sake, is *Chuck*. *He* dumped *me!* And what's worse is that if I get hit by a meteor tomorrow, he's on my permanent record as the last guy I was with! Oh my God." She took another long drink of wine. She looked dazed.

"I don't think they're expecting meteors tomorrow," Monroe said.

"Well now, *that* is a shame, because I think I could *really* use one to hit me right...here," she said, tapping her index finger hard on her forehead. The thought of it made her giggle. "God, I can't believe I'm talking about this. I've said too much. You're going to think I'm loose."

Monroe took a sip of his wine. Still awful. But it was making him feel warm inside, which he liked. "I'd be thrilled if I could say it had only been a year," he said.

Ava's gaze shifted heavily to Monroe. "That stinks," she said. "How long has it been?"

"Um...a while. I've kinda lost track."

"You're kidding. Come on. How long?"

"I really don't know."

"Yes you do, liar. Everyone knows how long it's been since their last time. Tell me."

"Twelve years."

"Twelve *years*? Seriously?"

"Yeah."

"You must be wound tighter than a Swiss watch."

"I don't even really think about it," he said.

"You are such a *liar*," she said, smacking him on the shoulder with an open palm. "'Oh, I don't even really think about it,'" she said, imitating his voice. "Right. You're a man. Men are programmed from birth to think about it."

"I guess. Um, listen, I don't mean to be rude, but it's really late..."

"Who was she?"

"Who was who?"

"The girl. Twelve years ago. Was she pretty?"

"Um...yeah," Monroe said with a shrug.

"What was her name?"

Monroe thought of the first name that came to his head. "Patty Halladay," he said.

"Patty, huh?" Ava said with obvious distaste. "I have an aunt named Patty. She's bigger than most football players. What did she look like? Your Patty?"

Monroe took another sip of his wine. He was starting to get the slightest bit used to it. "Dark brown hair. Long. Pretty. Good figure." He shrugged again.

"How did you meet? Did you date for a long time?"

"Uh...we met in class. In college. English class. We were study partners. Eventually we started going out. Didn't last long. A few months."

"Then what happened?"

"She started dating a guy on the football team."

"She just started dating this guy? Did she even tell you?"

"Well...yeah. I mean, yeah. She broke up with me and...you know, started going out with him." He took another drink from his cup.

Ava eyed Monroe sideways for a few moments. "You're not much of a storyteller," she said.

"Sorry."

"I won't hold it against you," she said, taking another long drink from her wine. "Actually, no, I will hold it against you."

"You will?"

"Yes. I'm tired of men lying to me. I don't believe your story about Sally what's-her-slut."

"Patty."

"Whatever. You're lying. I can tell."

"You can?"

"Yes. You're a horrible liar. You shouldn't try it. Now come on, I was honest with you – way more honest than I should have been – so you be honest with me. And by the way, you are *not* allowed to tell any of the guys about what I said about Chuck. I'm not that kind of girl. I just…got too lonely for my own good. And in my defense, I thought at first that he had promise. Ugh. Anyway, I want the truth from you. I at least need to feel like I can trust *one* of the men on this trip."

"I don't know. I mean, I don't want to lie to you, but the truth…it's not something I want to discuss."

"Don't care," Ava replied, waving her half-empty cup. "Spill it."

"Ava…"

"Nope. Come on. I have told you a lot about me. Even admitted to things that I really shouldn't have. You have to even the score."

"If I tell you this, you can't tell anyone. I mean it. I'll tell everyone about Chuck. And I'll embellish the story. A lot."

She criss-crossed her chest with her index finger and made a very solemn face. "Tell me. Even though I think I know what you're about to say."

"What do you think I'm about to say?"

"That you're a virgin."

He groaned. "It's that obvious, huh?"

"When you try to cover it up with stories, yeah. But I doubt your grocer can tell." She looked at his face. "Ehh, maybe he can."

"Hey," Monroe said.

"I'm kidding," she said, squeezing his knee. Her touch sent a shiver through him. "Actually, I find it a little hard to believe. It's not like you have a humpback."

"Thanks. I guess."

"Come on. You're not a bad-looking guy. Nobody showed interest in you back in school?"

Monroe shrugged. "Nobody good," he said. "I only attracted the fat girls."

"That's so mean!" Ava said.

"Well, it's true. There was this one girl, Becky Osborne, who was just plain huge. She had this big crush on me and didn't make a secret of it. Everyone started calling me Jack Sprat when they found out about it."

"Was she nice, at least?"

"She was obnoxious. Kept following me around the halls. One day I got tired of it and told her to get lost."

"What happened?"

"She hit me in the head with her history book. After I stopped bleeding, the whole side of my head turned purple."

"Oh."

"That was mostly it. Girls never showed any interest in me otherwise. They went for the guys who smoked and rode motorcycles, or played football."

"Yeah. I went through my share of those."

"See? Nobody wants the skinny smart kid. Human wallpaper," he said, pointing to himself. He took another drink of the wine.

"You're too hard on yourself," Ava said. "I'm sure you'll find the right girl. Give it time. Don't be afraid of them, though. Nobody will go out with you if you don't ask."

"Easy for you to say. You don't have to do the asking."

"No, I just have to sit around and wait for someone to ask me. At least you have some control over it."

"Think I should buy a motorcycle?" Monroe asked.

"You?" Ava laughed. "Um, sorry. No."

"Don't laugh."

"I'm sorry," she said, forcing herself to stop. She looked at Monroe, tried saying something, then burst out laughing again.

"See, this is why I don't talk to people," Monroe said, getting up.

"Wait, wait, sit down," Ava said. "I'm sorry. I won't laugh any...oh God," she said, bursting into laughter again. "I'm sorry. It's really not that funny..." She started doubling over.

She was laughing so hard that, despite himself, Monroe started laughing with her. "You're drunk," he said.

"Yeah, I think I am," Ava said, wiping tears from her eyes. "I'm sorry. I don't mean to laugh. But thank you," she added, standing up. "I needed that. Seriously, though, please don't buy a motorcycle. Okay?"

"I'd have probably crashed it anyway," he said with a shrug.

"Thanks for letting me keep you up," she said. "I need to go to sleep now." She walked unsteadily toward the door. "Good night, Arthur."

"Good night."

She opened the door and left the room, leaving the door open behind her. "Motorcycle," he could hear her saying to herself as she walked back to her room. He watched her go, enjoyed the view of her butt as she laughed some more and used her key to get into her room.

~

Monroe heard her laughing some more to herself as she undressed in her room. Then she started singing a little, something that sounded vaguely like a Beatles song. He heard her click off her light. He waited a couple minutes more and was rewarded for his patience as he began to hear sounds of her moving slightly on her mattress. After a minute, her breathing became louder and heavier, and the mattress sounds increased, until she cried out softly, then again a few seconds later, and after that, her room was quiet until the sound of her steady breathing was all he could hear.

Five minutes later, Monroe was spent as well, and could finally sleep.

Chapter 17

"What on earth happened to you?" Westcott asked the next morning when he saw Coleman, who was, as usual, sitting in his chair in the lab. Also as usual, Westcott was the last to arrive for work.

The agent's forehead was almost entirely covered by an ugly, though colorful, bruise.

"Glory," Coleman replied. "Glory happened. Where's my gun?"

"How should I know?"

"Pipsqueak and Chubby say you have it."

"I'm not chubby!" Kendall shrieked.

Westcott looked at Monroe, who shrugged. "Sometimes lying feels like too much work."

"What a surprise," Westcott growled. He turned back to Coleman. "Your weapon is somewhere safe. You don't need it."

"Give it back or I find another gun and shoot you with it."

Westcott pointed to Kendall, who was busily shoving his third powdered-sugar donut of the morning into his mouth. "He's the one who knocked you out. Shoot him."

"Hey!" Kendall said, splurting powdered sugar onto his shirt.

"Considering it," Coleman said. "Where is it?"

"Forget it," Westcott said, trying to look brave but not entirely pulling it off. "You're not getting it."

"Yes I am."

"You can't touch me," Westcott said. "That's why you missed so badly yesterday and shot the cat instead of me. You need me to do this job. If I get hurt, you have to go back to Langley and explain that the job didn't get done because you blew your top and shot the doctor."

Coleman said nothing. He sipped his coffee without taking his eyes from Westcott.

"That's what I thought," Westcott said. "Now can we quit screwing around with all this nonsense and get to work?"

The sounds of coughing, then gagging, then loud vomiting, came from the bathroom.

"What's that?" Westcott asked.

"Ava's not feeling very good today," Monroe said. "Go easy on her today. She had a long night."

"I'll let you know when I start asking you for advice on how to treat my employees," Westcott said.

"I mean it," Monroe replied.

Coleman's eyebrows shot up. Kendall stopped chewing for nearly an entire second.

"Mind your place, son," Westcott said. "You just stick to your erector sets. I'll worry about my assistant." He looked around at Coleman and Kendall. "You're all nuts this morning." He walked into his office and closed the door.

A moment later, the toilet flushed and Ava came out of the bathroom, looking pale and sweaty. "Sorry about that, everyone," she said. "God, how embarrassing."

"Don't worry about it," Monroe said.

"Mom says the best cure for a hangover is more liquor," Kendall said, earning himself a dirty look from Ava.

"Sorry," Kendall said. "Mom's kind of a drunk."

Ava said nothing more and went into the operating room.

"Hey, Monroe," Coleman said, fishing into his pocket.

"Yeah?" Monroe replied.

Coleman pulled the van keys from his pocket and tossed them at the startled Monroe. "Hang on to those for me. From now on, you drive the van."

~

As it turned out, having the keys on him was handy for Monroe. Having largely completed the job of developing the electronics that would be implanted, Monroe and Kendall turned their attention to building out the electronics they would need to have in the van to covertly capture whatever their acoustic kitties recorded. It was a big job, one that would take them the better part of a month. Fortunately, the weather had started to improve, and working outside was a welcome change for the two of them.

By late morning, Monroe was ready for a break. He told Kendall he'd be right back and climbed the fire escape to the lab.

Coleman was nowhere to be found. Monroe absent-mindedly wondered how much it had hurt when Coleman had head-butted George into unconsciousness. Coleman hadn't seemed to feel it at all.

He thought, not for the first time, that there was no way he would ever make even a passable field agent.

The door to the medical area was open, and inside, Monroe could see that the door to Westcott's office was closed. Ava was in the operating room, trying to get Adams to sit still on the table.

"Need some help?" he asked.

"Thanks," Ava said weakly. "Could you help hold him down? I need to check his vitals, and I'm not really feeling up to wrestling with him right now."

"You okay?"

"I've thrown up six times since we got here."

"Oh."

"Believe it or not, I'm feeling slightly better than I did when I woke up. I am not ever drinking that much wine again. I forgot how bad wine hangovers are."

"You were having fun, at least. You looked like you were, anyway."

"You referring to the part where the fat guy almost brained me with the pool cue, or the part where I admitted too many sordid details about my past to you?"

"Both, I guess."

"Mmm."

"At least it took your mind off of your problems for a little while," Monroe offered.

"Yeah, I suppose it did. Unfortunately, then I woke up. Nauseous. And with a pounding headache. So my problems are still here, and now I've added new ones."

"I'll stop trying to cheer you up."

"It's okay. I'm sorry. Okay, hold him still for a minute."

"Sure."

They didn't talk while Ava listened to various parts of Adams' body with a stethoscope. To his pleasant surprise, Monroe noticed that he could look straight down her shirt while she was working. Her bra was powder blue and lacy.

When they were almost finished, Coleman barged his way in. He held a paper bag in one hand, the kind that liquor bottles are put into. He set it on the end of the table and looked at Ava with an expression of pride in a job well done.

The two of them stared at each other for a moment.

"Is that for me?" Ava asked.

"Affirmative."

"What is it?"

"Wine." He pulled it from the bag with a flourish. "It's even the kind you like – yellow."

"Um," Ava said, "that's very sweet. But I really don't feel good today, and it's because of wine, so it might help if you maybe put that someplace where I can't see it."

"I bought cups," Coleman said. "They're in the other room. Didn't want them to spoil the surprise."

"You want to open this now?"

"Sure. Kendall's drunken lush mom is right," he said. "Hair of the dog that bit you, and all that." He managed to force his mouth into a grin. It was like watching a game show host pass a kidney stone.

"Thanks," Ava said, "but I'll save it for later."

Coleman's smile wavered. "Fair enough, toots. You just let me know. I'll help you drink it." He winked at her and continued grinning in a manner Monroe found extremely creepy.

"You drink wine?" Ava asked.

"Negative. It's for pansies. But I'm happy to drink it with you, because you have outstanding breasts and are saucy."

"Hey," Monroe said.

"It's okay," Coleman said, holding a hand up at Monroe. "Saucy is a compliment. I know what you mean, though. I wasn't sure at first either."

"No," Monroe said, "that's not it. You shouldn't say the other thing."

"That she has outstanding breasts?"

"Yes."

"You disagree that her breasts are outstanding?" Coleman asked.

"Guys," Ava said with more than a little exasperation.

Monroe's mouth flapped open a few times before he could stammer anything. "Wha, uhh, that…isn't what I meant," he said. "I meant…"

"Then we're agreed." He turned back to Ava. "Your breasts are spectacular. Two out of two men agree."

"Okay, enough about that, please!" Ava said, crossing her arms over the breasts in question. "Thank you for the gift. We will not be drinking it together. I'll save it for another time. Maybe we all can share it. Maybe when we get a working prototype. How's that sound?"

"Terrible. That's eight testicles and only two breasts."

"Coleman!" Ava shouted.

"What? It's true. That's an unhealthy ratio."

"Okay, get out," Ava ordered. "Come back when we're ready to operate. I'm not talking to you any more."

Coleman looked insulted. He jutted a thumb at Monroe. "Does he have to leave, too?"

"He can stay."

"Your decision is questionable."

"He doesn't talk about my anatomy," Ava said.

"Why not?" Coleman asked Monroe. "You're not...you know...one of those?"

"Coleman, get out," Monroe said.

Coleman looked at the two of them for a moment, then started to leave. "This is why I need my gun," he said.

Ava rolled her eyes. "Great," she said, putting the bottle into a cabinet. "All I need is him chasing me around. This day just keeps on getting better."

"Are you going to share it with him?" Monroe asked.

"I like my idea better," she replied. "I'll share it with everyone when we get a prototype working."

"Good," Monroe said, mostly to himself.

Chapter 18

Yevgeny winced and groaned in pain as he sat on the park bench. The day was overcast, but the weather was warm as he and Boris settled in to eat their lunch.

Boris noticed the wincing. "I keep telling you that you should see the doctor, Yevgeny," he said.

"I do not need to see a doctor."

"You are moving like an old man today."

"I am an old man."

"But your condition, it is treatable. They have an ointment. I have used it myself."

"Please, Boris. I am about to eat my lunch. I do not want to hear about you applying ointment."

"It is very soothing. Before the ointment, I could barely tolerate sitting in my office. Afterwards, I wished I were at the stables at home so that I could ride a great stallion."

"Boris. Can we please discuss this later? I cannot enjoy my sandwich."

They fell silent for a moment.

"What kind of sandwich have you brought?" Boris asked.

"Peanut butter."

"Peanut butter?"

"Yes. Peanut butter. It is popular in America. I have heard good things."

"You have no meat?"

Yevgeny sighed. "No, Boris. There is no meat on this sandwich. I was hoping that by not having meat, you would not demand to eat half of it."

"I would never do such a thing," Boris said. "Why would you think that?"

Yevgeny said nothing. They fell silent again. Yevgeny took a bite of his sandwich and chewed.

"I would be curious to try it," Boris said.

"This is why I brought a second sandwich," Yevgeny said, handing his paper bag to Boris.

Chapter 19

A couple hours later, Westcott was ready to operate again. Monroe had spent the time between prepping Adams and the operation working on the van with Kendall.

Kendall had been beside himself the entire time, constantly distracting Monroe with incessant amounts of whimpering. When Monroe pointed out that he'd never seen Kendall so much as petting Adams a single time, Kendall stopped whimpering for a few minutes, then resumed.

Coleman had gone to a furniture store after buying the bottle of wine and had bought three bar stools for the operating room, so that he, Monroe and Kendall would have a better view of the "surgical action." Kendall had said that he wasn't sure he wanted to see surgical action. Coleman had called him a pantywaist.

As Westcott and Ava prepared for surgery, Monroe was a bit surprised to see Kendall perch himself on one of the barstools.

"I thought you didn't want to watch," Monroe said.

"I'm not a pantywaist," Kendall said quietly.

"Before I get started," Westcott said, glancing at Coleman, "is anyone in the room today armed?"

"No," said Kendall.

"No," said Monroe.

"Don't need a gun to shoot you," Coleman said, drawing looks from Monroe, Kendall, and Ava. "CIA," Coleman said, looking at them all as he pointed his thumb toward his chest.

Westcott rolled his eyes. "Okay, let's get started," he said.

A half hour later, having managed not to sever any important arteries, Westcott was ready to implant the remote-control array Kendall had designed. It was delicate work, and while Westcott often had to pause to consider his next move, he seemed to be making good progress. For the first time since they'd arrived, Monroe found himself encouraged. He even started to get accustomed to the sight of seeing a cat's innards splayed open in front of him.

He couldn't help but notice, though, that Westcott's hands shook. Not badly, but more than it seemed like they should. He wondered if

Westcott's hands had been shaking during Washington's operation. Westcott also seemed to be sweating profusely.

"Poor guy," Kendall said. "I can't believe that something I designed is getting shoved inside a cat. I feel like Hitler."

"Really?" Monroe asked.

"Maybe not Hitler," Kendall said. "Kitty Hitler, maybe."

"Kitty Hitler," Monroe said.

"Yeah," Kendall said. He realized Monroe was looking at him. "Not that there was one."

"Right."

They went back to watching the operation.

"Doctor," Ava suddenly said, "I think you just cut one of the wires."

Westcott paused and used his sleeve to wipe beads of sweat off of his brow. "I did not."

"You cut one of the wires?" Kendall said.

"No," Westcott said.

"Yes, you did," Ava said. "See? There."

"You need to stop," Kendall said, waving his hands. "Those wires could…"

Sparks suddenly jumped from inside the cat. "Ow! Shit!" Westcott said, yanking his hands back.

With a spectacular flare, Adams burst into flame.

"Oh!" Kendall shouted. "Oh! Bad!"

"Jesus Christ!" Westcott shouted.

Ava shrieked. Everyone was shouting and jumping out of the way. Westcott dropped his instruments and bolted from the room.

"Fire extinguisher!" Coleman screamed at Monroe, jabbing at him with his cane and gesturing toward the object in question, which was sitting on the floor in a corner. The order snapped Monroe out of his sense of panic. He ran to the extinguisher and picked it up. "How do you work this thing?" he screamed.

"Give it here!" Ava shouted, grabbing it from him. She used it to douse Adams in a matter of seconds. With the flames out, Adams began spewing smoke from his freshly charred incision.

"That was bad, right?" Coleman said.

A phone started ringing.

Monroe looked around. "Is that a phone?" he asked.

"Oh!" Coleman said, hopping off his stool. "Yes, the phone." He exited the room briskly.

"We have a phone here?" Kendall asked.

"Apparently." Monroe said.

"Where?"

"I don't know. Let's go look." He and Kendall followed Coleman.

"Don't worry," Ava said, "I'll just take care of the smoldering body here."

"Thanks!" Kendall replied with genuine cheer.

Kendall and Monroe found Coleman opening the fuse box, which sat on the wall above the chair where he sometimes sat and mostly slept. The phone was inside it, and Coleman picked up the receiver.

"Coleman speaking," he said. He stiffened a bit. "Affirmative. I'll hold."

"I didn't know there was a phone in there," Kendall said. "Did you?"

"I assumed it was the fuse box," Monroe said.

"Yeah. Me, too."

"Yes, sir," Coleman said into the phone. "Hello, sir."

"Makes me wonder what else is stashed around here," Kendall said.

"I bet there's at least one corn dog hidden somewhere," Monroe said.

"You think?" Kendall said, scanning the room enthusiastically.

"Yes, sir," Coleman continued. "We're making excellent progress. We had our second surgery today...It's proving challenging, but we're on course. Very glorious."

"He can't have corn dogs around here," Kendall said, deflating after having spotted no previously unnoticed corn dogs. "They'd rot. You'd smell them."

"I suppose," Monroe said.

"I'd advise against it, sir," Coleman said. "There's nothing to see just yet. Maybe once we get an initial working prototype... I'd estimate another few weeks, at least."

"I wish there were nudie magazines hidden," Kendall said. "I have a hard time pooping without nudies."

"It seems like a lot of your life revolves around poop," Monroe said.

"Intestinal health is important," Kendall replied.

"Yeah," Monroe said.

"Yes, I understand, sir," said Coleman, rubbing his brow. "We're working as fast as we can. Seven days a week. ...No sir, I don't think that's necessary."

"I can't keep nudies in my room," Kendall said. "The maid might find them."

"So what if she does?" Monroe asked. "She doesn't know who you are."

"Yes, sir," Coleman said. "We'll work as quickly as possible. I'll provide frequent updates."

"I know," Kendall said, "but Carmelita's nice. I see her in the office a lot when I hit the vending machine."

"Carmelita? You know her name?" Monroe asked.

"It's on her name tag," Kendall replied with a shrug.

"Yes, sir," Coleman said. "I understand." He hung up.

"You have a crush on the maid," Monroe said, teasing.

"I do not," Kendall said, but his tone was unconvincing.

"Carmelita's a fine woman," Coleman interrupted. "More adventurous in bed than one would expect from a native of Guatemala. You'd be wise to corral her."

Kendall gaped at Coleman. "You slept with her?" he asked.

"Only twice. Enough for me. Have at her, lad."

Kendall wore the expression of a man who just realized he was wearing another man's underwear. "Thanks," he said.

"Who was on the phone?" Monroe asked.

"Oh, that was Henderson," Coleman replied. "We have one month to get a prototype ready to show him or we're all fired. Anyone else hungry?"

"A month?" Monroe said. "That's crazy! Westcott hasn't even gotten to the point of stitching a cat back up yet."

"Fear not, lad," Coleman said. "The Central Intelligence Agency was built on unrealistic deadlines. There's glory in it, just like there's glory in having uninhibited, tendon-damaging sex with Guatemalan housekeepers. Which I still highly recommend you try," he said, pointing to Kendall.

"Thanks," Kendall said, too stunned to elaborate.

"Coleman," Monroe said, "there's no way we'll be ready to show a prototype in a month. You have to ask for more time."

"What are you talking about?" Ava said, coming out of the operating room. "Did I hear you say we need a prototype in one month?"

"Or we're all fired," Monroe said.

"Oh, there you all are," Westcott interrupted. He was climbing through the window from the fire escape. "I'm glad to see none of you were hurt. Wonderful day out there."

"I suppose you thought we kept the fire extinguisher back at the motel," Ava said.

"I was simply keeping the best interests of the project in mind," Westcott said. He raised his hands, which were still covered with bloody rubber surgical gloves, and wiggled his fingers. "Indispensable, you know."

"Well, Mr. Indispensable, you need to get a hell of a lot better in a hurry," Ava said. "We just found out that we have to produce a prototype in a month."

"Or we all get fired," Kendall said, still dazed but somehow coherent enough to grasp the concept of his impending professional doom.

"You mean you all get fired," Westcott said. He popped off the surgical gloves, looked around for a trash can, found none, and tossed the gloves on the floor. "I am not an employee of the CIA."

Coleman pulled a small piece of paper out of his pocket, unfolded it, and read. "*Washington Post*," he said. "Carl Bernstein, 202-546-1977. Up and comer, I hear. Bad with money. Hairy. Likely a hippie. Likely to despise animal testing. *The New York Times...*"

"Do you have to cart out that same threat all the time?" Westcott said.

"Oh God," Ava said. "I'm going to end up unemployed."

"You will not," Westcott said, waving his hand dismissively. "We can be done in a month. With a prototype, anyway. All we need is to be able to have something to prop up for Walter. It doesn't have to be perfect. We can do it."

"I thought you were friends with that guy," Ava said. "You're willing to basically lie to him?"

"Let's just say that I'm less concerned about maintaining my friendship with Walter than I once was. We'll convince him that we have a prototype."

"I wish I had your confidence," Ava said.

"Hey," Westcott said, "is that a phone? I thought that was a fuse box."

"Can't leave a fuse box unsecured like that," Coleman said. "Fuse box is over here," he added, knocking on a section of wall about three feet to the left of the phone.

"Behind the drywall?" Monroe asked.

"Exactly," Coleman replied.

"What if we blow a fuse?"

Coleman looked at the wall for a moment. "New rule," he said, turning back to the group. "No blowing fuses."

~

An hour later, Monroe and Kendall were in the van, driving Adams' corpse to the woodsy spot where they'd dumped Washington.

"We got closer today," Kendall said. "At least that's something."

"I suppose," Monroe said.

"I didn't think cats burned that quickly."

"Me neither."

"He really went up fast."

"Yeah."

"You think we're going to lose our jobs?"

"I think there's a decent chance of it, yeah."

They drove in silence for a moment.

"I don't know what I'll do if I get fired," Kendall said. "I've never been fired. I was employee of the month for twenty straight months when I worked at the IGA. They gave me a plaque. It was a little gold grocery cart. But not real gold. It turned green and gave me a rash whenever I touched it."

"Hey Jimmy," Monroe said, "did you see Westcott's hands during the operation today?"

"What about them?"

"They were shaking."

"They were?"

"Yeah."

"I didn't notice," Kendall said. "You know who always had shaky hands? My Uncle Weaver. Every time he tried to light a cigarette, he'd end up setting his mustache on fire. I kept telling him, why don't you shave your mustache? But every time I asked, he'd punch me in the kidney. Anyway, Uncle Weaver's hands shook because of all the Jim Beam he drank all the time. I once saw him pour it over pancakes. Stunk up the whole kitchen."

"Your stories are always so great."

"You think? I hated Uncle Weaver. But he's dead now, so it's okay."

They drove for a few more minutes in silence. "Here we go," Monroe said, pulling over. "This is the spot."

They got Adams – like Washington, he was wadded up into several sheets – out of the back. Unlike Washington's body, Adams' was stiff as a board. It smelled vaguely like overcooked chicken.

"You want to say something this time?" Kendall asked.

"No."

"Okay. I'll do it." He closed his eyes, then held out his palms like a priest saying a prayer during Mass. "Goodbye Adams. May the fish in Heaven be slow and plentiful, and may you not ever catch fire again. Amen."

They tossed him into the woods, where he landed a few feet away from Washington's lumpy sheets.

"Whew," Kendall said. "Already stinks back here."

~

That night, after eating at a restaurant called the Starving Aardvark, which Kendall had insisted on patronizing, and which had turned out to be as bad as one might expect from a restaurant named after an animal that eats insects when it is in fact starving, Monroe sat in his room and listened to his coworkers settle in for the night.

Coleman once again turned out to be frustratingly silent. No television, no phone conversations, nothing. Monroe wondered how he missed Coleman's romps with Carmelita. Maybe they hadn't happened in Coleman's room. Maybe they hadn't happened at all. You simply couldn't trust people to tell the truth. That's why it was helpful to listen to them.

A noise caught Monroe's attention. Coleman was making some kind of noise. He was...humming. It was hard at first for Monroe to figure out what song it was, even though it was vaguely familiar.

When Monroe finally identified the song, he rolled his eyes. Coleman was humming the national anthem. Monroe flipped over to Westcott's room.

The first voice he heard was that of the same mystery visitor he'd heard the night before. "Okay, you know, I'm tired of this shit," the man said. "You need to tell me what happened today. I don't like it when you're evasive."

"I am not being evasive," Westcott replied. "And I need another drink."

"Morton, if you—"

"Don't you Morton me, you queen."

"—if you don't tell me what happened right now, I'm going back to my motel and packing my bags. I mean it this time."

"I mean it this time," Westcott repeated in a mocking tone. He was slurring his words slightly.

"Fine. Fuck you then. I'm leaving."

"Sit down, God damn it," Westcott moaned. "You're making a federal case out of nothing. Can't I ever choose to not talk about work?"

"Listen to you," the other man said. "You're shitfaced."

"I am not. And besides, you like it when I'm shitfaced."

"I like it when you've had a few drinks. When you're shitfaced you can't even get it up."

"Fuck you."

"Not likely. So what happened today?"

"Jesus, Thomas, you are one relentless bitch."

"I can't help it if I always get what I want," Thomas replied. "So spill it."

Westcott sighed. "It's nothing. The cat I was operating on caught...a little bit...on...well, on fire."

Thomas gasped. "On fire? On fire?! What do you mean, on fire?"

"It caught on fire. You are familiar with the concept of fire?"

"Don't get snippy with me. Oh my God, that poor kitty. Is it okay?"

"I don't want to get into this."

"Morton Westcott, you tell me this instant. How is the kitty? You know I'll find out sooner or later."

After a long pause, Westcott said, "It's dead."

Thomas made sort of a choking sob kind of noise.

"Jesus, here we go," Westcott grumbled.

The noise from Thomas escalated to a low moan, then a high squeal.

"There is no need to get all blubbery," Westcott said.

"Blubbery?" Thomas blubbered. "Blubbery? An innocent animal is butchered and set on fire and you are so cold-hearted about it that you can call me blubbery?"

"It wasn't my fault, dammit. The electronics, they were faulty. As soon as I put them in, they shorted out and ignited the oxygen from the breathing mask. The whole damn cat just went up."

Thomas gasped again, wetly this time.

"I said it wasn't my fault. It was those damn incompetent electronics morons from the CIA. They're hopeless. I can't help it if I'm stuck working with idiots."

"But..." Thomas said between racking sobs, "...you performed the operation. You know I don't like it when you kill kitties." Thomas' voice went up with each word, eventually turning his voice into a squeaky sound not unlike the sort a mouse makes when it is being crushed.

"A cat catches on fire right in front of me, practically explodes, and all you're worried about is the fucking cat," Westcott said. "Don't be worried about me, asshole."

"You shut up! You know I don't like this part of your work."

"It's just a fucking *cat!*"

Thomas gasped. "A cat? *Just* a cat? I suppose next you're going to say that Judy Garland is *just* an actress!"

"You're insane."

"Oh, I am, am I? Fine. You know what? You can just suck your own cock tonight, because I'm out of here!"

"Jesus fucking Christ, calm down, will you?"

The door opened. "Fuck off, you old drunk!" Thomas said as he slammed the door loudly enough to make Monroe's ears sting.

Monroe slid the headphones off. He pushed his curtains aside so that he could see the parking lot. After a moment, a man with short salt-and-pepper hair and a goatee emerged from the breezeway that led to the rooms in the back of the building. As the man got into his car, Monroe could see that he had tears streaming down his face. He sat in the car for a moment, lit a cigarette, then pulled away.

Monroe slid the headphones back on and was greeted by the sound of Westcott loudly vomiting in the bathroom. He pulled them off again.

Monroe thought for a moment. Kendall's story about his Uncle Weaver was stuck in Monroe's mind. Maybe it wasn't Westcott's surgical skills that were the problem. Maybe it was that the man was tossing back a fifth of scotch every night.

He was jarred from his train of thought by the sound of a phone ringing. It took him a moment to realize that the sound was coming through his headphones. He slipped them back on.

The phone rang several more times before Westcott picked up. "Hello," he said slowly, sounding very much like a man who had just vomited a mixture of scotch and stomach acid. "Oh, it's you. Yeah, yeah, hi, hon. ...Huh? You bought what? ...What do you mean? An actual monkey? ...No, I don't want it in my house. Christ almighty, Ethel. I don't care if Margie got one. Margie's nuts. She's fat, she has a moustache, and she's nuts. And she probably can afford to pay someone to clean up after it. ...No, I have not been 'drinking *again*.' I have had *a* drink or two, so what? Don't talk to me like that. ...No, it's not like having a baby around the house. It's like having a monkey around the house. Just because it wears a diaper and shits itself, that doesn't make it a baby. It goes back tomorrow. ...Yes, it does. ...No. No! Dammit,

Ethel, I will not allow a monkey to live in my house. I do not want to come back to a house full of monkey diapers! ...No. I'm hanging up now. ...Yes, I am. And when I talk to you next time, I expect there *not* to be monkey noises coming from your end. Good night!"

Monroe yanked off his headphones before Westcott slammed down the phone. He turned off the listening station. After a moment, he dialed Kendall's room.

"Hello?" Kendall sounded entirely bewildered that somebody would actually be calling his room.

"Kendall, it's me, Monroe."

"Oh. Hi, Artie. Whatcha doin? Do you hear more sex?"

"No. Listen, I have a favor to ask of you."

"Okay."

"Will you see Carmelita tomorrow morning?"

"Probably. She's usually there when I get donuts out of the vending machine in the office. Why?"

"I need you to ask her something about Westcott. Ask her if she finds empty liquor bottles in his room when she cleans it."

Kendall hesitated before speaking. "I don't know, Artie. You're asking me to have her spy on Westcott, kinda. I'm not sure that's ethical."

"Jimmy, she's a housekeeper, not a lawyer. She doesn't have codes of ethics. Give her ten bucks or something."

"Ten bucks! Are you kidding? You give her ten bucks!"

"I would, but she doesn't know me. She might tell you. I'll even give you the ten bucks."

"I don't know. Why do you want to have her snooping in Westcott's room, anyway?"

"I think you might have been onto something when you mentioned your uncle today. I'm worried that Westcott's hands are shaky because he's drinking every night."

"He is? How do you know?"

"I'm pretty sure I smelled liquor on his breath this morning. Oh, and have you noticed that he never comes out with us to dinner or anything else?"

"I thought that was because he knows we hate him."

"Well, yeah, that's part of it, but he's never asked to go out with us even once. I think he's been staying in his room and getting tanked every night." Among other things, he thought to himself.

"If he's drinking like that," Kendall said, "he's not going to be very good at the cat surgery, huh?"

"Exactly. But I can't confront him about it unless I'm sure. I need you to ask Carmelita."

Kendall sighed. "Okay. You know talking to women makes me sweaty."

"You'll be fine. Think of it as an excuse to talk to her."

"Okay. Think I can just give her five dollars, though? Then I can keep the other five. My donut expenses are starting to rack up."

"Sure. See ya."

"Bye."

Monroe hung up and laid on his bed. If he was right, they had a problem. And it wouldn't be easy to get Westcott to give up the booze.

He flipped on his listening station and toggled to Ava's room. He heard the shower running. That was pretty much all he needed.

Five minutes later, he was fast asleep.

Chapter 20

Monroe waited until they got to the lab the next morning before asking Kendall about his assignment. Kendall had been acting a bit out of sorts on the walk over, which made Monroe concerned that the conversation with Carmelita hadn't gone as well as hoped.

Ava and Westcott started prepping the O.R., and Ava asked Monroe to pick out a Jefferson. Coleman hobbled to his usual spot on his chair and stared intently at a rock that he'd brought with him and placed on his right knee. He fell asleep, as usual, a few minutes later, but Monroe knew better than to think he could speak freely around a sleeping Coleman.

He went to Kendall's workstation. "So," he said in a low voice. "How'd it go with Carmelita this morning?"

Kendall peered around Monroe at Coleman. "It was...weird," he finally said.

"How so?"

"She...um...she gave me...you know," he said, pointing toward his belt.

"She gave you what? Jimmy..."

"She gave me...she did..." Kendall said as he pointed more insistently.

Monroe shook his head in exasperation.

Kendall looked around, then leaned toward Monroe and whispered, "She did oral sex on me."

"*What?*" Monroe said aloud. He covered his mouth, realizing his mistake, but Coleman only snorted a bit and continued sleeping. He turned back to Kendall. "Jimmy...what the hell?" he said, more quietly.

"I didn't mean it, I swear," Kendall said.

"Jimmy, I sent you to ask about bottles in Westcott's room. How does that convert into...you know, *that?*"

"It wasn't my fault. I...I think she misunderstood me."

"Go on," Monroe said.

"I went to go buy my donuts out of the vending machine, right? And at first, I was worried, because Carmelita wasn't around. But then she came in, and she smiled and waved at me a little, and you know, she's Guatemalan and all, but she's pretty. You know?"

"I haven't noticed."

"Well, she is. So, well, I went ahead and started talking to her. I said hi, and she said hi back, except she didn't say hi, she said hola, and then I said that I need to ask her a favor. And she nodded. And I asked her about Westcott's room, and she nodded. And I asked if she's ever cleaned bottles out of his room, and she kinda looked confused, and she frowned a little. And so I thought she didn't want to tell me, so I reached into my pocket and I realized that all I had was a pair of tens, and that I forgot to come get a five from you beforehand. So I figured I didn't have a choice, so I gave her one of the tens and asked if it helped. And she looked at it kinda funny, and then she looked at me and said, 'more.' And I thought, geez, Carmelita's not as sweet as I thought, and that she was extorting me for twenty whole dollars."

"Okay," Monroe said. "So what did she say?"

"Well, she didn't really say anything. She looked around the office, and nobody else was there, so she grabbed my hand and took me out of the office, and took me to this room near the back of the motel where they keep the mops and sheets and cleaning stuff. And...uhh..." Kendall seemed on the verge of tears.

"And?"

"And, she started undoing my pants, and I swear, I didn't know what to do, I was *completely* confused, and she...you know...did the thing."

"Oh my God," Monroe said. "She's a hooker?"

"Uh huh," Kendall said, burying his face in his hands. "My mother would kill me if she knew. A *hooker*! A housekeeper hooker! I'm so mortified. What if I get the crabs?"

"She doesn't speak English, does she?"

"Not a word. Other than things like 'yes' and 'no' and 'more.' Oh, and 'your manhood is magnanimous.' But I'm not really sure what she meant by that."

"Why didn't you stop her?"

Kendall shrugged. "She's good."

Monroe considered this for a moment. "Yeah, okay," he said. "But did you get to even ask her about the bottles?"

"No. But when she was...you know, busy, I saw this on the wall and took it." Kendall reached into the front pocket of his slacks and fished out a key.

Monroe recognized it. It was a master key, just like the one he'd pilfered before he planted the bugs in everyone's rooms.

It occurred to Monroe that he really needed to plant a bug in the housekeeping supply room.

"I think it's a master key," Kendall said, putting it back into his slacks.

Monroe patted him on the shoulder and grinned broadly at the stroke of luck. "Nice job, soldier," he said. "Done like a true employee of the CIA."

"Huh, yeah, I guess you're right. Wonder if that's what it's like to be a field agent."

"I somehow doubt it."

"Yeah."

"At least now we know how Coleman got her," Monroe said. And why none of the action had taken place in Coleman's room.

"I feel so dirty," Kendall moaned.

"Okay, we need to make up an excuse to get out of here. Then we can go back to Westcott's room and get any bottles we see in there. We need to go before Carmelita cleans his room."

"Will I be able to go to church any more? I don't want to get struck down."

"Come on. We should get going."

"I'm defiled."

Monroe looked at Kendall for a moment. "On second thought, I'll go by myself. Give me the key."

"Oh God, and she was with Coleman before she was with me," Kendall said, absent-mindedly handing the key to Monroe.

Monroe pocketed the key. "If anyone notices I'm gone, just tell them I forgot something in my room, and that I'll be right back."

"I hope I don't have any Coleman on me," Kendall moaned, looking mournfully at his groin.

Monroe rolled his eyes and left Kendall alone with his thoughts. He was halfway out the window when he felt a tap on his shoulder. He turned around, expecting to see Kendall.

But it wasn't Kendall who had tapped his shoulder. It was Coleman. The sight of him made Monroe jump.

"Jesus," Monroe said, catching his breath. "Don't sneak up on people like that."

Coleman's eyebrows shot up. "I'm supposed to sneak up on people. CIA," he said, jabbing his thumb into his chest.

"Right. So, um, did you need something?"

"Where you going?"

Monroe glanced at Kendall, who was continuing to stare blankly into space. "I forgot something in my room," Monroe said. "I'll be right back."

"Negative. Request denied."

"Coleman, I wasn't asking you. I just need to run across the street. I'll be right back."

"Son, you are one terrible liar."

Monroe blinked several times, much like a bad liar would when caught telling a bad lie. "I'm not lying," he attempted.

"As I said, you're a terrible liar."

Monroe hesitated, tried to think of something else to say, but gave up. "So I'm told," he said, defeated.

"Skullduggery," Coleman said, tapping his nose.

"Huh?"

"A skilled agent of the Central Intelligence Agency can smell skullduggery from a mile away. You and Chubby are up to skullduggery."

"Hey! I heard that!" Kendall said.

"Let's go, pipsqueak," Coleman said. "I'm coming with you."

~

"So spill it," Coleman said once they were in the alley.

"Can I trust you?" Monroe asked.

"I'm an employee of the Central Intelligence Agency."

"That's not really an answer."

"It's not meant to be," Coleman replied. "The CIA is allowed to know everything. Trust, or a lack of trust, is irrelevant. Either you tell me what you're after or you don't get it." He looked at Monroe and tapped his own temple. "Smarter than you," he said.

Monroe weighed his options for a moment as they walked. He decided to talk. "I think Westcott's hitting the booze hard at night," he said. "I noticed yesterday that his hands were shaking during the operation. He's not going to be able to get this job done if he has shaky hands all the time."

"I saw the shaky hands, too. He's old. Maybe he has a condition. Might be crazy."

"He's not that old. And if he had a condition, Ava would have said something about it by now. He's drinking and it's affecting him. At least, that's what I think."

They finished crossing the street and had reached the motel's parking lot. "And what does all this have to do with needing to go back to the hotel?" Coleman asked.

Monroe dug into his pocket. "I came into possession of one of these," he said sheepishly, holding up the master key.

Coleman's eyes widened like a small boy seeing a stripper for the first time. "A break-in!" he exclaimed, eyeing the key.

"No no, not a break-in," Monroe said, trying not to sound panicky. "A...a peek."

"Seeking evidence," Coleman said. He took the key and stared at it. He almost seemed to be talking to himself. "On the trail. On the hunt. Thrill of the chase, pipsqueak, thrill of the chase. I'm in."

"Does that make what we're about to do any less illegal?"

"Not at all. No warrant. Entirely illegal. Something about civil rights. Not important. We're going in."

"Great."

Coleman took a quick look at Monroe. "I didn't know you had it in you, pipsqueak," he said.

"Yeah, well...desperate times, I guess."

"There's glory in desperate times," Coleman said. He was practically aroused with anticipation. "I'll try hard not to destroy anything, but I can't make any promises."

"We have a key. There shouldn't be a need to break anything. I'm just hoping to find a couple empty bottles."

"I wish I had my gun," Coleman said. "Remind me to grab it when I get back to the lab. I need to shoot Westcott and I keep forgetting to." He slapped Monroe on the shoulder. "Come on, lad, the game is afoot."

~

There was nobody around when Coleman and Monroe got to Westcott's room. "Act casual," Coleman said, "and give me the key."

Monroe rolled his eyes and handed Coleman the key. Coleman opened the door and ducked inside with Monroe close behind. Coleman peeked through the window shades to make sure they hadn't been seen.

Monroe walked to one of the nightstands and turned on a lamp.

Coleman dove headlong across the room, swatting the lamp off the nightstand and sending it crashing into a wall. The bulb popped, sending sparks flying as the lamp shattered.

"What the hell did you do that for?" Monroe shouted.

"Shhhhh!" Coleman said. He was laying flat on the floor and cocking an ear. "No lights on during a break-in!" he whispered. Didn't you learn that during your training?"

"My training mostly consisted of someone showing me where the bathrooms were," Monroe shot back.

"Agency's going straight to shit these days," Coleman said, rolling onto his back.

"So you don't want the lights on, but you're okay with smashing a lamp loud enough to be heard from the parking lot?" Monroe asked.

"Son, never question an agent during a mission," Coleman said, gathering his cane and getting back to his feet. "Okay, so what do we got?"

"I think we're in luck. The maid hasn't cleaned his room yet."

"Toss the room!" Coleman shouted.

"Coleman," Monroe said. "I don't think we need to." He picked up two bottles of Glenlivet from the dresser. One was empty, and the other was nearly empty.

"Damn."

"What's wrong?"

"I wanted to toss the room."

"Sorry."

Coleman yanked one of the drawers out of the dresser. He turned it over and spilled its contents, mostly socks and boxers, across the room.

"Feel better?" Monroe asked. "Can we go now?"

"I suppose. Are you sure you don't need to find anything else?"

"Whoa," said Monroe, looking at the dresser. "Maybe I do, yeah."

"Yeah? I'll go tear apart the bathroom."

"No no, look over here," Monroe said. He pointed to the open space in the dresser where the underwear drawer had been. The drawer beneath it, now visible, contained three full bottles of Glenlivet.

"We should pour those down the sink before we go back," Coleman said. "Then shatter the bottles in the bathtub."

"Yes to the pouring, no to the shattering."

"You leave a lot to be desired as a partner," Coleman said, yanking the drawer open and grabbing the bottles.

~

"I'll lead the interrogation when we return," Coleman said once they were walking back to the lab.

"I don't know. That might get a little too confrontational."

"Confrontation is a good thing, son. Helps get people shot."

"What is it with you and shooting people?"

"People need shooting. Not all, but many. You're not one of these hippie 'guns kill people' people, are you? I shoot hippies."

"It just seems like a lot of overkill when you're dealing with a doctor, an assistant, and two electronics engineers."

"I don't believe in overkill."

"Maybe I should be the one to talk to Westcott."

"Negative. Lead negotiator: CIA," he said, thumbing himself in the chest.

"At least don't make a huge deal out of it, okay? I don't think he'll respond well if he thinks he's being publicly humiliated."

"Son," Coleman said, "you have a lot to learn about negotiating."

"Great."

~

They found Westcott in his office, where he appeared to be consulting a text of some kind. Coleman didn't knock on his door before opening it.

Westcott immediately saw the bottles they were carrying. "What's going on?" he asked.

"Found all these in your room, drunkard," Coleman said, setting three bottles on Westcott's desk one at a time with enough force to create a loud *clunk* with each one.

"You broke into my room?" Westcott said. His face darkened. "What do you think gives you the right to break into my room?"

"No breaking in involved, lush," Coleman said, putting his free hand on Westcott's desk and leaning forward over it. "We had a key."

"A key? How did you get a key?"

"Central Intelligence Agency," Coleman said, straightening and pointing to himself.

"You had no right to go in there! You didn't have a warrant, you had no reason to go into my room! This is insanity! I could have you arrested!"

"Did you not hear the 'Central Intelligence Agency' part?" Coleman said.

"What is your point, Coleman? You lunatic! So you found some scotch in my room. You wanted to steal my scotch?"

"No. Just pour it down the sink."

Westcott's mouth moved, but it took a few seconds for words to start coming out of it. "You...you...you poured out my *scotch*?"

"I knew that was a good idea," Coleman said to Monroe.

"You poured out *Glenlivet*? Do you have any idea how much Glenlivet *costs*? Probably more than you make in a month, you overblown civil servant!" Westcott's entire head was turning a deep shade of red.

"What's going on in here?" Ava said, standing in the doorway. She saw the bottles in Monroe's arms. "What's with the bottles?"

"They stole my scotch from my motel room!" Westcott cried, pointing at Coleman. "These people are insane! And what, you were in on it, too, Monroe?"

"Uh..." Monroe stammered. He glanced at Ava, who was looking at him as if she were just as interested in his answer as Westcott was. "Kinda."

"Don't be shy, lad," Coleman said. "Capture glory where the glory is due. This entire mission was his conception. Kudos!"

"This was *your* idea?" Westcott bellowed at Monroe.

"Arthur, what is going on?" Ava asked.

"His hands were shaking yesterday," Monroe blurted.

Ava shot a look at Westcott.

"My hands were not shaking!" Westcott yelled.

"Yes they were," Ava said quietly. "During both operations."

"Ah ha!" Coleman yelled.

"So I had a little case of nerves," Westcott protested. "I'm not allowed to be human?"

"I'd believe you if we hadn't found all these bottles," Monroe said. "Your hands are shaking because you're hung over. I wouldn't care – none of us would care – if we didn't need you to be able to get this job done. I don't want to lose my job, Doctor."

"Hey," Kendall cried from the hallway, where his head was bobbing as he tried to see over Ava, "what's going on in there? Nobody told me we were having a meeting."

"You people are insane!" Westcott shouted. "Just because a man enjoys a drink or two at night to help him relax, it doesn't mean he's a drunk! I can handle my liquor, and it has nothing to do with my skills as a surgeon! You're all going to lose your jobs now anyway, even if this project succeeds! I'll have you all arrested! Better yet, I'll sue every one of you until you're penniless! Get out of my office with this ridiculous *nonsense!*"

"Okay then," Ava said, "prove to us that it's nonsense. Stay off the scotch for a week. If you're telling the truth, then all you've lost is a week of drinks. And you can have all our heads on a plate."

"I can't see!" Kendall said.

"You, of all people, will not dictate terms to me, do you understand?" Westcott screamed at Ava. "You work for me, and if I hear one more word out of you about this preposterous nonsense, I'll fire you on the spot! Get out of my office!"

Ava looked furious, but she remained silent for a moment as she stared hard at Westcott. It was the kind of look people have on their faces before they rip other people's arms off and wield them like big, messy nightsticks.

"Guys?" Monroe said, breaking the silence. "Maybe you could give me a moment to talk to the doc."

"Arthur, this is my fight," Ava said.

"I know," Monroe replied. "But I need to have a word with the doctor."

"I'm not talking to you either, pencil-neck," Westcott growled.

"With all due respect, Dr. Westcott," Monroe replied. "I think you will want to hear what I have to say."

Something about the way he said it stopped Westcott from replying. He stared back at Monroe, suddenly suspicious.

"Look at the stones on this one, huh?" Coleman bellowed, slapping Monroe on the shoulder. "I wasn't going to let you negotiate, but I'm starting to think this could be fun. If you find my gun in here, I'm fine with you shooting him."

"Arthur?" Ava said.

"What's going on?" Kendall said from the hall. "Somebody let me in!"

"Come on, Chubby," Coleman said as he tried to herd Ava out of the office, "let's go frighten the cats."

"You're mean," Kendall said.

Ava hesitated, looking at Monroe, then allowed Coleman to move her into the hall before he shut the door. "If he pins you, shout the word 'Albuquerque,' and I'll send in reinforcements!" Coleman shouted through the door.

Monroe sat in one of the chairs on the opposite side of the desk from Westcott, whose face was still deep red as he eyed Monroe warily, like a boxer who realizes that the rules of the fight have just changed, but has no idea what the new rules are.

"Have a seat, doc," Monroe said. "You and I need to talk."

Westcott said nothing, but he slowly sat down.

"I know about Thomas," Monroe said.

Westcott blinked. "Thomas who?" he asked.

"The Thomas who keeps visiting your room at night. The one who is staying at a nearby motel, but who comes over every night while the rest of us are out. I kept wondering why you insisted on having a room in the back of the motel. It was so nobody would notice Thomas coming and going."

"Thomas is a business associate. We often meet at night because I'm so busy with the project during the day."

"Then why did you pretend not to know who he was a moment ago?"

"I didn't realize that he was who you meant."

"So if I called Ethel and asked her about Thomas, she'd back up your story?"

"Of course. Mr. Monroe, I think you had better leave. I don't like what you're insinuating. And trust me, you are barking up a very dangerous tree here."

"What's her number?"

"Whose number?"

"Your wife's. I could go call her from the fuse box phone. Just to back up your story."

"I'm not giving you her number."

"No problem. I'll get it from Coleman. I'm sure he has it on file somewhere." Monroe stood up and reached for the door.

"Wait," Westcott said. "Sit down."

Monroe turned and looked at Westcott. He sat back down. "You're going to go cold turkey."

Westcott glared at Monroe. "I still think this is ridiculous. I do not have a drinking problem."

"Then giving up the booze for a couple months won't kill you."

"A couple months? I thought we were just talking about a couple weeks."

"I want you off the booze until the project is done. And if you try sneaking in a drink here or there, I'll know about it and our deal is off."

Westcott rubbed his eyes. He sat like that, with his hands over his eyes, for what felt like a very long time. "I suppose we have a deal," he said at last.

Monroe took a deep breath. "There's more," he said.

Westcott looked up from his hands. "Oh no. I go cold turkey, you keep quiet. That's the deal."

"I'll call Ethel. For that matter, I'll tell Henderson, too."

"You wouldn't."

"I would."

Westcott leaned back in his chair. "What is it that you want?"

"I want Coleman's gun."

"Why? You're not going to give it back to him, are you?"

"No. I'm not sure what I'm going to do with it. I won't let him shoot you, if that's what you're worried about."

Westcott glared at Monroe for a moment, then reached into his pocket for a set of keys. He unlocked a small filing cabinet next to his desk, reached inside, and pulled out Coleman's revolver. He set it on the desk between them.

"Is it loaded?" Monroe asked.

"No. I threw the bullets away."

"Okay. Good." He took the gun and put it into his back pocket.

"Anything else?" Westcott asked.

"Actually, yeah. I want you to double Ava's salary. And pay for all of her son's medical expenses."

"You must be joking. Do you know how much that will cost me?"

"Do you want everyone to know your secret?"

Westcott sighed again. "Okay. Agreed. But don't get greedy."

"Don't worry. That's all I'm going to ask for. Oh, except I want you to be nice to Ava from now on. No yelling at her, or treating her like dirt. Deal?"

"I have your word that what you have learned is strictly and permanently between us?"

"Yes. And for all I care, you can continue his visits if you want. I won't tell him either. He won't know I exist, for that matter. So we have a deal?"

Westcott hesitated, then extended his hand. "Deal."

Monroe shook Westcott's hand, then stood up again and reached for the door.

"Mr. Monroe."

Monroe stopped. "Yes?"

"I just wanted to say that I underestimated you. I'm actually a tiny bit impressed. This is the kind of thing I might have done to a business rival in my younger days."

"Thanks. I guess."

"Before you let it go to your head," Westcott continued, "you need to keep something in mind. You now have changed the rules for yourself. Nobody here is going to underestimate you any more. And though I will cooperate with your terms, and in some ways am even grateful for them, make no mistake about it, where you used to only have friends on this project, now you have an enemy."

"I know."

"One more thing, before you leave."

"Yes?"

"How did you find out?"

Monroe shrugged as he opened the door. "Central Intelligence Agency," he said.

~

Ava waited in the lab with Kendall and Coleman, who passed the time by arguing about whether or not Kendall was in fact chubby. She could hear Monroe and Westcott talking but couldn't make out what they were saying. Monroe seemed to be doing most of the talking. That was all she knew. She was surprised that their voices never raised above a conversational tone, especially after all the screaming that had happened when they were all in there.

When the door opened and Monroe walked casually into the lab, Ava jumped up. Coleman and Kendall cut short their conversation.

"Well?" Ava asked.

"He's agreed to go cold turkey for as long as we're working on the project," Monroe said. "After that, he's free to down as much scotch as he can get his hands on."

Ava, Kendall and Coleman stared at him.

"Um," Monroe said, "...and that's pretty much it. I told him I'd tell you guys. He's feeling a little, well, I think he wanted to not have to discuss it any more."

"How do we know he won't go back on his word?" Ava asked.

"He won't," Monroe said.

"What on earth did you say to him?" Ava asked.

"Uh…we just talked. You know, man to man."

"Man to man!" Coleman barked. "No better conversation than that. Unless it's woman to woman. And the women are Danish."

"That's it? You talked man to man?" Ava asked.

Monroe shrugged. "I promised to keep it between us. But trust me, he's on the wagon. And I expect he'll be a bit more civil from here on in."

"He will?" Ava replied. "Arthur, what did you say to him?"

"Really, I can't say. But everything's fine. Really."

"Darlin'," Coleman said, placing an arm around Ava, "they reached a gentlemen's agreement. You're just going to have to respect that. It's the law of the West."

She shrugged Coleman's arm off of her. "I don't understand you men."

"I don't think you're supposed to," Monroe said. "Anyone else hungry?"

"Me," Kendall and Coleman said simultaneously.

Chapter 21

"Yevgeny," Boris said, "I am troubled."

"What is it now?" Yevgeny said as he unwrapped his meatball sandwich.

"I viewed an American motion picture last night."

Yevgeny took a large bite of his sandwich. He had learned that if he ate quickly, he lost less of his lunch to Boris. "And?" he said around his mouthful of meatball meat.

"And these Americans, they are a disturbing people."

"This is something you have just discovered?"

"In this movie, a young man is courting a young woman. And the woman's mother makes…advances…toward the young man. In Russia, this would not happen."

"Boris, there are strange people in every country. Including Russia. We are home to twice as many people as America. I am certain that at least one of them has had an inappropriate conversation with their daughter's lover."

Boris sat with his unwrapped pastrami-on-rye sandwich on his lap. "I do not doubt that every nation has its share of deviants," he said. "But this is not what troubles me."

"What, then?" Yevgeny asked, taking another bite that caused over half of his remaining sandwich to disappear into his mouth.

"The mother, she had beautiful legs. And lovely hair. She was very pretty. Prettier than the daughter."

"And this disturbed you?"

"In Russia, no mother looks like that. In Russia, mothers look like old men. They have hairy chins and breasts that hang below their waists. They are hunched over and foul-smelling."

Yevgeny stopped chewing for a moment. "This is true," he said. "My mother, my God bless her spirit, looked not unlike Premier Khrushchev near the end. She had arms like a bear."

"Exactly!" Boris said, jabbing his index finger in the air. "Here in America, the mothers look like daughters. How is this possible? What are we doing wrong?"

Yevgeny was feeling full, but still managed to wedge the remainder of his sandwich into one bulging cheek. "I do not know. You should commission a study."

"Perhaps I should."

"So the young man in this corrupt American movie about mother whores – how did he respond?"

"He ran away."

Yevgeny rolled his eyes. "Americans. Such idiots."

Chapter 22

As much as they hated losing the time, the team had agreed to Westcott's request to give him a few days to adjust to his "new lifestyle" before attempting a surgery on Jefferson.

The change in Westcott was astounding. Ava could hardly believe how much, and how quickly, Westcott seemed to change. In the years she had been working for him, she had never seen him behave like he was. While he didn't exactly become cooperative, he stopped being belligerent. He became much more quiet in general than he had been, and no longer protested every idea that wasn't his. He seemed to relinquish control over the project without reservation.

Ava kept asking Monroe how he had done it, but he held fast, refusing to let even a single detail slip. After a while, Coleman and Kendall started asking as well, but he had resisted their inquiries, too. Kendall in particular seemed hurt that Monroe wouldn't divulge his secrets.

Westcott was being true to his word about giving up the scotch. Monroe spent a great deal of time listening to him at night, and he heard none of the telltale glass-clinking sounds. Unfortunately, Westcott seemed to be saving his nasty disposition for times when he was away from the project; on two of his first three nights sober, Thomas stormed out after lengthy arguments.

On the third night after the confrontation with Westcott, Monroe heard a knock on his door. He quickly scrambled to hide his listening equipment – Carmelita was very vocally providing her services to a man who apparently could not stop himself from repeating the phrase "heavens to Betsy" the entire time – and looked through the peephole. It was Ava.

"Hey there," he said to her as he opened the door.

"Hi," she said, holding up another bottle of wine in one hand and a pair of plastic cups in the other. "Care to split another one with me? I promise not to chug this time."

"Sure. Come on in."

She sat in the chair and poured them each a cup, filling them slightly less than halfway. "Sorry about the plastic," she said.

"Why?"

She looked at him. "You're supposed to drink wine in a glass. Tastes better."

"Oh." He took the cup she offered him.

"Not much of a wine aficionado, huh?"

"No. I'm not really much of a drinker, period."

"Thanks for humoring me, then."

"No problem."

"I hope you don't mind, my barging in here like this," she said. "I was bored in my room, and…oh, and I sometimes just need company after talking to Robby."

Monroe had heard her conversation with Robby. It hadn't seemed to go badly at all, so he meant it genuinely when he asked, "What happened?"

"Nothing," she said. "The last week or so, when I've spoken with him, he hasn't cried on the phone, hasn't begged me to come home. Even my mom has given up on asking me when I think I'll be home."

"That's good, though, isn't it?"

"No," she said, her eyes suddenly wet. "Dammit," she said with a sniff. "I told myself I was not going to cry in your room again."

"It's okay."

"You probably think I'm crazy."

"I work with Coleman and Kendall."

She laughed. "Good point."

He gave her a moment to pull herself together. "So what's wrong?" he asked.

"Something occurred to me tonight," she said. "He's getting used to life without me. I've been gone so long that he's starting to move on. He doesn't need me," she said, fighting back a sob.

"Oh."

Ava sniffed and tried to compose herself. "But that's not why I came over here. I came over here to distract myself from that. I don't think I could bear to dwell on it tonight. Let's just have some wine and not talk about bad stuff." She took a drink. "Deal?"

"Yeah, deal. But he still needs you."

"I know. But not as much as he did a week ago."

"He's just learning that he has to be patient."

"I guess."

"You'll get to see him soon. One way or another, we're home in just under a month."

"You don't know that," she said. "If Westcott gets better with surgery now that he's off the sauce, and we suddenly start churning out successful prototypes, we might be here for a lot longer than a month. We only get sent home if we fail, and then I go home to swarms of investigative reporters asking me why I shoot hair spray into bunnies' faces."

"You do that?"

"Yeah. They don't like it, in case you're wondering. And if you ever find yourself in possession of a can of the new formulation of Magic Net, don't ever ever ever spray it in your eyes."

"Okay. What would happen?"

"Your eyes would probably melt."

"Oh. What would the old formulation do?"

"It would make your eyes bleed for a few hours." She reached for a tissue and used it to dab the tears from her cheeks. "Then they'd melt."

"Oh."

"Anyway, if the reporters show up, I'm probably out of a job not much longer after that."

"We just need to make sure we succeed then," he said, taking another sip. Tonight's wine was a little better than the last bottle. It was a bit sweeter. And like the other one, it made him warm.

"I wish I had your confidence," she said.

"Things usually work out."

"Spoken like somebody who's always had things work out for him," she said.

Monroe shrugged.

"Sorry, I don't mean to sound bitter," Ava said, taking a sip. "I've had too many things go wrong in my life to still be able to see any glass as being half full. The only way a glass is half full is if somebody's spit in it."

Monroe looked down at his cup of wine, which thankfully was much less than half full. "Things don't always go wrong," he said.

"They go wrong often enough."

"Well, I think we have a good team working on this. Believe it or not, Kendall's good at his job. I like to think I'm good at mine. I know you're good. Westcott's stopped drinking. Now we just need to make sure Coleman doesn't shoot anyone, and we're set."

"Funny. Heck, the way Westcott's acting lately, I wouldn't be surprised if he was the one to snap and start shooting."

"Nah, he's harmless. Besides, he doesn't have the gun anymore."

"He doesn't?"

"Nope. I have it."

"You do? How did you get it?"

"Asked for it."

She lowered her cup to her lap as her jaw dropped. "Monroe, what on earth did you do to Westcott? You got him on the wagon *and* you got the gun? Did you find naked pictures of him with a young boy or something?"

"Nope."

"You're going to have to spill your secrets one of these days," she said, grinning even though her puffy eyes and still-damp cheeks told a different story. "I'll find out."

"Nope. I'm sworn to secrecy."

"Arthur, if a woman wants a man's secrets, she'll get them."

"I don't doubt that," he said, trying not to sound as nervous as he suddenly felt.

"I have to say, Arthur, I'm starting to feel like you're an iceberg."

"An iceberg?"

"Yeah. All below the surface. There is so much more going on with you than everybody knows. I thought I was starting to get to know you, but after the thing with Westcott, I feel like I'm only becoming more aware of what I don't know about you."

Monroe was blushing. "I'm not that complicated."

"Everybody's complicated," she said, taking a longer sip. "Everybody's screwed up, at least a little bit. In Coleman's case, a lot."

"To be honest, I've never done anything like what happened the other day. I'm kind of surprised at myself, actually."

"That makes two of us. You know, speaking of all this...can I ask you a question?"

"Sure."

"Did you say something to Westcott about me?"

"Like what?"

"The way he's been acting...he's different with everyone since your little chat, but he's actually been *nice* to me. Of all the things Westcott has always been, he has never, ever been nice. Did you put him up to that?"

Monroe hesitated. "I got tired of seeing him treat you like garbage," he said, looking at his cup. "I didn't like the way he talked to you."

Suddenly her hand was under his chin, lifting his face. Her eyes were wet again, but this time she was smiling. "Thanks," she said. "A lot."

She leaned forward and kissed his cheek. Her lips felt soft and just a little wet on his cheek. She smelled like the wine, but mixed with something sweeter. Perfume. It evoked a response that he felt deep inside him. His heart began pounding, causing his hands to shake in turn.

All that, and she had only kissed his cheek.

She sat back into her chair. "That was a really sweet thing to do, and I wanted you to know that I appreciate it."

He started to speak, but his throat seized on him. He was startled by how close he came to vomiting on himself. The taste of it entirely ruined the spell of the kiss. Story of my life, he thought. "You're welcome," he finally croaked.

"So, tell me about your family," she said.

"You want to know about my family?"

"The way I see it, we still have most of a bottle of wine to kill, and I'm tired of talking about work, so sure, let's talk about your family. There have got to be some truly twisted tales in there."

"What makes you say that?"

"Do I need to bring up the virginity thing?"

"No."

Monroe took another sip of his wine, a longer one this time, and started telling Ava about his family. It took him a while to get going, but once he did, he talked for hours.

Chapter 23

"You are giving him a proper military burial, are you not?" Coleman asked.

Monroe and Kendall stopped walking toward the fire escape. Both of them happened to glance at the garbage bag in Kendall's hand, which contained the remains of the cat who came to be named, albeit for a fairly short time, Jefferson.

As things had turned out, sobriety suited Westcott the surgeon well, even if it very much did not suit Westcott the alcoholic. He had been able to successfully implant the electronics into Jefferson, making it his first successful surgery since Eisenhower was in office, but it soon became apparent that Jefferson's body was rejecting the new improvements. He didn't survive his first night as the world's first acoustic kitty, and what was left him was resting stiffly in the garbage bag Kendall was holding.

"Does throwing him into the woods count as a proper military burial?" Monroe asked.

"Good lord, son," Coleman said, throwing his hands in the air. "That soldier was killed in action. He gave his life for his country. You can't just toss him in the weeds like he's some kind of freshly battered hippie."

Monroe and Kendall glanced at each other, but neither decided to ask the question they were both thinking.

"Come on, you dipshits," Coleman said, rising from his chair with great effort. "We're going to do this right. Is there still room in the van for all three of us?"

"Sure," Kendall said. "We had to take out the benches to make room for everything, but you can sit on the floor."

"Got a better idea, son," Coleman said as he climbed out to the fire escape. "You sit on the damn floor."

"Aww," Kendall moaned.

"Quit your bitching. Monroe, find us a hardware store. We need to buy some wood and white paint to make the crosses."

"We're making crosses?" Monroe asked.

"Can't have a military burial without a cross, son," Coleman replied.

"It's going to be a long day," Monroe said under his breath to Kendall.

"Tell me about it," Kendall said. "These slacks always chafe my thighs when I get hot. I'm going to be miserable."

"Great."

Chapter 24

With Madison, the fourth cat chosen for participation in the project, the team got even closer to its goal. Kendall and Monroe made adjustments to the electronics, coating them in a thicker layer of plastic to prevent rejection, and Westcott was once again able to implant them without trouble. Monroe and Ava noticed that Westcott's mood seemed to brighten with each successful surgery.

The team was cheered to discover that Madison had survived his first night with the implants. By the end of the second day after surgery, he was up and about, and on the third day, with just under three weeks until Henderson's visit, the team gathered to conduct the first in-lab test of the controls.

Kendall scratched Madison behind the ears as the cat sat in the middle of the lab with everyone gathered around. "All right, Madison," Kendall said, "time to make us proud." He grabbed the remote control from his workstation.

"What do you think you're doing?" Coleman asked.

"I'm going to give it a shot, to see if everything's working," Kendall said.

"CIA," Coleman said, jutting a thumb toward his chest.

"What's that supposed to mean?"

"CIA is always in charge," Coleman replied, holding out his hand. "I drive."

"I'm CIA, too," Kendall said, clutching the remote to his chest.

"Yeah, but not real CIA."

"Yes I am."

"Ever kick a Russian operative in the testicles on the streets of Geneva?"

"No."

"Hand it over."

"Coleman, come on," Ava said. "Let Jimmy give it the first try. He designed it."

Coleman paused for a moment, looked from Ava to Kendall and back. "This is why field agents are supposed to be armed," he groused.

"Okay," Kendall said. "Oh. Hey, Monroe. Give him a nudge. He'll probably be more responsive if he's on his feet."

"Okay." Monroe nudged Madison, and on cue, the cat got off its haunches and walked in a semi-circle, wondering what it had done to deserve the indignity of being forced to get up.

"Here goes," Kendall said. He flipped on the remote's power switch. Madison looked at Kendall and stopped walking.

Kendall pushed the fore/aft control stick forward. The cat didn't respond and simply continued staring at Kendall.

"It's not doing anything," Coleman said. "Make it do something."

"I'm trying," Kendall said. "The light on the remote is working. We should have power."

"Oh," Monroe said.

"I don't understand," Kendall said. "Maybe the array got damaged during the operation."

"It didn't get damaged," said Westcott, perched on a barstool near the window. "I can vouch for that."

"Um, guys?" Monroe said.

Kendall jerked the fore/aft stick back and forth, then did the same with the left/right stick. "Come on, do something," he said.

"Kendall," Monroe said. "I think he's dead."

"Huh?" Kendall stopped fiddling and looked at Madison, who continued to stare into space. "No way. We just started!"

Ava crouched near the cat and stroked it. It didn't move. "Yep, he's dead."

"Shit," Monroe said.

"Gross," Kendall moaned.

"Funeral duty!" Coleman barked. "Pick 'em up and move 'em out!"

~

"We're never going to have a kitty ready in time," Kendall said from his spot on the floor of the van on the way back from Madison's burial, during which he and Monroe did most of the work while Coleman threw rocks at squirrels in the hope of "at least killing something this week."

"I think we'll make it," Monroe said. "We still have more than three weeks until Henderson gets here. We're getting close already."

"I fried Madison's brain, just like it was an egg," Kendall moaned. "All he wanted to do was grow his hair back and spend the rest of his years sleeping, and instead I flipped on my remote and cooked his little kitty brain. Just like that. Dead! I don't think I can take this." He pulled a ham sandwich from his pocket, unwrapped it, and took a massive bite.

Monroe looked back at Kendall. "That was in your pocket the entire time?" he asked.

"Yeff," Kendall tried to say around the half-chewed ham and bread.

"Why?"

"No reason."

"You can take all you want," Coleman barked from the passenger seat, "but you gotta eat what you take. Wiser words have never been spoken. You keep that in mind when you're enjoying that chow, son."

Kendall stopped chewing for a moment. "Fankth," he said, spraying bread crumbs.

"Look, Jimmy, we couldn't expect to get everything right on the first couple tries," Monroe said. "Westcott knew that. Why do you think he ordered twenty cats?"

"Westcott didn't order the cats," Coleman said. "CIA ordered the cats."

"What difference does it make?" Monroe asked.

"Accuracy is a critical element in any successful mission," Coleman replied.

"Thanks for the accuracy, then."

"Besides, Westcott wanted fifty cats," Coleman said. "I denied the request. That many cats, bad for troop morale. Can't underestimate the role of morale."

Kendall swallowed the last bite of sandwich. Crumbs littered the front of his shirt. "Westcott thought we'd need fifty cats to make one successful acoustic kitty?" he asked.

"Affirmative. He said we'd need that many to find one that was suitable for field work."

"What does that mean?" Monroe asked.

"Son, you ever teach a cat to roll over or play dead?" Coleman asked.

"No."

"Not easy," Coleman said. "We're trying to teach a cat to conduct surveillance." He shook his head slowly. "Grim task ahead of us. Very grim. I once tried to train a cat to tear out the throat of a Czech politician. All it did was scratch the man's ankle."

Monroe and Kendall stared at Coleman.

"Cats are poor leapers," he said, by way of explanation.

"You're right, Jimmy," Monroe said. "We're screwed."

Kendall whimpered. "I'm going to have to eat government cheese," he said.

Coleman banged his cane loudly on the van's dash, causing Monroe and Kendall to both jump. "Cheer up, boys!" he commanded, looking them both in the eye. "Troop morale, very important," he added, almost to himself, as he leaned back again.

A moment later, he slumped over in his seat, his jaw fell slack, and he began to snore.

"It really is almost creepy how he can do that," Kendall said, flicking a crumb off of his shirt.

~

Monroe found Ava working in the OR when they returned. "Good, you're back," she said when she saw him. "I need help prepping another cat. Westcott wants to operate again tomorrow."

"Okay. Hey, uh, is there any particular quality I should look for in the next one?"

Ava stopped cleaning her instruments and looked at him. "Like what?"

"Like, a certain amount of alertness, or ability to listen?"

"I suppose a lethargic cat wouldn't be the best choice," Ava said. "Why?"

"Coleman mentioned that cats are hard to train. I don't want to pick one that won't be able to do what we need him to do."

"Cats certainly are a little more challenging to train," Ava said, "but not impossible. I'm not sure there's any way to know without trying to train it."

"Do you really think we'll be able to get one trained in 22 days, though?"

"No. But I'm assuming Henderson doesn't need to see a fully trained and functional prototype. I think we can show him that the electronics work, and they don't kill the cat, and that it can at least go in one direction upon command. Hopefully that will be enough for him. If he is requiring us to make the cat do something more complicated like, ohh, I don't know…"

"Like tearing open the throat of a Czech politician?"

Ava gave Monroe a strange look. "Um, okay, I was going to suggest something a little less dark, but okay. Anyway, if he wants us to have the cat do something of any complexity, we're probably dead in the water."

Monroe thought for a moment. "I guess we'll just have to do what we can. My hunch is that if we can just show Henderson that we can get the kitty to go forward on command and stop on command, we'd probably buy ourselves at least a few more months."

She sighed. "Yep."

"Oh. That's not really good for you, huh?" It wasn't really a question.

"At this point, nothing about this project is good for me," she replied. "I just need to not think about it. So why don't you go get us a new cat to prep?"

"Okay," he said. He got to the door and paused. "Ava?"

"Yeah?"

"When this is over...whenever it's over...none of us will probably see each other very much, huh? I mean, I'll see Kendall once in a while, and it's possible I might bump into Coleman, God forbid, but it's not like we'll all be working together."

"We may not be working together," she said, "but there's no reason why we can't stay in touch. But if I invite you for a barbecue and you bring Coleman, I'll never forgive you."

"Yeah," Monroe said. "I suppose we'd...stay in touch. Okay. Hey, who was the fifth President?"

"Oh. Uh, let me think. Washington, Adams, Jefferson, Madison...oh, hah, you know who it is?"

"Who?"

"Monroe."

Monroe rolled his eyes. "That's a bad omen if ever I heard one," he said.

"Or a good one," she said. "Glass half full, Arthur."

"Yeah," he muttered to himself as he went in search of his feline namesake. "Glass half full."

~

Monroe found that he had a hard time picking the next cat. Upon realizing that this particular cat would share his name, the choice seemed to take on greater meaning. He spent a good hour approaching each of the 15 remaining cats, which was a bit of a challenge since the cats had become increasingly wary of the people around them. Perhaps, surmised Monroe, the scent of Adams flambé had put them off.

After a great deal of consideration, Monroe chose the cat that kept hanging around his desk. The one that had, in recent weeks, found itself unable to stop rubbing its sides against the nearest wall. The one that would pick bits of food out of one of the large community feeding dishes, carry them in his mouth across the lab, then drop them in a pile in the opposite corner before eating them. As odd as cat behavior was in general, this particular cat seemed to be functioning on a higher plane of oddity.

Monroe's assumption was that this was the single worst cat to choose for the program. And that is why he chose it.

~

Carmelita had been particularly entertaining that night. She had managed to find a john who seemed to only speak some kind of Nordic language – Monroe couldn't tell which one – leading to some rather confusing moments for the multiply satisfied customer as Carmelita, speaking entirely in Spanish, somehow got Nordic Man to realize that he was, in fact, a customer. It was almost impossible to tell whether or not Nordic Man paid up, but since Monroe heard no sounds that would indicate an assault on Carmelita's part, he assumed that she must have been adequately compensated for her time.

An hour later, Carmelita returned to the supply room, but this time the second person's voice was female.

"Oh, you do it in here?" the voice said. "Ahh, spare mattresses. Nice touch. Well, it isn't exactly the Hilton, but right now I could care less."

Carmelita said something in Spanish.

"Honey, I can't understand a word you're saying," the other voice said, "but right now I really don't care…ohh…oh my, that's nice…"

Monroe sat forward on his chair and gripped the headphones against his ears. "This is the single greatest moment of my life," Monroe muttered to himself.

He heard a knock on his door and nearly jumped out of his skin. He yanked off the headphones, then realized that the knock wasn't on his door, it was on Ava's, the next room over.

Monroe started to put his headphones back on, but hesitated. A loud squeal of girl-on-girl joy called to him from the little speakers, but he fought the urge to put the headphones back on for just a moment.

He heard Ava's door open. She said something brief, probably a hello. Then he heard a male voice talking. Coleman's voice.

"Oh, *mannn…*" Monroe groaned, looking at his headphones. He reached for the dial on his listening station, then stopped. He heard another squeal, followed by a long, throaty moan, from his headphones.

"Oh, you have got to be *kidding* me," he said in frustration and indecision.

He heard Coleman's voice again, this time through the wall between his room and Ava's. He was in her room. "Shit," Monroe said, flipping the dial over to Ava's room and cramming his headphones on. "He better be quick about this."

"…very nice of you, Coleman," Ava was saying, "but really, you don't need to."

"Women like wine," Coleman replied.

"Yes, well, that's true," Ava said. "But I haven't even drank the first bottle yet. Or the second."

"Why not? That's good wine. The fat woman at the liquor store said so. Plump women know edibles."

"I'm sure she's right about that. Like I said, it's appreciated. We'll all drink some of it once we have a successful test. Now is there…Coleman? What are you doing?"

"I'm staring at your breasts. Your left nipple is erect."

The door opened. "Ooookay, thank you, Agent Coleman, but I think I'll be fine by myself this evening," Ava said.

"I can do forty pushups," Coleman offered.

"Good for you, but really, you're making me uncomfortable. I don't want everyone to talk."

"Hogwash. I've seen Monroe come out of your room, and nobody talks about that."

"That's different. Arthur and I are friends."

"Ahh, I see," Coleman said. "I have a rival for your affections. And your erect left nipple."

"Will you please stop saying 'nipple?' And for that matter, stop saying 'erect.'"

"A battle between bulls for the warm embrace of the cow," Coleman said. "Only room for one alpha male in this herd, of course. Ah, or have both the pipsqueak and I already been beaten to the punch by the good doctor?"

"Westcott?" Ava laughed. "Please."

"You have not had relations with the doctor?" Coleman asked.

"Oh my God, no," Ava said. "He's my boss. What kind of a girl do you think I am?"

"A girl with an erect left nipple."

"Agent Coleman! Can you please get out now?"

"So it's just me and the pipsqueak," Coleman said.

"No, it's not just you and anyone!" Ava said. "Look, I'm very flattered. Really. But I am here to work. I am not here to get romantically involved with coworkers."

"I see," Coleman said. "Hm, I've already lost to the pipsqueak. I may have to shoot him."

"Coleman."

"Okay, no shooting. But I know when I've been defeated. Sign of a good agent, you know."

"Good night, Coleman. And you have not been defeated. Nobody is 'winning' me. I'm here to work."

Monroe heard footsteps. Coleman was walking toward the door. "Remember, ma'am, that you're talking to a trained agent of the Central Intelligence Agency," he said.

"What's that supposed to mean?"

"I can tell when you're lying."

"And what do you think I'm lying about?"

"You are not here just to work. And I have been defeated."

"You don't know what you're talking about," Ava said, but something in her voice faltered as she said it.

"Yes, I do," Coleman said, his voice fading. He was outside, walking back to his room, apparently. "Good evening."

After a long moment, Ava's door closed softly.

Monroe listened to the silence in Ava's room for several more minutes, not realizing that he was smiling.

Suddenly, he bolted upright. "Shit!" he said, frantically turning the dial back to the supply room. He heard nothing but deep, relaxed breathing for a few seconds. "That was probably the single filthiest act I have ever participated in," the voice said. "I can't believe I actually just did that. And I have no idea how on earth you did that one thing." He heard the sounds of someone getting off the mattress. "Too bad we're driving the rest of the way to Florida in the morning. Well, sugar, I better get back before my husband comes back from dinner with the kids. You are worth every penny. See ya, hon."

"Adios, senora," Carmelita purred.

Monroe threw his hands up in frustration and tossed the headphones off. "I hate Coleman," he said to the walls of his room.

Chapter 25

Much to Monroe the human's chagrin, Monroe the cat turned out to be a surgical success. Not only did he survive the surgery, but he also healed quickly and seemed to desperately want to return to his beloved walls. As soon as the cat could walk, he went directly to the nearest wall and leaned against it for a half hour.

It soon became apparent to the team that calling the cat "Monroe" was problematic. Arthur found himself looking up every time Kendall tried to get the cat's attention, which was about once every forty seconds or so. They decided that because the human Monroe had the name first, that they should find some other name for the feline version.

"Let's just skip to the next President, John Quincy Adams," Monroe said, looking at the list he kept on his workstation.

"Absolutely not," Kendall said. "Skipping a President would be bad luck. Besides, it shares a name with you and with me, since that President's first name was James. There's just too much good luck there to start toying around with another President."

"So we'll call him James."

Kendall flinched so broadly that it looked like his entire body spasmed.

"What the hell was that?" Ava asked.

"Sorry. Mom calls me...that name. Gives me the heebie-jeebies when I hear it."

"So James is out," Ava said.

Kendall flinch-spasmed again. "Yes, please."

"Mr. President," Coleman blurted from his chair. "Call him Mr. President. That's how one addresses a true President."

Monroe looked at Kendall. "That's not bad. A little long, but technically we wouldn't be skipping any names."

"Okay," Kendall said. "Let's go with that. Hopefully the cat won't ever be in the same room as an actual President." He gasped. "Oooh, do you think our little acoustic kitty might actually meet a President someday?"

"What's he going to do, use it as a microphone?" Monroe asked.

"You never know."

"Mr. President it is," Coleman said. "Once again, the CIA solves a problem. So when do we take him for a spin?"

"Dr. Westcott wants to wait a couple days," Ava said. "He thinks the last cat might have been electrocuted because scar tissue hadn't sufficiently formed around the electronics. Just to be sure, he wants to give Monroe – I mean, Mr. President – a couple extra days."

"No good," Coleman said. "We're on the clock."

"Sorry. Doctor's orders. We forced him to quit drinking. The least we can do in return is respect his opinion."

"No, the least we can do is not shoot him," Coleman said. "Where is Dr. Death, anyway?"

"He said he was tired and went back to his room for a nap."

Coleman grunted. "Napping in the middle of the day," he said. "Pathetic."

Chapter 26

Ava and Kendall went to work on training Mr. President to respond to commands. By the end of the first day, Mr. President was responding to his name. The cat learned to approach people calling its name based on the promise of the treats Ava and Kendall offered to him. Unfortunately, as soon as the treat was eaten, Mr. President would immediately return to the nearest wall and meow four times.

The four-meow habit was a behavior that nobody could remember Mr. President exhibiting prior to his implantation surgery. Kendall pointed out that the number four was quite Presidential, since it matched the number of years in a full term, and that the cat was simply attempting to communicate that it appreciated its new name.

With little more than two weeks before Henderson was due to visit, Westcott gave the all-clear to test Mr. President's equipment. As the team gathered in the lab, the usual banter was in short supply. Most of them realized that if Mr. President got fried during his initial test, there was little chance of having a truly workable prototype in time for Henderson's visit.

Monroe gathered Mr. President and sat him on the floor between his workstation and Kendall's. "Okay, buddy," he said to the cat. "Show us what you got."

"I don't think I want to do this," Kendall said, looking at the remote control in his hands. "I fried a cat the last time."

"Nobody likes a sissy, Chubby," Coleman said.

"I am not chubby!" Kendall shouted.

"Here, I'll do it," Monroe said, taking the remote. "How do you power it up?"

"Flip the toggle switch on the top of the box," Kendall said. "And hope you don't smell cooked kitty."

"He'll be fine," Monroe said.

Kendall looked at him doubtfully.

"I have a good feeling," Monroe said with a shrug. "Okay," he said, turning to the cat. "Here goes nothing."

"Good luck," Ava said.

Monroe flipped the power switch. Kendall shrieked.

Mr. President stopped walking in circles for a moment and cocked his head.

Kendall shrieked again. "Oh God, he's dead!," Kendall squeaked. "I hear humming! He's simmering like a turkey! Make it stop!"

"No, look, he's still moving," Monroe said. "Kendall, the hum is coming from the remote."

"Oh yeah. I forgot. It hums."

"Pantywaist," Coleman muttered.

"I am not!" Kendall cried.

Mr. President meowed four times, then sat on his haunches and began gnawing on the toes of his right rear foot.

"So far so good," Ava said.

"What's he doing?" Kendall said. "That's gross. He's eating his own toejam."

"Okay, I'm going to try giving him a 'forward' command," Monroe said. "Here goes."

Monroe pushed forward on one of the remote's sticks. Mr. President's head jerked up and he meowed as he got up and looked around, as if he were trying to determine where the annoying jolt of electricity in his back was coming from. Not seeing anything, Mr. President tried to twist his head around enough to gnaw at the spot on his back where he felt the sensation.

"Not dead," Coleman said. "Not yet. Well done, soldier." This last comment was directed at the cat, which seemed oblivious to the compliment.

Monroe let go of the stick, allowing it to return to the center position. Mr. President stopped trying to reach the spot on his back. He looked around again, meowed four times, and headed toward the nearest wall, where he eyed the group of people warily.

"I'll be darned," Monroe said. "I think it worked."

"And he's not dead!" Kendall exclaimed.

Ava went over to Mr. President and used a stethoscope on him. "Heartbeat sounds normal," she said. She looked him over. "Things look fine. I think we just had a successful test."

"Hot damn," Coleman said. "We should celebrate. Ava, take off your shirt."

"Hey," Monroe said.

Coleman threw his hands up. "Whoa, sorry there, chief. But I didn't ask to play with 'em. Just wanted a look-see. No harm in that, is there? Those are fine American breasts she has there."

"She doesn't need you making those kind of comments, Coleman," Monroe said. "Let's just work."

"See?" Coleman said to Ava.

"See what?" Monroe said.

"Coleman, stop," Ava said.

"Central Intelligence Agency," Coleman said, pointing his thumb at his chest, then waving his index finger at Monroe and Ava. "I see it all. Trained eye."

"What are we even talking about?" Kendall said. "I'm confused. I got lost after the thing about seeing Ava's thingies."

"Good lord," Ava said, rubbing her temples. "I do not believe what I have to put up with on this project."

"Did I just say 'thingies?'" Kendall asked.

"Sure did," Monroe said, patting him on the back. "Welcome to junior high."

Kendall turned bright red and began tugging at his shirt. "Anyone else suddenly feel like throwing up?"

"Can we all just get back to work, please?" Westcott said, seeming truly bored with the conversation. "I don't want to be here all damn night."

"Yes, let's please change the subject to anything else," Ava said, crossing her arms in front of her chest.

"What we should be talking about," Westcott continued, "is the next step in this process, which is to train the cat to interpret the signals."

"I think we can start on that right away," Ava said. "We'll observe Mr. President for a couple hours to make sure he's not suffering any negative effects of the test. If he's okay, I don't see why we can't start training him this afternoon. We don't have the luxury of waiting longer than that."

"Teach it to find my damn gun," Coleman said. He glared at Westcott.

"Don't look at me, 007," Westcott said. He pointed at Monroe. "He has it."

Coleman's gaze shifted slowly over to Monroe. "You got my gun? How long have you had it? And why didn't you give it to me?"

"I didn't want you to shoot anybody with it."

"Boy, what else is the purpose of a gun other than to shoot people with it? What kind of cockamamie planet do you live on?"

"I prefer to live on one where you aren't armed. Don't worry, it's in a safe place. I'll give it back to you before we get back to Langley."

"I can cripple you with my pinky finger, you know."

"Then you don't need the gun, do you?"

Coleman sized Monroe up for a moment. "I liked you better when you were a pipsqueak," he said.

"Um, thanks, I think," Monroe said. "Anyway, the doctor's right. We need to work on training Mr. President."

Mr. President meowed, sneezed violently, and licked his nose.

"I'll help," Kendall said, raising his hand.

"You two have at it," Coleman said. "I got more important things to do."

"Yeah, like sleeping," Kendall said. He snorted a laugh and elbowed Monroe.

Coleman laughed, loud enough to be heard on the street below, then walked over to Kendall and slapped a hand on his shoulder.

"Ow!" Kendall shrieked. "Hey, I…." He fell silent as his eyes rolled back into his head and he collapsed in a heap on the floor.

"Oh my God!" Ava said, rushing to Kendall. "Coleman, what did you do?"

Coleman looked at Monroe. "Pinky finger," he said, holding the finger in question aloft.

~

"I'm not sure it's working," Kendall said as he tried to keep the icepack steady on his forehead.

"It's going to take some time," Ava said. "You need to be patient. Try it again, Arthur."

Monroe pushed the forward command on the remote. Mr. President hopped into the air several times, as if he suddenly found himself walking across a giant heated skillet.

"Here, Mr. President," Ava said, kneeling nearby and holding a treat in her hand. She waved the treat at the cat. "Here."

After several more hops, Mr. President spotted the treat and walked briskly forward to Ava. "Good kitty," she said, petting him and allowing him to eat the kibble. "That was good, except for the jumping."

"That's better than the spontaneous defecation thing he was doing earlier," Monroe said.

"Speaking of which," Kendall said, adjusting his ice pack, "I think I must have got some on me, because something smells."

"Why are men so fascinated by poop?" Ava asked. "You guys never stop talking about it."

"Poop's funny," Monroe said.

"No, it isn't," Ava said. "It's gross."

They looked at each other for a moment.

"I really don't know how to argue the point any better than that," Monroe said.

Ava rolled her eyes. "Anyway," she said, "if we can get him to do this a few more times, after a couple days we can try taking away the treat and repeating the command."

"A couple days?" Monroe asked. "Just to start learning to move forward?"

"I'm afraid so. Even that timeline is aggressive."

"We're never going to make it," Monroe said.

"Don't say that!" Kendall said, clamping his hands over his ears and yelping when he realized he'd just jammed an ice pack into his right ear. "It's bad luck."

"Luck or not, we just don't have enough time," Monroe said. "We need to ask Henderson for more."

"Not a good idea," Kendall said. "You know my friend Jerry Higginbotham? He once worked on a project for Henderson. He said they missed one deadline by just a single day and all got docked an entire month's pay, and the director on the project had to pick up Henderson's dry cleaning for two months just to save his job. Henderson wants things when he wants them."

Monroe sighed. "Then I guess we better keep working."

"We can't," Ava said. "Apparently I just used the last kitty treat." She held the bag upside down.

"The pet store isn't far," Monroe said. "I'll grab the keys."

"Mind some company?" Ava asked. "I could use some air."

"Uh, sure," Monroe said. "Kendall, you coming?"

"No," Kendall said. "My head still hurts. I'll stay here and play with Mr. President for a while."

Monroe grabbed the keys, and he and Ava climbed out of the window and down the fire escape. Monroe made sure he reached the bottom first so he could get a good look at Ava's butt as she climbed down.

Once they were in the van, Ava said, "I was thinking about what you said to me the other day, about none of us staying in touch after this is done."

"Yeah?"

"Yeah. And I don't see any reason why we couldn't stay in touch. Those of us who want to, that is. I don't see anybody clamoring to be friends with Dr. Westcott, but I wouldn't mind staying in touch with you guys. With the possible exception of Coleman. His love of weaponry is kind of a concern."

"That sounds good," Monroe said.

Ava looked at him. "That's it?" she asked. "It 'sounds good?'"

"Yeah," Monroe said with a shrug.

"You don't think we're likely to stay friends?"

"I...I don't know. It's possible."

Ava looked at him, awaiting further explanation.

"What?" Monroe asked.

"You're hedging."

"Sorry."

"If you don't want to stay in touch, that's fine," Ava said. "I thought after what you said the other day that it was something you were interested in."

"I am," Monroe said. He sighed, realizing she wasn't going to let him off the hook. "It's not that I wouldn't want to stay in touch. It's been my experience that...well, it doesn't happen. People get busy. Work. Kids. Other friends. You meet people, you're friends for a while, everyone moves on and makes other friends, and it just cycles like that."

"You don't have any friends that you've known for years and years?" Ava asked.

"No. Not really. I've had friends here and there, sure. But nobody I've known for a super long time."

"These people that you've been friends with along the way...did you ever call them? Or have lunch with them once in a while?"

"No."

"Then how do you expect to stay friends with them?"

"I don't know. I never thought about it that way, I guess."

"Wouldn't you like to have friends? People that you can do fun things with? Don't you get lonely?"

"I don't know. Sometimes I just like being by myself. I don't have to worry about doing things I don't want to do just because one of my friends wants to do it."

"That's why most people who are friends have common interests. That's what makes them friends."

"Most people I've met don't share my interests."

"What do you mean? You're not torturing animals in your basement or anything, are you?"

"No, I do that at work."

Ava sat back in her seat and watched the road for a moment. "Are all men like you? I mean, do they really all just want to be left alone?"

"I don't think so," Monroe said. "I can't imagine Kendall living alone for more than ten minutes without having a nervous breakdown. He told me his mom keeps forgetting to wear pants since she started back on Jim Beam, but he still isn't planning on moving out."

"That's creepy."

"It might not be so bad if she bothered to wear underwear."

They fell silent for a moment.

Monroe turned into the parking lot of the pet store. "I didn't sleep well for a few days after Kendall mentioned it. Don't worry. It passes."

Chapter 27

"Hey, you guys?" Kendall said. "I can't get him to pay attention."

"Kick him," Coleman said, looking up from his toes, which he had been intently picking. "Kick a thing, you have its attention." Westcott happened to be walking past on his way to the bathroom. Coleman kicked him in the leg.

"Ow!" Westcott yelped, grabbing his leg. "What the hell was that for?"

"See?" Coleman said.

"What's the problem, Jimmy?" Monroe asked.

"Well, look," Kendall said. He set down the remote and retrieved Mr. President from his cage. He put the cat in the middle of the room, where it sat for a moment. Over the past few days, with Ava, Monroe and Kendall teaching him for nearly 12 hours each day, Mr. President had made great strides. He had successfully made the connection between the impulses he felt in his back and the movements he was being asked to perform. The cat had learned quickly once he realized that if he did what was requested, he earned a snack. After a couple days, even with the snacks taken away, Mr. President continued moving according to the directions transmitted via the remote.

The one exception to the rule was the backward command. Whenever one of the team would use the remote to issue a "walk backward" command, Mr. President would not back up. Instead, he sat. Ava even started pushing him backwards while Kendall pulled back on the fore-aft stick, but it didn't matter. Mr. President simply refused to move backward. Monroe suggested that if they ever needed Mr. President to reverse directions, they could simply turn him to the left or right 180 degrees then have him go forward. Everyone agreed that this was a viable solution, and it also afforded them the unanticipated ability to order Mr. President to sit, which Coleman felt would come in handy in the field.

With Henderson's visit just ten days away, Monroe had found himself encouraged for a change. He'd almost become resigned to the possibility of losing his job at the end of the project, but with Mr.

President learning so quickly, he allowed himself to entertain the notion that he might still be employed in eleven days.

Kendall's announcement about Mr. President not paying attention, then, was a somewhat unexpected source of concern. "Show me what you mean," Monroe said.

"Okay. So Mr. President is sitting still, right? And I want to make him, say, walk over to Coleman's chair. He's been doing it all morning. But watch what happens."

Kendall toggled the remote, and upon command, Mr. President meowed – as he always did when he felt the first jolt of electricity in his back – and started walking toward the chair. After walking a few feet, however, Mr. President veered to the right, then began casually trotting toward the collection of cages located in the corner of the lab directly opposite from where he was supposed to go.

"See? I never turned off the 'forward' command, but he keeps wandering over by the cages for some reason." Kendall set the remote down and retrieved Mr. President before he could reach his cage.

"And you said he's been fine all morning?" Ava asked.

"Yeah. I've been repeating the commands over and over, just like you told me to do. All of a sudden he stopped working right."

"A good retriever would never perpetrate such a thing," Coleman sniffed.

"It looks like he's going for his cage," Monroe said. "Is there something in there that's attracting his attention?"

"I looked," Kendall said. "Nothing but his food dish and blanket."

"Maybe he's hungry," Ava said. "Let him go and see if he eats."

Kendall put Mr. President back on the floor. The cat coughed twice, then wandered to his cage and started eating.

"That's all it was," Ava said. "You've been working him all morning. He got hungry. He'll probably be fine in a few minutes."

"No good," Coleman said.

Everyone turned to him. "Why not?" Monroe asked.

"Can't have an agent wandering from his post simply because he's in the mood for chow," Coleman said. "Might get hungry in the middle of an important conversation. Surveillance takes time. Success is enjoyed only by the patient. He goes wandering off in search of the mess hall at the wrong time, he's AWOL."

"I hate to admit it, but he has a point," Monroe said.

"I once went six days without eating while hiding in a North Korean official's broom closet," Coleman said.

"We can't have Mr. President picking the wrong time to get hungry," Monroe said.

"What can we do about that, though?" Kendall asked. "We can't stop him from getting hungry."

"Actually, we probably can," Westcott interjected.

"We can?" Kendall asked.

"We *probably* can," Westcott said. "I'm not promising that it would actually work, but I could put something into the cat's stomach to stimulate it into thinking it's full. Or at least, to override the signal that tells Mr. President here that he's hungry. Wouldn't be very much fun for him, though, I'll tell you that. Not sure how we'd get him to eat if he doesn't ever think he's hungry. We might have to feed him through an IV line."

"That's horrible!" Kendall cried. "Absolutely not. I won't allow it."

"Not your call to make, Chubbs," Coleman said. "If I got distracted by a craving for cheeseburgers while on the job, I'd have 'em take my stomach clean out. Small sacrifice to make for national security. This fine patriotic cat, if he could talk, would almost certainly tell you that he won't think twice about doing what's needed to get the job done. Look at him. He's a patriot."

Mr. President was back out of his cage, having finished his snack, and was pressing his side against the wall behind his cage. Sensing everyone's eyes on him, he froze in place and stared back. It was not unlike the look a man stranded on a desert island gets when he realizes that the only other person on the island appears to be extremely hungry.

"Your country will remember your sacrifice, son," Coleman said to Mr. President.

"Are you sure there isn't another way?" Monroe said. "Would he even survive a procedure like that? It can't be easy to get an IV line into a cat."

"They don't like it, that's for sure," Ava said. "But we put IV lines into animals fairly often."

"Why don't we just make sure he's full before we send him out on surveillance?" Monroe asked.

"Cats sleep when they're full," Ava said. "It would be even harder to get him to pay attention. We could try to only feed him halfway to being full, but that's going to be hard to determine. Besides, if he has any room in his stomach, and, say, a mouse runs past him, he'll go after it. Cats are opportunistic eaters, designed by nature to eat until they're bloated."

Ava looked around the lab. "We hadn't thought of this problem because we're in an artificial environment," she continued. "There aren't any small animals or bits of trash laying around here. In a park, he'd be surrounded by things that look like they might taste good. I'm afraid Dr. Westcott is right. We need to remove the urge to eat."

"Like a patriot!" Coleman barked. From halfway across the room, the cat flinched and ran into his cage.

"Oh dear," Kendall said. "I feel sick. I think I'm cramping." He held his stomach for a moment. "Yep, I'm definitely cramping," he said, slowly doubling over.

"Guys," Monroe said, "we only have ten days until Henderson gets here. We can't have our cat starving to death on us. How long would it take Mr. President to heal from that kind of surgery, doc?"

"Normally I'd say a month," Westcott said. "But I'm guessing. I've never performed a procedure like this. We don't even have a month, so I think we need to do it as soon as possible if he's supposed to be up and about in ten days. And I need something electrical I can implant in his stomach to keep it irritated. If his tummy hurts, he won't want to eat, no matter how much he needs food. Kendall, think you can come up with something like that? It would need to be just like the ones we put in his back, but we'd probably need it to stay on all the time to keep his stomach off-kilter. And it has to be large enough to prevent him from passing it through his system."

"You want me to participate in this?" Kendall asked.

"Actually, I could give a shit if you participate or not," Westcott replied. "If we don't do the surgery, the project fails, and you all get fired. No skin off my nose. I'm just following orders here," he finished, shooting a look at Monroe.

"Project fails, you have problems of your own," Coleman said. "Don't forget that, chief."

"I already have problems of my own," Westcott said. "If this stupid cat works, great. If it doesn't, I'll survive. I'm tired of this shit. I don't know about you, but this whole thing didn't exactly turn out like I'd hoped."

"Somebody gets cranky when he's off the sauce," Coleman said.

"Kendall," Monroe said, "I know it's not exactly a fun job, but do you think you can work with Westcott to develop something quickly?"

"I'll try," Kendall said. "Poor Mr. President."

"Thanks," Monroe said. "You might as well get started now. We need all the time we can get."

"Yeah, okay," Kendall said. "But I want to go to the Starving Aardvark tonight if I do this."

"Fine. We'll go to the Aardvark."

"Negative," Coleman said.

"Why not?" Monroe asked.

"No steak there," Coleman said. "And unfriendly service. No can do."

"Coleman," Monroe said, "that waitress was not unfriendly. You goosed her. Of course she's going to slap your hand."

"That was an accident."

"It was like a proctology exam. You're lucky we didn't get thrown out."

"Can't throw out the Central Intelligence Agency."

"Okay. If Kendall wants to go to the Aardvark, we're going to the Aardvark. We're asking a huge favor of him here."

"Yeah," Kendall said, crossing his arms and glaring at Coleman.

"This is why I need my damn gun," Coleman said. He turned and walked back to his chair, dropping himself into it.

"Thank you," Monroe said. "Doc, can you tell Kendall what you need?"

"Sure. It'll be a thrill," Westcott said in a tone that indicated that it would in fact not be much of a thrill at all. "Let's go into my office. It stinks like cat pee out here. And the CIA."

Kendall inhaled deeply as they walked to Westcott's office. "Hey, you're right." He inhaled again. "Boy, that's really bad." He inhaled a third time.

"Kendall," Westcott said, holding the door to his office open.

"Oh, right. Sorry."

After they went into the office, Monroe went to his workstation and began gathering a few tools. The equipment in the van still needed a fair amount of work, and he had some time to kill.

After a moment, he realized that Ava had followed him to his workstation.

"You need something?" Monroe asked.

"Uh, no," Ava said. "I just wanted to say..." She stopped, looking over at Coleman. He was already sound asleep in his chair, or at least appeared to be. Ava lowered her voice anyway. "I wanted to say that I think what you're doing is good."

"What am I doing?"

"Everything. You're getting everyone working in the same direction. Coleman's not in charge of this project any more. Neither is Westcott. You are."

Monroe held up his hands. "No, no. I'm not in charge. I just want to save my job."

"You're too modest," Ava said. "You might not officially be in charge, but you are. You keep Coleman in check, you got Westcott to stop drinking, you even just got Kendall to help with doing something really unfortunate to a cat. You're the one keeping this thing from going off the rails."

"Well…thanks. I guess. I don't feel like I'm in charge. God, don't say anything like this in front of Coleman. He's pissed enough about the gun thing. If he didn't think he was in charge, he'd make me eat my own testicles."

"I seriously doubt that."

"No, I'm not kidding. He threatened to do that the other night when he asked to borrow ten bucks and I said I didn't have it."

"Oh."

"Yeah."

"Well, I just wanted to say thank you. And not just as a coworker, but as a…friend. You've been really nice to me. Nicer than you had to be. You've put up with my crying about Robby and everything."

Monroe felt himself turning red. "It's okay. I didn't mind."

"Well, I really do appreciate it," she said, reaching out and rubbing his forearm lightly. It was like having a small electric shock go through his body. He doubted that the shocks Mr. President received were quite as pleasant. As quickly as it happened, though, Ava's hand was once again withdrawn. "And I've decided that I'm going to make sure we stay friends after this is over," she said brightly, as if she hadn't just provided the highlight of Monroe's entire week.

"Okay," he said.

"You sound thrilled."

"I'm sorry. Yes, I'd like that." He paused. "A lot," he added.

Ava smiled, and Monroe realized she was looking directly into his eyes. "Well, I've decided," she said, finally relaxing her gaze, "that once we're done here, I'm going to cook you dinner."

"Yeah?"

"Yeah. You can meet Robby, and my mom if she's still there. I'll make my lasagna. You'll love it. It'll make you nice and fat."

"Sounds good."

"Okay. It's a deal." She looked over her shoulder, toward Westcott's office. "Well, I'm thinking I should go in there. I'm afraid of what might happen if I leave them on their own for too long."

"Probably a good idea."

"See ya."

"Yeah. See ya." He watched her go. For once, he didn't just stare at her butt.

~

Dinner that night was entertaining, if uneventful. Coleman never stopped complaining about the quality of the food at the Starving Aardvark's buffet, which mostly consisted of various casseroles and bottomless pits of fried chicken. He grumbled that it was nothing but "momma's boy food" and that "our ancestors would puke on themselves if they saw what has become of us."

Monroe didn't bother asking him to stop. He mostly replayed the conversation with Ava in his head over and over. He wondered if perhaps it was imagination, that she wasn't really very interested in him and was simply being nice. But no, that didn't seem to be it. The hand on the wrist. The look. Meeting Robby. A girl, a pretty girl, wanted to cook him dinner. And she wasn't a relative.

Ava noticed how distracted he was and teased him about it a little. They chatted, not in the same way as they did in the afternoon, but Monroe enjoyed it anyway. They talked about movies, none of which Monroe had seen, but he didn't care. Ava, he learned, was a movie buff, and in particular a fan of Tracy-Hepburn movies. They agreed that Monroe needed to see more movies, and Ava cheerfully volunteered to take him to some, as long as he didn't want to see monster or horror movies, which she patently dismissed as "a waste of celluloid."

By the time they all returned to the motel and went to their separate rooms, Monroe was in as good of a mood as he'd ever remembered. He even went so far as to consider walking down the street to the nearby liquor store, buying a bottle of wine, and asking Ava to split it with him. But he wasn't sure what kind of wine to buy, and he wasn't sure how much it would cost, so in the end, he decided to simply finish off the night with a bit of listening.

As always, he started by flipping to the housekeeping room to see if Carmelita was "working." Nothing but silence.

He flipped to Coleman's room. More silence. Again. Monroe wished for the fiftieth time that he could simply ask Coleman what he did in his room at night, but of course he couldn't.

He flipped to Westcott's room.

"I don't understand what you're doing," a voice said. It was Thomas.

"There's got to be an explanation," Westcott said. It sounded as though someone in the room was moving around rapidly. Monroe could also hear drawers quickly being opened, then shut.

"You're being paranoid, and it's getting on my nerves," Thomas said.

Westcott didn't respond. More drawers opened and then shut.

"You do realize that I am laying here naked, right?" Thomas said. "Boners like this one don't show up every day, you know. Look at that. It's magnificent."

Monroe reached for his knob and turned it to any other room but Westcott's. He ended up on Kendall's line.

Kendall was, as usual, blaring the television. He also was, as usual, farting loudly.

Monroe reached for the dial to flip to Ava's room. For once, he hesitated. He held his hand over the dial for a while, tapped on it with his fingers. Curiosity got the better of him, and he flipped.

She was in the middle of talking to Robby. It sounded like he was in a good mood, and so was she. She laughed several times, apparently at a story he was telling her about his day. It occurred to Monroe that he rarely heard Ava laugh, but he liked the sound of it. Maybe once they got back home, he would get to hear it more often. He wondered what kind of comedies she liked to see at the movies. She probably loved Cary Grant.

Monroe listened to her talk and laugh, even though it was all just small talk.

He had no idea how many minutes had passed when the sharp knocking on his door began. The noise was so loud and furious that he feared for a moment that it was the police.

"You son of a bitch!" Westcott yelled from the other side of the door. "Open this goddamned door, you motherfucking son of a bitch! I should have known!" He was pounding on the door as if he were trying to knock a hole in it. "*Open this fucking door!*" he screamed at the top of his lungs.

Monroe froze, but for just a moment. Then panic rushed through him; he quickly tore off his headphones and began furiously shoving the listening station and headphones under the bed. It got stuck for a moment, causing his panic to ratchet up a notch or two, before he realized he hadn't unplugged the listening station. He yanked the plug out of the wall and pushed everything as far under the bed as he could.

"Morton, stop this!" Thomas yelled. Apparently he was also right outside Monroe's door. "You're acting crazy! You don't even know what that thing is."

"I told you to stay in the room, God dammit!" Westcott bellowed at Thomas.

"And do what, knit you a sweater? I don't think so!"

"I don't care what…Jesus Christ! You couldn't at least have grabbed a towel?"

"Well, excuse me, Mr. Freak Out And Run From The Room Like You're Going To Kill Somebody! Maybe I was in such a rush to stop you that I didn't think about it until after the door locked behind me!"

"You didn't grab the key?"

"No, I didn't grab the fucking key!"

"Great! So we're locked out!"

"Well, that is hardly my fault, mister!"

Westcott screamed in frustration. He began pounding again, this time even harder than before. "Now I'm really pissed off!" he shouted. "Open the door, you little fucking asshole!"

"I'm not going to open the door when you're screaming like that!" Monroe shouted back through the door. He looked through the peephole. Westcott's head was such a deep color of red that it was almost purple. He was only wearing an undershirt. Try as he might to avoid looking at Thomas, Monroe noticed that the man was correct about his boner not lasting forever.

"You're gonna open this fucking door or I'm going to break it down!" Westcott said, continuing to pound. Monroe backed away from the shaking door.

"What seems to be the problem here?" Coleman's voice said. "And why is this man naked?"

"Hey," Thomas said. "This isn't a peep show, buddy. Eyes up here, where I can see them."

"Coleman!" Monroe shouted, keeping back from the door. "I don't know what's going on! He's gone nuts!"

"I'm nuts?" Westcott shouted. "*I'm* nuts?!? Fine, you want to know what's going on, Mister CIA? This is what's going on!"

They went silent for a moment. "What's your point?" Coleman asked.

Monroe felt his stomach drop. He had a horrible feeling he knew why Westcott was so furious.

"So, I found the damn thing in my room!" Westcott bellowed. "Were you in on this, too? It wouldn't surprise me. You probably all know about Thomas and can't wait to use it against me yourselves! Bunch of losers! Jealous of my station in life, are you? Huh?"

"What on earth is going on out here?" Ava asked. "I...Thomas? What are you...and you're...wow, completely...umm..."

"Oh, hi, Ava," Thomas said, his voice suddenly halting and nervous. "Funny running into you here, huh?"

"What are you doing here?" Ava asked. "And...um...where are your clothes?"

"Hey, that guy's naked," Kendall's voice said. "I heard all the shouting, but I was in the bathroom and I couldn't understand everything. Can you guys start over?"

"I...umm..." Thomas stammered. "You know, do you maybe have a towel in your room?"

"Actually, yes," Ava said. "I'll get it for you."

"I'm really confused," Kendall said. "Why is there a naked guy here?"

"My name is Thomas," Thomas said.

"Oh, hey there," Kendall replied. "I'm Jimmy. This is Coleman."

"Nice to meet you."

"Don't try to shake my hand, soldier," Coleman grunted.

"Yes sir," Thomas said.

Westcott started pounding on the door again. "Get out here, dammit! Now!"

Monroe stepped back from the door even further. His face went pale and he broke out in a cold sweat. His eyes began darting around the room, looking for some way to cover his tracks, some way to get rid of the listening station, but of course there wasn't. The room was small, and the only window was next to the only door, on the other side of which had gathered the people he'd been listening to for three months.

There must be a way out of this, he thought. There has to be.

"Here you go," he heard Ava say.

"Oh, are you sure? I don't want to take your robe."

"I insist," she said.

"You know this man?" Coleman asked.

"Believe it or not, yes," Ava replied. "We work together. Back in Virginia. Thomas is in Accounts Payable."

"Ooh, you have good taste," Thomas said. "This material is so *soft*."

"I'm so confused," Ava said.

"Me too!" Kendall shouted. "I still don't know what all the pounding and yelling is about."

"Don't ask me," Coleman's voice said. "I found him like this."

"I'll tell you what it's all about, you fat bag of grease," Westcott bellowed.

"Hey!" Kendall said. "I'm not greasy!"

"It's about this! I found this! In my room! Under my bed!" Westcott said.

Monroe felt another wave of panic. It was confirmed now.

"What is that?" Ava asked.

"A bug," Coleman said.

"You found a bug under your bed?" Ava asked.

"You mean that really is a little microphone?" Thomas said. "I thought he was being crazy."

"You were in Westcott's room?" Ava asked. "I don't...why were you...oh." She paused for a moment. "Ohhh," she repeated. "Oh, dear."

"It's, um, not what you think," Thomas blurted with the conviction of a government bureaucrat claiming that he once played quarterback for the Green Bay Packers.

"Um, okay, sure it's not," Ava said. "Listen, we don't have to talk about it. Really."

Coleman interrupted them. "You people stay here and make sure he doesn't leave his room."

"We're keeping Artie in his room?" Kendall asked. "Why are we keeping Artie in his room?"

"Just keep him in there," Coleman said, his voice farther away now.

"What is going on?" Kendall asked. "Why is there a bug under your bed?"

"I think that's a question we should be asking your friend in there," Westcott said. "The one who *isn't...coming...out!*" He pounded three times on the door as he said the last three words.

"Monroe didn't plant a bug in your room," Kendall said. "Why would he do that?"

"To blackmail me!" Westcott shouted. "God, are you actually as stupid as you look?"

"Hey!" Kendall shouted. "Are you actually as old as you look?"

"Wait, wait, stop shouting," Ava said. "Everybody just slow down. Dr. Westcott, who's blackmailing you? We don't understand what you're saying."

"He's blackmailing me!" Westcott said. "Monroe! He…well, he…look, I don't want to get into the particulars of it…"

"I think I'm going to go back to our…uhh, *my*, room now," Thomas said. "Thanks for the robe, Ava. I'll bring it back later."

"You know, you can just keep it," she replied.

"Oh, I couldn't. It's a nice robe."

"Trust me, Thomas, I don't think I'd have much use for it at this point."

"Oh, that is so nice of you. I promise, I'll pay you back."

"Can you please leave?" Westcott barked. "Now?"

"Okay, you know what, mister?" Thomas said, "that is the last time you tell me what to do. I don't work for you!"

"Yes, you do!" Westcott yelled.

"Oh yeah. Well, I still don't have to take orders from you."

"Will somebody please explain all of this to me?" Kendall wailed.

"Kendall," Ava said, "I don't think you want to know everything that's going on."

"Doc keeps talking about blackmail. Artie's not blackmailing anybody."

"Oh yes he is," Westcott said. "And now I know how he found out…well, what he knows."

"What is it that he knows?"

"You know," Thomas said, "I think I really will leave now. You guys have fun. Was great to see you, Ava."

"What, did Artie discover that you two are gay lovers?" Kendall said with a laugh.

"Great!" Westcott bellowed. "So everybody knows now?"

"Oh," Kendall said. "I was just joking. You mean…you're really…?"

"Yes, Jimmy," Ava said.

"Wow," Kendall said. "I didn't think I actually knew any gay people. Everybody thought my Uncle Fergus was gay, but he was never sober enough for any of us to tell for sure. We don't think his reproductive organs were functional. Mom said he had an inverted penis."

Everyone was silent for a long moment. "Oh my," Thomas said.

Ava's brow furrowed. "So, Thomas – the 'Daddy Bear' you keep mentioning in the lunch room…that's Dr. Westcott?"

"I cannot believe this is happening," Westcott said, burying his face in his hands.

"Wait," Ava said, starting to laugh in spite of herself, "hang on a second. That's how Monroe got you to give up drinking? He said he'd tell everyone about the two of you?"

Westcott sighed heavily. "Yes."

Ava's laughing slowed. "But...how did he...?" She fell silent for a moment. "Arthur?" she said through the door. "This isn't making sense. Let us in. Dr. Westcott's not going to hurt you."

"Oh yes I am," Westcott said.

"Oh, please," Thomas said. "I asked him to kill a roach in our room last night and he nearly soiled himself running away from it. I don't think you have anything to worry about, whoever you are behind that door."

"Doctor," Ava said, "he's not going to open the door if he thinks you're going to attack him."

"Ava," Coleman said, apparently having returned from wherever he'd gone, "I'd like to search your room."

"*My* room?" she asked. "I didn't do anything."

"I don't think you did. I found this hidden in the television in my room. I suspect there's one in your room as well."

"You found a microphone in your TV?" Ava asked.

"Yes. Clever, actually. He guessed I'd never turn the thing on. He was right. Nothing but garbage. Rot your brain. I'd like to search your room," Coleman said. His voice was low, and all business in a way that Monroe had never heard before.

"I'll go with you," Ava said. Monroe heard them walking away.

"Monroe?" Kendall said.

"Yeah," Monroe said.

"Did you bug my room, too?"

Monroe sighed. He felt like throwing up. "Yeah," he said.

"Wow," Kendall said.

"You're in big trouble, asshole," Westcott said. "Shouldn't go around blackmailing people if you have your own skeletons to keep in the closet."

"Boy," Thomas said. "And here you kept telling me all of *my* friends were fucked up."

"Your friends are fucked up," Westcott grumbled. "And that asshole in there, he's not my friend. In fact, he doesn't even have any friends."

"Sure he does," Kendall said. "I'm his friend."

"You are now," Westcott said. "But you weren't when you were all picked for this assignment. Or did you never wonder why Henderson chose you bunch of nitwits?"

"I don't know what you mean," Kendall said.

"You're all a bunch of freaks," Westcott spewed. "Loners. Weirdos. The people nobody else wants to work with. That's why you got this ridiculous project. Henderson didn't think you had a snowball's chance in hell of actually producing anything. He chose you guys so that when you failed, nobody would care if you lost your jobs over it. The fact that you idiots might actually pull this off is a minor miracle."

"But...that doesn't make any sense. The project was his idea. Why would he put people on it unless he thought they could pull it off?"

"It wasn't his idea. It came from upstairs somewhere. I don't know who He's hoping the project will fail so he can pin it on his superior and take his job from him."

"So we're here to fail," Monroe said from behind his door.

"Nobody's talking to you, asshole!" Westcott shouted. "Now get out here so I can strangle you!"

"I'm so confused," Kendall said. "Henderson doesn't want us to build an acoustic kitty?"

"Of course he doesn't, you moron," Westcott said.

"So why are you here?" Kendall said. "If you knew all this, why did you volunteer to help us?"

"Because he gets to spend lots of time with his friend out here in the boonies," Monroe said from behind the door. "He could sabotage the project and get away from his wife. For months on end."

"Wait," Thomas said. "Morton, is that true? You helped ruin these people's careers and took them away from their friends and family for months just to spend more time with me?"

Westcott hesitated. "Yes," he finally said.

"Oh," Thomas said, his voice cracking. "That's the sweetest thing anyone's ever done for me. You're a total prick, but that's so sweet."

"Excuse me, doctor," Ava said. She was back. "Arthur, open the door."

"And give me my gun," Coleman said. "I'm going to let her shoot you with it."

"Shut up, Coleman," Ava said. "Arthur, open the door."

Monroe said nothing. He leaned his back on the door and slid to the floor.

"Arthur, were you eavesdropping on all of us?" Ava asked. "On me?"

Monroe waited a long time before answering. "Yeah," he said.

"For how long?" she asked. Her voice was shaking, but whether it was from rage or crying, he couldn't be certain.

"A couple months," he said.

"Maybe I should just purchase a new sidearm," Coleman said.

"Arthur," Ava said. "Why?"

He considered her question for a moment. "I don't have a good reason," was all he could think of to say.

"That's not a very good answer, Arthur," she said. "You're sick. You're the worst kind of sick person. You make everyone believe you're good and honorable, and the entire time you're...you're doing something like this. Listening to people's private lives for, what, your entertainment? To satisfy some kind of...perversion? You invaded our private lives, Arthur." When she spoke again, her tone was harsher and she started spitting out her words. "I think...you owe us...at least...a reasonable *explanation!*"

"That's what I keep saying!" Westcott blurted.

"Shut up!" Ava and Thomas said at once.

Westcott glared at Thomas. "I wanted to hear her finish," Thomas said. "This is getting good."

"I didn't want to hurt you," Monroe said.

"And to think..." Ava said, but didn't continue. "I don't ever want to speak to you again. Ever! You *bastard!*" She slammed her hand against Monroe's door, then stormed off. She went into her room and slammed her door, hard.

Nobody spoke for a moment. Monroe felt like he'd been hit in the stomach with a baseball bat.

Coleman used his cane to rap on the door several times.

"Okay, pipsqueak, now that it's just us boys," Coleman said, "it really is time for me to shoot somebody. Go ahead and open up."

Monroe slowly stood back up, took a deep breath, and opened his door. He let it swing all the way open and left it there. He returned to the bed and sat back down on the end of it. "Gun's in the bottom drawer," he said, pointing to the dresser.

"I'm not going to have to dig under your unmentionables to get to it, am I?" Coleman asked.

"No. There's just a bunch of electronics stuff in there."

Coleman went to the dresser and pulled open a bottom drawer. "Ahh, come to papa," he said, lifting the revolver and kissing it. He turned to see Kendall and Westcott watching him. "Nothing wrong with love between a man and his firearm," Coleman said. "Not the same as…" he trailed off, gesturing toward Westcott and Thomas with the gun. He shivered. "Gives me the willies," he mumbled. "No offense."

"None taken," Thomas said, not meaning it.

"Are you going to shoot him?" Westcott asked.

"Want to," Coleman said. "Won't." He made sure the gun's safety was on, then tucked it into his slacks in the middle of his back.

"Then give it to me," Westcott said. "I'll shoot him."

"Don't think so. I just got it back."

"So he's just going to get away with this? At least bring him up on charges! What he did is a crime, isn't it?"

"I'm sure there's a crime in there somewhere," he said. "But I don't see a need to pursue."

"But he needs to be punished!" Westcott shouted.

Coleman gave Monroe a long look. Monroe simply sat on the end of the bed, staring at the floor.

"He has been," he said.

Chapter 28

The team left Monroe behind the next morning. He walked to the small diner next door to the motel; they ate elsewhere. Nobody bothered to tell him where. He didn't ask. For the first time since they arrived in Cape, he ate alone. He spent most of the time during breakfast looking out the window. Cars went by. Cars filled with people on their way to work. People without clouds over their heads. A part of him badly wanted to pay his bill, go outside, and just start walking, to see where he'd end up, where he'd make his fresh start.

Coleman had confiscated his listening station. He would have destroyed it if he hadn't been so impressed with its design. He thought somebody was very likely to find it extremely useful at some point. He'd noticed that one of the settings on the dial had been labeled with the letters "CA" and asked who they were. When Monroe had told him those were for Carmelita, he had said, "Good man," but didn't explain the comment any further.

It had taken a while for Coleman to convince Westcott that Monroe did not need to go to jail in order to "learn his lesson." Westcott had threatened to call the police, but as Coleman had pointed out, they'd already removed all the bugs and the chain of evidence was broken. Any decent lawyer would have the existence of the bugs thrown out of court.

Monroe wasn't entirely certain why Coleman had gone to such effort to protect him. Maybe he didn't believe in going against a fellow employee of the Agency. Maybe he didn't feel as violated as some of the others because he knew he never did anything remotely interesting in his room. Or maybe he simply didn't like Westcott and was getting even for the man having taken his gun away. As usual with Coleman, his motivations were a total mystery. Monroe figured that field agents probably prefer it that way.

Regardless of the reason, Monroe was grateful. He never really expected that he'd get caught – although in hindsight, the notion of never being caught now seemed entirely ludicrous – so the idea of possibly ending up in prison had simply never crossed his mind. Once Westcott started talking about it, suddenly the threat of prison time had seemed extremely real. Monroe wouldn't last a day in jail. He was certain that he'd end up somebody's entirely-too-skinny girlfriend. He wanted to thank Coleman for watching out for him, but he had the feeling that Coleman was not a person who ever really enjoyed being thanked.

Kendall hadn't said much to him. He'd seemed mostly confused by the entire thing, rather than angry. Kendall was one of the rare people on the planet with nothing to hide. He, like Coleman, hadn't had to worry about Monroe discovering anything embarrassing or damaging.

Monroe had considered knocking on Kendall's door last night, after Coleman had taken away all the equipment and everyone finally left. If any of them would have been willing to talk to him, it would have been Kendall. But Monroe hadn't gotten the courage. He felt ashamed, exposed. He'd once read that people with huge secrets often feel better after their secrets have been uncovered, because they at least could then live honestly and no longer worry about being caught. As far as Monroe was concerned, that theory was a steaming pile of shit.

He felt the worst about Ava. Because he couldn't find the courage to open the door and face her, he hadn't seen her since they got back to the motel after dinner. He seemed fairly certain that he was unlikely to ever see her again. That was what hurt the most. He had hoped that he at least would still be allowed to work with her, at least until the project was over, but when Coleman had called him in his room that morning and told him that he wouldn't be accompanying them to the lab that day, even that small glimmer of clear sky had clouded over.

Monroe paid his bill at the diner and walked outside. It was sunny, but not overly hot. The cars continued to speed by on the two-lane highway in front of him. He wondered briefly if he should simply walk out in front of one of them and get it over with. As unhappy as he was, though, he wasn't that unhappy. He'd been alone before – most of his adult life – and he could go back to it. The project had always been temporary anyway. Besides, he assumed that being run over by a car likely would hurt like a motherfucker.

Monroe looked to his left, where the motel was, then looked to his right, which was the way toward the denser, more commercialized part of town. It was likely he could find a bank there, he reckoned, so it was in that direction, mid-morning on a Monday, that he started walking.

~

He happened to walk past a bank after about an hour and, on a lark, decided to go inside. The teller had looked at him like he was some kind of drifter. He wasn't surprised, considering he'd walked into a bank branch he'd never set foot in before, breathing hard and covered in sweat, and had handed over a check for $1,019.41, made out to "cash." According to his records, the withdrawal left him with exactly $13 left in his account. Monroe thought the number was somehow appropriate.

By early afternoon he'd stumbled across the bowling alley, and that seemed as good a place as any to stop and get off his feet for a while. He wished that he had at least had the wherewithal to go back to the motel and change into his tennis shoes before he set off walking however many miles he'd just walked. His loafers felt like cast iron on his feet, and he was certain that he'd developed blisters on both heels.

The bowling alley was air conditioned and felt wonderful. Much better than being outside, where the warm spring temperatures conspired with his long walk to render him soaked-through-the-shirt sweaty. The exercise as a whole had reminded him how out of shape he was.

Monroe wandered into the bar. He hadn't been there since the night Ava had picked a fight with…what was that guy's name? Dennis? Gary? Neither of those seemed right. Monroe hated how hard it was for him to remember names. Al? No.

He wondered if the bartender would recognize him and throw him out, but he did neither. There was one patron in the place, sitting at one end of the bar and watching the television. Monroe ordered a beer and sat at the other end. He saw that "General Hospital" was playing. A nurse was making out with a patient. She was hot. Only on television are nurses hot, he mused. The last time he was in the hospital, when he'd had his tonsils removed at 13, his nurses had been universally built like linebackers, elephants, or both.

"Stupid fuckin' tart," said the man at the other end of the bar. He was scruffy, harshly tanned, and indistinguishably middle aged. He looked like the type who was twenty years younger than he looked. His plaid flannel shirt looked like it had been neither washed nor ironed in quite a while, and his dark gray hair jutted in every imaginable direction. Monroe wondered if the man was homeless, senile, or both.

"Try to watch the language, Mel," drawled the bartender, a lanky man whose angular face was partially hidden under a short blonde beard. He had a grimy St. Louis Cardinals hat perched on his head. It was only slightly cleaner than his plain white t-shirt.

"It's a fuckin' bar, Frankie!" Mel protested. "Besides, she's a stupid fuckin' tart," he added, gesturing at the television. "Don't blame me."

"I got another paying customer, is all," Frankie said. "Try not to scare him off."

Mel shifted his weight so he could look at Monroe. "Hey there, fella. Didn't see you there. You mind if I call that retarded slut a stupid fuckin' tart?"

"The nurse?" Monroe asked. "Um, no."

"Thank you," Mel said. "Happy, Frankie?"

"Just watch your show, Mel," Frankie replied, leaning against the back bar and crossing his arms as he turned his attention back to the TV.

The nurse stopped kissing the patient. They talked for a while. She was telling him that she could never stay angry with him. She had spectacular breasts, half of which were exposed by her nurse's uniform. It was yet another blow to daytime television's reputation for realism.

"He fucked her sister, you know," Mel said. Monroe realized he was talking to him.

"The guy in the hospital bed?" Monroe asked.

"Yeah. The tart found out about it and chased them out of the house. They sped off in his car, and he ended up crashing. The slut sister dies – which I am personally pissed off about, because she had legs like you would not believe – and he gets cracked in the head. But he's been in a coma for a year now."

"That's some coma."

"Tell me about it. All from one lousy bump on the head. It's like these morons who write these shows don't know that it takes a little more than a little crack on the head to knock a guy out for an entire friggin' year. Anyway, so now, she realizes, now that he almost died, that she can't live without him, blah blah blah. So he fucks her sister, and she still loves him and is taking him back. Ergo, she's a fuckin' retard."

"Ergo?" Frankie asked in a mocking tone.

"Yeah," Mel replied. "Ergo. It's a fuckin' word. Latin. Get a vocabulary, will ya?"

Frankie waved a dismissive hand at Mel and returned to toweling off a glass he'd just cleaned.

"Maybe he's a good guy," Monroe said.

"Who, the coma guy?" Mel asked.

"Yeah."

"He fucked her sister! If I fucked my wife's sister – back when I had a wife – she'd have put my nuts in the blender, then made me drink 'em through a straw. Not that I'd want to fuck my wife's sister. My wife's sister looks like Art Carney."

"Maybe it was just a mistake…"

"No no no," Mel interrupted. "A mistake is forgetting to carry the one when you're doing your taxes. Doing the deed with your fiancee's sister, ho ho, that is something else entirely. Now granted, her sister was a filthy whore and practically shoved her goodies in his face until he had no choice but to play with 'em, but he did ultimately choose to play with 'em. It was not a mistake. It was a choice. This is something that people in this society today do not understand."

"Here we go," Frankie said. "The poor choice lecture."

Mel ignored him. "A poor choice is not a mistake," he said. "It is a poor choice, plain and simple, and when you make a poor choice, you have to live with the consequences. Hippies want to smoke pot and not get thrown in jail for it. Girls want to have sex and not get pregnant. Kids want to drop out of school and still make good money. But then people like this realize that they have completely and utterly screwed up their lives, and they want other people to bail them out of their messes because, according to them, they simply made a mistake, and they shouldn't have to live screwed-up lives because of it. Well, too bad. Life does not work that way." Having finished, Mel took a sip off his drink and looked back at the TV. The nurse and coma patient were gone, replaced by a middle aged couple arguing about something. "Speaking of filthy whores," he said, pointing to the woman and disregarding the fact that nobody had actually been speaking of filthy whores, "that one's the worst. She's got forty years of whoring under her belt. Whore!"

"You'd still fuck her," Frankie said.

"Damn straight," Mel replied, holding up his glass in a toast and taking another sip. "Whores know what they're doing."

"You'll have to forgive him," Frankie said to Monroe. "He likes to lecture when he's drunk."

"I am not drunk," Mel said.

"Yeah, and I'm Mickey Mantle," Frankie retorted.

"It's okay," Monroe said. "I actually agree with him."

"Oh, sweet Jesus, don't tell him that," Frankie said. "You'll never get him to shut up now."

"Frankie," Mel said, "I like you. I really do. But fuck you. And I need another." He pushed his glass forward.

"So you're here a lot?" Monroe asked.

"Here and there," Mel said.

"Every day," Frankie corrected. He placed a fresh glass in front of Mel and poured scotch into it. "I think he don't have a TV at his place or something."

"First of all," Mel said, pulling the glass of scotch toward him, "it's 'doesn't have a TV,' and second, I actually do own a television, thank you very much. I simply enjoy getting out of the house once in a while."

"So you come here every day?" Monroe asked.

"Here and there," Mel said, sipping his scotch.

"I don't want to seem rude, but...do you work?"

"I do not," Mel said. "Used to. Got tired of it."

Monroe decided not to press the topic. "I can understand," he said, sipping his beer. "What kind of work did you do, when you were working?"

Mel's eyes were on the TV. He didn't answer at first. Monroe started to wonder if he was going to. "I was a minister," he said.

"Really?"

"Really," he said. "First United Baptist Church. I assume you're not from around here?"

"No."

"Mmm. It's not far from here. On the south end of town. Nice church. Nice people. A few whores here and there, but that can't be helped. Whores like to go to church. Helps them forget they're whores."

"You remind me of a friend of mine," Monroe said.

"Your friend a whore?"

"No. But I'm guessing he holds them in the same esteem you do."

"Sounds like a smart fellow. Well, I see I've chatted my way right up to the commercial break, so I am going to take a break of my own. Be right back, gentlemen, and no, Frankie, you may not take my glass."

"Try not to get it on your shoes, old-timer," Frankie said.

"Fuck you, Frankie."

Frankie chuckled as he went back to cleaning glasses. Mel headed for the bathroom.

"He's a character," Monroe said. His beer was almost empty.

"You can say that," Frankie said. "You ready for another?"

"Yeah, what the hell. Hit me."

Frankie held a clean glass under the tap and poured Monroe's beer. "We keep an eye out for him here," he said.

"Mel?"

"Yeah. Poor guy, his wife died in a car accident a few years ago. Happened right out in front of the alley here. Some drunk was going the wrong way, hit her head-on. Middle of the afternoon."

"Jesus."

"He stuck with the minister thing for a while. That church is the biggest one in town. Everybody was, you know, trying to make him feel better and all that. But they never had kids, so he really didn't have nothing left, you know? About a month later, he started showing up here. First it was just once a week, then a couple days, then he just up and quit the church and started planting himself here every day. Started watching the soaps because his wife was addicted to them, from what he says. He says he likes being here because he feels Clara here. That's his wife. Was his wife, I should say. Anyway, he just hangs out here now, every day, and that's about it."

"Poor guy."

"Shit, I'm surprised he lasted this long. As much scotch as he's put away over the last couple years, his liver can't be in good shape. One day he ain't gonna show up, ya know? I just hope he don't keel over in here."

"He must really miss his wife."

"Suppose so. He can't let her go. My wife, hell, I'd love to let her go. I'd pack her damn bags. But he don't wanna let go of Clara. I told him he should find himself some nice widow to take him in and cook him dinner and stuff. But he always says no. Says he'd rather be here with just a tiny bit of Clara than be somewhere else with all of some other woman. Ask me, he's crazy. But hey, he pays his tab, so what do I care?"

"Where does he get the money from, if he hasn't worked in all that time?"

"Life insurance. He showed me the check once, before he cashed it. I guess he figures he won't last as long as the money."

"He must have been really attached to her," Monroe said.

"I guess. Maybe he just wanted an excuse to chuck it all and be a drunk. No pressure in that."

"I suppose not."

"Hell, I'd do it m'self if I didn't have a kid. Bein' a drunk, shit, that's easy."

Monroe saw Mel's reflection in the bar's mirror as he returned from the john. He dropped onto his stool and swung his legs around so he was facing the TV again. "Frankie, you retard," he said. "I told you not to take my glass."

"I didn't," Frankie said. "It's right in front of you, you old shit. Use your eyes."

Mel looked harder at the bar. "Oh. Sure enough." He lifted the glass and sipped his scotch. "I'd apologize if I liked you."

Frankie looked at Monroe and rolled his eyes.

"So, my friend," Mel said, looking over at Monroe, "what brings you into this rather loathsome establishment this afternoon? I know it wasn't the soaps. Or the service."

Frankie flipped him the bird. Mel didn't bother to look.

"I just ended up here," Monroe said. It was the truth.

"At 2 o'clock in the afternoon? People don't drink at 2 o'clock in the afternoon without a good reason. You get fired today or something?"

"I guess you could say that."

"Son, being employed is like being pregnant. You either are or you aren't."

"I think I might be fired. If not already, then soon. I suppose technically I'm still employed."

"And you aren't there because?"

"Very, very bad day at the office," Monroe said, drinking his beer.

"Mmm," Mel said. "Frankie, set me up here. I'm dry."

"Sir, yes sir," Frankie said flatly, grabbing a bottle of scotch.

"You're too young to give up, you know," Mel said to Monroe.

"I didn't say I was giving up," Monroe said.

"You look like you're giving up," Mel said. "Look at you. What did you do, wrestle a bear in the parking lot? You're not the kind of guy who drinks at 2 o'clock in the afternoon."

"Neither are you."

"Sure I am. Watch me," Mel said. He slurped his drink loudly.

Monroe opened his mouth to speak, but thought better of it and took a sip of his beer instead.

"What?" Mel asked.

"Nothing."

"Speak your mind, son. Otherwise you end up going through life pissed off."

Monroe took another sip. "Never mind."

Mel stared at him for a long moment. Monroe waited for him to look away, but he didn't. He could see the older man out of the corner of his eye. Mel was just sitting there, staring at the side of Monroe's head.

Finally, Monroe couldn't take it any more. "You won't like it," he said.

"Take your best shot," Mel said.

"You gave up. That's what I was going to say. It's not a very nice thing to say, so I didn't want to say it. But you made me be the bad guy and say it anyway."

Mel snorted out a laugh. "I didn't make you do anything. I just wanted to know what you said."

"Well, it wasn't a very nice thing to say, so I'm sorry," Monroe snapped.

Mel thought for a moment. "Maybe I did give up. What do you think, Frankie?"

"You gave up," Frankie said.

"Okay, yeah, looks like I gave up," Mel said. "You were right. No shame in that. So what do you think?" He held out his arms, showing himself to Monroe. "Does it suit you? This is what giving up is."

"I'm not giving up," Monroe said. "I'm…taking a break."

"Oh," Mel said. "Man's just taking a break," he said to Frankie. "Okay then. All right. I'll get off your case."

"Thank you."

"When are you leaving?"

"Excuse me?"

"When. Are. You. Leaving?"

Monroe shrugged. "I don't know. I'm only on my second beer."

"So you're going back to work tomorrow."

"I don't know. Geez. Are you always this nosy?"

"Frankie, am I always this nosy?"

"Yes," Frankie said. "That's why nobody else ever comes in here."

"Looks like you were right again, my friend," Mel said to Monroe. "So? When you going back to work?"

"Why do you care?"

"I don't. So when are you going?"

"I don't know! Geez! Just let me drink my beer, okay?"

"Come on, Mel," Frankie said. "Guy's a paying customer. Leave him alone. Just watch your shows, a'right?"

"Sorry," Mel said, holding up his hands and trying to look as offended as possible. "Just having a conversation. I will go back to watching my shows, as you so deprecatingly refer to them."

The three of them fell silent for a few minutes. Frankie focused on washing a few more glasses, while Monroe and Mel sipped their drinks. "Dark Shadows" was playing. Monroe watched it, even though he'd never even heard of the show and had no idea what was going on. The few minutes he watched were incredibly bad. He marveled that anybody could stand to watch it at all.

Mel shifted in his chair and looked at Monroe. "Why did you say I've given up? Did Frankie spill my life story to you?"

"Uhh…" Monroe stammered, looking at Frankie, not wanting to get the bartender in trouble.

"I just told him about Clara, that's all, Mel," Frankie said.

"Mmm," Mel said. He looked back at the TV and took another drink.

"I'm sorry about your wife," Monroe said.

"Me too," Mel replied, still looking at the TV.

"Think you'll ever go back to the church?" Monroe asked. "Go back to work?"

"It's possible," Mel said, "but I strongly doubt it. Too many whores."

They fell silent again.

"She was everything to me," Mel said, still looking at the TV. "She kept it all going. We were together for 36 years."

"I'm sorry you lost her," Monroe said.

"Yeah," Mel said. "But I'd do it all over again, even knowing she'd be taken from me too soon. Was worth it."

Monroe looked down at his glass. "I eavesdropped on my friends, and now they all hate me," he said.

Mel looked at Monroe. "I assume there's more to the story than that."

"I eavesdropped by planting bugs in their motel rooms."

"Bugs? Like James Bond? Little microphones?"

"Yeah. That's what I do for a living. I make bugs."

"Well no shit," Mel said, openly impressed. "This is getting good. So why did you put bugs in their rooms?"

Monroe shrugged. "I don't know. It's what I do."

"Jesus, don't start bullshitting me now," Mel said, swinging around to face Monroe. "You can do better than that."

"I suppose…I like it."

"I think we all knew that already. Why?"

"I don't know. I…I guess because I don't have any friends. I don't have anyone to talk to. I like hearing about people, what they're doing."

"I thought you said your friends hated you. Then you say you don't have friends. You lost me."

"I didn't have friends. Then I started working on this…project. I got to know some of them, and we got to be friends. I told myself that I'd stop listening to them, but it never really happened. I kept on listening. Last night, they found the bugs, and this morning they all went to work without me. So I guess I'm off the project now, and what few friends I had are probably not my friends any more."

"Have you talked to them about it? Tried to apologize?"

"No."

"Why not?"

"What's the point? They caught me spying on them. I invaded their privacy. Would you talk to someone if you found out he spied on you?"

"Maybe. Maybe not. Depends on the circumstances."

"You're a minister."

"*Was* a minister," Mel corrected. "What's your point?"

"You're supposed to be forgiving. You know, like Jesus."

"Look, you asked me a question, I answered it. I might trust that person again. Other people might not. But you never know, and you'll really never know if you don't go back to work and face those people again."

Monroe took another long drink from his beer. "I don't think so."

"What's the worst they could do?"

"You don't know my friends."

Mel sighed. "Okay. I tried. But if you're ever going to have a chance with her, you should go back."

"Well, I…hey, I didn't say anything about a her," Monroe said.

"What am I, retarded? Of course there's a her. Men never worry about whether other men trust them. None of us trust each other, period. Trust is only an issue with women, mostly because no woman's going to screw you if she doesn't trust you. Is she pretty?"

Monroe realized that it was becoming pointless for him to continue denying the existence of a her. "Yeah," he said.

"Nice tits?"

"You don't talk like a minister."

"I'm not a minister any more. Jesus. Get over it. So, does she have nice tits?"

"I don't…I'm not answering that."

Mel gave Frankie an incredulous look. "I'm not asking you her favorite position, kid," he said to Monroe. "I just want to know if she has a nice rack."

"They're good, yeah. Happy?"

"You should bring her down here. Sounds like a nice gal. Not sure why she's tangled up with the likes of you."

"Well, she's not. So don't expect to see her here."

"Don't give up on her, kid. That's all I'm saying. Of course, if you do give up on her, at least I have a new drinking buddy. I wore my last one out."

"What do you mean?"

"There used to be another regular here for years," Frankie said. "Cyrus McCready."

"Good old Cyrus," Mel said.

"What happened to him?"

"He died," Frankie said. "Liver failure. Right where you're sitting, actually."

Monroe looked down at his stool. He slid his beer over and moved onto the next one to his right.

Chapter 29

Monroe spent the night in a motel near the bowling alley. He wished that he had packed his stuff and brought it with him. Walking back for it seemed like too much hassle, and taking a cab would cut into his precious drinking money, so he decided to just wear the same clothes for a few days, then weigh his options.

That was his new attitude. One day, one minute at a time. Don't worry about anything that's not a problem right now.

The lack of wardrobe change did not go unnoticed the next day at the bar. Mel didn't seem surprised that Monroe was back for a second day, but he did give him trouble about smelling funny, even though Monroe couldn't detect any odor himself. He sniffed hard at his pits every time he went to the bathroom, but detected nothing. He decided Mel was either making it up or smelling his own brand of old-drunk scent.

The few days after that started to blur. Monroe got drunk each day, ate bowling-alley food for dinner, then continued drinking until he was fairly certain that he was starting to embarrass himself. Unfortunately, the alcohol blurred his judgment as well as his speech, and in reality he embarrassed himself each night long before he bothered to notice that he was drunk.

After that first day, Mel stopped pushing Monroe to return to work. The topic didn't even come up in conversation. Monroe had felt better after admitting out loud that he'd spied on his friends, but he still didn't feel good. He tried not to think about it. That got easier with each passing day and each passing drink.

By the third night, Monroe felt at home. He had started to get a feel for the flow of the alley, the way it was sparsely populated during the day, but overflowing with people of all walks of life at night. Families, couples, partiers, white collar, blue collar, they all came to bowl. And from their permanent seats at the bar, Mel and Monroe made fun of almost every one of them. Mel also went to great pains to discuss the bodies of the female patrons and which of them would look best in a cavegirl outfit.

During the days, Monroe started to follow the soaps. Mel caught him up on all the back stories, having watched every episode of his favorites – or at least, Clara's favorites – for the last couple years. Monroe kept expecting that he would, at some point, start enjoying the shows, but he soon came to realize that soap opera scripts were universally atrocious and clearly intended to entertain only those who were willing to ignore the preposterousness of, say, a woman's long-lost (and diabolically evil) identical twin arriving in town exactly one hour after her sister was struck by a car and knocked into a coma while traveling alone in Tahiti.

Despite his distaste for the absurd shows, Monroe never said a disparaging word about them. He felt it was the least he could do for the memory of Mel's wife.

On the third night, Monroe and Mel were ignoring the TV. Once the bar became relatively full, the noise of the crowd made it impossible to hear anything on the aging Zenith, and "Gunsmoke" just didn't work as a silent movie.

Monroe was enjoying the new outfit he'd bought for himself that day. Tired of wearing the same clothes, and realizing he needed something to change into if he ever hoped to take the first outfit to a laundromat, he'd walked to a small men's clothing store near his new motel. The store was run by a shriveled man in a ridiculously large cowboy hat, and accordingly, most of the clothing in the store seemed best suited for wearing to a cattle drive. It had taken him some time, but eventually Monroe found a plain white button-down shirt and a pair of jeans. It was the first pair of blue jeans he could remember wearing since he was in high school. And to top it off, he'd splurged on a $50 pair of honest-to-goodness shit-kicking cowboy boots. He couldn't decide if they looked ridiculous on him or if he simply wasn't accustomed to seeing himself in anything besides loafers and tennis shoes. But it was a change, a big change, so he went with it.

As he sat on his stool with his back to the bar, he caught Mel looking at his new boots for what seemed like the twentieth time. "Come on," Monroe said. "You know you want a pair."

"I do not," Mel replied. "I merely am fascinated by how much of a fairy you look like in them."

"You know, God hears you when you say things like 'fairy.'"

"Fuck off," Mel said.

Monroe wiggled his boot-laden feet. "I'm starting to think I like them," he said. "They make me taller. They're comfortable, too."

"I'm sure the boys in the bath houses will love them," Mel said, looking back out over the bar. A woman with an extra-healthy pair of hips was leaning over the pool table, trying to line up a shot. "Whoa ho ho," Mel said. "Now that is my kind of caboose."

Monroe looked. "You have lousy taste," he said.

"Gotta have something to hang onto, my friend," Mel said. "Besides, girls with big butts are a little more grateful to have you around. Show me a girl who looks like Marilyn Monroe and I'll show you a slut who can't stay in the same bed for more than a month. Hey, you related to her?"

"Marilyn Monroe?"

"Yeah. You have the same last name."

"Hers was fake. Her real name was Norma Jean Baker."

"No shit?" Mel said. "Hmph. I didn't know that. So every time I pretended my wife was Marilyn Monroe, I was imagining that I was screwing a girl named Norma?"

"Norma Jean, yeah."

Mel grunted. "And so, my life gets just a tiny bit more depressing," he said, taking a sip of his scotch.

Monroe grinned. He was fairly drunk, he realized. Little surprise, considering he'd been drinking since 2 p.m. and it had to be getting close to 8:00.

A large man walking into the bar caught his attention. The guy was big, with a gut large enough to shade a water buffalo. He looked dirty, like he hadn't showered in a couple days, and his sleeveless t-shirt had what appeared to be a large coffee stain in the middle of the back. The man crossed the bar to the pool table, upon which he set a quarter to indicate that he wanted to play the winner. As he did, Monroe noticed that the man had a nasty welt in the middle of his forehead, just under the spot covered by his grimy mesh baseball cap.

Monroe froze.

George. His name was George.

He was the guy Ava had beaten at pool a few weeks before. The one Coleman had hit with a pool cue and head-butted into oblivion.

And he was headed straight toward the bar.

Monroe whirled around quickly and faced the bar, putting his head down.

"You about to get sick or something?" Mel asked.

"No. Don't talk to me for a second."

"What the hell did I do?"

"Nothing. Just…hang on, I'll explain in a minute. Shh."

George ambled up to the bar. He was standing right next to Mel.

"Budweiser," George said to Frankie.

"You're shushing me?" Mel said. It occurred to Monroe that Mel might even be drunker than he was. "Can't shush a man without good cause, son."

Monroe said nothing and kept his head down.

"What the hell is the matter with you? You're about to throw up, admit it."

"Hey," Frankie said as he finished pouring George's beer, "if you're gonna puke, Artie, you need to take it into the bathroom."

"Will you guys both just shut *up*," Monroe said, trying to keep his voice down.

"Don't you tell me to shut up," Mel said. "I'll kick your balls straight out of your nut-sack, smart guy."

Monroe looked up. "Mel, just be quiet for a one damn minute, will you? I don't want…" His eyes darted to George's face and he froze in mid-sentence.

George was looking right at him.

"Don't want what?" Mel spat. "My foot in your ass? 'Cause I'm not gonna feel bad about putting it there. Done it before."

George kept staring at Monroe, who was too terrified to look away. Suddenly, George's eyes didn't exactly widen, but did become noticeably less beady. "I know you," he said, wagging a finger in the air.

Mel spun around and looked up at George. "Who, me?"

"No," George said. He pointed at Monroe. "Him."

"Oh," Mel said. He looked back and forth between Monroe and George. "Really? No offense, buddy, but you guys don't look like you're from the same parish, you know?"

"You owe me eighty bucks, shithead," George growled. "You and that bitch friend of yours."

"Did he just call me a bitch?" Mel asked.

"It was only sixty," Monroe stammered. "She gave one of the twenties back to you."

"Where is she?" George said. He turned and began scanning the bar.

"She's not here," Monroe was relieved to say.

"That's too bad," George growled. "I was looking forward to breaking her face."

"Artie, you have strange friends," Mel said.

"Shut up," George ordered. "You owe me eighty bucks, buddy," he said to Monroe. "Either you pay in cash or you pay in bones."

Normally, Monroe never carried more than ten in his wallet. Fresh off his shopping spree, however, he thought that he might still have eighty in there. He dug through his wallet, frantically counting bills.

He pulled a stack of them out and put them on the bar, pushing them toward George. "Here," he said. "Eighty dollars. You can count it."

George continued staring at Monroe.

"Go on, take the money, go find a nice girl to assault," Mel said, pushing the stack even closer to George.

Without looking away from Monroe, George reached out and took the money. He shoved it into the pocket of his jeans. "So I guess you decided to pay in broken bones, huh?" he said. "Fine with me."

"Hey," Mel said. "You just took the man's cash. It's in your damn pocket. Get lost."

George's glare shifted from Monroe to Mel. "I thought I told you to shut up," he said.

"And I told you to get lost," Mel said, turning his back to the man and facing Monroe. He thumbed over his shoulder in George's direction. "Ten bucks says he's from Kentucky," he said.

Before Monroe could realize it was happening, George had grabbed Mel by the shoulders and thrown him halfway across the bar. Mel yelped in pain as he landed hard on the floor and slid into a beer-laden table.

There was nothing between Monroe and George. Monroe got to his feet, knocking his barstool over in the process as he tried to edge away from the enormous man. Panic was starting to well up inside him. He hadn't been in a fistfight since he was in the second grade. And even then, he'd been pummeled. He wondered how much it was going to hurt when George started pounding him. He wondered if he would even be conscious, or alive for that matter, by the time George finished.

Everyone was yelling. Frankie was yelling something about taking it outside. Others were yelling the word "fight" repeatedly.

Mel had found his lungs again and was yelling something about boots.

The boots. Monroe was wearing boots. Cowboy boots.

Shit-kicking boots.

And then, a thing happened.

In less than a heartbeat, everything welled up inside Arthur Monroe all at once. Anger, fear, frustration, rage, the project, the ass-whipping he'd received in second grade, the years of being ignored by women and tortured by men, and the improbable reality of his feet being clad in rock-solid cowboy boots, it all exploded in him, all at once. His eyes lost focus. His lips peeled back from his teeth.

George saw the look in Monroe's eyes. His own eyes widened as it occurred to him that he might just have made the classic bar-brawler's mistake of picking a fight with a crazy person. Not that this knowledge, gleaned just a moment too late, did him any good.

With the force of a sledgehammer and the speed of a championship boxer, Arthur shot his right boot forward and kicked George squarely in the testicles.

Hard.

Five times.

The gasp from the collection of onlookers seemed to suck every ounce of breathable air from the room. Everything went silent as George took a single step forward, his face turning a shade of red that seemed to deepen with each passing second, then crumpled in a heap on the floor.

Monroe gaped at the large man gasping for breath on the floor in front of him. All the rage, the hysteria, was suddenly gone, replaced by shaking legs and a growing sensation of nausea. After a moment, he realized that everyone in the bar was staring at him. Women's jaws were dropped. Men whistled in a combination of admiration for the swiftness of the victory and the empathy that every man feels when a fellow male has just been kicked squarely in the junk.

Near the door, Coleman was leaning on his cane and giving Monroe an enormous thumbs-up with his free hand.

Monroe blinked. "Coleman?"

"Affirmative!" he bellowed. "And nicely done, even though you look like a moron in those boots."

"That's what I said," Mel added, dusting himself off as he tried to get up.

"Hey! Assholes!" Frankie yelled from behind the bar. "Get out of my damn bar. Regulars or no, there's no fighting in here! Get out now or I call the cops!"

"Stand down, citizen," Coleman said. He jabbed his thumb into his chest. "Central Intelligence Agency." He looked around the room. Everyone was still watching. "Not that any of you should remember that," he said, waving his cane around. "Resume your questionable and potentially subversive activities."

"Guys," Frankie pleaded, "go on, get out of here." He pointed to George, who was still doubled over in pain. "He's gonna get up any minute now. Go tear up somebody else's joint."

"Come on, pipsqueak," Coleman said to Monroe. "You're with me."

"You know this guy?" Mel asked.

"Uh...yeah," Monroe said. "He's one of the people I work with."

Mel's eyebrows shot up. "So you really are with the CIA?"

"Yeah," Monroe said. "I told you that."

"I know, but I never believed you."

"Gee, thanks."

"You told him you're CIA?" Coleman asked.

"Yeah," Monroe said. "So? You just announced it to the entire bar."

"That's different. I'm armed. Who's this?"

"Oh. Sorry. Coleman, this is Mel. Mel, Agent Wyman Coleman."

"Any friend of Artie's is a friend of mine," Mel said, offering his hand.

Coleman shook it. "I enjoy shooting things," he said.

"I enjoy drinking things," Mel said.

The two men stared at each other for a moment.

"Let's go," Coleman said to Monroe.

"Where are we going?" Monroe asked.

"Lab. We hit a snag and need your help. And the fat one keeps whining about you and I'm about to shoot him in the head twenty times to make him stop. Figured this was the better solution."

"But...I thought I was fired. Everyone hates me."

"True on both points. But the first one was never really made official, and the second one, it's mostly the girl and Doctor Twinkletoes who are still mad at you. They'll get over it."

"Guys," Mel said, looking at George, "he's getting up."

"Excuse me," Coleman said. He hobbled over to George, who was laboring to his feet but had only made it about halfway up. Coleman smacked him on the shoulder, and he looked up.

"Remember me?" Coleman asked.

George was in too much pain to speak, but the low moan he made indicated that he did indeed recognize the man standing over him.

"Good," Coleman said. "Just checking." He quickly reached down and pinched a hunk of the large man's shoulder. An instant later, George dropped back to the floor with an enormous thud, out cold.

"What the hell was that?" Mel said, staring at George's limp form. "Did you kill him?"

"Pinky finger," Coleman said, holding the digit in question upright. "Fear not, he's alive. Agency frowns on killing on domestic soil. That pinky finger trick was something I learned from a double agent in Prague. She was attractive. We had sex. So," he said to Monroe, "we're off then."

"Coleman, I don't know if I can go back," Monroe said.

"Nonsense," Coleman said. "And I'm not asking."

"I'm not sure I can face everybody again. I don't want to go. Maybe I should just go home."

"I really don't want to have to shoot you, but…actually, shooting you might be fun. In the leg, maybe?"

"Let's not go crazy shooting folks here," Mel said. "Look. Artie. You need to go. Go and face it and move on."

"Mel…"

"Shut up. Listen. I know you regret what you did. You should. But you're a solid guy. Weird as shit, and a lousy dresser, but a solid guy. If you don't go and face this, you start to forfeit that a little. At least go try to make it right. If it doesn't work out, hey, you can come back here. Shit, you should come back here anyway. And bring the girl. I wanna see those titties for myself."

"They're nice," Coleman said.

"So I hear," Mel replied.

"He's sweet on her," Coleman said, jabbing a thumb toward Monroe.

"You think he has a shot?"

"Not at all."

"Okay, guys, that's enough," Monroe said. He sighed deeply and ran his hand through his hair. "Fine," he said. "Let's go, I guess."

"Good man," Coleman and Mel said simultaneously. They gave each other an odd look, like old men who begin to suspect that they may somehow be related.

"What about him?" Monroe asked, looking at George's prone form by the bar.

"I'll buy him a beer when he comes to," Mel said. "I'd recommend you gents be long gone by then."

"Good idea," Monroe said. "Okay, Coleman. Let's go."

Chapter 30

"You missed a lot," Coleman said once they were in the van.

"I've only been gone three days," Monroe replied.

"CIA works fast," Coleman said. "Not a lot of time here, so I'll brief you quickly. Chubby figured out a device to keep kitty from getting the munchies. Doc got it implanted just fine, but since then, kitty isn't eating."

"He isn't eating?"

"Affirmative. Had to put him on a tube. Intravenous feedings, four times a day."

"Geez."

"Son, we don't say 'geez' in Field Ops."

"Sorry."

"We also don't say 'sorry.' Much worse than 'geez.' Sign of weakness. When we're sorry about something, we shoot."

"Maybe we can focus on continuing to get me up to speed."

"Ah yes. Excellent tactic. So the kitty is not doing well, but it is getting better at following orders."

"Okay. That's good."

"Walks sort of crooked, but otherwise works fine."

"So what was the problem that made you come get me?"

"Yesterday, we took kitty to the roof for an outdoor test. Everything was working, until kitty got more than about 20 feet away. After that, we couldn't hear anything from the bug. Range is too limited."

"That's strange," Monroe said. "I reduced the power output on the bug so that it wouldn't kill the cat if it shorted out. I didn't think it would reduce the effective range down to 20 feet, though. It shouldn't, anyway. There must be something else going on."

"Chubby kept saying that he wouldn't know how to rewire one of your bugs to see what was wrong."

"He's not chubby."

"Don't start with me, soldier. Doc said at this point there's not enough time to pull the current bug out and put a new one in anyway. And he doesn't think kitty would survive another operation in his current state. We're stuck."

"Okay."

"Son, I could use a little more reassurance than 'okay.' You gonna be able to fix this?"

"I don't know. I'll need to run some diagnostics. I need to figure out what's causing the problem first."

"I'm still not reassured."

"It's the best I can tell you for now. Hey, so why is Westcott still helping out? His secret is out. We lost our leverage."

"Son, you underestimate the formidable nature of an extremely pissed off woman. Chubby told Ava about Westcott setting up this whole field trip just so he could have playtime with that other fella. She convinced him that it was in his best interest to keep helping."

"What did she do, threaten to shoot him?"

"No, but that would have been my suggestion. She threatened to tell his wife."

"Oh yeah. I forgot about her. I should have thought of that."

"The entire affair has led me to decide never to cross Ava. Frightening woman when angered."

"I know."

Coleman glanced at Monroe. After a moment, he said, "I believe her also to be forgiving."

"I don't know about that. I'm not going to count on it, that's for sure."

"Buck up, soldier. You'll just have to win her over. I'm happy to give you tips on how to do it."

Monroe laughed. Coleman stared at him.

"Oh," Monroe said. "You were serious."

"Field agents are trained in the art of persuasion."

"Do any of your tips not involve a gun?"

Coleman thought for a moment. "No."

"Great," Monroe replied.

They drove in silence for a bit.

"Caused a bit of a ruckus when we figured out you were gone," Coleman said. "Tried you at home, tried you at work, tried you at your momma's house."

"Oh God," Monroe said. "You called my mom?"

"Affirmative. Pleasant gal. Sounds plump."

"Did you tell her I was missing?"

"Of course."

"Great. Now I'm going to get a thousand phone calls from her. I knew taking off would turn out to be a bad idea."

"Agreed. Running from problems is bad business, son. When in doubt, aim and fire."

"What else did you tell her?"

"Little. But she's right. You really should call her more often. Go visit at Christmas. That sort of thing. A good man is good to his mother. I take flowers to my mother every Sunday."

"Not since you've been on this project."

Coleman fell silent for a moment. "Shit," he said.

"How did you know I was at the bowling alley?"

"Central Intelligence Agency," Coleman said

"No, really. How did you find me?"

"You weren't at home, weren't at work, weren't in your hotel, weren't at momma's. It was the only place left that I could think of. I was going to start checking the morgues next. Unpleasant business, checking morgues. Once encountered a live octopus in a morgue in Bombay."

"So you got lucky."

"Nothing lucky about finding an octopus in a morgue."

"No, I meant you got lucky when you found me at the bowling alley."

"Son, if there is one thing that is completely absent at the Central Intelligence Agency, it's luck."

"You got me there."

The conversation took another pause as Monroe gazed out the window. He realized they were getting close to the lab. "So," he said, "how's Ava?"

"Seems healthy. She's a sturdy woman."

"No, I meant...you know, never mind."

They fell silent again. This time it was Coleman who spoke first. "She hasn't said much the last few days," he said. "Chubby keeps trying to cheer her up. Isn't really working."

"She's not going to be very happy to see me."

"Agreed."

"I'm nervous."

"You have good reason to be. She might hit you. If she asks for my gun, I'll have no choice but to give it to her. Women have the right to shoot people, too, you know. Susan B. Anthony and all that."

"Is that supposed to make me feel better?"

Coleman considered this. "No. Should it?"

"No," Monroe said, looking out the window. "I guess not."

~

It was after 9 p.m. when the van pulled into the alley. Coleman explained that the team felt it was under the gun, with Henderson arriving in just a few days, so everyone had agreed to work into the night.

"Are you sure everybody really wants me to come back?" Monroe said as they got out of the van and began climbing the fire escape. "I left. I abandoned everyone. And what I did...spying on everyone...that was really bad."

"True. But we can't do this without you. No other choice."

"You could have called in one of the other guys from Langley. I'm not the only bug guy in the Agency."

"Calling in another bug guy would have alerted Henderson that there were problems. Besides, you were already in town." He started climbing the ladder from the alley.

"Westcott said I got picked for this project because I'm a freak," Monroe said.

Coleman stopped climbing. "Affirmative," he said.

"Hard to find another expendable Agency guy who could build bugs, huh? Everybody else has wives and kids and friends, and it would be bad if they got fired. So it was better to track me down. Right?"

"Son," Coleman said, not looking down, "we all got picked for this mission for the same reason."

"Jimmy and me, you mean."

"No," Coleman replied. "All of us."

"Oh," Monroe said. "I always assumed you and Henderson worked together to select the team."

"Negative."

"Oh."

Neither man spoke for a moment. Then Coleman resumed climbing. "Time to get the job done, soldier," he said. "Quit your belly aching."

"Yes sir," Monroe said with little enthusiasm.

~

"Monroe!" Kendall shrieked from his workstation. He knocked over his stool in his rush to give Monroe a long and somewhat uncomfortable bear hug. "I never thought we'd see you again! Coleman, you found him! You're the best!"

"No hugs," Coleman warned.

Kendall finally stepped back and looked Monroe over from head to toe. "What's with the cowboy getup?"

"It's not a cowboy getup. I just bought some jeans and boots."

"Boots that have administered a glorious beating," Coleman interjected. "I was witness to it myself."

"You look like you're trying to be a cowboy," Kendall said. "It's going to be hard for you to be taken seriously as an engineer looking like a cowboy."

"I'm not...," Monroe began. He stopped in mid-sentence and sighed. "Coleman said you were having problems with Mr. President."

"Don't you want to know how I've been?" Kendall asked.

"Okay, sure. How have you been?"

"Shitty! You left me here with Coleman and Westcott. I can't believe you did that to me. Shithead!"

"I'm sorry," Monroe said. "And...I'm sorry about the thing with the bugs. In the motel."

Kendall waved his hand in a dismissive gesture. "What do I care? It's kinda creepy, but I'm not mad or anything. Just don't do it again. It isn't nice."

"Thanks, Jimmy," Monroe said, genuinely surprised. "I won't leave again. Promise." He held out his hand.

Kendall took it. His hand was sweaty and cold, a combination that Monroe found tremendously off-putting. He shook firmly anyway. "Listen," Kendall said, lowering his voice, "about all that stuff. Coleman and I are the forgiving type, but I don't think you're going to have as much luck with the medical community here. You might want to lay low as much as possible."

"Thanks," Monroe said. The tension in his stomach had immediately returned. "Where are they?"

"In the operating room. Giving Mr. President his IV feeding."

"Okay." He took a deep breath. "I guess if I'm going to run some diagnostics on the bug, I better get started, huh?"

"Affirmative," Coleman said. "Time's wasting. Come on." He led the way to the operating room. Monroe and Kendall followed.

They found Westcott and Ava – and to Monroe's surprise, Thomas – inside. They appeared to be removing the IV from the anesthetized cat.

"Found him," Coleman announced, getting their attention. Monroe found it hard to look them in the eye, but he forced himself to do it. When Westcott and Ava saw him, their expressions turned hard.

"Hi there," Thomas said with a wave.

"Don't be nice to him," Westcott snapped.

"Fuck off," Thomas said. "I don't have an axe to grind with the man. Besides, he has a boyish charm about him."

Monroe gave Coleman a confused look. "He knew all there was to know," Coleman said. "Figured we might as well let him hang around. He's been helping with the kitties. Besides, if he's here, he's not off running his mouth about it."

"And it is such a pleasure working with you, too," Thomas said.

"You're lucky I don't grab Coleman's gun and shoot you with it, you little freak," Westcott said to Monroe. "So let's just get one thing clear. I am not happy about having to work with you again. Just do your fucking job and stay out of my fucking way."

"You're over-using the word 'fuck,'" Thomas said. "It has less impact that way, you know."

Westcott ignored him. "I don't want to see you or hear you any more than I have to," he said. "And Coleman, I don't want him staying at the same motel or eating with us."

"You don't give the orders, Frankenstein," Coleman said.

"No, it's okay," Monroe said. "I don't blame him for being upset. I'll stay at the place by the bowling alley. I have a few things there already. I'll be fine." He was trying to see Ava's expression, but she was keeping her head down and doing her best to completely ignore him.

"So fix him, fuckhead," Westcott said, gesturing toward Mr. President. "That's what you're here for. Get to work." He stormed past them and went to his office, closing his door.

"I've always thought it was unfair that he was the only one who had an office," Kendall said.

"You really want to be around him all the time?" Coleman asked.

"Ah," Kendall replied. "Good thinking."

"Central Intelligence Agency."

Monroe approached the table where Mr. President lay. "Is he done?" he asked Ava. "Can I take him?" He watched her intently.

She didn't bother looking up at him, just continued putting away her instruments. "He's fed. You can take him. He needs to be fed again in about four hours. He should come around in about 30 minutes." There was an edge in her voice, and as she spoke, she began setting things down more loudly.

"Thanks," he said, scooping up Mr. President. "Ava..."

"Don't," she said. "I don't want to hear it. Go fix the problem."

"In case you hadn't noticed," Thomas said in a loud whisper, "she's insanely pissed off at you. Isn't she just so sexy when she's angry?"

"Thomas," Ava warned.

"I think she might be ragging, too," Thomas whispered loudly to Monroe, earning himself an even angrier glare from Ava.

Monroe said nothing as he took Mr. President out to the lab area. Kendall and Coleman followed.

"Boy was that awkward," Kendall said a little too loudly.

"Was it?" Coleman asked. "Damn, I wish I could tell."

Monroe set Mr. President down on his workstation. "So tell me again what's happening," he said.

"Oh," Kendall said. "Uh, well, when he gets more than 20 or 30 feet away from us, we lose the signal from the bug. We can't hear anything."

"Do you hear increased static, or just silence?"

"Static, definitely."

Monroe furrowed his brow. "I don't get it. It should transmit a clear signal for a couple hundred feet at least."

"Maybe it's broken," Coleman said.

"That's possible," Monroe said. "But then it likely wouldn't be transmitting a signal at all. Maybe the scar tissue around the bug is causing some kind of problem."

"Well, I do have one theory," Kendall said. "Maybe it's getting too much interference between the control array and the device we put in his stomach. The thing in his stomach...it gives off a steady series of electric pulses. Westcott said that would irritate the stomach enough so that he doesn't feel hunger pangs. Poor guy, his stomach must hurt all the time."

"Pain endured in the service of one's country is glorious," Coleman said to nobody in particular.

"I guess that could be it," Monroe said. "It could be as simple as an interference issue. I can think of one way to know for sure."

"An antenna," Kendall said.

"Yep," Monroe replied.

"Can't have an antenna sticking out of kitty's head," Coleman said. "Ruins the surprise."

"True," Monroe said. He studied the cat on the table in front of him, trying not to notice the numerous scars on his back and belly, and the splotchy fur that came as the result of being shaved in preparation for various procedures. "I suppose…maybe we could put it in his tail?" he said.

"Wouldn't it look weird if his tail was sticking straight up?" Kendall asked.

"Would make him easier to pick up," Coleman said. "Like a handle."

"I can just use a wire," Monroe said. "I wouldn't have to encase it. Assuming Westcott can put a wire in a cat's tail."

"Henderson will be here in three days," Kendall said. "Think that's enough time to do another surgery and get him back on his feet? Can he even survive another surgery?"

"I don't think we have a choice," Monroe said. "I guess I'll get to work on the antenna. Tell Westcott I should have it ready in a few hours at the most. He can do the surgery then. We'll have to take our chances."

"Okay," Kendall said, heading toward Westcott's office. "It's good to have you back, Art," he added.

"I wish everyone felt that way," Monroe said, too low for Kendall to hear.

"She'll come around," Coleman said.

"I doubt it."

"You're right. Give up. I was trying to be nice."

"Thanks."

Chapter 31

Westcott performed the operation in the wee hours of the night. Kendall and Coleman observed the operation, but Monroe passed the time by trying to sleep in Coleman's chair. He hadn't felt comfortable being in the same room as Ava. At least, he assumed that she would prefer he not be there.

He wasn't able to get any sleep. He wondered how it was possible for Coleman to sleep in the chair. It was hard, and the back was at a rigid 90-degree angle from the seat, forcing him to sit in it with his spine perfectly vertical. Leaning back didn't help, as it was difficult to lean without tipping over. He ultimately gave up and laid down on the floor.

As he lay there, listening to the sounds of low conversation coming from the operating room, a black cat approached him. Monroe watched as the cat sniffed around at his shirt, then looked intently at his armpit for several moments, and finally wandered toward his boots, which the cat licked several times.

"You better hope we all get fired, pal," he said. "You and all your buddies here."

The cat meowed at him.

"You could have an antenna in your tail," Monroe said to it. "And some weird shocker thing in your stomach. You'd be a nightmare on feet."

The cat stared.

"That doesn't bother you?"

The cat sat down, seemed to ponder something, then started gnawing on its haunches with more than a little sense of urgency.

"Well, it should," Monroe said.

The door to the operating room opened. Coleman, Kendall, Westcott and Thomas came out. Westcott said nothing and simply headed for the window. He opened it and climbed out.

Thomas waved at him. "Have a good night, Arthur," he said cheerfully.

"Bye," Monroe said quietly.

"Come on, pipsqueak," Coleman said. "Operation's done, nothing to do here tonight. We're heading back to the motel. I'll drop you off at your other place."

"You know, I'll just stay here," Monroe said. "I'll be fine."

Coleman and Kendall shared a look. "You sure?" Kendall asked. "Because, um, she's staying to watch Mr. President," he said, gesturing toward the operating room.

"Oh," Monroe said. He thought for a moment. "You know, I'll be fine. I'll stay out of her way."

Kendall started beaming. "I knew you guys would work it out," he said.

"Work what out?" Monroe asked. "Jimmy, nothing's been worked out. At all."

"Yeah, but it will. Okay, we'll see you. Come on, Coleman, let's leave them alone."

"Jimmy, relax," Monroe said. "There's nothing to leave us alone for."

"That's what you think. I've seen the way she's behaved the last few days. You destroyed her," he said with a huge grin.

"Gee, thanks, Kendall," Monroe said. "You really know how to cheer a guy up."

"You can't hurt somebody that bad unless she has a little something extra in her heart for you," Kendall said. "It's a good sign."

"Chubby, you sound like a greeting card," Coleman said.

"I am not chubby!" Kendall shrieked. "Now come on. We're leaving. I'm tired."

"Yeah yeah," Coleman said. "Okay, pipsqueak. We'll be back around 8:00. Good luck." He fished the van keys out of his pocket and tossed them at Monroe. "In case she starts shooting," he said.

"Thanks."

Coleman crawled out the window, then Kendall, and soon after that Monroe could hear nothing but silence from the alley. He walked around, turning off a few of the lights. He always preferred his lab to be a bit dark anyway.

The door to the operating room opened and Ava stuck her head out. "Oh," she said, surprised. She glanced around the room. "You're still here," she said with no warmth in her voice.

"I promise, I won't bother you," Monroe said. "I didn't think I'd be able to sleep. I figured I could get a little more work done."

"Fine," Ava said. She ducked back into the operating room and shut the door firmly.

Monroe watched the door for a moment. He ran a hand through his hair and rubbed his eyes. Staying was a mistake, he thought. He slowly started fishing the van keys out of his pocket.

The operating room door was yanked open again. "What kind of person are you, Arthur, hmm? What kind of person does that to people?"

Monroe froze in mid-fish. He could feel himself turning pale. "I...I don't know. I'm sorry. I wish I'd never done it. I don't know why I did it."

"Then fuck you," she said, slamming the door.

Monroe stared at the door for a moment. He resumed fishing.

The door flew open again. "No. I'm not accepting your answer. I need better than 'I don't know.' I deserve better. Wouldn't you say that I deserve better?"

"Yes," he said. He felt like he was being scolded by his grade-school principal.

"Then why? I mean, you *invaded* my *privacy*. I realize that's what you do on a daily basis, but you're supposed to do it in defense of our country, not because you want to snoop on people for...I don't know, for fun? My God, Arthur, now I have to wonder what you heard and what you didn't! Were you listening to me the entire time?"

"No. Sometimes I listened to the other rooms."

"But it was mostly mine, wasn't it?"

"A lot, yeah." He didn't want to admit that he probably spent more time listening to Carmelita, or listening to the housekeeping room and hoping that Carmelita would show up in it, than he did listening to the other rooms.

"Great," Ava said. "That is just fucking *great*." She slammed the door again.

Monroe gave her a few moments this time before he started trying to dig the keys out of his pocket again.

The door flew open once more. This time, Ava had a look of horror on her face. "Oh my *God*, Arthur!" she shouted. "Oh my God! I was...I did some *extremely* private things in my room. You listened to that, too?"

"Uh...I don't know what you mean..."

"Yes you do. You know exactly what I mean. Did. You. Hear. That. Too?"

"Um. Yeah," he said. He was looking at the floor. He didn't dare look at her. His face went from pale to burning red.

"Oh my *God!*" Ava screamed, slamming the door again.

The door flew open yet again. Monroe was getting used to it. "I can't believe you, Arthur! I can't believe you would do that to me! And to think that…uhhhrrrrrr, to think…to *think!*"

He could feel her staring at him, expecting him to say something. "I…I don't…I'm really, really sorry."

"I don't care! You invaded my privacy! You lied to me. But you know what the worst part is? You betrayed me. You betrayed our friendship. You…" She trailed off. "You mother fucking prick," she said, her voice breaking. Monroe didn't see it, because he was staring a hole through the floor, but she looked directly at him as she said it. She closed the door again, not slamming it this time. The non-slam was far worse than he slams.

The door stayed closed for several minutes. Monroe sat down on his stool, looking at the various tools of his trade, neatly tucked away into their respective places on his desk. It occurred to him that one of the reasons he liked his tools so much is that they were never mad at him, never expected him to behave a certain way, never looked at him with disappointment or hurt or disdain or in their eyes. They simply didn't care what he did, and they certainly never demanded to know why he did it.

Nor would they care if he packed them up and left with them.

The boxes the equipment came in were stacked in the corner behind Kendall's workstation. Monroe sifted through them, finding a larger one, and set it quietly on the floor next to his stool. Being careful not to make much noise, he began putting some of the gear into the box.

The door opened again. Monroe shot upright and pretended to be puttering with a spool of wire. He couldn't help glancing up at Ava. She wasn't looking at him as she walked toward the bathroom. "I am not talking to you any more, so don't even say anything," she ordered, making an effort to keep her eyes forward. She marched straight into the bathroom and slammed the door.

Monroe exhaled heavily. He sat at his workstation, not moving. He could hear her in the bathroom.

"I really hope you are not sitting out there listening to me pee," Ava barked. "Or maybe you'd like to shove a microphone under the door so you can hear a little better?"

Monroe didn't say anything. He couldn't help but hear the sounds from the bathroom. He covered his ears with his hands and clamped his eyes shut.

Ava came out of the bathroom. "Did you even hear what I..." she started, but stopped herself. "What's that?"

Monroe lowered his hands and opened his eyes. She was standing between his workstation and the bathroom door, and was pointing to the box on the floor next to him.

"It's nothing," he said. "I was just cleaning up a little."

Ava peered inside the box. "No you're not. That thingy there, you use it every day. What is that thing?"

"It's a soldering iron."

"Yeah. The soldering iron. What are you doing? And this time, for once in your life, Arthur, this time, tell me the real answer. You owe that much to me."

Monroe stared at the soldering iron in the cardboard box for what felt like a very long time. "I was packing a few things," he said in a very low voice. "I thought it might be best if I left."

"Over my dead body."

Monroe looked up. "Huh?"

"I said, over my dead body. You are not leaving."

"I thought you'd be happy."

"Why would I be happy about you leaving? Yes, I'm mad at you, Arthur. You did...a terrible, terrible thing. I don't think we will ever be like we were before. I don't think I can be around you very much any more. But you are needed on this project. You built half the crap that's inside that poor cat in there. You know how it works, and you know what to do if it goes bad. You are part of a *team* here, Arthur. You can't just leave everybody high and dry. You already did that once, and it was almost a huge mess."

She paced a little. Monroe thought she looked extremely tired. "You can't just disappear as soon as something gets rough in your life," she said. "That's not how it works. Not if you really want to be around people. And I think you do. I know you do. You're not very good at it, for whatever reason, but deep down I think you're a decent guy who's become so screwed up that he can't figure out how to actually relate to people. But that doesn't mean you should give up trying. Not if it's something you want. If you give up trying to get the things you want, then you're just wasting your life. Whether you realize it or not, you want to make this project succeed. I at least know that. Whatever else you want, hell, I don't know. But I know that you want this thing to succeed. Heck, otherwise we've done horrible things to these poor animals for no good reason. So take your soda-ing…thing…"

"Soldering iron."

"Yes, that, and put it back on your desk. You are staying."

"Okay," Monroe said.

Ava stared at him.

"What?" he asked.

"Put it back on your desk."

"Oh. Okay." He reached into the box and pulled out the iron.

"Good," she said. "Now. Since we are going to have to work together, hopefully for more than just the next few days, we are going to need some rules. First, we will separate work stuff from personal issues. We will be civil to each other when it comes to getting the project done. Second, if it is not work-related, you will not talk to me. At all. About anything. We are colleagues, not friends. The fact that I'm talking to you right now should not be construed as friendliness, because a big part of me wants to find something heavy and beat you with it. Got it?"

"Ava…I'm sorry," he said.

"No," she said, waving a finger at him. Her eyes started to well up. "No, you don't get to say that any more. That's off limits. I don't trust you, Arthur. Whether or not that will ever change, I don't know, but I don't have high hopes. So take your sorrys and keep them to yourself. Shove them up your ass and keep them there. Are we clear?"

Monroe tried to speak, but what came out sounded more like a croak. He cleared his throat. "Yeah," he said. "I'm…uh, we're clear."

"Okay. This is the last time we're going to talk about anything but work. Is there anything you would like to say before we're completely done here?"

"Well…"

"Other than you're sorry? Because that part is up your ass."

"Oh. Uh, no. I don't have anything else."

Ava looked at Monroe for a moment. He tried to interpret the expression on her face but couldn't. "Okay then," she said, straightening. "I have to go watch Mr. President. I'll see you in the morning. I suggest you get some sleep."

"We could take shifts. You could wake me up in a couple hours. If something goes wrong with Mr. President, I could come get you."

Ava hesitated, then looked at her watch. "I'll wake you at 4:00 a.m. I suggest you try to get some sleep. Won't do any good if you fall asleep on your watch."

"Okay. Uh...good night, I guess."

Ava said nothing. She went back to the operating room and closed the door.

Chapter 32

Monroe heard noise coming from the alley. He checked his watch. 8:23. He rubbed the fatigue from his eyes and checked Mr. President once again. He was still sleeping, and all his vitals seemed fine. Ava had shown him how to check them.

The three hours of sleep he'd gotten had not seemed like nearly enough. He had felt almost nauseous when he'd woken up. But he hadn't dared to ask Ava for more time. He'd said nothing, willing himself awake and forcing himself to pay close attention while she explained what he needed to do. Then she had gone to Westcott's office to sleep, closing the door behind her.

The next four hours had been mind-numbingly dull. Mr. President was sedated, Ava had explained, and wasn't supposed to wake up until mid-morning. Monroe's job, for four consecutive hours, was to watch a cat sleep.

Mr. President didn't look good. The new bandages around his tail, combined with the new ones over his shoulders, where the bug had been originally implanted, made him look like Wile E. Coyote at the end of a cartoon, after the Road Runner had tricked him into blowing himself up or impaling his own skull with a crowbar.

Looking at Mr. President, he understood why the Warner Brothers folks had cleaned up Wile E. between every scene, so that he appeared to be full of good cheer as he prepared to receive his next set of horrific injuries. Otherwise he'd have looked like Mr. President did, with bandages piled upon bandages and scars piled upon scars. The overall result was a little too grim to be considered humor.

Bored, he'd started wandering around the lab, trying to keep himself entertained. He didn't feel like working, but there really wasn't anything else to do. He certainly didn't dare attempt to watch Ava sleep, though the thought had crossed his mind. He wondered if she had undressed at all in order to get comfortable. He started to picture her sleeping in Westcott's office wearing just a bra and panties, but he forced himself to stop. He wasn't allowed to think about that any more.

He could hear Coleman and Kendall talking to each other in the alley and decided to try knocking on Westcott's office door. "Ava? The guys are here." He heard nothing from inside the office. "You know, in case you want to...I don't know, get yourself together. I guess." He still heard nothing. He wasn't sure what to do. He could hear the ladder to the fire escape being pulled down and looked toward the window as he started to knock again.

Just as he did, Ava opened the door, and Monroe knocked on her face.

"Ow!" Ava said, recoiling and grabbing her nose.

"Oh shit, I'm sorry," Monroe said.

"Jesus. That hurt!"

"I'm...uh, I didn't mean it. I didn't know you were there. I couldn't hear you."

Her hair, he noticed, was a disaster. It was all stacked up on one side. She saw what he was looking at and glared at him. "Don't you say a word about the hair," she said. "I'm going to freshen up." She crossed the lab and went into the bathroom.

"Cat dead yet?" Coleman boomed from the window as he crawled through it.

"No," Monroe replied.

"It's a good day then." He breathed deeply, in then out. "Yes sir, good day."

"Coleman, move," Kendall said. "I can't get in with you standing right there."

"Can't rush a man the morning after coitus, my portly friend," Coleman said, moving slowly away from the window.

"I am not portly!" Kendall said as he wedged himself through the window. "And ew, I don't want to hear about your coitus."

"The human sexual act is a glorious thing, Chubbs. You should try it sometime."

"I have tried it, thank you very much. I just don't want to hear about you trying it."

"Carmelita?" Monroe asked.

"Carmelita," Coleman confirmed, firing a finger-gun at Monroe. "That's a fine woman. Flexible. Sturdy. And, I assume, entirely lacking the sense of taste."

"Ew," Monroe said.

"Where's Ava?" Kendall asked.

"Bathroom," Monroe replied.

Behind Coleman and Kendall, Westcott climbed in through the window. "Cat's still alive?" he asked.

"Affirmative. We are a 'go,'" Coleman said.

"Wonderful," Westcott replied unenthusiastically. "I'll go check on him."

"When can we take him for another test drive?" Coleman asked.

Westcott shrugged. "Depends on how quickly he recovers. He's had a lot of invasive surgery over the last few weeks. Normally I'd have tried spacing out these surgeries over a span of months. He's not exactly going to hop off of the table this morning."

"Henderson's here on Friday," Coleman said. "Two days."

"I know how to count," Westcott said. "You're going to have to be patient and hope for the best. It's possible that you may not get to test him again until Henderson gets here."

"Not acceptable," Coleman said. "We need at least one day of testing in a park, somewhere outdoors, no later than tomorrow."

"Ooh, I love parks," Thomas said, crawling through the window. "You'll forgive me if I don't explain that comment any further."

"I can't make the cat magically walk," Westcott said, ignoring Thomas. "Not unless I start shoving wires up his ass."

Coleman's eyebrows shot up.

"No," Westcott said. "Jesus, I was making a joke. Sick bastard."

"I'm not the one making his living by spraying toothpaste into bunnies' eyeballs, doc," Coleman said.

"No, you just turn cats into television antennas."

"In the service of America, damn straight I do."

"Morning, boys," Ava said with a yawn as she came out of the bathroom. Monroe was amazed at how much better she looked. She looked good, period. Seeing her in her freshened state made his chest ache a little.

"Mr. President's doing fine," Ava said. "His vitals were steady this morning. He's hanging in there pretty well, all things considered."

"Tough bastard," Coleman said. "Like me. I like that."

"Yeah, well, even so, I think he's going to be really weak when he wakes up," Ava said. "Did I hear you say something about wanting to test him tomorrow?"

"Affirmative."

She glanced at Westcott. "It's really the doctor's decision, but I think the risk is too great. He might be able to handle some activity tomorrow, but at the risk of him being exhausted again come Friday when Henderson's here. If you ask me, you should wait until Friday. I think he'll do fine. He knows the commands. It's not like you need to re-teach him anything. Unless we're worried about the new antenna shorting out..."

"It won't," Monroe said.

"Then I would advise waiting until Friday," Ava concluded.

"I think she's right, Coleman," Monroe said.

"Nobody cares what you think, Arthur," Ava snapped. Everybody seemed to freeze when she said it. The sudden smack of her remark sucked the air out of the entire room.

"Now, Agent Coleman, if you don't mind," she said, "I'd like to take the van to get some breakfast."

"Um, he has the keys," Coleman said, pointing at Monroe.

Ava glared at Monroe and held out her hand. He sheepishly dug the keys out of his pocket and gave them to her.

"Blatant displays of authority turn me on, you know," Coleman said as Ava walked past.

"Pig," she replied as she crawled out the window. "You're all pigs. And by the way, Arthur, those boots are ridiculous."

After she was gone, Coleman turned to Monroe. "Soldier, I think that woman has it in for you. But she's right about the boots."

"I don't want to talk about it," Monroe said.

"I just realized that I'm glad you're back," Westcott said as he walked toward the operating room. "She's so pissed at you that she's forgotten all about being mad at me."

"I'm still mad at you," Thomas said, following him.

"What the hell for?"

"General principle." They disappeared into the operating room.

"Why did she call me a pig?" Kendall asked. "I'm not a pig."

"Sure you are," Coleman said.

"Will you cut it out with the chubby jokes?" Kendall cried.

"Look, guys," Monroe interrupted. "After Friday, no matter what happens, I'm going home. If Henderson's happy and continues the project, you'll have time to bring in somebody else and train them up."

"America hates a quitter, son," Coleman said.

"She'll get over it, Artie," Kendall said. "Give her time."

"No," Monroe said. "It's not going to work. Me being here is not going to work. You guys will be better off. It's fine. Besides, I can't live like this. I just want to go back home and go back to the way my life used to be. This is...it's too much. I'm sorry, guys. I've made up my mind."

"Come on, Artie," Kendall said. He was starting to look genuinely upset. "Don't go. Please. I actually like the boots. They kinda remind me of cowboy movies."

"I'm sorry, Kendall," Monroe replied. "I can't."

"This week sucks," Kendall said, grabbing a pencil from his workstation and throwing it across the room. It struck a cat, who yelped in surprise and hissed at all of them, just to make sure that its bases were covered. "See?" Kendall said, gesturing toward the cat. "It sucks. We have a cloud over us now. Nothing's working out."

"Pull your panties out of your crack, son," Coleman said. "We're on course with the project. That's all that matters. Everything else is irrelevant."

"I still say there's a curse on this project," Kendall moaned. "This sucks. Everything sucks. My life sucks." He sighed. "I want a corn dog."

"Guys?" Westcott said, poking his head out the operating room door. "Cat's awake. You should come see it."

The three of them traded concerned glances as they followed Westcott. Mr. President was sitting on the operating table and seemed…wrong. His eyes were only half open. He appeared to be leaning a bit to the left. His tongue was poking out from his mouth, exposing about an inch of bright pink flesh. As they watched, Mr. President raised a paw to his mouth and began cleaning it, not by running his tongue along the paw, but rather by holding his head in place and running the paw over the tongue.

"Ever see a cat do that before?" Coleman asked.

"Nope," Westcott replied.

"Me neither," Thomas said. "It's funny, though. If he lives, can I keep him?"

"No," Coleman said. "Can you make it stop doing that? I find it disturbing."

As if on cue, the cat fell over in mid-lick. He paused for a moment, the resumed dragging his paw over his tongue.

Coleman looked at Westcott.

"I've never seen that either," Westcott said.

"What's wrong with him?" Kendall asked.

"Hell if I know," Westcott replied. "Best guess, he's been under anesthesia too many times recently. He's exhausted, he's in pain, and he's disoriented. Not sure what else to tell you. I certainly don't have the time or resources to run exhaustive tests at this point."

"He'll be ready for Friday," Coleman said. It wasn't a question.

"Maybe," Westcott replied, tossing a stethoscope onto a table. "Maybe not. I'll do what I can to get him in better shape, but I'm not making any promises."

"What if I threatened to shoot you if the cat's not ready?" Coleman asked.

Westcott glared at him.

"Shit," Coleman said. "Can you at least make him look better? Maybe take off the bandages, give him a little more hair, that sort of thing?"

"Agent Coleman, if I remove the bandages too soon, he'll bleed all over himself. As for the hair, there's nothing I can do about that. It will just have to grow back. Besides, even if I could figure out a way to attach some new hair, where would I get it? They don't sell it at the hardware store."

Coleman peered out into the lab, where several cats were in view, sleeping the morning away. He looked back at Westcott with raised eyebrows.

"You're joking," Westcott said.

"I don't tell jokes," Coleman replied. "Not capable of it. Comes from my mother's side of the family."

"Jesus," Westcott said. "Fine, I'll see what I can do. But no promises."

"Your country is proud of you," Coleman said.

"Yeah yeah," Westcott replied.

~

The rest of the day passed slowly but quietly. Nobody spoke much. Ava took her time returning from breakfast, not actually coming back until after lunch. She appeared to have gone back to the motel and showered. When she came back, she didn't even look at Monroe and mostly spent her day in the operating room with Mr. President.

Monroe passed the time by tinkering with his equipment and checking on the gear he and Kendall had installed in the van. Most of the real work had already been done, so Monroe was mostly just trying to look busy. Being in the van also kept him out of the lab. All he wanted to do was leave. Being around Ava and seeing how angry she was at him was getting harder by the minute. He didn't understand the outburst in front of everyone else. He thought they had at least said their piece when they had been alone. The sudden flare-up and public rebuke left him feeling that she was only becoming more angry, not less.

He thought ahead, beyond the next couple days. Despite Mr. President's relatively poor condition, Monroe was still optimistic that the test would go off without a hitch. If Mr. President had proven anything over the past couple months, it was that he was a tough little son of a bitch. If any cat could put on a show for Henderson, it was Mr. President.

Once the test was over, he'd have Coleman drive him to the bus station. Maybe once he was home again he could try getting his superintendent job back in his building. Being the super helped pass the time in the evenings, especially when there wasn't much to listen to. Assuming he even wanted to listen any more. It occurred to him that for the first time in months, he was starting to miss Marie and her antics. Clueless, horny Marie. He wondered if Dick was still in the picture. Probably not. Marie didn't tend to keep boyfriends around that long. And the kind of men she dated didn't seem to mind.

He could get his job back working for Kricks. A successful performance in the Acoustic Kitty project would certainly assure him of that. Being back in his old lab at Langley seemed nice. Familiar. Comfortable.

Just one more day, he reminded himself. One more day, and it will all be over. It will all be right again. One more day.

Chapter 33

If Boris doesn't stop scratching himself like that, Yevgeny thought, I'm going to strike him.

Boris did not seem to notice how annoyed his companion was becoming as they settled in for another lunch on their favorite park bench. A complete lack of self-awareness was one of Boris's defining personality traits. His hand, therefore, stayed inside his pants, digging and scratching, for a good thirty seconds before it emerged again.

"Perhaps you should see a doctor," Yevgeny said.

"Why?" Boris asked.

"Why?" Yevgeny said, exasperated. "Your hand, all day it is rooting around in your pants. It is like you are keeping a rat in there."

"What interest is it of yours if I occasionally have an itch? Is it wrong for me to scratch an itch?"

"It is not wrong to scratch an itch," Yevgeny, his voice starting to rise. "It is wrong to assault your groin while someone sitting right next to you is attempting to eat!"

"So I see. What kind of sandwich is it you have today?"

"Boris, you pig-headed old man, I am trying to tell you that I do not want to see you scratching yourself throughout our lunch again today. Three days I have had to endure it. See a doctor."

Boris huffed and shifted on the bench a bit. "It is these American toilets," he said. "I am sure I gained an infection from one of them."

"Yes, of course," Yevgeny said, rolling his eyes, "it must be the toilets."

"It most certainly could come from the corrupt American toilets. I have never liked the toilets here. They are too low."

"Boris, no Americans have ever used the toilets in our embassy. It is not the Americans."

"They built it. I am sure one of their lazy workers soiled it with his vermin before we occupied the building."

"The building is forty years old. It is not the toilets."

"What is it you are implying? That I have acquired an itch from a prostitute? Because I most certainly have not been consorting with prostitutes."

"Who said anything about prostitutes? All I suggested was that you see a doctor so I do not have to worry about what is on your hands while we eat. Please, see the doctor. Today."

Boris huffed again. "If it bothers you so much, I will see the doctor. I am sorry I have been such a burden."

"Thank you," Yevgeny said, taking a bite of his sandwich.

The two men sat in silence for a moment, enjoying the slight breeze blowing through the park.

"Was the prostitute at least worth the trouble?" Yevgeny asked.

"Indeed she was," Boris replied, shoving his hand down the front of his pants.

Chapter 34

Monroe heard the van approach and went outside. Staying at the other motel made him feel more like an outsider every day, so he was glad that at most, he'd only have to do it for one more night. He was hopeful that he could catch a bus back home that night and not even have to come back to the motel other than to gather his things.

Coleman saw him approach the van but honked anyway, three times. Monroe waved in his direction sheepishly. He could see through the window that the man was grinning like an idiot. Big day, he supposed.

"Big day!" Coleman practically shouted when Monroe opened the side door.

"Thank God," Monroe said as he got in. "Good morning, by the way."

"Spectacular morning," Coleman said.

"What time does Henderson arrive?"

"About an hour. He landed in St. Louis last night and is driving down this morning. Glory is but sixty minutes away, lad."

Monroe took a deep breath. "Think we'll pull this off?"

"Without a doubt," Coleman said. "Nothing to it today. Henderson arrives, we show him how the cat moves around the lab, do some right turns and left turns, have him do surveillance on Westcott's office, done. Henderson is filled with joy, the project is extended, we go down in the annals of the Agency as having done what nobody thought could be done. Glory!"

"I suppose when you put it that way, it doesn't sound so bad," Monroe said. "Think he'll notice the splotchy fur?"

"Don't worry about the fur," Coleman said. "I took care of the fur."

Monroe looked at him.

"Fear not, kitty will get the job done," Coleman said, turning the van into the alley. "You worry too much. We should be...oh."

"What is it?"

Coleman was staring through the windshield. "He's here."

Monroe looked. Sure enough, a black sedan sat idling in the alley, directly in front of the fire escape.

"You said we still had an hour," Monroe said.

"It would appear that he arrived early. Not a problem. We're ready. Right?"

Monroe thought Coleman, for once, actually looked a tiny bit nervous. "Right," he replied.

Coleman slapped him on the shoulder. It hurt. Monroe slapped Coleman's shoulder in return, hard. Coleman didn't seem to notice.

As they got out, the rear passenger door to the sedan glided open. Henderson stepped out of the car. He was dressed in a three-piece suit and peered disapprovingly at the various puddles in the alley. He walked in a crooked path toward the van in order to avoid stepping into any of the water. "Good morning, Agent Coleman," he said without a trace of warmth. Monroe had forgotten how the man spoke, the way he implied, simply with the tone of his voice, that nobody else in the room was his equal. "Ready to go?"

"Yes sir," Coleman replied, pulling the fire escape ladder down. "Follow me."

"Up there?"

"Yes sir. Secret lab, sir."

Henderson rolled his eyes. "Yes, of course it is. Look, Agent Coleman, I paid a small fortune for this suit. It's Italian. It was custom-tailored by an actual Italian. I am not going up a fire escape in it. Besides, I'm not here to see some lab test. I want to see your prototype in action. In the field. Can't rely on a thing that hasn't been tested in the field."

"The field?" Coleman asked.

"Absolutely. We passed a park not far from here. Perfect location."

"Sir...while we're confident that Mr. President is up to the task..."

Henderson held up his hand, interrupting Coleman. "I'm sorry," he said. "Did you say Mr. President?"

"Ah, yes, sir. Mr. President. That's the test subject's name."

"Good lord," Henderson said, shaking his head and rolling his eyes. "I suppose I should have expected something like that. After the test is over, we will be renaming him. Get your subject and follow us."

"But, sir, with all due respect..."

"Agent Coleman, I did not travel all this way to climb up a fire escape and watch a test in some decrepit laboratory. I'm sure your people here are just fine with working in that kind of environment, but it's not suitable for this test. Get the cat and follow us. Am I being clear enough, Agent Coleman?"

"Yes, sir. Give me a moment to retrieve the subject."

"I'll go with you," Monroe said. "We need to be careful bringing him down."

"Why?" Henderson asked. "Is something wrong with him?"

Monroe and Coleman glanced at each other. Coleman spoke first. "He's had considerable amounts of surgery and isn't quite himself yet," he said. "We just want to err on the side of caution."

Henderson's brow furrowed. "Coleman, I thought you said this prototype was ready."

"He is ready," Coleman said. "He simply needs more time to get back to peak form. Sir."

Henderson glared at the two of them with barely concealed suspicion. "Just get the cat."

~

The park Henderson chose was near the center of town and was surrounded by busy streets on all four sides. It covered only a few blocks. Although the weather was pleasant, a small playground on the north end of the park had only attracted a few kids thus far. The few park benches were similarly abandoned, except for one near the western side. On it sat a young couple, chatting and sharing a sandwich.

On the drive over, the team had discussed how to approach the field test. Everyone agreed that they needed to keep the test as short and basic as possible. Have Mr. President approach someone, listen for a few minutes, then return. Nothing else beyond that. They all hoped that would be enough to make Henderson happy.

Coleman had nominated himself to be Mr. President's handler in the park. Kendall had argued that he should do it, since he was the one who developed the array and knew best how to control the cat, but Coleman kicked him in each of his shins, and it was pretty much settled after that.

The van and sedan were parked in metered spots along the park's eastern side. Cars passed by as Monroe and Kendall started turning on the listening equipment lining the back of the van.

"This isn't exactly the most secure location he could have chosen," Westcott said, watching through the windshield at the cars going past.

"Sometimes the best place to hide is out in the open," Coleman said. "I once conducted a strip-search in the middle of a crowded plaza in Düsseldorf. Nobody noticed. Ahh, Düsseldorf."

"I still think a more secluded spot might have been better," Westcott grumbled. "The damn cat walks like it's drunk and crippled. Probably going to scare the shit out of a few kids."

In his carrier, which was perched on Ava's lap in the front passenger seat, Mr. President meowed.

"He can hear you," Kendall said. "Be nice."

"If I wanted to be nice to him, I'd pump him full of pentobarbital."

"What's that?"

"It's what you use to put animals to sleep," Ava said.

Kendall gasped. "That is *not* being nice!" he shouted to Westcott.

"Keep it down, Chubby," Coleman said, as he shrugged a trench coat onto his shoulders.

"I am not chubby!" Kendall whispered loudly. "And what's with the coat?"

"Blending in," he responded. He fished a pair of sunglasses out of the pocket of the coat and put them on.

"But it's warm outside. You're going to look like a flasher if you step out there in a trench coat and sunglasses."

"Son, let me tell you something. I have forgotten more about working in the field than you've ever remembered with your entire chubby little finger." He looked at Monroe. "Is that how it goes?"

"I doubt it," Monroe replied.

"No matter." He turned back to Kendall. "Give me my remote."

"We're all gonna get fired," Kendall said glumly as he handed the remote to Coleman.

"Positive attitude, son!" Coleman barked. "Glory is upon us. Positive attitude."

"It's okay, Jimmy," Monroe said. "I have a good feeling about this. Mr. President can do it."

"So now you care about the project?" Ava said, still looking forward. "When did that happen? Last I heard, you were just some shithead who was only worried about himself."

Monroe had no idea how to respond, so he simply said nothing. Ava continued staring forward anyway, as if she'd expected no response in the first place.

"I wish you guys could get along," Kendall said softly.

Monroe wanted to tell Kendall not to worry about it, but he thought better of it and stayed silent.

There was a loud knock on the driver's window. It was Henderson. Coleman rolled down the window. "Yes sir?" he asked.

"What's the holdup?" Henderson said. "I've been waiting in my car. Let's get this done. I have an afternoon flight back to D.C., you know. Can't sit around here in the sticks all day with you people."

"Yes sir," Coleman said. "We're just warming up the equipment. Ready to go now."

"Good." Henderson paused for a moment as he noticed what Coleman's garb. "You're wearing a trench coat?"

"Of course, sir."

Henderson rubbed the bridge of his nose and sighed. "Fine. So what will I be seeing this morning?"

"Sir, I will carry Mr. President to that park bench over there," Coleman said, pointing to a bench in an empty corner of the park, not far from where the van sat. "I will release him. I'll then have him go forward approximately 50 feet, make a left turn, then another left turn, and return to me. The technical team in the van will monitor the signal and record everything the subject hears. The medical team will monitor the subject and ensure that the testing is within established medical parameters."

"In other words, we'll be able to tell when it falls over dead," Westcott muttered in the back of the van, low enough that only Monroe and Kendall could hear him.

"After that," Coleman said, "we'll return to the lab for a full analysis."

"That's it?" Henderson asked.

"Uh…yes, that is the plan, sir."

Henderson exhaled sharply. "Agent Coleman, I can't possibly be able to brief the Director about this project if I don't have more definitive results. We need to record a conversation. I need a real test. There's a couple over there on that bench. Have the cat listen to them."

"Sir, that's a considerable distance from the bench where I'll be sitting. The subject is not adequately recovered…"

"Hogwash, Coleman. I want to see a real test. I didn't fund this project for nothing. I need results. Have the cat listen to that couple. That's an order. I'm going to go observe from my car. Get going."

Coleman rolled the window back up as Henderson returned to his car. "Okay, you heard the man," he said. "Give me Mr. President."

Ava opened the door to the carrier. "I don't know if he's up to this, Coleman," she said. "He's not in very good shape."

"Excuses, excuses," Coleman said. "Think I got a chance to whine my way out of it when I was locked in a Pakistani jail cell with nothing but a tin cup and a standard-issue stapler? I had to carry that stapler in my rectum for three months before I could escape. But did you hear me whine about new variables? This is the United States of America we're trying to protect here."

Coleman took Mr. President out of his carrier. He looked atrocious. Westcott had done his best to glue hair from a few of the other cats over his remaining bandages, but all it did was make the cat look like a feline version of a B-movie zombie. Any self-respecting veterinarian would have euthanized the cat at first sight, using whatever was handy to get the job done.

Coleman held Mr. President up so that their eyes met, Coleman's hidden by his dark sunglasses and Mr. President's seeming to loll around just a little. "Do you understand me, soldier? It's time to get the job done for your country. Sacrifices may have to be made, but when they are made in the defense of your sacred motherland, no sacrifice is for naught. Are you with me?"

Mr. President's eyes lolled a little more.

"Okay then. Let's go," Coleman said, throwing his door open.

"We're all going to get fired," Kendall said.

"We'll be fine," Monroe whispered.

"Oh, listen to that, more talk from Arthur, acting like he cares," Ava barked. She was still facing toward the windshield, watching Coleman make his way to the park bench, dressed in his trench coat, a wriggling Mr. President draped over one arm. "None of this matters to you anyway, right?"

Monroe wasn't sure whether to speak or not. He decided to throw caution to the wind. "Of course it matters to me," he said.

"No, it doesn't. You're leaving after today anyway, aren't you?"

"Huh? I didn't..." he started to say, but stopped. He glared at Kendall.

"I'm sorry," he squeaked. "It slipped out during breakfast."

"Dammit, Jimmy."

"Don't be mad at him," Ava said. "At least he tells me the truth. Something you seem to have a very poor grasp of."

"Okay, fine, I admit it, I'm quitting after today. I'm sorry I let everybody down. I'm clearly not cut out for this. Okay? I admit it. You guys will all be better off anyway. Nobody wants me here."

"Says who?" Ava said, swiveling around at him. Her eyes were wide with anger. "You *are* cut out for this, Arthur Monroe. You just choose not to be. You could be a good guy, you could stick things out through thick and thin. You choose not to. If you want out, fine. But be a man about it for once. Tell the truth about it for once. It's always you sneaking off or running away once things get hard. So if that's what you want, fine. Go die alone, you prick."

"I'm feeling really uncomfortable here," Kendall said softly.

"What the hell do you want from me?" Monroe said, trying not to shout. "I don't understand you! You're angry with me for leaving, but then if I stay, you get angry with me for that. Ever since I came back it's been made very clear that certain people would rather not have me here. Am I right, Doc?"

"I'd like to hammer your skull until you stop twitching," Westcott said.

"See?" Monroe said to Ava. "You clearly feel the same way."

"I don't want to...," Ava said, her expression changing. "That's not what I want."

"No, but you don't want me here. I'd say you've made that fairly obvious. Why not just admit it? You hate me. You absolutely hate me. I like you, and I guess I started getting this stupid idea that you liked me too, but you don't. Not now, anyway. You *hate* me, and I can't take it any more. Why should I stick around just so you can hate me?"

Ava froze, her mouth open. Her eyes were welling up.

"As entertaining as this little lover's quarrel is," Westcott said, "I should point out that Coleman is sitting on the bench and seems to be waiting for us. If you two are in the mood to actually get some work done here."

Ava and Monroe looked out the windows. Coleman was on the bench, the only person in the park wearing a trench coat on a sunny early summer morning, with Mr. President on his lap. Coleman appeared to be saying something to Mr. President, though his gaze was fixed on the van.

"What's he doing?" Kendall asked.

"Oh. Shit," Monroe said, yanking his headphones on, suddenly very grateful for the distraction. "He's trying to make sure the mic on Mr. President is working." Monroe turned to his board, a real board, not the miniature, bare-bones version he'd become accustomed to using in the motel room, and potted up the signal from Mr. President.

Coleman's voice came through crisply over the headphones. "...in, Sylvester, this is Tweety, I repeat, if all is clear, give a signal...come in, Sylvester, this is Tweety..."

Kendall was listening through his own pair of headphones. "Is he calling us Sylvester?"

"I think so," Monroe said. "Apparently he's Tweety."

"Did we discuss using code names?"

"No."

"I wish he'd discussed it with us. I hate Sylvester. He's not even funny. I'd have rather been Foghorn Leghorn."

"Foghorn Leghorn isn't funny, either."

"Sure he is. He's funnier than Sylvester, at least."

"Guys," Ava snapped. "What's he saying?"

"Oh. He's waiting for a signal," Monroe said.

"What kind of signal?" she asked.

"He's not saying."

"God, just for once it would be nice if he didn't have to play spy," Ava said. She reached over and flashed the headlights of the van twice.

"Ten-four," Coleman said into the cat. "Sylvester, I see your signal and acknowledge it. Commencing field exercise. I am now releasing the prototype. I repeat, I am releasing the prototype."

"At least we know the microphone is working," Westcott said.

"Of course it's working," Kendall said. "Artie built it."

Outside, Coleman set Mr. President on the ground. He sat up for a moment, then fell over.

In Monroe's ears, it sounded like a tree had fallen on Mr. President's head. "What was that?"

"Subject is down!" Coleman shouted, though the sound was muffled in Monroe's ears, since the bug was now half-covered by park grass. "I repeat, subject is down!"

"Good lord, he fell over," Ava said. Mr. President was in the grass, waving his paws in the air as though he were fingerpainting a very low ceiling.

"He fell over?" Kendall cried.

"If he has a heart attack, I'm leaving," Westcott said.

"Quiet," Ava snapped, earning her a glare from Westcott but nothing more than that.

Coleman quickly grabbed Mr. President and set him upright. Once he felt certain that the cat was stable, he slowly sat back up on the bench. "Subject is stabilized," Coleman said. "Extracting remote control."

"Here we go," Monroe said.

Coleman held the remote close to his lap and used his foot to nudge Mr. President until the cat shifted around and was facing away from the bench. He took a deep breath and toggled the remote to move the cat forward.

Nothing happened. For a long moment, absolutely nothing happened.

Then Mr. President got to all fours and began walking forward. Everyone in the van fell completely silent. All of them, even Westcott, watched the cat's every move.

Mr. President's steps were anything but the precise ones normally exhibited by healthy cats. His rear end bumped up every time he brought his back legs forward. He seemed to slant a bit to the right, as if he were about to fall over again at any moment. Still, he persevered and managed to walk more than halfway toward the bench where the young couple sat.

Even better, Monroe could clearly hear what Mr. President was hearing. The sound of the breeze. The heavy, awkwardly spaced padding of the cat's footsteps in the grass. The shrieks of the children on the other side of the park. Monroe could barely contain the sudden wave of excitement flowing through him. It was working! Mr. President, the world's first functional Acoustic Kitty, was working! Monroe wanted to whoop with excitement, but he didn't dare drown out the soft noises coming through his headphones.

He suddenly heard an unusual chittering kind of noise that he didn't recognize. The chittering stopped, then started again. When it stopped the second time, so had the sounds of Mr. President's feet in the grass.

"He stopped," Ava said. "It looks like he sees something, but I don't...oh. It's a squirrel. Go on, squirrel. Shoo." She looked at Coleman. He clearly was continuing to push forward on the remote and was staring at Mr. President as intently as Mr. President was staring at the squirrel. The squirrel, having noticed the rather surprising presence of one of its natural predators in its favorite food-gathering spot, was staring just as intently at Mr. President.

For a brief moment, everything in the park stopped. The air stopped moving. The leaves in the trees stopped rustling. The squirrel, the cat, Coleman, and everyone in the van, stopped breathing. Life, for one almost imperceptible moment, froze in place.

And then, the squirrel twitched.

"Ohhhhh, *shit.*" Ava whispered.

When it happened, it happened fast. The squirrel bolted to its left at full throttle, making a panicked run for whatever hidey-hole it thought was nearby. Mr. President leaped after it, ignoring the pain shooting through his surgery-wracked limbs as well as the shocks emanating from his spine. He sprinted after the squirrel, his butt bouncing into the air with every poorly coordinated leap.

The sounds in Monroe's ears changed radically. All he heard was the whooshing of wind. "What's going on?"

"He's chasing the squirrel!" Ava shouted. She banged on the window. "Stop, Mr. President! Stop!"

"No, kitty!" Kendall shrieked. He threw off his headphones and flung the rear doors of the van open, nearly knocking Westcott into the street in the process.

The squirrel spotted a tree and dashed for it, not noticing the two-lane road between itself and the tree in question, nor the large colorful objects that sped left and right across its intended route. It was an unfortunate fact of nature that the typical squirrel's tiny brain was capable of comprehending the safety of trees, and the tasty crunch of the nut, but not the concept of looking both ways before crossing a very busy street.

Mr. President saw nothing past the squirrel. All he saw, all he knew, was the thrill of the hunt. Mr. President was a cat that had spent almost his entire life indoors. And he had been perfectly content to live indoors, for he knew no different. Life, as far as he knew, was a series of naps and feedings, and the occasional satisfying scratch. Until, that is, strange things had started happening to him, and he had felt pain, plenty of pain, and strange jolts of burning electricity, like the ones screaming through his spine at that very moment. Somewhere in his little brain, he was aware that the jolts meant that the people wanted him to do something. Under other circumstances, he would have been content to follow orders.

But not now.

He had seen a squirrel. And the squirrel had looked, well, tasty. And deep inside him, something awoke. Something he had never known was even there. Something primal. Something that told him that he was a member of a species whose primary reason for being was to chase down anything smaller than itself, kill it, and eat it.

It was that primal urge that had set Mr. President free.

And it was that same primal urge that caused Mr. President to forget the pain in his joints, and the pains shooting down his spine, and think one thought, and one thought only: *I am going to catch that thing, and I am going to kill it. And then I am going to eat it. Because that is what I do.*

Nothing else mattered. Not the pain, not the screaming people, and certainly not the brightly colored cars on the road.

Coleman leapt into action as well, tossing the remote control aside and sprinting at full speed for about a dozen steps before remembering that his left knee was entirely devoid of cartilage. It was the searing pain in that knee, as bone ground hard against bone, that reminded him, causing him to instinctively pull his left leg into the air, which in turn caused him to crash hard to the grass, thus ending his attempt to prevent disaster.

Unaware of Coleman's left knee, as well as the entire lack of cartilage therein, the squirrel barreled into the street, just ahead of a rather sporty blue Cadillac.

Mr. President barreled into the street directly behind the squirrel.

Just in time to be barreled into by the sporty blue Cadillac.

In Monroe's ears, it sounded like Mr. President had triggered a land mine.

"Noooooooooooo!" Kendall screamed as the Cadillac screeched to a halt. "Mr. President!"

Ava threw open her door and ran to the back of the van. When she saw what was left of the cat, she flinched and covered her eyes.

Westcott saw it, too. "Lucky son of a bitch," he said, to nobody in particular.

The driver of the Cadillac, a businessman in a tailored suit, got out and looked at the remains on the street behind his car. "Shit!" he shouted. He quickly ran to the front of his car and began inspecting the bumper for cat-related damage. In the lane behind him, traffic had stopped, and impatient drivers almost immediately began leaning on their horns.

The couple on the park bench heard the noise and paused in their conversation as they looked toward the road. Somebody had run over a cat and was now blocking traffic. The young man suggested they finish their conversation elsewhere, and the young woman agreed. The park was normally so unpopulated that it was a perfect spot for them to discuss details of the memos she typed every day at the nearby Air Force base. It wouldn't be good if a bunch of motorists spotted them together. That would be very hard to explain to her husband.

Coleman hopped on one leg toward Mr. President's flattened body as fast as he could. "Nothing...to see...here...good citizen!" he shouted between hops. "I'd...advise...you...to...return...to...your... vehicle!"

"Was that your cat I ran over?" the driver said, looking up from his bumper. "Because I've got some damage here. You really shouldn't let cats run loose in this park."

Coleman stopped hopping. He glared at the motorist for a moment, huffing hard in an attempt to catch his breath. Then he pulled out his gun. "Stand still," he said, raising his weapon.

Later, when reporting his run-in with the crazed, one-legged cat owner in the trench coat, the businessman would explain to the police that when the crazed man had pulled a gun on him, he had immediately jumped into his car and sped away at fast as possible. He decided it was not relevant to mention the fact that he'd gotten several miles away before he realized that he'd soiled his tailored suit, as well as the front seat of his sporty blue Cadillac.

Coleman took off his trench coat as he hopped slowly toward what was left of Mr. President. The cars had stopped honking as soon as he had pulled his gun. The motorists now waited patiently for the one-legged man with the sunglasses and large handgun while he used his trench coat to hastily scoop up the remains of a cat that looked like it had been unattractive even before being run over. They didn't even start honking when a chubby man with tears streaming down his face ran up to the crazy one-legged man and insisted on seeing the gruesome contents of the folded-up trench coat. The police who later questioned the first two motorists in the line, the only ones who got a good look at the crazy man in the sunglasses, decided that the story the motorists told was just a bit too bizarre to be true. Particularly since nobody saw the white van in question anywhere around town after that morning.

The first motorist in the line of cars also mentioned that he was certain he saw a black sedan parked in front of the white van, but that it had driven away while the crazy man with the gory trench coat was trying to get the chubby man to calm down. He swore up and down that the black sedan had government plates on it.

All the more reason, surmised the police, not to bother investigating the matter of the lunatic with the dead cat in his trench coat any further.

Chapter 35

Arthur Monroe shivered the snow off of his coat as he checked his mail. As usual, it included no shortage of bills, but the junk mail, for once, was starting to outnumber the bills. That was new. The perils of holding a business license that has your home address on it, he supposed.

"Hey there, Artie," a voice called from down the hall. It was Marie. Despite the 25-degree weather outside, she was wearing a tank top and very skimpy silk pajama bottoms. "I thought it sounded like you."

"Hey, Marie. Still too hot in your apartment, huh?"

"Yeah. This is the most I've had on all night. Do you think you could pleeeeease come in and take a look at my radiator?"

"Marie, that's Mr. Leftridge's job now. You really should ask him."

"I know, but he's been here three times and it's still not really fixed. I asked Fred to take a look at it, but he doesn't know shit about fixing things. He's not very good with his hands, I'm sorry to say." Fred was her latest boyfriend. She almost broke up with him after he tried to slide a hand up her sister's skirt during Thanksgiving dinner. Monroe had heard all about it the night he had fixed the drain on her kitchen sink.

He had long since stopped fixing things for the other residents, no matter how hard they complained about the incompetence of Mr. Leftridge, the new super. Marie was the only one who could still talk him into it, mostly because she entertained him with stories about her seemingly endless number of brief relationships, and partially because she almost never wore a bra around her apartment.

"Marie, I'm really tired," he said. "I just did a thirteen-hour day at the store."

"Oh, you and that store. The building's not the same since you quit being the super. Come on, if you fix it, I'll even pay you. I can't keep walking around my apartment naked."

Monroe exhaled, but his exasperation was more for show than anything else. "Tell you what. Tomorrow's Saturday, and I close early on

Saturdays. I'll come by tomorrow night and fix it. You don't have to pay me, but you can cook me dinner."

Marie grinned. "You're the best, Artie. But I suck at cooking. How about I order us something from Nico's? Do you like Italian?"

"Order the biggest lasagna they have. I get the leftovers."

"Artie Monroe, I do believe we have a date. See you tomorrow, okay? I'm going back inside – it's freezing in this hallway. See ya."

Shaking his head and grinning to himself, Monroe watched her scamper back down the hall before he headed up to his apartment.

~

The bell over the door rang as Monroe walked through the front door of K&M Specialty Electronics the next morning. Monroe looked up at the bell, momentarily confused. "Jimmy?" he called, turning his attention toward the store. "You here?"

"Yeah, I'm here," Kendall shouted from the back of the shop.

"Jimmy," Monroe said, stamping the snow off of his cowboy boots, "you left the door unlocked again."

Kendall appeared behind the counter. "But I'm here. I was just in the back, that's all."

"I know, but we don't open for another fifteen minutes. The door really needs to stay locked when we're closed. It only takes a second for somebody to slip in here and grab something. This is expensive stuff we're stocking."

"Yeah, I know. That's why I installed the bell over the door. Just did it this morning. Nobody's going to sneak in here when I'm around. I have ears like a cat."

Monroe sighed. "I guess. I'm not sure I like the bell, though. Makes the shop sound like a mom-and-pop liquor store. People who come in here, they don't want the place to sound like a grocery store. They want cloak and dagger. James Bond."

He glanced up at the bell again. It had flowers on it. "There's no glory in a grocery store," he said.

"Aww," Kendall said.

"Jimmy. There are flowers on it, for God's sake."

"It was the only one they had at the flea market," Kendall moaned. "If I can find something without flowers, can I still have a bell? Maybe I can find something cooler, like a gong. I promise, I'll still keep the door locked if I get here first."

Monroe rubbed the bridge of his nose. It was a gesture he did frequently when he was around Kendall. "Okay. But no gongs. We're not running a Chinese restaurant."

"Thank God. I look terrible in red. Mom says red makes me look like a Christmas candle."

"That's great, Jimmy," Monroe said, rubbing the bridge of his nose.

~

"I think I'm going to go get some lunch," Kendall said.

Monroe glanced at his watch. "It's almost 2 o'clock. You didn't eat yet?"

"Nope," Kendall said. "I had a big breakfast. Besides, I've been wanting to try that new diner over on Fourth, and it's always crowded right at noon. I hear they have good corn dogs."

"Okay. I'm sure I can handle the rush," Monroe said as he looked at the empty store. It actually had already been a good day. Four customers, three of them paying, each of them buying nearly $1,000 worth of merchandise. K&M Specialty Electronics wasn't a haven for amateurs, although they were welcome to browse. Most folks, when they see how much surveillance equipment costs – the good stuff, anyway – they lose interest in spying on their neighbors and spouses. K&M mostly catered to pros like Coleman.

"I'll be back in a while then," Kendall said. "If my mom calls…"

"I know. Tell her that you're not buying any more Jim Beam for her."

"She really does need to go back to Jack Daniel's. She doesn't get all crazy on Jack."

"I'll do what I can."

"Thanks. See ya."

The door jingled as Kendall left. With an hour to kill before the shop closed for the afternoon, Monroe decided it was time to stop procrastinating on the bills. He went to the small office in the back of the store and groaned when he saw the sheer number of bills in his "in" tray. Paying all the bills that came with running a business was torturous work as far as he was concerned. But in the end it was his business, his and Kendall's, and there was nobody else to do the paperwork but him. Jimmy was the salesperson. Monroe was the paperwork guy.

The bell on the front door rang again. Monroe smiled; the sound meant he was saved, temporarily, from the stack of bills, even though it was probably just Kendall coming back because he forgot something.

"Your mom called," he shouted. "She said she's going to eat your birds if you don't bring her three fifths of Beam."

"It's a good thing I don't own any birds then," a woman's voice called back.

"Shit," Monroe muttered to himself. "I'm sorry," he said more loudly as he walked toward the front of the store again. "I thought you were my…"

He stopped in mid-sentence when he saw who was standing just inside the door. It was Ava. In front of her, busily shaking the snow off his heavy wool hat, was a little boy, about six years old. His hair was more of a sandy color, but otherwise he was the spitting image of his mother. He was a little too thin for a kid his age, and his eyes were the dark, sunken eyes of one who has had things a bit too hard during his short life.

But none of that seemed to be on the boy's mind at the moment. All he cared about was getting the cold snow off of his hat.

"Are you going to say hi?" Ava asked, drawing Monroe's attention back to her.

"Uh, yeah. Hi. I'm sorry. I…you surprised me."

"This is Robby," she said, shaking the boy's shoulder. "Robby, this is Arthur. He's a friend of Mommy's."

"Hi," Robby said. His attention immediately wandered to the various pieces of equipment in the display cases mounted on the walls. "Mommy, what is this stuff?"

Her brow furrowed as she looked around. "I actually don't even know how to describe what this stuff is, Robby," she said.

"You like James Bond?" Monroe asked.

"I'm not allowed to see James Bond movies," Robby said.

"You don't *need* to see James Bond movies," Ava said to him. "They aren't that good anymore, anyway. I'm surprised they still bother to make them."

"But he's cool," Robby said. "My friend Carl, his dad took him to see one, and he said it was neato. Except that he kissed lots of girls in it. Oh, but he also had a car that turned into a submarine. I want a car that turns into a submarine when I grow up."

"Well, we don't have any submarine cars here," Monroe said, "but this stuff is what we call surveillance equipment. At least, that's what it says in the yellow pages about us. But you know what it really is?"

"No," Robby said. "What?"

"Spy stuff."

"It is?" The boy's eyes went wide as he looked around the store with greatly renewed interest. "Do you have x-ray glasses and stuff like that?"

"Well, no, there's no such thing as x-ray glasses…"

"Sure there is. My friend Carl has a pair. He can see bones through them, and women's underwear."

"Robby!" Ava said.

"That's what he said, Mom! But I tried them on and I couldn't even see Carl's underwear. They don't work for me. Makes me mad."

"Okay, buddy," Ava said, patting him on the shoulder and trying not to laugh. "Tell you what, why don't you look around a little bit? Then we can go find someplace to eat."

"Can I get ice cream for dessert?"

"Sure. But only if you're good while Mommy is here. And only if you eat something green first. Okay?"

"Okay." He pressed his hands against the glass of one of the cabinets, smearing it, as he peered at the various bugs inside it.

Ava watched him for a moment, with the kind of look that mothers have for their children. Adoring, but also making sure they aren't wiping their noses on a stranger's display glass.

She turned to Monroe. They looked at each other for an awkward moment.

"So," Monroe said, breaking the silence, "what brings you down here? Or did you just happen to be in the market for a camera that looks like a briefcase?"

"No, thankfully, I'm out of the spy business," she said. "Hopefully for good. Once was enough for me." She undid a couple of the buttons on her coat. "I, um, I actually wanted to see how you were doing."

"Oh. Wow. Well…I'm good." He stopped for a moment. "Kendall set this up, didn't he?"

Ava smiled. "Yeah, he did. He called me a few weeks ago, suggested I swing by sometime. Told me all about the store and how well things are going. Who knew there was a market for this stuff?"

He followed her gaze as she looked around. He enjoyed showing off the store to people who were seeing it for the first time. "My old bosses at the Agency weren't real thrilled about it," he said, "but there really wasn't anything they could do. Besides, most of this stuff is about five years behind the technology we had at the Agency. And you can't get it anywhere else, except one or two places in New York, and a couple small shops in Europe. We have customers driving in from all over. Private investigation is big business these days. And we do get the occasional horny rich kid who wants to look up his classmates' skirts."

"That's disgusting."

Monroe shrugged. "Spying isn't always pretty. The money all spends the same, and I have lots of bills."

Ava glanced around, as if she were looking for something and couldn't find it. "Should I be glad I'm not wearing a skirt today?"

"No. Don't worry. I don't have anything like that here. I only sell it now. And occasionally do the custom job for people I know. I'm out of the business of using it."

Ava sized him up. "I'm glad you learned that lesson."

The smile faded from Monroe's face. Suddenly he didn't know where to look. His eyes settled on Robby. "I know you don't want to hear it, but I am sorry," he said quietly.

"I know."

"You're still mad at me."

"Yes. A little. I probably will always get a little mad when I think about it. It was so…disappointing. I had come to think very highly of you, Arthur."

"I let a lot of people down."

"I don't think I've ever been as mad at a man in my life."

"Even more than the guy that started beating you up?"

Ava glanced at Robby, still infatuated with the gizmos behind the glass. "I know he gave me my son, but the guy was a piece of garbage," she said. "I didn't care about him."

"But you're saying I'm worse than that guy?"

"No. I'm saying I didn't care about him."

Monroe shut up. It was dawning on him, what she was trying to say.

Ava took a step toward him. "I started to care about you, Arthur," she said softly.

He caught the look in her eyes. The familiar warmth came to Monroe's face as he turned car-crash-bruise red. "Oh," he said.

"You seemed like a nice guy," she said. "A good guy. With a good heart. Guys like that are hard to find. It took me a while to figure that out, but I did. So…I came down here to make a peace offering, I guess. I was thinking I could make you dinner sometime."

"Really? I didn't know you could cook."

"I make exactly four dishes well. Everything else is hot dogs and Frosted Flakes. But I will make one of the four for you."

"Do I get to pick?"

"Nope. I'm cooking, I get to pick. You bring a bottle of wine. Good stuff, at least ten bucks."

"I can handle that. I don't know anything about wine, but I can ask Coleman."

"Coleman knows wine?"

"Sure. He never told you about the four months he did undercover work as a waiter in Nice?"

"Let me guess. It ended with him shooting someone."

"A Chinese spy, I think it was, yeah. The guy was his roommate. Both kneecaps, as I recall."

"That sounds like Coleman, all right. So you've stayed in touch with him?"

"Yeah."

"How's he doing?"

"Good. He had a rough go of it for a while, after Henderson forced an early retirement on him."

"He did? That doesn't seem fair."

"Henderson had to make somebody his fall guy. Otherwise he might have ended up on the street."

"So was it a big stink when you guys got back to Langley? I never heard anything. Apparently Westcott and Henderson had a falling out over the project and they stopped talking to each other. After that, I didn't hear a peep about you guys or the Agency. I actually hadn't thought about the project in quite a while until Kendall called the other day."

"I'm sure you were thrilled to have the memory dredged up."

"I was very pleasantly surprised, to tell the truth," Ava said. "When the project ended, I felt like I never wanted to see any of you guys again, but talking to Jimmy made me realize that...well, that I actually missed you idiots."

"We're an acquired taste, I think."

"Yeah."

"So did Jimmy tell you what you've missed?"

"Actually, no," Ava replied, peering into one of the cases of equipment. "I think he was really nervous about calling me. You know how he gets."

"Yes, I do. Did he suddenly say he had to go?"

"Yeah."

"Probably the bowels, then."

"Yeah, that's what I figured. So, what's been going on? Are you and Coleman actually friends now?"

"I suppose you could say that, yeah," Monroe said. "Although you never really know what's going on in Coleman's head."

"So I recall."

"He's a private investigator now, you know."

"No kidding."

"Yep. Opened a private investigations company of his own. He mostly spies on guys cheating on their wives, so it's not quite like the old days overseas, but suspicious wives tend to pay well for that kind of thing. It doesn't hurt that his job involves watching people screw."

"Umm, you said a bad word," Robby said, still by the display cases.

"Sorry," Monroe said. "Won't happen again."

"Robby, don't eavesdrop," Ava said.

"Okay. Sorry, Mom." Satisfied, he went back to perusing the goods.

Ava smiled. "I think he's impressed with you. It's normally very hard for me to get him to talk to strangers."

"He just hasn't learned to hate me yet. How's he doing?"

"Better," she said. "He'll always have to take his medicines, but I'm okay with that, as long as it keeps him around. Still lots of doctor visits, though. Fortunately, Westcott stuck to his word and gave me the raise you extorted from him. Thanks for that, by the way. Why didn't you tell me?"

"You wouldn't have let me do it."

"True. Westcott didn't tell me right away that it was your idea. He said he thought I had earned it. He left his wife, by the way."

"No shit."

"Bad word!" Robby said.

"Sorry. I'm sorry," Monroe said, holding his hands up. "I'm not used to being around kids."

Robby shrugged. "It's okay." He went back to checking out the microphones disguised as lipstick tubes.

"He left his wife, huh?" Monroe asked. "To be with Thomas?"

"Nope. Those two fought like cats and dogs for a couple months after we all got back. Eventually Thomas quit and moved to California. Westcott's with another guy now. William. They go to lunch together sometimes. It's actually kind of cute, in a very disturbing way. Dr.

Westcott isn't as grouchy, so I guess that's good. Don't get me wrong, he's still a big jerk, but he's not as bad as before."

"I've been watching the papers to see news about the company. Did I miss it?"

"No. I guess Henderson didn't bother following through on his threats. Nobody ever came by with a microphone or a camera. But we also didn't get paid a dime by the Agency. All that time for nothing."

"That's the Agency for you."

"Yeah. Get this, though. Westcott pulled me aside a few weeks ago and said he's wanting to retire in a couple years, and that he wants me to take over when he does."

"No kidding? Wow. That's really great, Ava."

"Yeah, but I'm not going to do it."

"You aren't? Why not?"

"Too much pressure," she said. "Besides, what we do…I'm really tired of doing it. I'm ready for something else. I just don't know what that something else will be yet. I figure I can take my time figuring that out."

"Well, good for you," Monroe said. "Sometimes it's good to take stock of your situation and make a change for the better."

"I can see that," she said, glancing around the store again. "So when did all this happen, Mr. Business Mogul?"

"I never bothered going back to the Agency, other than to get my stuff. I just couldn't do it. I had a little money saved up and lived off that for a little while, and got my job back as my building's super to make a little money. I was talking to Coleman one night when we were out bowling…"

"You guys still bowl?"

"Oh, yeah. Every Thursday. I'm absolutely awful."

"Funny. So, go on."

"Anyway, Coleman had started doing PI work, and he kept asking me to build him stuff that he could use on the job, and he was complaining that what he needed was really impossible to find. Gave me the idea for this place. Took me another month to talk Jimmy into being my partner, and two months after that we opened. Coleman's my best customer."

"Wow. It's frightening to think that you three are friends."

Monroe shrugged. "We share a common bond of dysfunctional personalities."

"Apparently," she said, smiling. "So do you think you can make it? To dinner?"

"I'd like that a lot. Yes."

"I'm going to try to trust you again, Arthur. I shouldn't. My Mom thinks I'm asking for trouble by doing this."

"I'm not the same person I was during that project. I mean, I am, but I'm not. I feel good. And I realize that I'm not going to get a third chance. I don't want to screw up again."

"You know," Ava said, "the moment I walked in, even through your stunned expression upon seeing me, I could tell that something had changed about you. Whatever it is, it looks good on you."

Monroe smiled. "You think?"

"Yes, I do." She looked down. "I have to say…dear God, you're still wearing those boots?"

"There is nothing wrong with these boots," he said with mock indignation.

"I'm sorry, Arthur, but those have got to go. You are not a cowboy."

"Sorry, darlin', but the boots stay," he said in a horrible Western accent. "These boots and I have been through a lot. Can't turn my back on 'em now. Besides, they remind me of a friend."

"Who?"

"A guy I met in Missouri. You didn't know him. Good guy. Kinda helped set me straight."

"Sounds like a good person to stay in touch with. You still talk to him?"

"No," Monroe said.

"Arthur, there's no law against calling people once in a while."

"It's not that. He passed away in September."

"Oh God, Arthur. Oh, I'm sorry. I didn't mean…"

"It's okay. I know you didn't."

"That's really sad," Ava said. "I'm so sorry, Arthur."

"Actually, I think he's a lot happier now. But thanks."

"Those are cool boots," Robby said, interrupting them. "What are they made of?"

"Snakeskin," Monroe said. "I think."

"Whoa," Robby said, staring at the boots. "I wish I had some. Mommy, I want some for my next birthday."

Ava rolled her eyes. "Men. All the same. Come on, Robby, let's go eat."

"Yay!" Robby shouted. "I'm hungry!" He looked at Monroe. "What's your name again?"

"Arthur."

"Mr. Arthur, if you come to dinner, can you bring some of this stuff for me to play with?"

"Sure." Monroe looked at Ava. "But, uh, no bugs."

"Thank you," she said.

Monroe looked back at Robby. "How about a hidden camera, though?"

"Yeah! Cool!"

"It's a deal," Monroe said. "I'll see you then, okay?"

"Okay. Bye, Mr. Arthur." He waved and went out the door as Ava held it for him. Monroe could feel the burst of cold air blowing in.

"See you soon," Ava said. "And no fair standing me up. I will find you and shoot you."

"Coleman would approve."

She laughed. "Bye," she said as she smiled at him, really smiled, and then the floral bell was clinging at him again as the door closed. They both waved at him through the window.

Monroe watched her go. After she and Robby were out of sight, he looked around the street until he was certain nobody was coming. The day had turned miserable, though, and he saw no one.

He stood by himself in the store and marveled at how much had changed since he'd last seen Ava. Being alone used to always be accompanied by a hollow feeling, a sense of unwanted isolation, even though he had come to seek out solitude over the years. Even though he was alone in his store, he felt, finally felt, that he was where he was supposed to be.

For the first time since he was a little boy, Arthur Monroe shoved his hands in his pockets and did a little backwards skip in a circle around the middle of the store. It was something he did all the time as a child, having picked it up from watching Curly do the same thing on "The Three Stooges."

It had been a long time since he had done the Curly shuffle.

He reveled in the moment...until he slipped on a patch of melting snow and crashed to the floor in a crumpled heap.

"Stupid fuckin boots," he moaned.

Acknowledgements

To Niky Roberts, Dave Collett, Alyssa Royse, and Stephanie Mulherin, who read early drafts of this steaming pile and returned with desperately needed words of encouragement, and in some cases, even more desperately needed fixes.

To Delaney, Lexie and Madison, who left me alone long enough to work on this book and distracted me like a pack of monkeys when I needed a break.

And most of all to my wife Colette, who is both my staunchest supporter and bluntest critic. Without her this work would never have been finished, plain and simple. She inspires me in more ways than I can count.

Oh, and I shouldn't forget to thank you for buying this book in the first place. I sincerely hope that you enjoyed reading it.

About the Author

Bob Rybarczyk is tall and has almost no vertical leaping ability. He is a vice president at a public relations agency and has written a weekly humor column for the online version of the *St. Louis Post-Dispatch* since 2001. His column, called *Suburban Fringe*, can be found at www.stltoday.com/fringe. He is a native of St. Louis, where he lives with his wife, three daughters, and a startlingly overweight cat. Feel free to annoy him at brybarczyk@sbcglobal.net.

Printed in the United States
99837LV00002B/35/A